TAKE ONE CANDLE
LIGHT A ROOM

TAKE ONE CANDLE
LIGHT A ROOM

SUSAN STRAIGHT

Pantheon Books, New York

*This is a work of fiction. Names, characters, places, and incidents either
are the product of the author's imagination or are used fictitiously.
Any resemblance to actual persons, living or dead, events, or locales
is entirely coincidental.*

Library of Congress Cataloging-in-Publication Data
Straight, Susan.
Take one candle light a room / Susan Straight.
p.   cm.
ISBN 978-0-307-37914-6
1. Identity (Psychology)—Fiction. 2. Travel writers—Fiction. 3. Family
secrets—Fiction. 4. Blacks—Race identity—Fiction. I. Title.
PS3569.T6795T35 2010   813'.54—dc22   2010012683

www.pantheonbooks.com

Printed in the United States of America

First Edition

2   4   6   8   9   7   5   3   1

In memory of my father-in-law, General Roscoe Conklin Sims Jr., Stanford Lanier Sims, Charles Sims, Tommie Chatham Jr., Stan Davis, John E. Murphy, Emory Elliott, Oscar Harper, John "Newcat" Bratton, and especially my brother, Jeffrey Paul Watson.

For Dwayne Sims, General RC Sims III, Carnell Sims, Derrick Sims, Eddie Chandler Jr., Trent Chatham, and all the men in the driveway; for my nephews, General IV, Aanais, Evan, Richard "Stuxx" and Jarrod, Leroy and Tony, Corey and Cortez, EJ III and Marcus and David and Kendall, and especially for Sensei Sims.

PART ONE

There are places we fear, places we dream, places whose exiles we became and never learned it until, sometimes, too late.

—THOMAS PYNCHON,
Against the Day

APACHE

I KEEP THE TWO PHOTOS on the ebony sideboard in my small dining room.

The first is black-and-white, but has taken on that edgy silvery-brown look of a gelatin print. It is Louisiana, 1958. The five young women stand beside a truck with a curved hood, the word *Apache* in chrome letters beside my mother's hip.

They are sixteen. They are leaving their homes.

Their faces are stark and somber, varying shades of amber and gray in the cold winter light. Claudine, with hooded eyes, a plumpness around her jaw from the baby, her arms crossed over breasts swollen like bags of rice under her shirt. Felonise, hair in a pompadour over her thin face, her coat collar too big around her flowerstem neck. Mary, black eyes fierce and slanted, the dark scar still visible on her face where his ring gouged out a kernel of skin on her left cheekbone. Zizi, whose light gray eyes are clear as water, her thick black braid askew on her head. And my mother, Marie-Claire, her face pale and round as a tortilla, her dark brows like tadpoles swimming toward each other, the only one who tried to smile for the camera.

He hadn't gotten her, or Felonise. Mr. McQuine.

It was my mother who told me the story, so that I would stay home, safe, and never trust the outside world, or the white people in that world.

If he operated now, he'd be called a serial rapist or night stalker with a nickname like the Hillside Strangler or the Westside Rapist. But back then, in rural Louisiana in the 1950s, he didn't even make the news. He had only his own name, and that was enough. He was Mr. McQuine, and everyone knew to be afraid of him and his light blue car skimming along the road past the houses. In the dark, my mother said, the car was like a garfish swimming at night, the front grille its teeth bared. But in the daytime, the car was even worse, because it faded into the color of the pale sky and the dust cloud around it when Mr. McQuine drove slowly past people's yards to look for smoke rising from a chimney and a girl who might have stayed home from school.

After he took the first three girls—Claudine and Zizi and Mary— and the sheriff wouldn't even come out, they knew. No one cared. No one would make him stop.

Claudine was walking home from her aunt's house. She'd stayed out of school to help her aunt with a new baby. Mr. McQuine caught her on the road from Seven Oaks where it winds along the bayou and then cuts through the woods to Sarrat.

He kept her all night. When she made the porch of her house, she could barely walk. No one had phones, so they thought she'd stayed at her aunt's with the baby.

She had her own baby in the fall. Eyes pale gold as corn shucks. Her mother held it, but she wouldn't. Her father took it away to a cousin somewhere. When he came back he wouldn't say where.

Mr. McQuine caught Zizi in her house, when she played sick to miss church, and after she tried to hit him with an iron he grabbed her wrist and broke it.

He caught Mary hanging laundry in the yard behind her mother's house, when everyone else was out weeding the cane. She fought, too, and he slapped her across the face. Blood welled into the dent left by the sapphire.

It was that scar like a brand that made my father, Enrique, crazy.

He said his grandmother used to tell him about her mother, Moinette Antoine, who was a slave, and the brand burned into her shoulder by the man who said he owned her.

My father went hunting for Mr. McQuine. He went to the Time Out, where Mr. McQuine and the other white men drank, but the men only laughed and told him to buy beer at the back porch. Mr. McQuine knew, though, what Enrique wanted. Weeks later, Enrique waited in the dark kitchen at Seven Oaks after midnight, when everyone was asleep. But when the blue Chevrolet parked in the gravel, Mr. McQuine came into the kitchen with his gun already out, and he made Enrique put his own gun on the antique wooden table. He lay three envelopes on the table, moved his gun to make Enrique open each envelope and pull out the long strands. The first black and curled as moss; the second wavy and brown; the third Indian-straight and thick as horsetail.

Claudine, Zizi, Mary.

Mr. McQuine sat at his kitchen table, his gun and Enrique's in either hand. He said, "I smell you when I come in. Trespassing punishable by death." Mr. McQuine was near sixty, so fat that his stomach folded like a mushroom inside the white shirt, and his black tie pointed to a pool of sweat that made the cotton transparent.

Enrique waited for him to shoot.

But Mr. McQuine laughed. He told Enrique when he pulled the hair from their heads it was part of an experiment. It was science. The hair of a child might have turned out blond, if the blood had been improved. But he hadn't been able to check the hair, because the baby was gone. Then he told Enrique to go home.

Next time, Mr. McQuine said.

Blond hair next time. That would have been my mother.

They packed up the girls in the night, in that old white truck named Apache, where they sat huddled in the metal bed, hidden under blankets and sacks of rice, driven in the dark from Sarrat to Baton Rouge, where they caught a Greyhound bus that took them to Rio Seco, California, to live with Mrs. Herbert Batiste, who had left Baton Rouge years ago. She ran a boardinghouse where they would be safe.

After the girls left, that winter day in 1958, my father, Enrique Antoine, had the photo of them developed, and he studied it every night. All the time he planted cane, weeded the rows, and then set the fields on fire the following winter for the harvest, he thought of Marie-Claire, the one he had wanted to marry, and the way she wasn't on the porch or lingering in the field, where her fingers used to brush his when he got a cup of water.

The only one who stayed behind was Anjolie. She was the most beautiful, too, with a golden face and full lips and so much black wavy hair her mother kept it in a thick braid coiled like a nest on her head. Her mother wouldn't let her leave for California. She said she couldn't live without her only child. So she kept Anjolie inside, with all the doors and windows locked. Her father built an armoire for the bedroom and whenever he left for the fields, if any car came down the road, Anjolie was locked into the armoire until her mother could see through the risen dust or falling rain who was in the yard. For more than a year Anjolie never left the house, not even for school or church, until Mr. McQuine finally died while driving back to his house after he'd been drinking all night, his blue car on fire in a ditch by the side of the road.

The newspaper said Mr. Daniel McQuine was a fifth-generation planter whose grandfather had cleared hundreds of acres given to him by Iberville. The article said he died with no wife or heirs, and that his cousin would donate the house and land to a historic trust. The photo showed Mr. McQuine on his tractor.

Everyone in Sarrat remembered only his car, and the chrome grille-teeth that Enrique had crept around in the bar's gravel parking lot, where he cut the brake lines with a knife and spat on the trunk. It had taken him more than a year to find the right night. He left his saliva like a little white cloud there before he ran back to the woods to wait for the car to end in the ditch after the curve in the bayou road. But when he peered into the wrecked car, he saw Mr. McQuine's eyes still moving and his mouth opening to say something, and my father finished him. Then he walked through the trees for miles, back to Sarrat, where there were no girls hanging up laundry or laughing in their bedrooms while they combed each other's hair. There were no girls for a long time, because even though it was safe after Mr. McQuine was buried, Anjolie never left her house, because she was used to it, and the other girls never came back. Enrique Antoine and the man he thought of as his brother, Gustave Picard, went to California. After a few years, Gustave Picard came back and married Anjolie.

But before that, every day she opened the curtains and sat in a chair to look out at the fields and the pecan trees and the edge of the road that led somewhere else.

The other photo is of us. Their daughters. Five young women, standing on my mother's porch in southern California, wearing the shirts we bought senior year. Maroon and gold, with "Class of 83—Always Wild and Free." We are seventeen and eighteen. No one ever thought we would leave the little community my father and Gustave had made in the orange groves.

Bettina looks like her mother, Claudine—pink skin and green eyes and huge breasts under the maroon T-shirt. Clarette like her mother, Mary—implacable dark eyes, high cheekbones, and thick black hair in a halo around her forehead. Cerise is thin and wary, Felonise's girl, hair braided in a bun, arm wiry on my shoulder. I am vague and taupe and smudged, my hair invisible in the chignon behind my head, my face turned slightly toward Glorette.

She was not the daughter of Zizi, who had died of leukemia when she was twenty. Glorette was the only child of Anjolie. She was even more beautiful than her mother. Her face was hammered gold, polished over her bones. Her eyebrows like hummingbird feathers, precise and dark, and her eyes the purple of night.

We are standing on the porch after graduation, under my mother's bougainvillea with the smallest white stars inside the blooms, but Glorette didn't graduate. She had just given birth to Victor, whom my mother held off to the side of the photo. Glorette's face is blurred and turned toward the sound of crying. He couldn't be quieted, I remember.

In the end, we were the only two who left our childhood homes.

I was the only one of us who didn't have children. The spinster. Maiden aunt. The godmother. Marraine, in Louisiana French, was what they called me.

Glorette was like my sister. And she had died August 25, 2000. Five years ago tomorrow. Her small body folded in on itself by someone who'd left her in a shopping cart in an alley behind a taqueria, her long black hair tangled around her beautiful face and falling through the metal mesh that left marks on her cheek.

TOY DISTRICT

"YOU A LIE!" someone shouted from the alleyway near where I walked downtown, where homeless men had congregated, and it sent me directly to my childhood. "You a damn lie!"

That was how people accused each other back in Rio Seco. Not "That's a lie," or "You're a liar."

You *were* the lie.

"I ain't no lie, you drunk-ass—"

The shouts faded when I left the hot sidewalk that smelled faintly of beer and pee and onions, off Spring Street, and went into the lobby of a beautifully restored building that used to be a toy factory. Two people were already in the elevator. The young woman held the door for me and smiled.

"Hi, I'm Donovan," she said. "I'm the publicist's assistant. What a great building!"

"It used to be like a Third World country on this block," the man said. Perfect pressed shirt. Artful stubble. He nodded. "Jeremiah. I'm one of Arthur's lawyers."

They looked at me expectantly. "FX Antoine," I said.

Donovan, whose hair was a shining auburn bob, said, "Oh, I loved your last article in *Vogue*! It was on Belize, right?"

Jeremiah looked sideways at me. "Your mom named you FX?" he said.

I smiled. People from my childhood didn't know the initials I used for my travel essays, because no one from home ever read them. I had just finished one about Oaxaca for *Vogue,* and an article on Bath for *Travel and Leisure.* At noon today, I'd gotten off a plane from Zurich. I was working on a Switzerland piece for *Immerse,* the funky travel magazine where I had regular assignments.

No one who read my essays or assigned them knew my real name.

"She did," I said to Jeremiah as the elevator door opened.

The loft had cement floors the color and texture of limestone cliffs, and ebony-wood furniture, and grass growing in pots. Arthur Graves's new place. He'd made a career by moving to a different city each year and writing a book, always about himself—a man who searched for the right apartment or house where he could paint, who always found a local woman to cook for him and another local woman to love him. He'd done Rio de Janeiro, Lisbon, San Francisco, and Avignon. After a year, he'd leave for another place. Another love.

Arthur Graves actually looked like his jacket photo—white-blond hair combed severely back from his tanned forehead and curling like commas behind his ears, black horn-rimmed glasses. Very British. He stood near a table piled with empanadas and fruit, his new book propped on a side table with a vase full of white roses. He'd been in Argentina this time. Not Buenos Aires but Córdoba, and the first chapter had been published in *Immerse.* So here we were—magazine writers, editors and publicists, people from the *Los Angeles Times,* and people from Hollywood because this book was being made into a movie.

I was headed for the empanadas when my phone rang. Rick, my editor at *Immerse.* "Hey, FX, you at the launch party?"

"Yes," I said.

"Tony's there with you?"

"No," I said, bending to get a plate.

"Come on, get him out of the house. This guy from *The Wall Street Journal* said he might come. He wants to cover *Immerse,* and if Tony's at the party, that makes it worthwhile."

Tony had just won a Pulitzer for a photo essay on children without fathers—he'd gone to rural Mexico, Nigeria, Kentucky, Montana, and Iraq and shot pictures of children holding cell phones, talking to the absent fathers whose portraits were beside them. "Tony doesn't go out on Wednesdays. And I'm not staying long—I need to go home and sleep. I only came to check out some new connections."

"Try," Rick said. "I'll be there in a while."

I stood near a window, looking outside at the heat waves shimmering off the skyline and the parked cars below glinting like silver teeth. We were on the fifth floor. Down there, homeless men were gathering in an alley, settling along the wall though it was not near sunset yet. From here, the green pup tents, brown cardboard squares, and shopping carts made the alley look like a cul-de-sac with absolute boundaries and property lines. Two men were shirtless, their dark backs wide with muscle.

Grady Jackson might be out there, arranging cardboard or sleeping however he had in the streets for so many years. Grady Jackson, who'd been a walking fool, who'd made me know I was a walking fool way back when I was fifteen. He brought me here to LA the first time, when he stole a car and I climbed into the backseat. I had thought of Grady every day of my life since then. But he was a fool for love, too, and I would never be. He was homeless, living somewhere in an alley or under an overpass, and I lived in Los Feliz in an Art Deco apartment building.

We had been kids together, and he fell in love with Glorette. Then he'd stolen something from her—the man she loved—so she'd have to marry him. But she could never love him, and when she left him, he lost his mind. He came here and lived on Skid Row. Glorette had lost her heart, and filled the emptiness every day with the smoky vapors of crack.

Tomorrow was five years since she died. She'd been killed on her thirty-fifth birthday.

Maybe Grady was dead now, too. Below, the two men were setting up a domino game. When I turned, a woman was just behind me, holding dark wine in a big goblet. The red swayed, and the low sun reflected a patch of light that swayed, too. Arthur Graves came between us and said, "Look at it! The windows were black with grime, I remember. Absolutely *black*."

The woman had hair the color of champagne and a silky dress like lime sorbet. She smiled at me without showing her teeth, and my phone rang in my pocket.

I smiled back and rolled my eyes, mouthing "Excuse me" while I turned.

"You comin?" Cerise said. Not hello, how are you? She was my sister-in-law. Even though my two older brothers had left my two childhood friends, the women they'd married right when we got out of high school, Clarette and Cerise were still my sisters. "Tomorrow is five years, Fantine. They lookin for you to come home. Your maman and mine cookin right now."

"I'm at a work thing," I said softly. "And I just got off a plane. I'll be there tomorrow." I walked to the bar, picked up a glass of the red wine, and moved to a different window, hearing laughter.

"Where you been?" she said. That was the question I heard every time from my family. Wherever I'd been, it wasn't as important as being home.

"Switzerland and France." I knew she wouldn't ask me anything about either place.

"So you might drop by, huh? If you ain't too busy." Cerise sounded pissed, like she did every single time we talked. She was mad at me for being in LA, mad at my brother Lafayette for leaving her and their kids, and mad at Glorette for being dead.

"Fantine!" she whispered harshly. "You didn't never see her anymore! But I saw her all the time." Cerise was crying now. "If I went to get my nails done. Or at Rite Aid. She went in there for a break."

I didn't know what to say. I tried to imagine what Glorette had looked like by then.

"She would just smile and say, 'Hey, girl,' like it wasn't no big thang she had a bruise on her neck."

"Cerise," I said. "I'm coming tomorrow."

"Shit, Fantine," she said, her voice sharpened, clearing of sobs. I knew it was always good that she could hate on me for a minute. "Fly round the damn world every week and cain't drive sixty-two miles home. Uh-huh."

"I'll be there tomorrow," I said, and she hung up.

I took two long swallows of the wine. The sour fullness washed my throat, went behind my eyes. An older man smiled at me and lifted his own glass. "Lovely merlot from the Rio Negro Valley in Patagonia. They made sure to buy Argentinean wines."

I nodded and took another sip. He said, "Are you working with Arthur? Are you with the publisher?"

"No," I said. "I work for magazines."

"Ah!" He stood beside me now. His face was that classic combination of silver eyebrows, blue eyes, and pinkish cheeks. The blush was really a mesh of fine red veins, a net of blood rising to the skin.

"I'm with his publisher now. I've finished my first book. Arthur teases me by calling it another Greatest Generation tome. World War Two, you know."

The last swallow of wine settled in my chest. "My father was in the war," I said.

His eyebrows moved like pale moths. "Really? Which front?"

"In France somewhere. He never said the place."

"He didn't talk about his experiences," he said, nodding.

I put down the empty glass on a beautiful ebony-wood table and gave him my best sigh and rueful grin. "He's not much of a talker."

"Well, he could have been traumatized. Where does he live now?" the man asked.

"Here," I said, moving back toward the bar. "California."

"You're a Los Angeles native?" Clearly he wasn't.

"No, I'm from Rio Seco. An hour east of here." And a different universe. He held out a card, and I took it. GERALD JOHN FITZGERALD. PROFESSOR EMERITUS — BOSTON COLLEGE, DEPARTMENT OF HISTORY. "THE WORTH OF THE WAR."

"My da had a sense of humor when he named me," he said, smiling so widely the little string separating his front teeth showed.

My hand was engulfed in his. "FX Antoine," I said.

"No! With that name, you've got some Irish in you, too. And Spanish, no doubt."

"It could be," I said, and then my phone rang again. I looked down at the number. "I'm so sorry—this is my godson. I'll be right back."

"Your godson?" He didn't believe me. His whole face collapsed, the blushing cheeks redder. "Well, yes. As always, with the Electronic Generation." He actually bowed and turned away.

My own face was hot when I flipped open the phone and sat on the little black leather bench near the front door. "Victor?"

"Marraine! Where you been?" He was in a car. The music was so loud it vibrated through the phone like a dull roaring. "I think I called you six times," he said.

"Switzerland," I said. "I just got back today."

"You see paintings?" He always asked what I'd done, and I tried to describe the museums and mountains and buildings to him. I usually brought him a print, but I had gotten him something bigger this time.

"I saw a panoramic painting. It was what came before movies."

"What was it about?" He was trying not to shout.

"War." I closed my eyes. "It's called *The Bourbaki,* and it takes up the whole top floor of a building." The painting circled around my friend

Jane and me. Moroccan soldiers in their tasseled uniforms, their red fezzes like biscuits on their heads. Surrendering in the snow of Switzerland in 1871.

"That's all you gon tell me?"

"Hundreds of soldiers coming back from a battle in winter during the Franco-Prussian War and being taken care of by Swiss villagers. Dead horses. Blood in the snow."

He was silent, but that just meant he was thinking. Like me. Then he said, "You didn't tell me about The Who. Professor Zelman gave me 'Baba O'Riley.'"

"What?"

He started singing into the phone. "'Out here in the fields, I fight for my meals! I get my back into my livin!'"

Someone in the car yelled, "Shut up, nigga. Fitty Cent just came on. Let him sing."

"If you call that singin," Victor shouted back.

"Who are you with?" I asked, trying to sound neutral.

"Zee and Fonso."

Jazen and Alfonso. He'd never hung out with them in high school. Alfonso had just gotten out of prison; Clarette, who was a correctional officer, had told me. Jazen and his Navigator owned the streets near where Glorette was killed. Didn't Victor know they might have sold his mother the rock she'd smoked that night? Boys—no, they weren't children anymore. Glorette had Victor when we were seniors in high school. Bettina had Alfonso the year before. They were young men. But no one ever used those words anymore. They were dudes, bangers, bros, guys. Fools.

Victor said, "You gave me the hookup with the iPod and Professor Zelman gave me the hookup to The Who. They rock."

"He's pretty cool for a professor," I said. Zelman had given him an award for best essay and for top honors student at the city college in Rio Seco. Victor had just graduated in June.

"'I don't need to fight—to prove I'm right—I don't need to be forgiven!'"

A deep voice came from the background. "Fool, I ain't tellin you again." Jazen. He drove the Navigator, and ran the show.

Victor was silent for a moment. The room was nearly full of people now, and two more women came through the open door. The leather bench was so low to the floor all I could see were knees and shoes. Strappy green sandals and sensible pumps.

"Marraine," he said. "I need to talk to you."

"Where are you?" I said.

"We're comin to LA! I won tickets to a concert, and we gotta pick em up." But then he must have held the phone closer. He whispered, "I was so happy about the tix cause I been thinkin about tomorrow. You know. And I just wanted to—tell you."

I said carefully, "About tomorrow? Are you okay?"

He said softly, "I stayed at Fonso's mama's house last night. She got faded on some Hennessy. You know what she said? She said she saw my pops play the flute once at a club, with my moms. I put some Yusuf Lateef on my headphones and I was thinking about it all night. He didn't even stay till I was born. Hated me before I even came out. And I can't even sing."

I closed my eyes and saw his father. Sere Dakar. Perfect Afro like a black dandelion. His long fingers on the flute.

Victor said, "Wanted to tell you about The Who. Can't tell nobody else."

We stayed quiet for a minute, inside the drumbeats.

Then Victor said, "Can I stay at your place for a while?"

"What?" I felt the humming fatigue in my head, and the thumping music from the phone made it worse. "Today?"

"Yeah. The concert's on Saturday."

"Victor," I said. "I don't know. I just got off a plane. I'm at a reception."

"Is the conversation desultory or erudite?" he said, his voice light again.

"Very funny." I was the one who'd taught him the SAT words, for the test he never got to take. "Let me call you back."

His voice rose. "You know The Who said the F word on the radio? Way back then?" Then he whispered, his mouth right up on the phone, "Marraine—you light a candle? For my maman? Do you still pray? I don't."

He hung up.

My back pressed against the wall covered with textured plaster. The entry foyer had a dark rattan rug and, across from me, a wooden pew with carvings on the armrests. Above it was a wooden figure, sitting on a shelf. The ceilings were so high that the room felt like church. The Virgin Mary looked down on me.

Who are you—Who-oo? Who-oo? Tell me who the fuck are you?

Victor had written some good essays for Professor Zelman—on the violin used in the Creole music his grandfather loved, on how the Red Hot Chili Peppers and Average White Band were white guys even a black guy could love. He wrote a great piece on falsetto love songs of the 1970s and '80s and how they worked on women of a certain age— Cerise, Clarette, and me. Not his mother.

But I didn't want Jazen and Alfonso anywhere near my place. I wanted to be alone, thinking about the *Bourbaki* panorama painting and the Aare River, red geraniums like fireworks in the window boxes. I could pick up Victor in Rio Seco tomorrow, when I drove out there. I leaned my head against the wall.

Mary's blue robe was decorated with the fleur-de-lis. The royal lily.

I had been in a cathedral in Reims, France, with a group from college, during our semester abroad. The guide with her lovely French accent showed us the stained glass windows. I was staring at the colors and the light, and she said, "That figure was created during the crowning of the dauphin. Do you see the yellow bits on the blue robe? The fleur-de-lis—they are reserved for the royalty." Her voice was so proud. I first thought of Marie Antoinette, because I was nineteen and still believed royalty was romantic, and then I heard my ancestor's name in my forehead.

Moinette Antoine. She was branded on the shoulder with the fleur-de-lis after she ran away and was captured. She had escaped to find her mother. Which shoulder? Like livestock. Live. Stock.

I stood up and felt dizzy. Arthur Graves said to someone, "I've heard the Los Angeles River is over there, amid the tangle of those warehouses, but I can't be sure, of course, because it's not as if it's an actual body of running water, right? You tell me, darling."

Out here in the fields, Victor sang. I fight for my meals. Moinette Antoine had been out in the cane fields. After the branding, her friend Fantine had tied a piece of salt meat on the burn—the flower. The two women who gave me my name.

I went back to the bar and took an empanada with another glass of wine. I wanted to wash out my skull. I'd had coffee and breakfast in Zurich, and water and tomato juice on the plane ride. The wine crased some of the hot sand resting behind my eyes. Back at the tall windows, I looked outside at the alley, the homeless men. Even from here I could see the big guy holding up his palms to the sky in a gesture like surrender to his laughing friend. His palms were pink as roses.

The phone shook again in my hand, and when I opened it, Victor said in a low voice, "Marraine? Don't forget me. I need to get out of here. I need to be in LA with you."

Before I could say anything, he hung up.

When Glorette showed him to me for the first time his eyes were tight lines like knife slits in a skull, and his mouth was open wide with cries. No teeth—the screaming rode down a flume of pink tongue.

I hadn't paid attention when Bettina had Alfonso, but Glorette with Victor scared me so badly that I never wanted to have sex again, never wanted to think that the mouth fastened on my neck—Marcus Thompson's mouth—and the tongue sweeping along my collarbone would deliver me into a baby. My own teeth imprinted on Marcus's neck, so that everyone would know we'd been together—we both needed that badge back then.

Don't forget me—Victor's voice quiet and clotted with sadness. I was not his mother. I had never been a mother. I hadn't even slept with a man for almost a year. I hadn't stayed anywhere long enough, and hadn't found anyone interesting enough.

I closed my eyes and listened to the sentences moving around the pale cement walls. Because where I had grown up, the older people spoke French most of the time, and even their English sounded French, many times I heard American phrases as if I were from another country.

"Oh my God, did you get her galleys? The new memoir? What a wack job."

"Whoa," someone else said. "You're shitting me. The guy said that?"

"Yeah, no, absolutely," a woman answered. "I can't wrap my mind around it."

In the bathroom, I ran cold water on my fingers and dragged them across my throat. It had been rainy in Thun and Bern, when I followed the Aare River. I called Tony.

"Please come to this stupid party," I said. "Rick really wants you here. And I haven't seen you in two weeks." He was the one person I wanted to talk to. Not Victor. I leaned my forehead against the lime-stone counter.

"It's Wednesday," he said. I heard the TV. The loft walls were so thick that party noise only entered under the door, like a cartoon ribbon of laughter.

In the mirror, my hair was held firmly by shiny gel in a tight bun, my collar still crisp and white. "I know," I said. "But you can't keep mourning like this."

"Why?" Tony said, his voice blurred and angry. Scotch. "You left me a message that you had to go to some five-year anniversary of death tomorrow."

"Yeah," I said. "You're right. But can I come by?"

"In a while," he said, and hung up abruptly. I smelled the white candle burning on the counter. Jasmine? Gardenia?

I returned to the window. Arthur Graves had a different woman in tow, pulling her toward the view. She smiled wide at me and said, "LA's not much of a skyline. Even if *everybody's* moving downtown." She was messing with him. She leaned in close to me, long silver drop earrings brushing her bare shoulders. "I love your shirt," she said. "Where did you get it?"

Arthur Graves focused on my face and said, "And who is this lovely vision? You look as if you've just arrived from Buenos Aires! Doesn't she?"

I smiled, and they waited. I did look Argentinean. Or Andalusian. Maybe a tanned Angeleno.

The woman touched my sleeve. "Thanks," I said. I had twenty different white cotton or linen shirts, and twenty black ones, and that was all I wore. I had gotten the idea when I was sixteen, looking at photos of Carolina Herrera and Audrey Hepburn. My face was taupe. Neutral. I held up the sleeve, which was edged with shiny whiter embroidery. "Oaxaca. They have beautiful clothes."

"I love Oaxaca! Is that where you're from?" she asked, leaning closer. "Mexico? I went to Oaxaca on this shoot for *Elle* once." She put out her hand. "I'm Jesse James Miller."

"FX Antoine."

Her voice was excited but confused. "*You're* FX Antoine?" She was trying to reconcile my face with what I wrote. My photo was never in magazines. I wrote odd narratives about people and food and landscape, and I never mentioned myself. She said, "I loved your piece on Bath." She was studying my hair.

I could be Saudi or Hawaiian, Mexican or Italian.

"You wrote that great piece on South Carthay for *Angelena.* God, I was sad when that magazine went under."

I nodded. I'd written a monthly column about different neighborhoods where LA women might like to spend a day—unexpected places like South Carthay, Beverlywood, Palms. Places no one might have thought of for lunch.

"Wait—you wrote that piece on Springsteen's Jersey Shore. Where Tony Volpe's from. You work with him, right? He's amazing. Is he coming by?" The wineglass trembled a bit in her hand. She was a Tony fan. Everyone was a Tony fan.

"Probably not," I said.

"So, are you from Oaxaca?"

The wine was so dark it looked like cherry Kool-Aid, and I tasted that chemical sweetness on my back teeth. Glorette and I used to drink black cherry Kool-Aid on my mother's porch. Our arms sealed together by sweat, our backs against the wood shingles of the house, singing Chaka Khan. "'Tell me somethin good—tell me, tell me, tell me . . .'"

And then those voices stored inside the memory of my cell phone, in my pocket, next to my thigh—they said, Fantine. You comin home? Your maman cook for everyone. Fantine. Call me. Call me. Don't forget me. Tell me somethin good.

"Louisiana," I said. "My parents are from Louisiana." I wanted to bite back the words as soon as they'd left my mouth. The sun was hot on my back, through the window. In my pocket was a boarding pass from Zurich, but also a coffee bean for luck, from my mother.

Jesse James Miller said, "Wow—and is that where you're still based? New Orleans?"

What was she? Blond, but with streaks of brown. Her nose was wider and flatter than it could have been, and her lips were framed by those smoker tributaries in the skin. Her voice was the honey-nicotine kind, her camisole top silky and purple.

"I grew up in California, in Rio Seco," I said. I should shut up now. Now. "A world away from here."

She grinned widely again. "Oh, I know exactly what you mean. I'm from Anaheim, a little tract house. Need I say more?"

But whenever anyone said something like that—I'm from Fresno, I'm from the Valley, oh my God I know what you mean—they didn't know what I meant. I wasn't from LA, with millions of people, or even Rio Seco, which was big enough, with a population of 300,000. Drive out farther, to the very edge of the city limits, to the orange groves near the river, and go down a long dirt road. Inside the trees was Sarrat, a place unto itself, a place my father had made on his own, for his people.

I should just walk home now—from here to Los Feliz, and then I'd sleep. Grady Jackson had taught me to walk that far. We were walkin fools.

"I'm sorry," I said. "I have to get going."

She grinned. Her teeth were perfect. She handed me a card. "I'd love to work with you sometime."

"The outlaw Jesse James," I said, and reached for her hand. "Nice to meet you."

Outside on the terrace I called Rick. "Hey—I'm going home."

"It's that bad?" he said.

I looked at the shadows moving inside the loft. "No. Not bad. Kind of desultory."

"No Tony?" he said.

Rick didn't know about Tony's ritual. He would have thought it excessive and sentimental. "He's really tired," I said.

"Okay. Come by the office and get coffee and talk about some new pieces."

The homeless men below were laughing and shouting at the domino game. Three concrete circles stood on the terrace, way above the earth, filled with grass as green as antifreeze.

I made my way to the door. Jesse James Miller was in the hallway. Near the bar, Gerald John Fitzgerald bowed in farewell. I lifted my hand and called out to him, "I'd like to call you. About the war. I'm going to write tonight about the Franco-Prussian conflict."

He opened his mouth in surprise. I opened the door.

The Greatest Generation. My father and Gustave and all the men from their generation had fought in that war, too. They left their little villages in Louisiana and Georgia and Mississippi, and returned to the country that still hated them and wouldn't let them drink water from

white porcelain and silver faucet, or release water into stained porcelain and silver handle. My father and Gustave had gotten back from
killing strangers in Europe, but they couldn't send girls walking down
a road without danger.

They came to California and re-created their villages or towns, like
everyone else. I took the stairs. The dank stairwell still smelled of toy
factory. Who'd made the toys?

It was California, but all the little villages the fathers and mothers
made, with their food and music and fears, were carried around inside
us. We'd been born here, the people of my generation, gone to school
together in the '70s and '80s, eaten the same cafeteria brown gravy and
mashed potatoes, read the same books and kicked the same balls, but
even though we wore platform shoes and bell bottoms and tight Qiana
shirts, we carried around our individual villages, and what our parents
gave us—their caution and fear and anger and vigilance and stories.
No one left Sarrat except Glorette, and me.

I had not lit a candle for her. On the sidewalk, the light had barely
changed. It was three thirty and August—the sun wouldn't go down
for a long time.

MITLA

THE *IMMERSE* OFFICE WAS on Eighth, near Hill. On Eighth and
Olive was a bar called the Golden Gopher. Five years ago, that's where
Grady Jackson had told me how he stole Sere Dakar from Glorette.

I should tell Victor the truth. I'd known it for this long and hadn't
ever told him. How did you tell a story like that now, all these years
later? Your father didn't abandon you—he was murdered. How would
that make Victor feel better? Even Glorette had never known.

When Victor was growing up, Glorette had always been high or
sleeping, and she might have told him stories, but she didn't know that
one. She'd told him about her palm tree sparkler, and the barn owls, the
Perseid meteor shower in August, and coyotes. Sometimes he'd stayed
with his grandfather, and he heard stories there for sure, but Gustave
and my father didn't know about Grady and Sere Dakar.

I couldn't call him now and tell him anything, while he was in the
Navigator. But I'd see him tomorrow, and I could judge whether the
truth would help him or hurt him.

At the mouth of the alley, I paused and listened to the men. People
were still passing in waves on the sidewalk, leaving work early. Then
the door opened on a Porta-Potty at the back of the alley, and a woman
propped herself against the blue plastic wall. She leaned there, her
palm pressed to her temple as if she were trying to keep something from
falling out of her head. Her black hair was like dead seaweed, and her
knees ashy gray as rain puddles. A man approached, and she pulled
him nearer to the door.

She was working. She stared at me and I moved past the alley.

I walked down Spring Street toward Third. Construction workers
were gutting an old bank and a SRO hotel. Signs for luxury lofts were
lit with spotlights on the roofs. Thousands of homeless people had
packed their tents and bags and boxes and coats and melted into invis-

ibility when the sun rose high enough—now they came out with the approaching end of the workday like emissaries sent among the rest of us.

I headed down Third toward Broadway. I'd meet with Rick and then walk home. It would feel good.

Nobody walked home from Downtown to Los Feliz. Only a walkin fool.

On Broadway, the butt mannequins showed off curvier jeans than you'd see on Melrose or Rodeo. Just the bottom half, cheeks turned to shoppers. All the stereos blasting cumbia and salesmen calling out and jewelry flashing gold.

All over the world, wherever I walked, I had my uniform for moving through a city. My black leather bag, holding only my thin wallet and a small notebook and pen. Nothing flashy, nothing too money or too poor. A woman walking for miles and miles—you had to look like you had somewhere to go. Not like you were rich and ready to be robbed, and not like a man-magnet with cleavage and jewelry.

And just as every time I walked, settling into a rhythm of long even strides so that I could think—about the Aare River and the wooden houses perched high on the steep slopes above it—first I thought of Grady. Maybe he was still alive, and maybe his sister Hattie was still at the Golden Gopher.

No one would ever kill for me, like Grady Jackson had killed for Glorette.

No one looked at me. My earrings plain silver hoops, my only makeup black eyeliner and a lip gloss called Fig. My eyes slanted and opaque.

But Glorette—even if she'd worn a sack, men stared at her. She was nearly iridescent—when I'd first learned the word in junior high, I knew it meant Glorette.

Another alley, and a homeless woman lay in a heap, curled tight as a dog around herself. Glorette—her face so lovely that her life was ruined, and my face so bland and neutral that I had always been allowed to lie to people, and imagine myself.

We could have been twins, when we were children. But then we turned fourteen and everything changed—her face rearranged itself, and her body moved differently. Her eyelashes, her legs, her breasts.

Our Barbies sat on the shelf above her bed, their sharp feet dangling over us, and she brushed mascara onto her lashes while I watched.

Glorette, walking the two miles to school beside me, her stride slow and measured as a gazelle's, her legs long and thin, the crescent of white underneath the purple-black iris that somehow made her seem as if she were sleepily studying everyone, and the men could not look away. Every day our mothers coiled our long hair into buns high on our skulls. All day, men imagined pulling the pins from Glorette's hair and the river falling down along her back, tangled in their hands.

Junior high—one day a hand pulled Glorette into a broom closet while she paused in the hallway. I left her behind on my way to class. She'd been tying her shoe. I glanced back to see her looking up, as if someone had spoken to her, and then moving toward a doorway. Then she disappeared.

When we walked home that afternoon, a hickey marked the back of her neck. A cloud of blood that teeth had sucked toward the surface. I wished someone would want to touch his lips to my neck. But she said nothing. And it was the back of her neck—why would someone stand behind her?

That weekend, she showed me the five-dollar bill. We never had more than quarters. She held it in her palm, like a dead leaf, and said, "Mr. Darmand. That janitor. The young one. He stood behind me. Did something behind me. On my jeans. He ain't touched no other part a me, cept my hair. Pulled back my hair and held on to my neck." She put her fingers over her eyes, a visor against the light in the room, and then she sat on the floor. "Like I was a shadow. Like—the picture of me."

I didn't understand until a long time later. I felt sick at the idea of him pushing and pushing at her from behind, but by then I never wanted to bring it up again.

Two homeless men started shoving each other in the street, and the pedestrians in the crosswalk swerved like ants around a pebble, and the cars brayed like huge donkeys.

All the men here downtown—sleeping with outstretched fingers near my heels, pushing carts, doing ballet moves between the stalled cars—a Mexican man with a handlebar mustache and no teeth under it who grinned at me, and a man my age, with skin like mine, his hair

dreaded up in a non-hip way. Like bad coral. He sat down on the curb
and stared at the tires of the nearest cars.

Where was Grady?

I pushed the button on the intercom in the doorway, and Rick said,
"I'm coming down. Need coffee."

He bounded down the stairs and said, "See the new place next door?"

It was a tiny restaurant with MITLA stenciled on the window. The
ancient ruins of a Mayan kingdom that I'd seen in Oaxaca. I touched
the electric blue stucco walls—the texture felt fresh and prickly. Burnt
umber curtains at the window, and the door was actually gold. Spray-
painted?

Rick grinned. "You said Oaxaca had great coffee, and you weren't
kidding." When he hugged me, his arms were the same as when I'd met
him five years ago. Slender, but gym-toned. He was maybe an inch
taller than me, his black hair cut short like broom bristles, standing up
with gel. He grinned and said, "I missed you." Then I heard the gentle
moo of his phone on vibrate, and he turned toward the doorway and
waved me in. "Damn. Gotta take this one, FX. Advertiser."

I sat down at the table near the window, and a man bent and smiled.
"Café con leche, por favor," I said, smiling back.

His Mayan face—eyes dark and sharp as oleander leaves—looked
down at me while I sipped the coffee, and he said, "Bueno, no?"

So good—cinnamon and nighttime and something secret. "Que bueno," I said, and he might have thought I was Honduran, or Panamanian.

The first time I met Rick, he'd said, "I've been reading your stuff
forever. Since you're a world traveler with a hundred bylines but no
contributor's photo, I always wondered where you were from."

"Here," I'd said.

"LA?"

"Rio Seco."

I remember how he had studied me. "Where's that?"

"Have you been to Palm Springs?"

"Of course! I love midcentury architecture."

"Then you passed Rio Seco," I'd told him, and that was it.

When he got to the reception, would he meet Jesse James Miller?
Would she say, "So is FX black? Louisiana, wow. I never would have
guessed from her work."

Rick dropped into the seat, out of breath. "So damn hot out there."

"Remember when we first met, and you said you were from Brooklyn all defensive, like I wouldn't know shit about it, and then you said, Fort Greene, and I said Tillie's was a great coffeehouse?"

"I was impressed," he said. The waiter brought him black coffee without being asked, and Rick grinned wide. "Can you tell I've been here a few times?"

Back then, he'd said, "Can you find somewhere different to go, to immerse yourself completely? That's what I want this magazine to be about."

Immersion. I finished my coffee. Too much liquid. The wine was wearing off. I said to the waiter, "Chilaquiles?" A dark man in a janitor's uniform was eating a plate full of torn soft tortillas in sauce and cheese. The waiter smiled again.

Rick's hair glistened like needles in the harsh light. "How was the Aare? Not a river I'd heard of. Worth it?"

"It was great. Little towns and cities in the shadow of the Alps."

"You gonna get anything good out of it?"

"If you pay me." He was waiting for the word I'd bring. I said, "Botz tunsig."

"I can't even guess that one."

"It's like oh-my-gosh," I said. "In some little village outside Thun. *Tunsig* is Swiss-German for thousand, and even Jane doesn't know what *bot* means."

"You saw Jane?"

"Yeah. She met me in Luzern for the day." I smiled. "She asked if you were still good at desultory conversation. I said not with me."

He laughed. "We never did desultory. Not since the first day we met."

"Yeah. I asked you if you'd ever been in love."

"And I said twice." Rick put his hands around the cup. "In high school, and she dumped me for a football player, and in college, and she dumped me for a professor."

"You told me you were in love with your job and your apartment," I said. That night, I'd realized why everyone I knew in LA made good money and ate good food and lived in great houses or apartments—because we were mostly not in love. Sometimes we fell in love with the idea of love, but it hardly ever worked out. Love was about having things already, trying to share those things or buying more things together, and then arguing about the things.

Except for Tony. He'd actually been in love.

Rick raised his eyebrows and said, "Found him yet?"

He meant the Intrepid Gentleman or the Unlikely Companion—the one who could accompany me on my travels and feature as a straight man in my essays. The man some other writers had. And as always, I said, "I wasn't looking."

The sidewalk outside was glittering as the sun shifted. He said, "I just bought a loft on Spring Street. Not far from Arthur Graves's place, actually."

"What?"

He shifted his body away from the table. The cloth was dark red. "How does he snare those women?"

"You bought this place? Aha—more room for Jenny."

He shrugged. Jenny was a photographer's assistant at the magazine— twenty-eight, that kind of dark-eyed messy-hairbun girl who went skiing in winter and mountain biking in summer.

But then he leaned forward. "It'll take me a year to ask her. You know it will. Shit. Six months to figure out the place as far as furniture and paint and another six before I get up the nerve. By then she'll be with some goddamn ski instructor."

See? I thought. It's not love. It's sharing things. I said, "So ask her now."

"Says the woman who's never told me anything serious about herself. Who remains a mystery."

I pushed the plate of chilaquiles toward him to taste. The red sauce spread along my tongue, the pebbly corn kernels nestled in my molars.

"I need the Oaxaca piece by September 20—we're running that one in December." He looked down at the plate. "You said they hardly ever use flour tortillas. Just corn. This is like bread pudding, only with tortillas. And spicy."

I said, "Rye bread, pumpernickel, baguettes, tortillas. What's the Ethiopian bread?"

"Injera."

"Yeah. Then you have places with no bread. Just rice."

"And I think of bagels."

This was how we always ended up. Knowledge for the sake of ourselves and no one else—the kind of conversation my family would never have. They would talk only about people and places we already knew and hated or loved.

Except Victor. He wanted *Bourbaki* and botz tunsig. He wanted chilaquiles.

Rick grinned. "So I was thinking of Turkey, or somewhere along the Dalmatian coast." Shifting into business, the other language we shared. "New beaches are good," he said. "And ports, for cruise advertisers. We need some water. Boats."

"Everybody wants to be around water." Then I looked at the indigo blue of the walls. Indigo—that smell kill Moinette's grandmère, my grandmother had said. Grow indigo to make them blue soldier coat, she said. So Lafitte pirate can kill them soldier. Lafitte pirate take away the maman of Moinette.

"There's always pirates," I said.

"What?" Rick said. "You're going Johnny Depp on me?"

"I went to Cornwall once, and they still talk about pirates. And in Belize some guy told me about pirates. Just thinking."

He left money on the table, and we got up to leave. "The romantic idea of pirates is hot now," I said. "The allure of the ports and coasts." Cinnamon scent. Spices from the Orient. "Family legend is we knew some pirates."

Rick folded his arms. "Come on. A, you're finally going to tell me something about yourself, and B, it's a pirate joke?"

If I said Lafitte, it meant Louisiana. I didn't want to go there again this afternoon.

My phone rang when we were on the sidewalk. Victor's voice was loud and deep. "Marraine? She's here. My moms. Her picture's here."

Rick mouthed, "The Tieless Companion?" I rolled my eyes.

Victor shouted, "I swear it's her. But it says sweet voodoo. Not her name. Marraine, you have to come to this club. In Burbank."

I said, "Burbank?" Rick studiously unwrapped some gum.

"Yeah—remember I won tickets? Zee brought me to get them from the radio station. Clear Channel. Hollywood Way. The place is called Dimples. I can't go in there—I knocked but the old guy just shook his head. Marraine, please. You have to find out why she's here."

"Okay," I said softly. "I'll be there."

"You gotta hurry," he said, quieter now, his hand muffling the sound.

"Lots of fools win tickets here and it's too many of em walkin around. We gotta go soon."

Jazen and Alfonso were ready for trouble at four o'clock on a Wednesday? I closed the phone and said, "Rick, can you give me a ride?"

DIMPLES

THE CAR WAS A midnight blue Beemer, hot as dragon breath, as my brothers used to say. Rick opened the windows and pushed in a CD. Fela Kuti. He said, "So you didn't drive downtown?"

"I came in a cab, pretty much from the airport," I said. The drums of West Africa knocked against my earlobes. I closed my eyes—for a moment, the rhythm sounded like the opening conga beats of William DeVaughn: *Though you may not drive a great big Cadillac—diggin the scene with a gangster lean.* Now Victor was riding in the Navigator, with Fifty Cent.

"Where are we headed? I get to see where the famous FX Antoine lives?"

"You know I live in Los Feliz," I said. "I need to go to Burbank for my godson."

"You have a godson? He works for the studios?"

Foolish to keep playing this game—a mysterious writer with no family. "He won concert tickets. The radio station's off Hollywood Way."

Rick headed toward Sunset. "Ay yi yi," he said. "Four twelve. Graves is reading at seven at that new bookstore downtown. I was going to talk you into coming with me."

"I'm sorry," I said. "I'll meet you there after I get my godson—straightened out."

Rick squinted at the freeway on-ramp. "It's a possibility." The traffic was still flowing. He said, "What's the concert?"

"Dave Matthews."

"What—your godson's forty?"

"He's twenty-two but he likes Dave Matthews," I said. Even though he's supposed to like Akon and Chamillionaire.

The ivy covering the freeway bridge above us was dusty and motionless. A rogue burst of bougainvillea spilled over a retaining wall. I wanted to be alone for an entire day, with no phone or people. I saw

myself beside the Limmat, in Zurich, yesterday. I wanted to eat Thai
food and read my new book.

I said, "I got this book by Tommaso Astarita—southern Italy. *Between
Salt Water and Holy Water*—great title, huh? Maybe Tony and I could
go to Naples."

Rick nodded. "Let me see who's done Italy recently. Hey—the Golden
State Freeway." He pointed up to the sign. "I forget it's called that. I'm
always on the 101 or the 10. We could take this all the way to Oregon."

On my right was the Los Angeles River, the water like a metallic
table runner stretched the length of the concrete channel. Closer to the
Los Feliz exit, the sloping cement banks were decorated with so much
graffiti they looked like crazy preschool rugs set down beside the river.
"What if this ever flooded?" I said, looking at the sweep of shallow
water.

"It can't." Rick was squinting again at the signs above us. "It's not
like the Mississippi. We have to take the Ventura Freeway, right?"

We followed the river companionably for a few more minutes, and
then it ducked under the asphalt and disappeared. Rick said, "Warner
Music Group—right there."

Off the exit, we were in a strange little residential area. Two gray
apartment buildings with foil-covered windows, like spaceships baking
in the heat. A few sherbet-colored stucco duplexes. Then we saw the
huge brick buildings across Olive Street. ABC, NBC. Lots of parked
cars, kids walking around. Rick said cautiously, "Can you find him?"

"He's probably waiting for me inside. Clear Channel—right there.
Thanks, Rick."

"I'll see you at the bookstore. Talk to Tony about Naples, the Dalmatian coast. You want to have breakfast at ten—the three of us?
Finalize the next two assignments?"

I closed the car door. "Sounds good. And you see if Jenny wants to go
to the party, and take a look at your cool downtown loft."

Until he drove away, I held the phone to my ear and moved my
mouth. No one did that in Switzerland, even in the big cities. Nothing
was wrong there with walking, looking at buildings or trees or faces,
just thinking about rivers. Being alone.

I waited at the crosswalk. NBC Studios. Atlantic Records. Rhino
Records. Where the hell was Dimples?

The sun was glaring hot on the sidewalk. Two groups of teenagers gathered around me suddenly as a herd of antelope, moving me forward in the green light. "Armando, you serious—you takin Malia to the concert?" a girl said loudly. "That puta? After I drove your ass here?" Her brows were drawn on long and thin, and her shoulder said *Payasa* in green cursive. Clown—feminine version. She threw up her hand. "Look at this! She just texted me." Her nails were wine-red claws around the cell phone she pushed in his face. "Get your own damn ride home, Mando."

The boy stopped in the stripes and said, "Just wait five minutes till I get the tickets—" but she started back the other way and he kept crossing doggedly, head down.

Someone behind me shouted, "Marraine!"

Down the dingy block I'd just left was a squat brown building with signs and appendages everywhere. Dimples Dance and Supper Club. I shaded my eyes. Showcase to Stardom! Who in the hell would believe that?

SING FOR YOUR TAPE—FREE TAPES TO VIRGINS. A black sign with white letters, high on the roof. The other big roof sign shouted KONTINUOUS KARAOKE!

When I crossed the street, along the exterior of the mud-brown wood-panel walls were black-and-white photos. The Beatles. James Dean. Elvis. A set of narrow stairs led to a dim second-floor landing with a door and another sign. SCREENING ROOM. Was this a joke? Would some girl really head up those rickety wooden stairs? I shivered, even in the glaring heat, thinking of the door opening to the janitor's closet, the way Glorette had tilted her head up from tying her shoe. The cement at the base of the stairs was spotted with discs of flattened gum like black quarters.

They waited on the sidewalk near the entrance. Jazen and Alfonso were both wearing huge jeans and heavy denim jackets in the August heat. Alfonso's hair was cut to stubble, and a tattoo made a greenish shadow at his temple. He was prettier than his mother, Bettina, with caramel-bright skin and neat features.

Jazen wore cornrows, stray hairs blurring the angled pattern. He looked like his mother. Juanita. I remembered her from freshman year, when she came from New Orleans. Jazen had glossy brown skin, what they called Chinese eyes, and a scar on his forehead. A thrown rock? A nail file? It was a small crater like a missing puzzle piece to his face.

Victor—he usually said something funny right off, but this time his face was closed, held so tight all the bones showed. He was pale, and his cheekbones were like Glorette's, sharp and distinct, small spades under his skin. He wore skinny jeans and a yellow T-shirt that said "Black Coral—Belize." His dreadlike twists stood up like sun rays. His iPod was clipped to his pants, the earpieces dangling around his neck. Three black males, I thought, walking toward me. That's what the cops see, and the corporate guy in the convertible stopped at the corner, and the kids gathering at the crosswalk. But Victor wasn't dressed like a gangster.

I saw the fear in his face, and the calculation in Alfonso's, and the swagger undercut with uncertainty in Jazen's.

We didn't hug. I had held him a few times the summer after he was born, when he was small and squirmy and froglike to me, before I went off to college; when I saw him next he was running and dirt-kneed and hard to catch, like all Sarrat kids. Years later, when his grandpère used to rescue him after Glorette was hospitalized or evicted, Victor would greet me gravely if I happened to come to Sarrat, but he never ran toward anyone for a hug or candy. Victor would sit on his grandfather's porch, watching for a long time before joining the others.

I said, "Nice hair," and touched his shoulder when he got close enough. He was tall, about six-one, and reed thin. His shoulder bone was wide and knobby under my hand. His eyes were his mother's— night-purple and soft.

But he didn't smile, casually, testing, as he usually did. His high forehead was grooved with three lines.

I looked at Jazen and Alfonso. "Hey, guys." Alfonso was from Sarrat—he knew old-school manners and said, "Auntie Fantine," but Jazen merely lifted his chin at me.

Victor propelled me forward into the dingy entrance, a long dim hallway lined by black-and-white publicity stills. "Appearing Nightly" was Tiffany, with the newest photo. Close to the street were blond girls, hair silver in the pictures, and that blond-girl look: pale blue eyes clear as water, teeth like baby refrigerators, boobs round and fake as grapefruit halves peeking out of camisoles. Aime. Angela. Angelle. But as we got closer to the door, the pictures were older and more faded. A Mexican-American girl. Conchita. I would have laughed, except then I saw the photo beside her. Browner with age, like those sepia portraits in a history book.

Gloria and Glorette. Gloria—her Chinese bob and full red lips and fake lashes, like someone out of a James Bond film. And Glorette—her mouth open and uncertain, her eyes shining. She looked fragile and sexy—like she needed the person gazing at her to save her. Every boy or man who had ever seen her looked at her that way. I am the one, he thought. The one she wants. The one she needs.

But she never wanted anyone except Sere Dakar. She loved Victor, this boy—the old word? Man-child?—standing with his throat so close to my temple, but he couldn't save her, and she couldn't save him.

"How'd you find this?" I asked.

"When we went by, I was like, I bet it's nothing but white girls, and then Fonso came down here and was like, Two sistas! Oh, shit, it's your moms." He was still staring at the picture, a little leap in his jaw like a tiny fish swimming under the skin.

Under the photo, white hand-inked words. Brown Sugar and Sweet Voodoo. Brown sugar—the two words I hated most. Just like a black girl should.

"Who's the other one?" he said. His voice was much deeper than his face and body—like his father's.

From the sidewalk, Jazen called, "We gotta go, nigga. I ain't got all day."

"Hattie Jackson," I said. "She was older than us. Her brother was Grady Jackson. He loved your mama. He married her after you were born."

He nodded. "Grady. Like Sanford and Son. This dude Chess always came to see my moms, and he'd talk about 'your big love, Trashman Grady.'"

I couldn't tell him now. Not here. "She called herself Gloria. She wanted to be an actress, and she must have gotten your mama to come up here."

He touched the dusty glass. His fingerprints hovered like three dark new moons above his mother's face. "They don't need this picture. It's like some historic archive. Like a museum." He went out to the sidewalk. "See the sign? This place doesn't open until six. But there's an old guy upstairs. He wouldn't open the door for me."

They're still here because they're black but light and sexy. I squinted in the sun. Brown sugar. Voodoo. Two hundred years of that shit, and it still works.

I went up the wooden stairs, baking in the sun, and got dizzy. I'd gone up dank cold stone castle steps in Switzerland two days ago. Screening Room. The door swung in, and on a video screen a young blond woman was licking an ice cream cone like it was something else, while onstage people laughed and clapped. An old white man peered out at me. He gave me a big smile until I got closer to him, and then he looked straight at my chest, slid his eyes up to my face, and said, "Hon, no offense, but you're a little long in the tooth. And the karaoke live feed doesn't start till eight."

I held back a laugh. "No. I wanted to ask you about a picture." I pointed downstairs. But I had to say the words. "Brown Sugar and Sweet Voodoo."

He squinted.

I said, "The black girls."

He shrugged. "Too many girls. And that one must be from when we first opened. Back in '83." Then Victor was behind me, and the man lifted his chin. "No rappers!" he shouted, and slammed the door.

Victor breathed hard. "He said '83?"

"Yeah." The year he was born.

"He said no rappers." Victor held out his hands. "What—I'm DJ Scholaptitude?" He turned and headed down the stairs to the sidewalk. "Old white dudes all look alike."

On the outside wall, the last picture was Gwen Stefani. "Yeah, discovered here, no doubt," I said to Victor.

He kept his head down and stood beside Jazen at the signal. Jazen ran his eyes over me one more time, dismissing me as useless and old. I looked back at him as my father had taught me by example. Eyes level with his, like staring at a pit bull—they say it enrages the dog, but that if you do it properly, with a dog that isn't insane yet, you have a chance.

"Jazen," I said. This was delicate. "You're from the Westside, right? Didn't your mama go to school with us?"

He looked back—same level. I was not a mother. I was wearing a foreign-looking white shirt. My nails were not painted. I lived in LA. "My moms went back to New Orleans after I was born. I stayed with my gramma in the Villas."

The Rio Seco version of a project. I said, "I got a ride here from a friend, so I better call a cab, Victor, and get back to work."

Victor said, "Come with me to STAR 98 to get the tickets. Then we can give you a ride home. You live right past that mountain."

He pointed up at Mount Wilson and Griffith Park. Good memory.

Joining us in the crosswalk were three business suits and two thirty-ish women wearing dresses and heels and looking out of place. Jazen and Alfonso held themselves stiff as lost people on a train. They were gangsters—never walked, never touched shoulders with anyone, and they seemed to hate being in LA.

"So we're doing the Target Christmas ads today and Thursday?" one of the women asked. "Are the other singers already here? Are we late?" She had very thick legs, straightened blond hair, and red lipstick. Backup singer?

One of the suited men said, "We're never late. You'll be fine. I can't believe they want us to record on a Wednesday."

Victor looked at a small piece of paper. "STAR 98," he said very softly. "Okay."

We were last inside. The elevator was half-full with the Target people, and we slid in beside them. They had watched us come with a mix of curiosity and dread that only three young black men can inspire.

Did they think I was the mother? Our reflections were all blurred in the etched metal elevator door. The suited men breathed shallowly. Then the blond singer said with a friendly smile, "So are you guys rappers? From LA?"

Jazen said, "Shit. Ain't from no LA. I'm from Rio Seco." His arms were folded, his legs spread wide, his jacket trembling in the jerky movement of the elevator.

She was still game. "Oh, is that in Texas? We're from Encino."

I said quickly, "Rio Seco's about an hour from here. On the way to Palm Springs."

But Jazen was bothered now. He said, "LA niggas ain't about shit." The elevator bumped to a stop.

In the silence before the door opened, Victor said, "Man, I'm sure she agrees, JZ, so chill."

He was too smart. No one got it. The door slid open and the women and I walked out first. Citrusy perfume and sweat. Then five wide jackets followed us. The men with boxy wool-silk coats; the boys with starched stiff denim, and Victor in his T-shirt. The right labels for each—Hugo Boss and G Unit.

"Shit, I make more money in a week than LA rappers make in a month," Jazen said loudly, recovered, but the Target group disappeared into an unmarked door.

The glass doors adjacent were crowded with teens. I saw the boy named Mando sitting on a round ottoman. His huge jacket crinkled when he moved. He said into a phone, "No, ese, she left me. I need a ride. Come on, carnal. Go tell my brother Moses to come get me. He's at my abuela's. The corner of César Chávez and St. Louis."

Then he looked up at us and his eyes narrowed. "I can't be hangin around, carnal."

Jazen and Alfonso said, "Hurry up, nigga," as if in chorus, and walked down the hallway to confer, glaring at the boy, while Victor pushed his way inside.

Air-conditioning caressed my forehead. The boy named Mando sat with his head leaning into his hands. His hair was oiled and combed straight back, glistening black with deep furrows. I realized the top hairs were so long that if they hung down they would have framed his face like ponytails. The shorter hairs underneath were like baby bird feathers.

Jazen and Alfonso leaned against the wall, staring with that odd insecure disdain. People avoided their eyes. They cared about nothing and no one not from their alley, their city, their car. In that, they were so much like my father and Gustave Picard that I wished I could have told them.

Victor loved to talk to strangers. He laughed at something the woman said when he signed his name, and then she laughed, too.

When he came out, holding an envelope with his name on it, he said, "Check me now. Victor Picard. Two tickets. Dave Matthews Band." His entire face had changed from the way it looked in the doorway of Dimples—he had Glorette's eyes, velvet and dark, but when she smiled, her cheekbones moved around her eyes, never changing them, and when Victor smiled big, like now, his eyes slanted up. He had his father's perfect teeth, like white Chiclets.

"Who are you taking?" I said.

Then his smile went lopsided. "I want to take Mayeli. But her moms is pissed cause she saw me in Jazen's car."

"Mayeli—the one from Belize?" He'd met her in college.

He nodded. "Hey—I can take you! You're not gonna trip on what it is." He paused, thinking. "Hootie and the Blowfish got a brotha frontin, but they're still whiter than Dave Matthews."

I said, "And you've been listening to Jimi Hendrix and The Who. You're gonna get wrecked. Just like me."

He looked into my eyes. "Marraine. I'm already fucked up." He held up his hands and bit his lips hard, so they nearly disappeared.

"Let's not put it that way," I said.

"You been drinkin the Kool-Aid?" he asked.

I didn't look away. "What's going on, Victor?"

He shrugged. "You didn't read it."

"Damn. You sent me an essay, right? The Kool-Aid."

He nodded. "I e-mailed it to you last week. But my laptop's been messing up. It's old. I thought you would call me." He let out a breath. "I want to send it to a magazine. If you know someone."

"Victor, I never check e-mail on the road. It takes me out of how I feel about a place. I just got back today." I put my hand on his shoulder, that knobby bone like a bottlecap. "Look, on Saturday we can go to the concert, and then you can hang out here in LA for a few days. You want to visit colleges, right? Tell me the plan."

"I have a 3.85," he said. "I got a B in math."

"Me, too," I said, smiling.

"The plan is I got the honors award, and some other stuff, but I need to fill out the applications by December. And Professor Zelman's gone."

"What do you mean?"

He looked at Jazen and Alfonso, who'd pushed off from the wall. "The plan is I need your help. I need to be out of Rio Seco."

After he graduated in June, we'd gone to USC for a day. "Okay," I said. "Next week we'll check out Occidental and UCLA. They should love a brotha like you. All wrecked."

Riding in the Navigator was like being on drugs, as I imagined it. I had never tried anything stronger than my father's rum.

But when I sat in the window-tinted back, the world slid by gangster-lean slow. No cheap speakers that fuzzed the air but an expensive system that sent the bass through the seat clean and layered as thunder.

The music was so deeply loud that it danced in my bone marrow. The drums were inside the flat bone over my heart. And the world looked absolutely different from when I walked. The sidewalks and buildings—the apartments, even the brick buildings with signs that read ELEKTRA and ATLANTIC RECORDS—were small and insignificant, and the people only puppets moving dispiritedly in the heat. It was like being in another country.

Victor lifted his chin when we passed Dimples and said something low under his breath. In the front seat, Alfonso watched everything, head moving smoothly left to right. He had a Chinese symbol tattooed on the left side of his skull, I saw now through the stubble. Jazen's sunglasses glinted in the rearview mirror.

Beside me, Victor craned his neck when we crossed over the LA River. He said softly, "I started working on a piece about rivers. You sent me that CD for my birthday. *Water Music.*" He leaned back against the seat. "I listened to it back here with the headphones, and Jazen was playing Lil Wayne, and the drums mixed up with the oboes. It was a trip. I read the liner notes, about King George and the Thames and the barge. This was like the barge, and we were driving on the freeway. Eight lanes. Black like water. Then we went off on a little tributary, and all the people were on the banks watching us go by."

I said, "Who are you writing the paper for?"

He said, "I got bored after graduation. I should have done my applications last year. But Grandpère was sick and I thought he was gonna die."

"He had pneumonia. I remember."

"You were in Belgium." He turned toward me now. "I wrote the papers for Zelman. He said the same thing happened to him when he graduated, so he gave me fake deadlines. He called them artificial assignments, and he was gonna send off the Kool-Aid paper to some journal. But he left."

"He left the college?"

He shook his head. "No. He got some grant to go to Brazil for a year and study rap in the favelas. He booked up last week."

Jazen said, "This the freeway?"

I leaned forward and said, "Right there." His cornrows were blurred and needed redoing. At home, Jazen and Alfonso drove through the alleys, watching their small empire, their rock stowed safely somewhere. Where had my brother Lafayette said they kept it—in a dryer at the Launderland?

What if they had drugs in the car now, and the cops stopped us?

They wouldn't be that stupid. Someone had to be holding their stuff at home. They couldn't have planned to do anything here.

Jazen kept up a steady stream of comment about the elevator. "She gon say am I a LA rapper. I'm from the Villas. Westside."

That singer had forgotten about Jazen the moment she stepped inside the glass door of the studio. The men had hardly noticed him, except to wonder whether he had a gun.

Of course he did. Somewhere in that big jacket? They always needed a gun.

He said, "Shit, it's all about the Dirty South now. Don't nobody care bout no LA niggas. It's all about Juvenile and Mystikal and Lil Wayne. New Orleans and the ATL. Don't nobody care about no Warner Brothers."

"You have about five exits," I said loudly.

We drove toward Los Feliz. *She got them big-ass triple Ds, but she still need to get on her knees.* Who was this singing? Sold on the market down in New Orleans. Brown sugar. We were still nothing. All of us. Glorette, me, Gloria. Tiffany. Breasts and ass and mouths. My arm was ghostly blue reflected in the window.

"Check that big old white house," Alfonso said, pointing. "Look like a plantation."

"Forest Lawn," I said.

"Oh, shit—the cemetery? A plantation fulla dead people," Alfonso said. "Look like Louisiana for a minute."

"You been to Louisiana?" Victor said.

"Hell, yeah, my moms used to send me there in the summer, when I got in trouble. Plenty trouble down there, too." Alfonso laughed softly. "I was way out in the country. Sarrat. But they had fools just like us."

Jazen said, "Man, I stayed in the Lafitte last summer in New Orleans. Call it the Bricks. Niggas was poppin each other there, too. Make LA look like kindergarten. VP, you never been?"

"Nope. Marraine, you been to New Orleans?"

I was still trying to process Lafitte. A project named for a pirate? Our pirate? I said, "I went to Azure, with your maman. Down south from New Orleans. But we were only ten."

Jazen said, "Wait—them horses?"

Fifteen feet from the freeway was a bridle path, and two people rode palominos whose long tails swished gently. "This shit don't even look like LA. I thought it would be clubs and stores. Hollywood," Jazen said.

"LA's so big you can't even see it all," Victor said. "It's forever." He sounded like a little kid. "The Getty Villa and Leimert Park. We saw poets there, right?"

"You're gonna exit on Los Feliz," I said. "We have stores."

"Marraine's crib is fit," Victor said. "Check it out."

Winding through the eucalyptus and magnolia that towered over us along Los Feliz Boulevard, then the beautiful pastel buildings along the street, they were all quiet until I pointed at a space along the curb.

"Nella Vista Street," Victor said. "I remember."

I loved my apartment building. It was like a small French chateau, but wrought-iron letters spelled out EL DORADO at the entry. The walls were buttery yellow, the steep mansard roof was all coppery and green, and I kept red geraniums in blue pots at the base of the steps.

When we walked into the courtyard, I wondered who was watching. Sherry was home. Her fan made the silky butternut curtains dance in the window. Violin music trailed from #6, where Jae, who played with the LA Phil, lived.

If people weren't sure what I was, they could speculate now, I thought, leading the way up the pebbly stairs with the three boys—I was just going to think of them that way, because I couldn't think of them otherwise. They were sons of people I knew and always would seem like boys to me, even though their feet shook the narrow steps.

EL DORADO

VICTOR WENT STRAIGHT to the pictures gathered in silver frames on the ebony sideboard. He picked up the one of the five of us, after graduation. Then he touched the smaller snapshot of Glorette holding him on his first birthday; he is nestled into her shoulder, looking suspiciously at me, the stranger home from college who held the camera. His cheek is fat, his hair is uncut tumbleweed, his eyes are slanted and glowing.

I saw his backpack, then, on the floor beside him. He thought he was staying. Tonight.

Jazen and Alfonso stood uncomfortably in the doorway.

I called out, "Come in and get something to drink."

In the kitchen, I got out bottles of iced tea. I looked out my kitchen window at the eucalyptus forest up the hill near the Griffith Observatory. Tony's house was up there. He'd been in Oaxaca doing the photos for my essay. I didn't want Victor here tonight. I wasn't ready to think about him being in LA.

Their voices floated through the arched entry to the kitchen.

"Nigga, you stayed up in here before? Yeah, my godmother hooked me up with a college visit. Shit. Two more years of school? For what? So I can still make more money than your ass? I make more money than your godmother, too. Bet. Hold up—Jojo callin. Jojo? Why you callin me again? I told you I got bidness in LA. Yeah. LA."

Jazen went out onto the balcony. The only man who ever came here was Tony. My neighbors—the only two I knew were Sherry and Jae—were probably past curious about these visitors. And if they'd seen Jazen's big jacket and Alfonso's tattoos, they were probably nervous.

Alfonso said to Victor, "He got so many bitches callin—" I put three glasses of iced tea on the coffee table, and Alfonso said, "Sorry, Auntie Fantine."

Because when Jazen was not in the room, Alfonso was still my nephew. Four of the women in that photo were his aunts. During his three years in prison, Clarette had kept an eye on him, kept him from too many fights.

I said, "And you've got two little girls, right?" I folded my arms and gave him my best imitation of Clarette's prison guard look. "No bitches."

Alfonso pulled down the neck of his white T-shirt. On each side of his collarbone rode a name: Egypt and Morocco. Twins. They were about five—I'd seen them at Bettina's, their braids thick as ropes.

He sat heavily on the couch and drank the entire glass of iced tea, his throat working. With his head thrown back, another tattoo was visible on his neck, but I couldn't read it.

Victor said, "This is my favorite picture. And I ain't in it."

I said, "You're right off to the side, in your grandma's arms. That's why your mom's glancing sideways."

"For real?" He held it close. "Was I bawlin?"

"Oh, yeah." I took the photo from him. "Always." I picked up the smaller one, of Glorette holding him, and said, "But not here."

Jazen came inside, closing his phone, his wide forehead furrowed with right angles. He'd look old fast, because he carried all that anger in the front of his head. Who told me that? An old man in Spain. He'd demonstrated on the forehead of his friend, in the small bar with a bowl of tiny dark olives near us.

Victor sat near the window, in the low-slung wooden chair with leather backing where I usually read. "This from Pottery Barn?" He grinned, and I saw his father's narrow gap between the front two teeth. The lie gap. The generous gap. Depended on which African-descended person you asked—my friends all disagreed.

"Very funny," I said. I'd told jokes about Pottery Barn when he was here before.

Jazen's eyes went from the chair to the window to his buzzing phone. "A barn? In LA? And fuckin horses everywhere?"

"It's a store," I said. "But that chair's from Indonesia. I got it from a friend."

Victor said, "Mayeli said we should go to Belize."

Alfonso said, "That fine short girl talk so funny? The one we saw at the store?"

"Yeah," Victor said, quietly. "Belize. Mayeli could show you all around. She says they got Indians, Amish people in those buggies, and brothas they call Garifunas."

"See the sights and shit," Alfonso said, but his head was drooping, as if he were going to fall asleep.

Victor stood up and went to the hallway, where I had hung twenty pictures in different-sized frames. I wanted it to look like Mrs. Mingott's stairway in *The Age of Innocence,* though I never told anyone that. "You got new ones," he said. "These are from Italy?"

"From everywhere." They were mostly museum catalogue photos, or large postcards I'd gotten from exhibits, or small posters I'd bought on my trips. An English landscape by Constable, a Renaissance landscape from Dosso Dossi. I put them in gilt frames and changed them often, except the very first print I'd ever bought, when I was eighteen—an etching of a desolate landscape with one tree, by Rembrandt.

"This from Africa?" Jazen held up a glossy silver-black vase with filigreed openings like flowers. He stood in the living room. He couldn't sit anywhere but his own car or his own couch—just like my father. "You been to Africa?"

"It's from Oaxaca," I said. "Mexico. A special kind of pottery made in only one tiny village. The kiln makes that black finish. I haven't been to Africa."

He put down the vase and walked over to the dining room table. "Why you ain't been to Africa?"

No use in lying, not in front of Victor. "I've been too nervous to go. African people can be pretty suspicious about Americans who look like me." Taupe. Vague. Nothing.

"So you write about clothes?" Alfonso looked at the magazines on the coffee table. *Immerse, Travel and Leisure, Elle, Vogue.*

"I write travel pieces about different places." It sounded foolish said aloud. I thought about how Tony always said our journeys were imaginary—people wanted to pretend they were there with us, so they didn't have to take all the trouble to go. "I try to tell stories about people and food and places most writers don't go."

Jazen said, "You should go to Africa. I always wanted to check Africa."

I couldn't help it. "The whole continent?"

He looked up from the table. "Hell, no. Just Senegal. That's where my gramma said her people was from. Call her gramma Singalee when they lived in New Orleans."

"Our people were from Senegal, too. My great-great-great-grand-mother. Marie-Therese, and her mother Amina. They came on the boat."

"Where these from?" He nodded at the three huge brown leaves in a line on the teakwood table. I'd filled the veined bowl of one leaf with coffee beans, one with pebbles from a beach in Italy, and one with three of my mother's wooden clothespins. Jazen actually sounded curious. "How you pack a damn leaf?"

"They're from Sarrat," I said. "From my father's sycamore tree in the yard. I picked them up in January." They were big as dinner plates, edges jagged, veins still vivid.

"Sarrat," he said dismissively. "How y'all always call that place by a name? Just some old houses."

Alfonso and Victor knew better.

"It's a neighborhood," I said. "Like this one."

"This place?" He looked out the window at the roofs of the other apartment buildings.

"You guys were in Burbank before. Now you're in Los Feliz."

"The happy place," Victor said.

Jazen's phone buzzed. He looked down at the number. "We gotta go. I gotta handle my bidness."

Alfonso opened his eyes and said, "Something smells good. Makes me hungry."

He was young again. He was Bettina's son, always hanging around my mother's table at dinnertime because his mother was out partying. "I can make you some rice," I said.

Victor was still in the hallway. "I don't remember this one."

"That's from 1636," I said. "A painter named Sebastien Bourdon. *The Encampment.* See what they're doing?" I pointed at the men sitting in the foreground. "It's like rock, paper, scissors. Called mora. It's just the hands. They're on the road, they don't have anything. Look at the tent—it's cloth strung up on those ruins."

"Who are they?" Victor said, leaning closer.

"I don't know. I counted eleven of them. They must be running from something." The painting was dark, the ruins shadowed, but the men were smiling. "I got it at a museum in Oberlin, Ohio. I did a piece on art collections in the Midwest."

"Nigga, you don't need no rice," Jazen said. His phone was a bee trapped in his big palm. He looked at the number. "Shit, I gotta talk to this one girl. No lie. She's gonna do my braids."

"Go out to the car and handle her," Alfonso said. "Lemme just get some rice. My auntie make some hella good rice."

Jazen went outside. The living room was quiet. I bent to pick up Alfonso's empty glass, and saw he was asleep, his head thrown back. Under his jawbone, small words curved—*Live My Life.*

Victor whispered, "Said he didn't sleep for three years inside. Fool falls asleep in a heartbeat." He put in his earpieces, turned on his iPod, and sat in the leather chair with a book of Brassai photos.

In the kitchen, I got out rice, saffron, Creole seasoning, garlic, and pepper. I sautéed the garlic in butter, added the rice and stirred until it was translucent, and turned the heat up high under the water. I'd been gone so much there was no meat, no eggs, no shrimp. Nothing but this and canned red beans.

My mother would shake her head. She cooked three full meals a day. Alfonso had eaten a hundred meals in my mother's kitchen. She never said no. Anyone could get a plate at my mother's table.

I stirred the rice. Fifteen minutes. I had never eaten a meal alone in my life until I went to college. I ate breakfast with my mother and brothers; my father and Gustave ate in the barn. At lunch, I ate at school with the girls. And dinner was with whoever stayed judiciously visiting in my mother's kitchen. Gumbo, etouffee, rice and beans, stewed chicken in sauce picante. The table never had fewer than ten people.

I picked up the Creole seasoning. Tony Chachere's. I hardly ever cooked—I ate out all the time. And my Calphalon pots were not my mother's heavy cast-iron pots. Iron gave everything a smoky, rich undertone.

Once, I'd read in a food magazine how old pots leached a little iron into the food, and I thought of how my ancestors—Amina, Marie-Therese, Moinette, and the other slaves—had survived. My brothers and I were always strong. We ate beans and rice, rabbit and wild pig and duck my father shot, and always oranges.

Victor came inside and said, "Smells good." He leaned against the refrigerator, holding one of the framed 5x7 prints from the hallway. The Constable.

"Why are you riding around with these guys?" I said.

"I got no hooptie," he said, palms up, joking. I folded my arms and gave him the look. The one my mother was so good at.

"It's—it's like runnin the world. Especially at night," he said, and his voice was low, his eyes distant on the flame under the pot. "Last night we were at Sundown Liquor, and I was thinkin about my moms. And this song came on. House of Pain. The drums, man, they were like— like a gong. Like, here we are. We were ridin and it's like bein inside this bubble, floatin down the street. Checkin people. Like—surveyin the world. And nobody can touch you. I kept thinkin about *Water Music,* and the Navigator."

"I thought you won the tickets last night?"

He grinned, and beside his eyes, a flourish of lines appeared. "I did. I had my headphones on later, cause they won't listen to that station, and I heard caller twenty and I got it." He went to the doorway and glanced out. "JZ still on the phone outside," he said. Then he sat down at the kitchen table and turned over the frame. I'd written the name of the painting on the back. "So tell me about *View on the Stour Near Dedham 1822.*"

"Dedham," I said. "Not dead ham." I had to laugh. I checked the rice. "Constable painted these huge landscapes for six years. All views of the river where he'd grown up. All at noon, I think. My friend Jane says there's going to be a big show of his landscapes next year in London."

"What does she do again?"

"She's a museum curator in Switzerland."

"She make good money?"

"Nope," I said. "But she likes it." I took coffee beans out of the refrigerator to warm. "So tell me about your Kool-Aid piece."

He put down the Constable and looked at my refrigerator door, which was blank and silver. "We were in class and some dude was all right-wing and Zelman said, He's got you drinking the Republican Kool-Aid. And somebody said, Yo, Zelman, you had us drinking the Led Zeppelin Kool-Aid."

"Why'd you write about that?"

Victor rubbed his hands through his hair. Brown and red and gold, the artful messiness and little twists at the ends. "I met this guy from

Oakland. His mom and grandma and aunt all died in Jonestown. He told me about it. They left him with his pops. His pops wouldn't go down there to Guyana. Kool-Aid. A crazy white dude with shades got all these black people to believe in him and go to Guyana and when it came down to the shit, he gave em a ghetto drink." He looked down at the River Stour, the limpid water, the small boat. "Now it's a joke. But I looked up the pictures. Where the words came from—dead people blowin up in the heat."

The front door closed, and he stood up. I peered through the arched doorway. Alfonso murmured, "She cool?" Jazen stood near the window, looking out at the roof of the next building. Victor passed me and sat down again on the leather chair.

I leaned against the doorway. Victor wrote in a small notebook. He was smiling again, saying, "So we could be DJ Sonic, DJ Phonic, and MC Catatonic."

"Shut up," Jazen said.

"Or you could be Laconic." Victor grinned up at me.

"SAT words," I said.

"Rappers could make a hella SAT test," he said. "Like Chamillion-aire." He pointed at Jazen. "I saw Yella Nigga in a magazine. I could be Ochre Fool, Fonso could be Burnt Umber Fool, and you could be—" He looked down at the notebook. "You said brothas call each other soldiers down in New Orleans. You could be Siena Soulja."

"Shut the fuck up." Jazen didn't move.

It was like they were speaking a code. But then Victor said to me, "We could go to Belize," he said. "Mayeli's from some little town called Teakettle. That's a story."

I nodded. *Travels with My Aunt*—like Graham Greene. That would be cute and magazine-acceptable if he were a kid—like Eloise. *Travels with Charley*—like Steinbeck. If he were a poodle.

He nodded his head to the beat inside his brain. "'Out here in the fields, I fight for my meals, I put my back into my living,'" he sang softly.

He was a twenty-two-year-old orphan, son of a man buried before he was born and a woman he held in his hands. He was a young brother with little dreads and eyes like velvet night, listening to The Who, remembering his SATs because he was sitting in my living room where he'd studied for them.

The smell of garlic and saffron floated among us. He pulled out his concert tickets. "This Sunday! August 28." He glanced down at the tickets again, and then put them in his pocket. "Home Depot Center. It never sounds as good as when guys used to say they were going to the Fabulous Forum. That was old school."

Jazen said, "We need to bounce. I gotta get my braids done."

Victor looked at me. "So the store's around the corner, right? I need to grab a couple things. If I'm hangin here. Or are you goin home later?"

"I'm going to Sarrat tomorrow," I said. But I looked down the hallway at my bedroom door. My suitcase was in there. My notes from Switzerland. Tony's gift.

I could take Victor to the Graves reading. He wasn't scary without Jazen or Alfonso. Not to me.

"The rice should be done," I said. In the kitchen, I turned off the flame. I was so tired. I hadn't listened to any music, hadn't laid out my notes. I'd spent an afternoon in a tiny village above Brienz with an old woman whose nephew brought her mushrooms. From the forest behind the wooden house. Mushrooms in a basket, and she weighed them with her two hands and clapped. If I didn't write that tonight— organize the piece on paper and in my mind—some of it would be lost.

I went back to the living room. "Why don't I meet you in Sarrat tomorrow night and you can come back up here after that? I'll talk to my neighbor—she's a history professor at Occidental. Maybe she'll take us on a tour. You can stay till the concert on the twenty-eighth. Then I'll probably be going to Italy."

"Yeah," he said. He bent to put back the Brassai. "You see the full moon was Friday?"

His T-shirt stretched tight over his shoulder blades when he kept his back to me, bending at the bookcase. Damn. Now he was sad.

I knew what he meant. His mother had taught him about palm tree sparklers, lit by the full moon. But Jazen said, "Nigga, shut up about the damn moon. Sound like a freak." His phone rang again. "I'm out." He went through the door without looking back.

"The rice is done," I said. "Let me get you a plate, Alfonso."

"When he say he out, he gone," Alfonso said. He actually sighed. "I hate Burger King." But he stood up, his pants so baggy he had to rehang them precisely on his hip bones. His jacket clanked against the doorway when he turned. "Thanks, Auntie," he said. "For the tea."

While they went down the stairs, Victor lingered in the hallway. He said, "The Huntington, huh?"

"I'm sorry, Victor, I'm just so tired. Tomorrow's better." I looked at the pictures above him. "We can go to the Huntington on Sunday."

"That's where this one's from." He held the Constable print. Not leaving yet. Stubborn. Trying not to be Jazen's boy. He said, "I like that one." He pointed at *The Annunciation*. "Baby Jesus got a halo like a little satellite dish."

Then he swooped past me and picked up the silver-framed picture of the five of us. He fit it onto the Constable. "I gotta borrow these two, okay? I'll bring them back."

"Victor," I said. "I'll make you a copy."

"I need them right now," he shouted, and ran down the stairs.

THE GOLDEN GOPHER

FIVE YEARS SINCE Glorette was murdered. I sat on the couch with rice in a blue and white bowl from Vietnam that Tony had given me.

The Navigator started up—drums and bass came through the stucco and shook the whole apartment. I went outside to the balcony, but I couldn't see the car. Lil Wayne's voice was dim and tribal. Everyone who lived here felt those drums, every day. All the kids played Fifty Cent and Lil Wayne. Everyone looked like what they thought black was, from inside their tinted windows. They all wanted to be Jazen and Alfonso—legends in their own minds, until they got to college class or to Starbucks.

The sounds faded. Victor had left behind his little notebook on the table, in his hurry. The picture of him in his mother's arms still there.

He wanted the picture without him.

What did he want? Did he want to be me? It flew through my mind—his hair, his height, his voice. He couldn't pass.

I wasn't passing. I was floating. I was invisible. He couldn't be invisible.

Glorette stared at me from the table. I picked up the photo. I had seen her only a few times in the last years before she died, and never in Los Feliz. But I had brought Victor here with me one weekend to study for the SAT.

It was March, and I was visiting my parents, sitting on the porch because the orange blossoms were like fragrant stars sending perfume through the yard. Victor had come out of his grandfather's house across the road with a huge book. SAT study guide.

DJ Laconic. Catatonic.

We'd sat at my mother's table, going over the word choices. I showed him how to use Latin roots, to think of all the French and Spanish and Italian words he already knew from common use. Not to panic when faced with a random list of freaky words.

Then he said, "I gotta go home and check on Moms. I been here at Grandpère's for a few days, cause she was gone."

He had been coming to stay with his grandparents since my brother Lafayette was on a plastering job and saw Victor alone on an apartment balcony, sitting with his back against the wall and his eyes closed, shirt filthy. He was four. Glorette had passed out in an alley and been taken to the hospital days before.

But Victor always went back home. Home was just his mother.

I drove him to the apartment. She was sleeping on the couch, her body curled like a cat, one hand dangling over the edge, fingers fanned elegant even when she was unconscious.

"Hey," she said, opening her eyes. That was the first word she always said to me. Hey. Like it had been a week. Not a year. She watched Victor go into the bedroom.

"Hey," I said. "How you been?"

She sat up and shrugged. Her collarbone was stark and the hollow in her throat deep. Like a model. No matter what she did to her body, she looked good. If I hadn't slept for two days, I got dark crescents under my eyes, but Glorette had lavender smudges over her eyelids that could pass for faded eye shadow. "You got your hair in a braid." She grinned faintly and lifted her chin. "You remember? That time?"

We could be eighty and still speak shorthand like this. I said, "Yeah." I wanted to sit on the couch, but it was heaped with clothes she was using as blankets. There was no chair, no coffee table, no other furniture except her favorite glass-topped round table, the one that looked like a patio set, in the linoleum patch that was the dining room.

I sat on the filthy carpet. "I remember."

"Clarette and Cerise braided our hair together that one time. We were twelve, huh?"

We each had an outside braid, and our skulls were held close together with a single thick braid, fat as an arm. They put us into one huge sweatshirt belonging to Bettina's mother and called us Siamese twins.

"We were exactly the same height," I said, as I always did. Glorette looked at the closed bedroom door, where Victor was. I looked at the fist-sized hole in the wall near the front window, where the white plaster looked like hard cracked frosting.

Even our bones matched, back then. Our wrists hung at the same distance from our shoulders. Our temples touched when we lurched forward in that sweatshirt. But then Glorette became beautiful, and I was still a child.

Beauty was the arrangement of the flesh on the bones, the way the mouth stayed still while the eyes moved under their fringe of lashes.

He had come out of the bedroom with a gym bag. He said to Glorette, "I'm gonna study for the SAT."

He'd slept here on this couch, after we studied all weekend at the teakwood table. We wrote hundreds of sentences, and broke down the words. Lucid. Lucidity. Elucidate. Liquidate. Luminous. Loquacious. Laconic. Ludicrous.

We got stuck for a while on the F words. Febrile, fervid, feverish. Fervent. The sentence I said: "Every woman wants a fervent declaration of love."

Victor had laughed. "Like the dude has a fever?"

I laughed and thought Jane Austen, Edith Wharton. "Like his words have a fever."

Then Victor said, "Who did you love? Back then?"

"Marcus Thompson. You knew that." It was awkward, because Marcus was his history teacher at the high school. I hadn't seen Marcus in a long time.

"But who else?"

I couldn't tell him. Because after Marcus, there was not love. There was Skeet Howard, in college. Then a young pianist in France, and Simon, who played the oboe and lived in Cambridge, and a basketball player I met for a day in Pisa. Now there were the few men I slept with during assignments, carefully, in hotel rooms.

"Nobody fervent, okay? You better tackle the L words again."

We'd sat here and watched TV that night, and he was still saying, "Liquid. Liquefy. Liquidation. Livid. Lipid."

I couldn't believe the easy way he played with the words, the way he could free-associate forever with me. Eventually, he fell asleep and I got up to go to bed. He turned over when I moved, and a long indentation from a pillow with braided cord ran along his cheek like a scar. How did blood work? He was Glorette's son—she was the only living child of Anjolie, who rarely used words aloud, though she might have thought thousands of them, and Gustave Picard, who had never known how to read or write.

My own father's mother, Antoinette Antoine, had never learned to read. She had worked cane all her short life. Her mother, Anjanae, could sign her name and write her children's names—in laborious capital letters. But her mother, Marie-Therese Antoine, though she had been born a slave, owned four books and could read. The books had been given to her by her mother, Moinette Antoine, my ancestor, who was taught to read by the young woman whose hair she curled on the plantation called Azure. It was named that for the color of the young woman's eyes.

When I was ten, we had visited Anjanae on the place still called Azure, and she showed me the four books. They were on a shelf high in her living room, next to pictures of Martin Luther King Jr., John and Robert Kennedy, and a Jesus who had been blond but had darkened with age and firesmoke to the color of us.

A Shakespeare collection, a novel called *The Blind Heart,* a book of Edgar Allan Poe poems, and the Bible.

When he was here, I had listened to Victor's lips pop softly, twice, in his sleep. Like two bubbles bursting inside his mouth. He would never startle if he felt safe, I realized, hovering over him with a blanket. But he'd slept around chaos and danger all his life. I'd seen Glorette's apartments—always one bedroom, and she slept on the couch, while he had the futon in the bedroom. He slept in his clothes, even his shoes on, so visiting crackheads couldn't steal them. He kept his headphones on all night for the same reason, and to erase the noise from his mother's friends in the other room. But his books were safe, he told me once. No one tried to steal those.

Maybe I should have let him stay tonight. But I was so tired. Too tired for words. I just wanted to sleep for a minute. I pushed myself off the couch, put my bowl in the kitchen, and went back to the bookcase near where Victor had sat in the leather chair. A pile of books on the floor. Victor had taken out the Brassai photos, and two books by my friend James Ralston, whose nom de plume was Jimmy Taco. His new book was *Handheld Heaven: A History of the Taco.* Victor had been reading his first: *National Treasure: A Cultural and Personal History of the Sandwich.*

Two pieces of paper fell out from the pages. Victor's tiny perfect handwriting. *You Can Eat It Dry: A Personal History of Ramen. Rock Cane Candy: A Cultural and Personal History of Crack in Southern California.*

I sat on the edge of the chair and laughed. Arthur Graves would read tonight about the Argentinean woman in a dry, astonished comic tone. Victor was probably funnier than he was. Maybe I could get him to write a piece for the *LA Times,* to start. Not a scary one.

I opened the second piece of folded paper.

The Villas—#24—The Balcony
What you don't understand
Is
The snarling jeweled nightbird can be
Beautiful
Even when it wakes you up at two
flying in circles
A silver rope a silver beam tied down? *tethered anchored*
No escape for the pilot
Either

Balcony. Tethered. Beautiful words.

He struggled with the seventh line. A rope. I had seen it over and over—the helicopter circling forever, as if held by a child. A kite. A lasso? Maybe that word.

He just loved words. Where did that impulse come from, deep inside his brain with its folds and crevices? His father had loved music. Maybe Sere Dakar's love for the notes and where they flew inside their lines, or outside, had been filtered down into his son.

That weekend, I'd taken him back Sunday night to the Riviera. It was near ten. We had stopped at the store for orange juice, his favorite Corn Pops, and a pack of #2 pencils with a small sharpener. His mother would have been out on the sidewalks near the Launderland and Sundown Liquor.

Thinking of Glorette, I brought my left wrist up to my face. No one could really see the tattoo unless I pointed it out, which I never did. The flowers on my skin might look tribal. Moroccan. Algerian. Berber.

Glorette and I had lain under the orange trees one summer when we were twelve. We had seen the jailhouse tattoos on Alphonse, Clarette's older brother, when he got out. He had a crude drawing of a woman on his forearm. He'd bragged to my brothers how a Mexican inmate did it—with an ink pen and a needle and a cassette recorder.

Somewhere in my mind I'd remembered the fleur-de-lis. The lily of

France on Moinette Antoine's shoulder. But I wanted something beautiful to mark me. And my sister. I brought one of my mother's larger sewing needles and a Bic pen. I broke the pen, emptied the ink into a plastic lid, and poked holes in our wrists. I moved the needle around a little to widen the holes. Glorette's face didn't move. I let tiny droplets of ink fall into the holes. The center of the flower. The pollen. Then I made five little scratches in a star shape around the dot. Orange blossoms.

Glorette. Glorette! Why hadn't I ever called her again, gone to see her, just sat for a few hours until the ghost people came to smoke some fog with her, said, "Hey, check this out," and laid our wrists aside each other to see if the indigo markings we'd made still matched perfectly?

I knew how to cry without making a sound or moving my face, from years of being in quiet hotel rooms next to Tony or in my own small bedroom back home. I kept as much of the trembling inside me as possible, and even though I shook and shook, it was silent, and the tears ran down my temples and cheeks and into my ears until it felt as if I were underwater.

Under water. Glorette and I had stared at the Mississippi River, on the levee, walking up with my father's aunt Almoinette from her tiny wooden house that must have been from slavery. What she called Back Then.

Dya. *That the spirit of the water people. They live under there. Faro. That the wind. The wind have a god, too. Tell you secrets. Messages. Ni. That the spirit inside your hair.*

I got my ligion. What they told me, my maman and tante and them. I got that Bible when I tite like you. I know every verse in that Bible. Make my morning devotion and evening devotion.

I let the priest say his piece. But we kept to ourselves. That how the gods stay with us. They right here. Dya *and* Faro. *They came over in the first one mouth. Amina. She tell her girl Marie-Therese, and Marie-Therese tell Moinette. She tell her girls. She call her girl Marie-Therese, too, after the mama. And then they tell their girls. That not a story. That the verse for them gods. No Bible for that. The ones we keep.*

They talk about voodoo, say we tell voodoo. That ain't no voodoo— we ain't never hurt nobody.

The first boy was Enrique. Your papa. The only son. He hear about them god, too. But the man don't tell the story most the time. We do.

———

I lay on the couch, holding the silver-framed photo of Glorette. How had her picture gotten onto that wall at Dimples? The only one to ask was Hattie, Grady's sister. Would she still be working at the Golden Gopher? Did I even want to know about whatever took them to Dimples?

I had to find out. At least I could tell Victor that.

He smelled hot and sour and milky when they handed him to me that day, when we took the pictures. His screams rolled against my shoulder and he banged his forehead on my collarbone. He was so angry that he wasn't in her arms. Eyes little black slits like watermelon seeds. He was not a human yet. That's what I'd thought, holding him. He was a tiny animal. I didn't want an animal. I'd never had one—no cat or hamster—and my mother's chickens, my father's dogs, meant nothing to me.

I closed my eyes, just for a moment, to see the Aare again. The water was blue as Windex, as if magical colorants had been dumped inside the mountain spring. I sat in a riverside restaurant in Thun, near the castle which loomed over me.

Two blond teenage boys had stealthily lowered themselves down the iron rungs of a ladder into the water, and another boy on the historic covered wooden bridge above them tossed down a line. They held the rope and suddenly stood up on surfboards, riding the current from the flume where the river made hydroelectric power. Like California. Everyone wanted to be from California. A small crowd of teenagers cheered from the opposite bank, and I shook my head and laughed. "Dude!" they called.

I dreamed of us swimming in the old canal that brought water to my father's orange groves. Cerise, Clarette, Bettina, Glorette, and me.

Our legs were golden under the surface of the canal. We kept lifting our feet from the water grass that grew along the bottom. It tickled. Then boys called to us from the eucalyptus windbreak near the canal. Boys were always shouting at us, on the way to junior high, in the street, at school. We were all beautiful. The five of us. Let me just get a taste of that! Come on, baby. You so fine. When they shouted, everyone but me crossed their arms over their chests, over the bathing suit tops with little flowers. But I floated down the canal to the footbridge and hid in the darkness under the wooden boards. The current was strong because it was summer. My father told us not to get carried under the footbridge because a metal grate was there. If a surge of water was released from the big canal, we could get trapped. A boy had drowned, farther down in Agua Dulce. His body pressed into the grate all night. I held on to the rope my father had nailed there, at the wooden bridge, just in case.

"FX? FX? You there?"

A man's voice startled me awake. The answering machine. I knocked it off the table near the front door when I stumbled to answer. He'd already hung up. Tony? I blinked at the reddish evening light in the window. The cool black canal water gone.

The phone rang again when I was in the bath. I grabbed a towel. "Fantine," the voice said. "Fantine. I know you there."

I said, "Hey, Clarette."

"You sleep?"

"No." I dried off and pulled on dark jeans. Indigo. Our legs had touched in my dream, under the water. Our knees had knocked hollow. "I'm coming tomorrow, but I have a breakfast meeting in the morning."

"A what?" Clarette snorted her breath through the phone so hard it was like I could feel it on my cheek. "So somebody gon cook and bring you a plate while you talk. Damn. Over here people just chomp on cereal and hide behind the box. So what time is this meeting?"

I knew where she was heading. "Ten." I buttoned a pleated white shirt, thin and gauzy, that I'd just bought in Luzern.

She snorted again. "Girl, by ten a.m. I been called bitch twenty-five times and had to break up at least one fight." Clarette worked at the prison in Chino. I waited for more. But then she sighed. "Five years."

"I dreamed about us just now. We were swimming in the canal. Those bathing suits we all got at Kmart."

Clarette was silent, and I could hear the kids murmuring near her. "I remember," she said finally. "Our first two-piece suits." She held her hand over the receiver and said something to the kids. "Unc Gustave stays over your maman's most the day now. She's makin gumbo. I got the sausage for her today at Andre's."

Because even though I was my mother's only daughter, I had not lived with her since I was eighteen. I visited about every six weeks or so, and I didn't run to the store for her.

Clarette said, "Your brother went and got all the shrimp." She paused and moved the phone closer to her mouth. "He stays in them old box houses now."

"Back home?" There were three small stone houses in my father's groves where the crate-makers had lived in the 1890s.

"Yeah," she said. Then she laughed. "Whatever. You ain't met nobody in Paris or wherever? Girl, you giving up? We forty this year. All of us."

"Don't start," I said, and warmth bubbled up behind my breastbone. "You have no idea what it is to get a man in LA. This waitress told me she did the online dating thing and she met a fine brother, but his picture had big circles on it. Holographs. From his driver's license."

When we laughed, it was like steel wool along my rib bones, scouring loose all the quiet of the last two days in the hotel room and on the plane.

"You still crazy," Clarette said. Then she told my niece and nephew, "You better get them shoes on now." She said to me, "I gotta get them over to your maman."

Then her voice changed. "Hey, I heard Victor never came home last night. He best not be hangin out with Alfonso and them. You remember I had Alfonso inside for three years? He just got out last month. Victor ain't called you?"

"He was here earlier," I said.

"Why would he go up there to LA?" Like everyone in my family, she pronounced the letters with disdain, as if the place were an alien compound.

"He won concert tickets," I said. "He should be on his way home."

"Better be," she said, distracted now. When we hung up, the laugh-glow was gone and I wanted it back.

I turned the heat up high under my mother's old roasting pan. I'd bought these coffee beans in Oaxaca. They wouldn't taste like my mother's coffee.

At the hotel—yesterday?—I'd sat at the white-cloth-covered table and ordered tea, as I always did in hotels because hotel coffee poured from silver urns made me powerfully sad. Three things—coffee, city flowers for sale in metal buckets, and peppermint candy—made me miss my mother with a kind of spearlike fear in my lungs that I would never see her again.

I shook the roasting pan, and the beans sent off a hiss of steam that went straight into my brain. When I was small, every morning meant coffee beans roasting black as anthracite, and the grits boiled in their white cloud. I was given one brown sugar lump by my mother, while I waited. I drank coffee turned golden with hot milk. When I was a teenager, I was handed the small cup of the adults, the coffee dark as oil inside.

Now I roasted beans from another country, packets with fine lettering and beautiful pictures from my travels.

In a hotel, I couldn't stand the thought of my mother, because if something happened to her or to me, I would be too far away. But here in LA, I was safe missing her—missing her painfully and still not wanting to drive the hour to Rio Seco to see her.

The beans were black and dimpled, and I put the pan on the piece of flagstone I'd found in an old quarry near Salem, New York. I felt my mother, the sound of her humming, the smells of coffee and smoke in her clothes, and her fingers in my hair.

Her fingers, and those of Cerise and Cerise's mother, Felonise. The thumbs tracing my skull, the wristbones twirling at my neck when someone braided, every weekend when we were young, getting ready for the night. But I knew what those hands in my hair meant. They were preparing me, with their own caresses, for a man. A boy, back then, who would become a man. My man. And I didn't want one. No. Uh-uh. Not me.

Because I'd seen what happened to Glorette. The teeth-bruise on the back of her neck. Then she fell in love with Sere Dakar, she got pregnant, he disappeared, and her life ended.

No. Not her life. That had ended five years ago. Her life was reduced, like butter and wine and sugar cooked to thick sweet smears—her son, her particular streets, her fingers holding the pipe and her lips pulling in the smoke, and dreaming of Sere Dakar through the scrim of movement and rock.

I'd been so afraid of a baby. When I went to her bedroom the first time, where she lay with Victor against her shoulder, his head was like a dark purple grapefruit, with black fur, and a depression in his skull. A pulsing there. I thought he was deformed. A hole in his head. Anjolie laid two fingers over the indentation and said something in French, and it scared me to death.

I sorted through my CDs. Nancy Wilson, recorded in 1963. *The Very Thought of You.* Sarah Vaughan. *April in Paris.* I had been listening to those songs since I was seventeen, seeing myself an expatriate in Paris and Marseille, sitting in a café wearing a dark coat and pearl earrings, my long hair rolled tightly in a chignon—even that word, *chignon,* meant that I knew, I knew—and drinking coffee from a thick white cup while I waited, looking at the gargoyles on the soot-stained buildings nearby. Then I would feel the man's fingers on the small of my back.

The right man.

I stood near the doorway, touching it. The small. Who had first called it that—the narrow portion below ribs and above hips?

I put in Debussy's *La Mer,* imagining the ocean off the coast of Italy or Spain. I lifted the perforated lid on the small roasting pan and poured the beans into the grinder, then put the powdery darkness into the French press and poured boiling water over it.

Making the coffee that would never be my mother's.

Then I listened to Al Green. The first eight beats of "Love and Happiness" and then the guttural thrill of the organ. Three o'clock in the morning. Talkin bout how she can make it right. Marcus pressing me against the eucalyptus leaves and whispering, Please. Please. Just a taste.

I wiped down the cast-iron pan my mother had brought with her in that Apache truck. Her mother had given it to her—told her she could make a living with one pan. That's what my grandmother had done. She had sold coffee and gumbo out of her house to people when they came in from the cane fields. In the old Sarrat, the one where girls were spirited away to California to keep them safe, while my father planned to erase the evil that would have crushed those girls. Maybe killed them.

The sun was still hovering in the haze of smog and amber evening. The restlessness surged through my thighs and ribs, as it always did when I needed to walk a long way. I wouldn't sleep if I didn't have movement and time.

Downtown was about three miles from here. Easy for me. I was a walkin fool. Maybe Hattie still worked at the Golden Gopher. She could tell me about the photo.

When I bent to pinch the dead geranium blossoms from the pots, Sherry called to me from the sidewalk. She carried a takeout bag from the Thai place. We'd been there a few times together—she told me about her work on women in World War I France.

"Hey—you're back! You had some visitors, huh?"

"Yeah." I dropped the blossoms. "I was interviewing them." You a lie.

"Oh. Yeah." Then she frowned. Her forehead was flushed red, her eyes traced with veins. "I was typing all day. But I looked out the window, and one of them ran down the stairs carrying something. Are you missing a picture?"

Victor. Shit. She thought he was a thief. I couldn't have this conversation right now.

I said, "No, I gave it to him. A gift." The intricate silver pendant at her throat was from Nepal. "He's a great kid."

I headed down Los Feliz Boulevard. I would tell her the rest tomorrow.

Nobody walks in LA. A whole song about it.

I walked past all the lovely buildings, the olive trees pruned like airborne poodles, the tiny rugs of lawn. No one looked out the window and said something about what I was wearing, or where I was going, or how thin I looked, because hardly anyone knew who I was, and I wanted to keep it that way.

Last night, Clarette would have brought the sausage to my mother, and every other person on Sarrat's single street would have checked to make sure the andouille was from Andre's Market. Then they would have given her coffee and asked how she felt about Glorette, and about me, because we had both disappeared.

I turned onto Vermont and passed the people sitting at sidewalk tables, dogs tethered to city trees, store windows with funky quilted

jackets and sequined purses, and one of my favorite bookstores—
Skylight—where Arthur Graves half smiled from a poster.

On Sunset Boulevard, the smells changed to engine oil and the vague
sweetness of blooming four-o'clocks planted in front of a botanica.
Coming toward me was the homeless woman who lived somewhere
nearby. Her shopping cart was full of her belongings and her small
dog—a rat terrier—rode where her purse would have been. She pushed
past me with her head down, and her scalp was pink as tinted pearls.

The only walkin fools I knew in LA were homeless people, and they
walked to pass the time or collect cans or find church people serving
food or erase momentarily the demons talking in their heads. They
needed air passing their ears like sharks needed water passing their
gills—to survive.

I was the same. I walked in that rhythm—my greatest oblivion and
comfort—and saw every person who passed me: two women pushing
strollers, their faces Mayan, plastic shopping bags like bulbous octopi
tied to the handles. Everything in the store windows—Silver Lake hip
gilded furniture next to blow-up dolls with fishnets, Echo Park panade-
rias with pink pan dulce and sugar skulls with eyebrows of icing.

I walked faster now, heading down Sunset toward Beverly. My
mother hadn't been allowed to walk far as a girl, when she was prey.
My father had walked hundreds of miles—when he was a homeless
child, when he worked the cane fields, when he was in the army—and
never mentioned joy in it.

A walkin fool.

My brothers and their friends named the fools, shouted them out,
when I was young. *Man, Detroit is one ballplayin fool. Don't do nothin
but dribble all day. I heard that. Cornelius tore up again—damn, that is
a drinkin fool. Got to have him that Olde English every day.*

And the worst kind? *Grady Jackson. Shit. Sprung fool. Ain't no sense
in gettin like that over a female. No female worth gettin that sprung. Not
even Glorette.*

My first time in England, Shakespeare was read aloud. *Fool, make
us laugh. Go tell the fool he is needed.* I saw it on the dessert menu.
Raspberry fool. I tasted the cream and cake, and thought of Grady
Jackson.

The houses and apartments of Echo Park loomed above me, and
beside me was a vacant lot tangled with morning glory blossoms closed

up for the evening, like handfuls of silver-blue cigars. I walked past the sheared-off cliffs below an old apartment complex, where shopping carts huddled like ponies under a Grand Canyon.

Glorette's body had been in a shopping cart. When we were small, and someone had left a cart in the canal, the mud and grass covered the metal skeleton until it looked like a shaggy burro under the water.

Through a gap in the hills, I could see downtown, buildings glittering like disco balls. No one knew I rarely drove. Everyone said, "Parking was a bitch today, huh?" and I nodded in agreement. I bet it was a bitch for them.

My hip bones felt like someone had poured hot oil inside the sockets, and my thighs hummed when I stopped at the corner of Eighth and Olive. A veil of coolness began to dry at my shoulders. It was warm here, but not half as hot as it would be in Rio Seco.

Across the street was the black tile wall, the dimly lit alcove of the Golden Gopher.

Grady Jackson used to wash that tile every night until it gleamed.

Grady and his sister Hattie were from Cleveland, Ohio, by way of Grenada, Mississippi. He hated his name. He was in my math class, though I was two years younger, and he wrote Breeze on top of his papers. Mr. Klein gave them back and said, "Write your proper name."

Grady said to me, "I want somebody call me Breeze. Say, I'm fittin to hat up, Breeze, you comin? Cause my mama name me for some sorry-ass uncle down in Jackson. Jackson, Missisippi, and my name Jackson. Fucked up. And your cousin—she in love with some fool name Detroit."

Glorette. We were sophomores, and a senior basketball player who had just moved here was talking to her every day. "Call me Detroit, baby. Where I'm from. Call me anything you want, cause you fine as wine and just my kind."

But Detroit had no car. Glorette smiled, her lips lifting only a little at the corners, and turned her head with the heavy pile of hair on top, her neck curved, and Detroit, who had reddish skin and five freckles on top of each cheek, said, "Damn, they grow some hella fine women out here in California."

He didn't even look at me.

One weekend, I was on my front porch when Grady Jackson pulled up in a car. My brothers Lafayette and Reynaldo had an old Chevy truck, and they jumped down from the cab. "Man, you got a Dodge Dart? Where the hell you get the money? You ain't had new kicks for a year. Still wearin them same Converse."

Grady looked up at me. "Glorette in your house? Her mama said she ain't home."

I saw his heavy brown cheeks, the fro that wouldn't grow no matter how he combed it out. Should have just called himself Missippi and made fun of it, learned to rap like old blues songs and figured himself out. But Cleveland had already messed him up.

I said, "She's home. She's waiting for Detroit to call her after his game."

He spun around and looked at Glorette's house, across the dirt street from mine, and said, "She think that fool gonna take her to LA? She keep sayin she want to go to LA. I got this ride, and I'm goin. You know what, Fantine? Tell her I come by here and I went to LA without her. Shit."

Then Lafayette said to him, "Grady, man, come in the barn and get a swallow."

My brothers had hidden a few beers in the barn. When Grady went with them, I didn't even hesitate. I'd wanted to go to Los Angeles my whole life. I got into the Dart and lay down on the floor in the back.

When Grady started the car, he turned the radio up real loud, so Glorette could hear it, I figured, and then he spun the wheels and called out to my brothers, "Man, I'ma check out some foxy ladies in LA!" His breath drifted into the back, smelling of pale sour beer. He turned the station to KDAY, and they played the Commodores and Cameo, and then he talked to himself for a long time. I knew the car must be on the freeway, by the long uninterrupted humming.

"She always talkin bout LA. Detroit don't know how to get to LA. He know Detroit. She coulda been checkin out a club. Checkin LA."

I fell asleep on the warm floor, and when the car jerked to a stop, I woke up. Grady was crying. His breath was ragged in his throat, I could smell the salt on his face, and his fists pounded the steering wheel. "There. I seen it, okay? And you didn't. You didn't see shit cause you waitin on some fool-ass brotha who just want to play you."

I sat up and saw Los Angeles. The City of Angels. But it was just a freeway exit and some narrow streets with hulking black buildings. I remembered one said Hotel Granada, windows with smoke stains like black scarves flying from the empty sills.

Grady looked back and said, "Fantine? What the hell you doin in here?"

I had come to the Golden Gopher five years ago, after Reynaldo called me about Glorette. "We don't know who gotted her."

I hadn't heard that for a while. She done got gotted. I had said, "What about Grady Jackson?"

My brother said, "Who?"

"Grady. The one she married after she got pregnant and the musician left her."

"What about Grady? That country-ass brotha been gone."

"He lives somewhere in LA. I should tell him."

"Only one might know is his sister. Remember? She was gon be on TV. She worked in some place called Rat or Squirrel. Some bar. Said it was just part-time while she was waitin to be in some movie about a jazz singer."

Maybe Hattie was inside. I had to ask her about the picture at Dimples. And tomorrow night, I'd bring Victor here, and tell him the truth about his father, and how I heard the story.

"Ma'am?" A goateed young guy in a black shirt that said SECURITY approached me. "I need you to move?"

I hadn't seen the film crew—three huge trucks parked on Eighth, a parade of black-shirted guys fanning out onto the street, lights being set up. Someone was taking video of the apartment building next to the bar—gargoyles, sooty cement, fire escapes. The place Hattie Jackson used to live. She'd had a pink curtain that blew out of the fourth-floor window. A young actor dressed in a camouflage jacket looked out from the window now—someplace he would never live. A place probably meant to be New York or Chicago.

Another security guy noticed me, in the middle of the street. A brother my age, with cheeks scarred as if acid had been thrown at him. His badge glinted in the lights. "Hey," he said. "Hey, baby—"

"I know—you're in the movies," I said, and crossed the street to go inside.

———

In front of me, blocking the narrow doorway of the Golden Gopher, two young men waited in line for the ID check, laughing and shouting, "It was a Zippo!" A street guy in a filthy bomber jacket looked each of the boys in the face and said, "Got a cigarette, bro?"

Twenty-four years ago, when Grady had brought me here accidentally, the Golden Gopher was a dive. There was no waiting to get in.

Hattie was twenty-two then, and Grady was eighteen, and I was still fifteen. He'd pulled me inside the club, past a knot of drunken men. One of the men put his palm on my ass, fit his fingers around my jeans pocket as if testing bread, and said, "How much?"

Grady jerked me away and up to the bar, and a man said, "You can't bring that in here. She underage."

A line of men sat at the bar, and someone knocked over a beer when he stood up. Then his sister spoke from behind the counter. She said, "Grady? What the hell?"

Hattie was beautiful. Not like Glorette. Hattie's face was round and brown-gold, her hair straightened into a shining curve that touched her cheeks. Her lips were full and red. Chinese, I thought back then. Black Chinese. Her dress with the mandarin collar.

She pushed three glasses of beer across the counter and someone reached past my neck and took them. Smoke and hair touched my cheek. I remembered. The bar was dark and smelled of spilled beer and a man was shouting in the doorway, "I'll fire you up!" Through an open back door I could hear someone vomiting in the alley.

"I wanted to come see you," Grady said. Sweat like burned biscuits at his armpits, staining his T-shirt. "See LA. The big city."

"Go home," Hattie said. "Right now, before somebody kicks your country ass. Take Lousana girl wit you."

Hattie's contempt was heated in her eyes. She thought I was Glorette. I said, "You know what? I was born in California, and I'm coming to live in LA pretty soon. But I'm not gonna work in a bar."

But she lifted her hand to dismiss me. "You probably not gonna work at all, babyface. One a them light-bright girls."

Grady pulled me back out the door as I was thinking Lite-Brite was a toy at Kmart, and this time the hand fit itself around my breast, and someone said, "Why buy the cow?"

Driving east, the moon was like a dirty dime in front of us, and we took a beautiful bridge over the Los Angeles River, which raced along the concrete, not like our river. Grady said, "We can't get on the freeway again."

"Why not?"

"Shit, Fantine, cause I stole this car, and you ain't but fifteen. John Law see me, I'm goin to jail."

He drove down side roads along the freeway, past factories and small houses and winding around hills. The Dart ran out of gas in Pomona. We were on Mission Boulevard, and Grady said, "You wanted to come. Now you gotta walk."

I stood in the darkened lounge. With the downtown renaissance, investors bought this scary dive and turned it into a hip dive. Two women wearing heels and camisole tops pushed past me impatiently, and two young actors I'd seen on commercials for *The OC* followed them into the bar.

It looked like Liberace had decorated—chandeliers and black pillars and little golden gopher statuettes on the tables. The jukebox was playing Johnny Cash. Farther in the long narrow space, the bartender leaned forward and squinted at me. "You okay?" he said. He had a two-tone bowling shirt, a porkpie hat and sideburns.

I gave him my impersonal traveling smile. He gave me that look— what is she, Brazilian?—and I went into the back part of the club, where small tables were set against the wall, and toward the alley.

I remembered the alley. Big couches covered with velvet and pillows lay at each end, and the OC boys were already collapsed on the cushions with two girls. It was cool to be in an alley, drinking Grey Goose martinis while the shouts of insane men circled above the walls. "Oh my God, did you see that one guy?" a girl said. "With the big fucking hole in his forehead?"

Grady used to get his dinner in the alley, back when there was a Mexican food place two doors down. Hattie had brought it to him here, every night at exactly six p.m., his only stop on the round of endless walking.

A little baroque gold table held an ashtray between the couches.

I looked straight up at the sky for a moment. Hazy as if sand flew through the air. "What is she doing?" one of the girls whispered. I knew better than to come to a place like the Golden Gopher alone. Places like these made anyone feel lonely.

My phone rang to redeem me. The girl rolled her eyes and looked away. Tony said, "FX? Where are you?"

"The Golden Gopher," I said.

"What? You okay?" His Jersey accent came back quickly when he wasn't joking.

"Yeah."

"Where the hell is the Golden Gopher?"

"Downtown. You'll have to come here sometime. Great pics."

"Come over."

In the bathroom, a gold vase held a single hibiscus. White, with a red throat. Where was Hattie? My hair had sprung loose like an aura around my forehead, from the heat and the walking.

How you get sprung like that over one woman? my brothers always said to Grady.

He came to the barn another night, and my brothers were working on a car. I had just taken them some coffee. Grady held his right hand wrapped in a rag, and he asked Lafayette, "She over there at her mama's?"

Lafayette said, "Man, she told me she was movin in with that flute player. Sere Dakar or whatever he call hisself. He playin them congas now, and he suppose to get a record deal. She's havin a baby, fool. Said they was gettin married."

Grady said, "He ain't fittin to marry her. I heard him say it. He was playin congos in a club, and I heard him tell somebody, 'I gotta book, man, I gotta get to LA or New York so I can get me a deal. Tired a this country-ass place.' So I hatted him up."

My brother said, "Damn, fool, your finger bleedin! He done bit off your finger?"

The red stain on the dirty rag. Grady said, "He pulled a knife on me. Man, I kicked his ass and told him to go. He was gon leave Glorette over and over—come back and then book again. I just—I told him to stay away." He was panting now, his upper lip silver with sweat. "Forever."

He pushed past me. I had already been accepted to college, and Glorette was pregnant with Sere Dakar's child—the swell was high up under her breasts, awkward on her body as when we used to put pillows inside our shirts inside that refrigerator house.

We never saw Dakar again. Grady had already been working for the city for a year—driving a trash truck—and he rented a little house and asked Glorette to marry him. He said he would love Victor as his own. But Glorette couldn't love him. After another year of still loving the man who got ghost on her, she left Grady to get sprung herself—on rock cocaine—and she refused to ever love anyone again.

Near the bar, a young woman—Paris Hilton–thin, blond over black hair, and a satin tank top—came out with a tray and squinted at me. "What do you want to drink?" she asked.

"Hattie Jackson?" I said, and then remembered. "I mean, Gloria Jones. Does she still work here?"

She shrugged. "Maybe she's that black lady in the go-bar."

The alcove. I went back to the counter, where Hattie was arranging bottles of Grey Goose and Ketel One. Her nails were not red now, but fuchsia pink. Her lips were pink, too, but thinner and ruffled at the edges. She looked so old.

"Don't call me by that name," she said, and sighed.

"I remember," I said. "Gloria."

She moved more bottles onto the counter. When I'd come, five years ago, she'd said, *I got myself to Hollywood, and they had been doin Pam Grier and Coffy and Cleo. My mama named me Hattie after the one in* Gone with the Wind. *Who the hell want to be called after a maid?*

A slave, I had told her.

Shit. Still a maid. I changed my name long time ago. After you was here the first time with my fool-ass brother.

Gloria Jones said, "Uh-uh, you ain't got no news for me. You told my brother about Glorette, and I ain't never seen him since. Five years. You might as well killed him."

A young guy with those unshaven filings clinging to his cheeks came up and said, "Hey, can I get a bottle of Grey Goose? And that—right there. *You know.*" His voice got all rapperish on the last two words, and he nodded toward a pack of condoms.

He handed her a hundred-dollar bill. She slid the things into a sleek black bag and gave him change. He said, "Thanks, Gloria. You always hook me up."

Her lips moved half an inch and her eyes not at all. And in the way he slapped his palm on the counter, lightly, dismissively, I saw it. She was the cool black madam, sex radiating out of the alcove, the funky agent for the bottle in the motel room.

Hattie looked straight at me. "Maybe it's cause there's no damn food around here anymore—why he doesn't come around. You know? Maybe after all those years, it was just the free food, and he done forgot who the hell I was." The blond waitress came by and raked Hattie with that glance. Hattie said, "And Miss Thang there done moved in with the bartender, and I heard her sister wants this job right here. Don't get much tips, cause people don't buy this shit till they ready for their private party."

Fake nails like pink almonds. "You've been here all this time," I said.

She shrugged. "Not much longer." She wore a wig. The hairs were perfect. "You know what? I left home and came up here, and I was fine as wine. But even the hookers in LA was somethin else. Hollywood was crazy, so I came downtown cause it was cheap and I thought I'd wait till I got me a movie. I did the dancing place for a month."

"The dancing place?"

"Over on Olympic. The men dance with you for ten dollars and they gotta buy you them expensive-ass drinks. But they smelled." She tapped all ten nails on the bar, as if piano keys were marked. "Lord, they all smelled different, and some of them, the heat comin off their underarms and neck and you could smell it comin up from their pants. Even if they had cologne, just made it worse. I couldn't do it. I came here, and I was tendin bar forever. The guys would tip me good, and that Mexican food place was so cheap. I would take my break, buy a plate, and go out front at six."

"After Grady finished washing the tiles."

"Two enchiladas and rice. One for him and one for me. I used to go to the movies on Broadway every night before work, and I lived next door."

"They're filming a movie there tonight."

She let a laugh out through her nose. "Yeah. They all down and dirty. Uh-huh." Her eyes were brown and muddy, as if washed in tea.

"I came to see you about Glorette," I said. "Her son went to this club. There was a picture of you and Glorette on the wall."

Now she frowned, so hard her eyebrows moved together like toy trains. "What?"

"Dimples."

Then she said, "Shit. Dimples. We went there one day. Yeah."

"Glorette was in LA?"

She laughed dismissively again. "Hell, no. I went home for Christmas to see my mama and them, and Glorette and Grady were livin in some lil house with the baby."

I looked at the hairs on her wig. What was underneath now? "Where he wanted to be. He was happy."

"Thought he was. Drivin a trash truck. I had this card from a dude came in here one night. He told me get a friend and come audition at Dimples. Make us stars. Grady brought me and Glorette out there the next day. Dude took our picture and then we got up there onstage, but Glorette—"

"She never sang."

"Not that." Hattie watched two customers pass, and her smile was perfect and curved then, her lashes moving. "We were standin there on the stage and they was movin the camera and all of a sudden her shirt is soakin wet."

I couldn't picture it. "She was crying?"

"Milk." She moved two bottles in circles. "Grady was sittin outside in the car with the baby, and somebody opened the door, and she musta heard cryin. Big old circles on her shirt, and you could see her—"

I knew.

"All the men in there was pantin. Shit. She run out and musta told Grady to leave, cause I sang my song and when I went out, that car was gone. I had to take a cab home." More customers went past the go-bar, and two waved at Gloria. She lifted her chin and said, "Hey, baby."

Her eyes were hard on mine. "They still got my tape over there, at the club."

Up there in a storage space? I thought. Behind the Screening Room?

"See, you could never get up there. You too boring." She took a sip from a glass and slid it back behind the register. "You were already gone to college then, but you never wore no makeup, nothin."

"You want me to apologize for going to college?" I laughed.

"See? Just like a high yella—" She sucked her teeth and turned to the bottles.

"Fuck you, Hattie," I said.

She whirled around, her hair swinging stiffly like a wing. "Oh, so now you got somethin to say? Not no big words? Just *fuck you*? Any dumb bitch can say that." She flicked her nails at me in dismissal. "My mama told Grady when he started goin out to Sarrat—Don't mess with them light-bright girls. You can't trust them breeds."

Breeds. Half-breeds.

She leaned forward, her cleavage trembling. "Neither fish nor fowl."

The blond girl came back. "I need change, Gloria."

She glared at me. I was old. No makeup. No man. No use.

Gloria handed her the ones, and the girl cut her eyes at us both.

"You got to buy something or go, Fantine."

"One cigarette," I said. Gloria laid it in my palm, and I gave her ten dollars.

"You didn't have to tell him," she said.

"He would have found out someday," I said.

"Shit," she said. "How? Wasn't nobody but you and me up here in LA." Her fingers were hard as a man's on my wrist. "I loved my brother. I never loved nobody else in the world, but every day I saw my brother and we ate together. I can't never go back home, but he came to me. And you took that away."

I pulled my arm from her grip. Her nails left half-moon smiles on my skin.

Grady had told me right here, outside near the neon sign.

I leaned against the shiny black tile, holding the cigarette. A skeletal finger.

That night, a bucket had slammed down on the sidewalk, and someone began to wash off the tile. A homeless guy. Green army coat, black sneakers glistening with fallen foam from his brush and rag, and black jeans shiny with wear and dirt. His hair was thick and matted, but a brown spot showed on the side of his head, like the entrance to an anthill.

He'd had ringworm in Mississippi, when he was a kid. He'd always combed his natural over that place. Grady? His hand moved back and forth over the tile, washing off fingerprints and smudges. Grady. He was missing half of his right ring finger.

I crossed the street. He squinted, and then he walked slowly toward me, steady, knees bending, arms moving easily at his sides. He stopped about ten feet from me and said, "Fantine?"

I nodded. He said, "I been waiting for you. All this time."

His hands were rimed with black, like my father's when he'd been picking oranges. His eyes were tiny, like sunflower seeds in the deep wrinkles. All that sun. All those miles.

"You told me you was gon come to LA. And you left for college. I married Glorette. I married her."

His four top teeth were gone, like an open gate to his mouth. He said, "We went to the courthouse. Me and her."

I said, "Grady, I came to tell you—"

"I knew you was somewhere in LA. Me and Glorette went to the courthouse after Sere Dakar was gone. He played the flute and the congos. But he wasn't African. I seen his ID one time. Name Marquis Parker. He was from Chicago. He coulda called hisself Chi-town. Told me he was goin to LA and play in a band. Glorette was havin a baby."

"He's seventeen," I said. "Her son."

But Grady stepped closer, the ripe too-sweet smell of urine and liquor and sweat rising from his coat. "No. My son. I was gon raise that boy. Dakar was gon leave her every time. So I got him in my truck."

I tried to remember. Grady had an old Pinto back then. "You didn't have a truck."

He trembled, and breathed hard through his mouth. "Fantine. All this time I waited to tell you. Cause I know you won't tell nobody. You never told nobody about the car. About when we walked from Pomona."

I shook my head. My brothers would have beat him down.

"I waited till Dakar came out that one bar where he played. Then I busted him in the head and put him in the trash truck. It was almost morning. I took the truck up the hill."

"Grady," Hattie said from behind me. "Shut up." She held a foil-wrapped plate of food. "Eat your dinner and shut up. You ain't done nothin like that."

"I did. It was a Thursday."

"You a lie. You never said nothin to me."

"Fantine—you was at the barn that night." He held up his hand, as if to stop me, but he was showing me his finger. "Chicago had a knife. I got to the dump and went to check the back of the truck, and he raised up and took a piece a me. But I had a tire iron. Fool thought he knew me. Called me Missippi and shit. But he didn't know."

I looked up at the slice of sky between buildings. Mississippi. Cleveland and Louisiana and Chicago. California. Men and brothers and fools.

Grady tucked the plate against his ribs like it was a football. He said, "I was waitin on Fantine. She can tell Glorette he didn't leave. I hatted him up permanent. But she still loved him. I don't love her now. I'm done." He brought the foil to his lips.

"You left him there?" I said. Sere Dakar—his real name Marquis Parker. A laughing, thin musician with a big natural and green eyes. "At the dump?"

Grady threw his head up to the black sky and dim streetlamps. His throat was scaly with dirt. "The truck was full. I hit the button. Raised it up and dumped it in the landfill. Every morning, the bulldozer covered the layers. Every morning. It was Thursday."

He stepped toward me. "He had my finger in there with him," he whispered. "I felt it for a long time. Like when I was layin in the bed at night, with Glorette, my finger was still bleedin in Dakar's hand." His eyes were hard to see. "Tell her."

I pictured Glorette lying on a table, my mother coiling her hair. Higher on her head than normal, because she couldn't lie on her back with all that hair gathered in a bun. "She's dead, Grady. I came to tell you. Somebody killed her back in Rio Seco. They don't know who. I'm going to see her tomorrow morning. You want me to take you?"

Sere Dakar lying under layers of trash. Glorette braiding her hair before we went to sleep—she whispered about how his long fingers played the flute, and then rested on the side of her neck. My eyes filled with tears, until the streetlamps faded to smears and I let down my eyelids. When I looked down, I saw the wet sidewalk.

Hattie went back inside without speaking to me, and she closed the black door hard. Grady whispered, "Where she get killed?"

"In an alley off Palm Avenue," I said, and his chest let out the air it had been holding. I couldn't lie. He knew what that meant. He knew what she would have been doing.

He walked away, that familiar dipping lope that I'd watched for hours and hours while just behind him, that night.

A homeless man crossed the street quickly and said, "You got another cigarette, sista?"

His hair had been braided a long time ago—clouds of new hair puffed around his forehead. We used to call that our baby hairs, all of us girls from Sarrat, and we plastered it down with Vaseline into complicated waves on our temples.

Fish nor fowl. Our scales. Our feathers.

Sista. He reached out his hand, cupped as if for water, and I put the cigarette inside.

The film crew moved like a black-clad army over the sidewalks and in and out of buildings. The older security guard studied me, stone-faced.

I called Victor. He said, "Hey."

I said, "Victor, where are you now? I'm sorry I was already booked tonight."

Then he said, "Gotcha—leave the digits. Late." A beep. That was his voicemail.

I put the phone in my pocket, and then slid it back out and turned it off. It had been so quiet in Brienz and even in Luzern. And I didn't want to hear from anyone else in Sarrat about why I wasn't there yet.

I moved down Eighth, the opposite way from the direction Grady had walked. I figured he just kept walking, after he knew she was dead. Maybe he walked all the way to Venice Beach and into the waves. Maybe he tried to walk home to Rio Seco and died of dehydration, and he was still somewhere in a field, under a quilt of tumbleweeds.

I moved quickly toward the Music Center, where well-dressed concertgoers lingered on the sidewalks. The sun was bronze, lowering itself into the smog. Construction site—my fingers bumped along a chain-link fence that glowed red as if it were on fire.

That night, when Grady ran out of gas in Pomona, we left the Dodge Dart beside the road and started walking down Mission Boulevard. The old Route 66—mythical asphalt.

"I been walkin all my life," Grady said. "Don't be sayin shit to me. Just keep up."

We left behind the auto shops and tire places, moved past vacant lots and tiny motor courts where one narrow walk led past doors behind which we could hear muffled televisions. Junkyard dogs threw themselves against chain-link. We moved easy and fast, me just behind Grady. Walking for miles, past strawberry fields where water ran like mercury in the furrows. Past a huge pepper tree with a hollow where an owl glided out, pumping its wings once and then gone.

That night, we walked like we lived in the Serengeti. And five years ago, Grady was still moving the same way, when I watched him disappear down Eighth Street into the darkness. Like pilgrims on the Roman roads of France. Like old men in England. Like Indians through rain forests, steady down the trail. Fools craving movement and no words and just the land, all the land, where we left our footprints if nothing else.

VERMONT

TONY HAD BEEN DRINKING when I called earlier—his teeth clicked like tiny castanets against glass. "You know exactly what I'm doing, FX," he said sadly. "I swear I need a black veil."

I took a cab back to Los Feliz and then walked up Vermont. Tony lived on the hill, near Griffith Park. The sidewalk was steep and broken by banyan tree roots. I pushed open the wrought-iron curlicued gate. His house was a big two-story classic Spanish-style with a heavy wood door. The first time I came over, years ago, he'd put his nose up to the small window in the door, behind three wrought-iron licorice sticks, and stuck his tongue onto the glass like a pink slug.

He had the windows open, the TV on. "Hey," I said.

"Hey," he said back.

Tony was the only person who knew almost everything about me— some of my life in Sarrat, and most everything else since. He sat on the couch with his feet up on the table. He held the small glass of scotch at his navel, as if it would catch drips from the ceiling.

"Two sips down, eight to go," he said.

His partner, Ian, had died last year. Ian was the pastry chef at a restaurant on La Brea, and on his way to work one morning at four a.m., a drunk driver going the wrong way on Sunset smashed into the Triumph and killed him.

I held up the wooden goat from Switzerland. "From Brienz, this little town at the edge of the Alps where they carve. Switzerland's famous for the cows with the bells, but one of these mountain goats butted me when I was hiking. Works for you, right?"

Tony smiled. "You writing the piece now? If Rick wants me to go, it'll be in two weeks, cause I have a shoot out in Palm Springs on Saturday. August 27 in Palm Springs. 114 at least. Shit." He petted the goat. "Then I have to go home. My nephew's wedding. Guess who's the photographer?"

I had to laugh. No one in my family ever asked me to write anything. The goat was big for a carving, the size of a chicken, actually. "You ever held a chicken?"

Tony shook his head. "You know my mamma was a city girl."

I stood the goat on the hearth of the huge slate fireplace. On winter nights when they were both home, he and Ian had sat in front of a fire. Ian was from England, some small village where he'd lived in a cold stone cottage. He loved fire. He used to say to Tony, "We need a dog for the hearth. Sleeping right there."

But Tony was always gone on a photo shoot, and Ian worked long hours at the restaurant, so they had a ceramic dog for a joke. And for a year now, I had brought a wooden or stone or ceramic animal from wherever I went. The hearth was crowded with chickens, dogs, a pig from Italy, a fantastic striped winged animal from Oaxaca. I made the goat kiss the pig.

On the couch beside him, I took off my boots. I could smell the scotch. "Never get used to it," he said. "Each sip is like fire, and then it goes straight to my dick. Which used to be a good thing."

"I know." I took the glass. One sip. So different from rum, the only thing my father and Gustave ever drank. They'd made their own, back in Louisiana. They called it something else, but it was sweet and dark. This was hot and gold.

Wednesday had been Ian's only day off. Every Wednesday that Tony was home, since Ian had died, he watched a movie from England and drank one glass of scotch whiskey and slept on the couch.

"You're going to be forty in November and I'm December," I said. I couldn't recognize anything about the movie. Stone house. An ocean. "What is this?"

"Hitchcock," he said. "*Rebecca.* That's really Carmel. I didn't know that until he told me." The waves crashed against the craggy coastline.

"Did you know there's an alligator in Lake Machado?" he said, sleepily. "They're trying to get some guy from Louisiana to catch it."

I laughed. The scotch was sharp on my molars.

Tony took another sip. His toes were long and brown. My toes were short and less brown. We had sat like this countless times, here and in hotel rooms and on ships. Sometimes we traveled separately—he went to Bath or Portland after I'd gone—and sometimes we were together.

"Conventional movie wisdom says we have a baby," he said softly.

"Yeah?" I put my anklebone next to his. "The craziest kid in the world? Obsessive in too many ways?" We had slept in the same bed a few times, when we could get only one room. But we had never awakened touching each other.

"Because we're both turning forty, and I haven't had sex all year, and we're supposed to regret not leaving behind our legacies." His long hair curled around his ear. Black loose spirals, like my mother's.

"We couldn't even handle a real dog," I said. I put out my hand and he gave me the glass. Heat in my chest.

"Everybody's still trying to set me up," Tony said. "They're always pissed—'How can you just stop having sex? It's unnatural!' I had a lot of sex with Ian. I'm done."

I hadn't had a lot of sex. I'd had enough sex. He was right. We could turn to each other and pretend, and try to have a baby. That would be a stupid movie.

He was the only person from my present to have been in my parents' house. Only the fourth white person to visit Sarrat. Maybe my mother thought he was black for a few minutes, until he started talking. His skin was darker than mine, because he was always tanned, and his eyes were black and shiny as the glazed ceramic panther on the hearth. But he talked to my mother about his own mother and her cooking, and he stayed in the kitchen long enough to make her love him a little.

I had been at his mother's house, in Asbury Park, New Jersey. She thought I was Italian and French. She had fed me his favorite soup— wedding soup, with chicken and meatballs and pasta and spinach— and joked with me about marriage. But I knew she knew about him, if not about me.

"I have to go home. Sarrat home. Glorette died five years ago tomorrow," I said. "Remember?"

Tony threw his head back and stared at the ceiling. His Adam's apple bobbed like a hummingbird trying to escape his throat. "I remember once when somebody else died. We were in France."

"Marseille." I slumped down in the couch and stared, too—the ceiling was textured plaster, buttery yellow. "We were in an alley talking about Marcel Pagnol and my father called. My brother Reynaldo and Clarette had a baby. A girl. She died after a week."

"They waited for you to come home. And you left."

I nodded. "I was going to be the godmother. I had to help bury her."

"You said they'd never forgive you if you didn't come home." His voice was soft and sleepy. "You said I was the only one who knew why you'd spend all that money."

"The Moors." I stared at the hearth crowded with animals.

"The Moors."

The fire—the table—the tribe. There was nothing else outside the circle that mattered. He knew.

Tony suddenly held up his thumb like he was hitchhiking to heaven. "Splinter," he said. "I forgot I was waiting for you to get it."

The kitchen light was bright. I held the needle over the stove flame. Tony sat at the long wooden table Ian had loved, with mazelike patterns of wormwood scars. I pulled his hand toward me. The left thumb was red at the tip.

The needle opened the flesh around the black dot. I moved aside skin. The tip of the needle—under the tiny dark piece of wood. A dart and it was out, smaller than an eyelash on my own palm.

"Stupid fence in the back is falling down," Tony said, his voice thick. Not with pain, but with longing. Ian had done the garden. "I keep having to prop it up."

I swabbed the raw hole with alcohol and blew on the skin.

How many times had I seen my mother and father close together at her table? I would hear them late at night, since my room was next to the kitchen, peer around my doorway to see them. She was fearless with splinters, and we had them all the time. She told us again and again, "Don't be no baby. You move, it hurt worse. I don't get it out now, you gon lose that finger."

Tony's eyes were closed. I dabbed the alcohol on the wound again and wrapped a Band-Aid around his thumb.

My mother would probe and probe, move aside the flesh on my father's palm, his thumb, his knuckle. Then the needle would flash. "La." She always held out her hand to show him the small source of pain. "Now you infected." She swabbed with alcohol, blew on his skin, and then my mother would hold my father's hand, helpless and upturned, in her own for a long time. "Dry now," she would whisper. "I can't have you lose no finger. I need you with all ten."

Once she kissed his palm.

I felt warmth behind the fly of my jeans. For someone to kiss the center of my hand. I closed Tony's fingers in on his palm, like when we were kids playing the spiderweb game. "Hey," I said. "Don't be a baby."

"I'm not," he said, opening his eyes. "I'm being a little kid."

"Shut up."

He stood up unsteadily. "A little kid who had some scotch. Damn."

While he was in the bathroom, I got out my notebook, thinking of Victor. I'd written notes about the Bourbaki panorama painting. The Moroccan soldiers, their skin bruise-dark against the white, white snow of Switzerland. Victor could be the Intrepid Godson. Godmothers were always cool—fairy godmothers! Lots of writers had great-aunts or patronesses. Victor could be the Reluctant Scholar. The Light-Bright Fool. The Dread Prince. "Hey," I called to Tony. "Have you ever been to the Dalmatian coast? Rick mentioned it."

He shook his head, smoothed the Band-Aid while we went back to the living room.

"What do you think about me taking my godson to Belize or on a cruise?"

"Rick doesn't have the budget to pay for someone else. If you could get *Vogue*—but not with a kid. Wait—he's in college?"

"Not right now. I talked to Rick about Italy for us. I have this book on Naples."

"We could go to Bernalda. My mom's grandmother was from there. She was a prostitute because some old guy in the Mafia raped her when she was sixteen." He took the last long sip of scotch. "Said once that ten minutes was over, she could never be anything different. Let's go write about that village."

He put his head back and closed his eyes. He had told me about this. In a bar in Rome. He told me about Bernalda, and I told him about the Apache, and Moinette Antoine's mother in Azure, Louisiana. How we were on this earth because women had been raped.

"Tony," I said. "We have to meet Rick in the morning. You've got shoots forever, but I need at least two more assignments. I have a Chicago piece for *The New York Times,* and I've got the monthly outing for *Los Angeles,* but that's only five hundred words."

He shrugged.

"Pirates. I told Rick we could do pirates."

"Pirates." Tony opened his eyes and frowned.

"Remember I told you about Jean Lafitte? Somehow he's one of my ancestors."

"You told Rick about Louisiana?"

"No." I'd told a total stranger at the party. Only said the word. "But everybody's into pirates now—Cornwall, the English pirates. My godson really wants Belize, and Belize had pirates."

"Cool." Tony put his hands behind his head and closed his eyes again. That meant we could talk about it later. We were the same—the idea needed time to move through our brains, like the dye florists added to the water of carnations. His cheeks had a sheen of sweat. The house was warm, and had never had air-conditioning. He said he would never sell it. He would live here until he died.

"KCAL News at nine is next," a woman said. "Our top story tonight—a twenty-year-old man was shot today near Warner Brothers studios. Melissa McCloud is there."

A blond woman gestured like a game show hostess at a blank wet spot of asphalt and said, "Earlier tonight, police kept onlookers from the crime scene while they worked to determine what happened this evening at around six."

Video footage showed three policemen holding up their hands and pushing back a crowd of people. Behind them, a body lay covered with something dark. Behind that was a row of black-and-white photos on a dingy brown wall.

Dimples. I leaned forward. The scotch burned in my stomach.

"Police have identified the victim as Armando Muniz. The victim's brother was on a cell phone with him at the time of the shooting. He says words were exchanged between the victim, who was on foot, and a group of males in a vehicle."

The blond woman was standing before the backdrop of the Warner Bros. buildings, but when she turned to sweep her arm toward the street, the light spun off the sign that said FREE TAPES TO VIRGINS.

Dimples.

"A gun was found beside the victim, and police found blood in an area approximately twenty feet from the body, so they're speculating that one of the assailants has also been shot. A dark-colored SUV was seen leaving the area. Anyone with information is asked to call the number at the bottom of the screen. This is Melissa McCloud reporting live from Burbank."

They'd gone back to Dimples. I saw Victor leaping down the last three steps below my apartment, holding the frames. He'd wanted his mother's picture.

I'd turned my phone off outside the Golden Gopher. I pushed the button. Three messages.

"Marraine. Marraine. Pick up. It's me."

"Marraine. It's Victor." I heard shouting. But he spoke low. "It's me."

"Okay. Did you jet off again? Damn." He paused. Then he sang in a whisper, "Tell me who the fuck are you?" The music behind him was loud, and then the line went dead.

THE RIVIERA

WHERE WOULD THEY GO? They wouldn't be in LA. I was the only one they knew here.

Blood on the asphalt. Someone had been shot. The boy named Mando was dead. I put my hands over my ears and heard the rushing of my own pulse. Victor with a gun?

No.

I didn't want to tell Tony. Not even him. This couch—I had come to sit here with Tony, not been willing to sit on my own couch with Victor. "What are you doing?" he said, sleepily, his head still thrown back. He couldn't drive. Too much scotch. I said, "I have to go home."

"See you tomorrow?"

"Yeah," I said.

On the cracked pavement, I walked fast, pushing callback on my phone. "Victor," I said. "I just saw the news. A shooting. What's going on? Are you okay? I'm in LA—if you're here, call me right now."

Three blocks to my place. Sweat laced my scalp when I got inside. My wood floor gleamed from the light in the courtyard.

They had to have gone back to Sarrat. My overnight bag—I threw in two pairs of indigo jeans. The white shirt I'd just bought in Zurich, gauzy cotton with seed pearls edging the collar, was still folded on the bed. Two more shirts from the closet. Then I picked up my laptop, and the messenger bag I'd bought for Victor.

Brown leather, nearly golden. The heavy buckle on the side. It could hold a laptop, books, anything. He had an ancient Dell that his grandfather bought him four years ago. He needed a new computer, too. I hadn't wanted to give the bag to Victor in front of Jazen and Alfonso. It meant college. Books. Dexterism. From *poindexter*—a nerd. Why not dexterity? I wanted to call him and say that. Where was he? He had to have gone home. He couldn't have shot anyone. He couldn't have been shot.

I called him again. "Victor. I'm coming home. I'll meet you at your grandpère's."

I hesitated in front of the chair where he'd sat. The Brassai. I put that book in the new bag, and the little notebook he'd left, and then I put in the Edgar Allan Poe.

The Corsica was clean, since it was always covered in the carport. I tossed everything in the back. If anyone saw me in an old car like this, they'd laugh. But I hardly ever drove it unless I went to Sarrat, and no one in Sarrat laughed at this car.

Dark blue. 1992. When I'd seen it for the first time, I said to my brothers, "You got me a pirate car."

Lafayette had said, "Why you always gotta say something crazy?"

"Lots of Corsicans were pirates. They lived on an island off France. Napoleon was born on Corsica."

"It's a car. Don't forget to change the oil," Lafayette said, and rolled his eyes.

I turned onto Los Feliz and headed toward the freeway. But at the on-ramp I went north, toward Burbank.

From the freeway, the red flashing lights of the police cars were visible, but I still got off and drove down the little side street before the club. At the corner, three patrol cars were parked sideways. The NBC building across the way.

The asphalt was black and gray and stained with oil and a thousand dark liquids. Whose blood? I made a three-point turn like someone who'd just been running an errand. No way would I be able to see down that dim doorway to an empty square on the wall.

In the parking lot beside Dimples, a huge satellite dish faced the sky. It was so old that holes were torn in the mesh, like an ancient flyswatter.

The river was on my left again when I headed south on the Golden State Freeway toward downtown. All the rivers where I'd sat drinking coffee with Jane or Tony or swans and strangers for company. The Danube. The Avon. The Seine, the Thames, the Limmat, the Rhine. The Aare a few days ago. The LA River twisted narrow and black as tar in its channel until it slid under the freeway again.

The César Chávez exit loomed up before me. Mando—the boy

with the feathery hair and too many girls—he'd said Chávez and St. Louis.

I took the off-ramp without thinking, and drove east. His long hair—had it come loose from the sweet oil and rested on his cheeks? He had lain in the street under the eyes of Gwen Stefani. Not Glorette. She was in Victor's hands—was she? Did Victor hold something else in his hands? No. Not the gun.

What could possibly have made them shoot at each other? A glare, a smudge on a stepped-on shoe. Anything.

Boyle Heights. The streets were narrow and steep, lined with small bungalows painted pink and yellow and turquoise. I'd been here many times with Jimmy Taco. He loved to take people out for birria, a goat stew, or tacos de lengua. Tongue tacos.

I stopped at the light. A crowd of people stood in front of a small lavender house on the corner. Two teenage boys were shouting, getting into a car. I pulled slowly through the intersection. Two young women stood in the street crying, their faces silver in the streetlight. One was the girl with the tadpole eyebrows and cursive tattoo. The one who hadn't wanted to give Mando a ride home.

I was shaking as I drove through the intersection and headed back toward the freeway.

The Pomona Freeway, where Grady had driven me while I hid in the back. Three more rivers until I got home. The moon was rising from behind the eastern mountains, in the center of my windshield. I passed over the Rio Hondo, banks tangled with wild grapevine, and the San Gabriel River, a vague ribbon edged by concrete chunks.

Sarah Vaughan's voice filled my car. *If I knew then, what I know now . . .*

I was coming up on the dump. La Paloma. I'd come here once with my father to empty a truckload of plastic containers someone had tossed in the groves. La Paloma rose up beside the freeway, a low mountain with its own ecosystem of spindly eucalyptus trees and fountain grass all around the base—to hide what the huge mound really was.

Our refuse. Our midden. The place someone would excavate to know about us in hundreds of years. And whose bones would be found?

Sere Dakar had chosen his own name. He'd told me that once, the only time I went to the club with Glorette to hear his band play. We were seventeen. She was pregnant but hadn't told him. The band was Serengeti. I already knew I was leaving. I had a scholarship to the East Coast. Brick buildings and snow.

When Glorette was in the bathroom, Sere Dakar sat next to me during a break. "Dakar is the capital of Senegal," I said, trying to be smart. A brainiac. He was twenty already. "I heard you were from Chicago."

He said, "Uh-huh. You never heard Soul Makossa? Or Hugh Masekela? I had a friend in Chi-town named Kenya Lumumba. I gave myself my own name, since my parents didn't have any imagination and I haven't seen them for twenty years."

But I never knew his real name until Grady told me. Marquis Parker.

Fire lit the top of La Paloma. Seagulls used to hover over the trash mountain, like a thousand white tissues drifting in the distance. Now the city had planted pampas grass that waved creamy plumes all along the roads the trash trucks drove. Natural gas came out through pipes at the summit of the steep hill, thirty years of refuse layered upon layer, and somewhere Sere Dakar might have been nothing—no hair or smile or fingers that played the flute, the heels of his hands that played the congas. Teeth? Ribs? Or was his essence rising still in vapors through the soil and burning now brightly in the torchlike flame that wavered at the top?

I had never wanted to tell Victor the story only I knew. Murder, not abandonment. His father hadn't left him before he was born. But now he was desperate, riding in the Navigator, holding pictures of his mother, nothing of his father, and maybe a gun. When I found him, I'd tell him everything.

He was in the backseat. He had to have been. He would have been listening to The Who on his headphones. The blood must be Alfonso's. Jazen would have shot Mando.

The Santa Ana River glittered faintly before me now as the car crossed the bridge that led into Rio Seco. Dry River. The narrow slide of water, with all the flood danger taken away by irrigation and dams and the levees of broken concrete—the river tangled through bamboo and wild grapevines and cottonwoods, heading west to the ocean, passing my father's orange groves. When I was a child and it used to rain hard for days, the angry currents swirled bank to bank like chocolate milk. Under me now, the water moved through the arrowweed—the tall straight-stemmed plant that my father said Indians used for their arrow shafts.

All the rivers, cutting through the cities and plains. All the people surrounding the water, brown or red or blue water, green or sluggish or white-capped—all the women reaching their hands into the water for cooking and washing, all the men reaching their hands into the water for fish or stones. You never been to Africa? The Nile. Man, my people from Egypt. Egyptian Lover—that had been one of Bettina's favorite rappers when we were teenagers. Maybe that's how Alfonso decided to name his girls.

The Mississippi—so wide and brown behind my great-aunt's house in Azure. Leaving New Orleans and all the boats and ships I'd seen as a child, then sliding past the small houses where men rode out into the bayous and bays for shrimp and oysters and fish. My father's aunt Almoinette holding shrimp curled like slick gray commas in her palm, saying to me, "That a tite bug in the water, oui, but he keep us alive. You catch so many bug, you can always eat. See he got eyes?"

I'd bent to see tiny black spots like peppercorns. "He got eyes, too. Just like you. Think about what he see before your papa catch him up. See the water all around him, but somethin in there we don't know. Some food for him, too, oui?"

My phone sat in my palm like a small black sunfish with a tiny fin.

I tried Victor again. Voicemail. I said, "Victor. I'm in Rio Seco now, so call me and I'll come get you. I've got my car. I'll be right there if you call me."

Home.

I called Cerise. She answered, "What—you done partying?"

"I just got off the freeway."

"Uh-huh. So you might stop by tonight, huh? If you ain't got another meeting." Music and voices were behind her.

"Cerise. Did Victor make it back yet?"

"Victor? He said he was goin up there to LA to stay with you."

"Yeah. He was with me earlier." It was always at least ten or fifteen degrees hotter in Rio Seco than in LA. I rolled my windows down when I got to Main Street. The Spanish-style buildings, the blank marquee above the old movie theater, the wood-fronted strip malls with dough-nut shops, pizza and nail salons. Anywhere in southern California.

"He left with Jazen and Alfonso," I said, turning on Palm and driving toward the Westside, where Glorette had always lived since she left Grady.

"What? He called his grandpère and said he was with you."

"He was. But—" Just at the edges of downtown was the long line of citrus-packing houses, where all of Rio Seco's wealth had once been delivered and sorted and boxed. The buildings were mostly empty. La Reina, where my father still delivered his oranges, was out near the river.

"I told him I'd meet him later," I said. Why hadn't I just kept him? Kept him—like a little kid. But he *was* a little kid—still curious and excited, no money, no car.

Long ago the freeway had split downtown into two, and the dank underpass was like a cave. WESTSIDE LOC was spray-painted along the tunnel, with KILLA and $$$. Like a crazy restaurant rating. On the other side, the arroyo separated the Westside from the orange groves. Cerise breathed on the line, inside those groves. No one in Sarrat would have seen the TV news, because they never watched it. That news was all LA.

"I'm swinging by Sundown and the taqueria," I said. "In case he's there. I'll bring him with me."

"I'll tell Unc Gustave," she said.

Esther Phillips sang, *Don't count stars, or you might stumble . . .* and suddenly I remembered Victor saying, "Sometimes I head to the Riviera, Marraine. Just like you do."

The Westside used to be a neighborhood of old Victorian houses and bungalows, but they'd been cut up long ago for boardinghouses and apartments, back in the forties when so many black people moved to Rio Seco from Texas and Oklahoma and Louisiana. In the sixties, some developer built the Villas—stucco apartment buildings in various pas-

tel colors in every vacant lot along the streets named Jacaranda, Oleander, Hyacinth, and Jessamine. The apartments were long shoeboxes
placed perpendicular to the streets, with wrought-iron railings and
cement courtyards, and on their bland entrances were their own inap-
propriate names: Jacaranda Villas, Jessamine Villas, Hyacinth Villas.
They couldn't make Oleander sound pretty since everybody knew it
was poisonous, so the pale blue complex with gang graffiti like black
ivy around the entrance was called the Riviera.

Victor had lived here before. When his mother showed him the palm
tree sparklers.

My phone rang, and I opened it without looking at the number. Rick
said, "Can I just say how much I hate the entire idea of spa travel? Hey,
you weren't at the bookstore."

I parked along the filthy sidewalk, where the curb was black with
tire marks and spilled liquids and fine dirt from the carob trees in the
parking strip. "Tony didn't feel good." No guys were hanging out in the
courtyard, but most of the lights were on, and the swamp coolers
hummed loudly, like each window had its own beehive. "Spa travel?"

"Yeah. Let's go to Slovakia for a tummy tuck. Let's not actually go
outside the windowless fortress of our medical building or meet anyone
from the city or eat real food. Let's go to Bratislava but only eat Jell-O
and soup."

I felt the heat rush into the open window, and the smell of marijuana
smoke and charred meat. On the balconies were little Weber grills like
landed spaceships. A block away, on the corner of Palm and Oleander,
two women walked in vague patterns. Glorette used to move along this
street, this alley, this corner. Glorette in her yoga pants and sports bra.
Red high heels.

"Sounds pretty painful."

Rick was driving. I heard the rush of traffic behind him. "Boring
even as these women were describing it to me after the reading. Are
you okay?"

"Yeah."

"So tomorrow?"

Breakfast. I'd find Victor, take him back to Sarrat, and spend the
night at my parents' house. Then he could come to LA with me in the
morning. We could talk about *The Personal and Social and Cultural*

History of Crack. We could start college applications. We could go to a movie. Something he'd never see in Rio Seco.

If he weren't bleeding.

"See you then," I said to Rick, rubbing my eyes until I saw red. I needed to firm up two more assignments. I needed that kind of cushion.

Victor had lived in #4 once. Two palm trees stood lonely in a courtyard planter like mine—this one had sparkly white rocks way back when, I remembered, but now just blackened dirt. I got out and walked slowly toward the trees. It had been so hot today that people were still cooking, and two of the grills glowed like campfires.

The moon had risen high enough to be behind the trees, the perfect place for what Glorette had shown me when we were kids in Sarrat, but these palm fronds didn't shift and toss and sparkle with silver electricity as they did in winter, when the moon was full and the sky was clean. Tonight the moon glowed like a dirty tangerine behind the lingering smog, blurry and tired above the dusty fronds, with nothing to reflect or move. Just the day's heat still trembling in the crown of the trees.

"What you lookin for?" A voice came from the stairwell. Same as Jazen's, but not him. Two embers floated in the darkness like red fireflies. As a child, I had looked everywhere for fireflies, and not seen them until I got to college.

"Nothing," I said, and went back to my car, my eyes floating in hot tears. Glorette, kneeling next to Victor on the balcony, showing him the way the trees looked like ghostly fireworks. If he didn't call me, I had no idea how to find him.

On Palm Avenue, the four-lane that went straight through the whole city, I stopped in front of Sundown Liquor. It was a tiny liquor store with posters of brown women with cleavage—Mexican girls wearing halter tops and cowboy hats, a light-skinned black woman with green eyes and a bottle of golden beer in her fingers.

Three men sat in folding chairs under the huge pepper tree in the back part of the parking lot. My brothers often came here in the evening, playing dominoes at the card table someone took home every night. But tonight my brothers were in Sarrat.

Chess Williams, who used to sit here every night, had been shot and killed not long after Glorette was murdered, some people said because he knew who did it. Of the three men at the table, I only knew Sidney Chabert. He squinted at me and raised his chin. He knew my car. I pulled into the parking lot, just next to the alley, and he said, "How you been, Fantine?"

"All right," I said, because that was the proper answer. "How about you?"

He shrugged. Sidney had been sprung for Glorette, but he'd never been with her, as far as I knew. Back when she was walking this alley, every Friday Chess used to give her fifty dollars as well as buying rock for her from someone he knew, and they stayed together all night. "In the morning, she makes him grits. Every Saturday," my brother Lafayette had said.

Sidney glanced up at me and said, "Five years." He was the one who'd found her body in the alley two blocks away from here, in the shopping cart. He'd wheeled the cart to this parking lot, to my brothers. They'd taken Glorette home in their truck.

"Yeah," I said. "You seen her son Victor tonight? With Jazen and Alfonso?"

The other two men were older. The one with silver threads in his rough natural said, "Them knuckleheads in the Navigator?"

I nodded.

"They come by about a hour ago and had a shoutin match in the alley. Some female owe a hundred bucks." The other man nodded. The dominoes were laid out like a skeletal X-ray in the dim light under the pepper branches. "Then they drove over to the Launderland. How they do."

Clarette had told me they stored their rocks in one particular dryer. I said, "Three knuckleheads?" and they both nodded. So Victor was still with them. Who was bleeding?

"They had to been fightin with Sisia," Sidney said, slanting his head toward the alley. "She always owe them. She probably still down there."

His eyes were muddy, and his breath smelled like malt liquor. "Five years. Sisia still walkin and Glorette layin in the ground." He said it like an old man.

I touched him on the shoulder. We used to sit next to each other in math. "I know," I said.

I got back in the car. A mural had been painted on the wall, to cover graffiti. The skeletons of Day of the Dead, with top hats. I felt that cold web of fear like a cape across my shoulders. In Luzern, two days ago, Jane and I had crossed the Kapellbrucke, the famous chapel bridge across the Reuss River where the ancient paintings on the triangular wood panels always featured a skeleton lurking, waiting, hiding—death was always there. Victor could be bleeding to death, in the back of the Navigator. Would Jazen and Alfonso take him to the hospital, where there were always cops?

I drove two blocks to where the Launderland was bright and day-like, the only person inside a Mexican woman wearing a pink apron and folding countless small shirts and socks like doll clothes.

Sisia. Turning down the side street, I saw her walking slowly away from me, in the alley. Her back was to me, but I knew she heard the car stop. The set of her shoulders changed, and her head rose so her neck straightened, and her butt shifted slightly under the tight lycra.

Black yoga pants, a black sports bra, and black high heels. Skin so dark you only knew it was skin because it shone glossy with lotion in the streetlights. She was like a parody of all those yoga moms I saw in LA every day, walking fast down the street with their phones and their toned muscles and their strollers like little wheelbarrows.

Sisia knew the car hadn't moved. She walked a few more steps, so the man she thought I was could see her body, how she looked like a cartoon-perfect woman, with narrow waist and long legs and ass for days, as the guys always said.

Then she turned and walked toward the car, her little red purse swinging, her gold hoops swaying, her breasts shifting loose and full inside the bra. She did it this way because her face was covered with acne scars, her beautiful cheeks turned to orange peel, her smooth fore-head to moonscape. But men still wanted that perfect body. I'd heard them way back in high school. "You close your eyes, fool. You ain't feelin her face."

She bent down slowly so I saw her lush breasts first, the valley between them ghostly white with baby powder, the tops glowing, spilling into the window. I was a shadow. I said, "Sisia. It's me. Fantine."

She dropped down to a crouch as if she'd been hit. "Shit, Fantine," she said. "Why you playin me?" The alley behind her was sandy and pale, two empty shopping carts huddled under a tobacco tree with yellow blossoms.

Then she lifted her chin. "Why you wastin my time?"

"You want a soda?"

"Fuckin hot all day. I gotta get me a Slurpee. I love them damn things."

She sat beside me, and her smell was Johnson's powder, cigarette smoke in her extensions, and fresh nail polish. Underneath was sweat.

"Where you stay now?" I fell into my second language so easily, even as I could still see the carved wooden pew and white roses in Arthur Graves's loft. We never said "Where do you live?" as that implied a permanence that hardly anyone had. Where do you stay? Right now, for a month, a year, a few minutes? Where have you perched for this moment, until times got better or worse?

"The Villas," she said carefully, looking at the dashboard. She wanted to know what I wanted. "You still stay up there in LA?"

"Yeah." No one from here ever asked me where particularly, since they didn't know or care about the difference between Silver Lake and Toluca Lake.

We passed the nail salon Cerise had mentioned this afternoon. The Vietnamese woman leaned in her doorway and watched my car. Sisia suddenly opened her purse and said, "Hey, you gon buy one a these?"

Prepaid phone cards—five of them worth ten dollars each. She held them in a stack on her outstretched palm, like an elegant layered pastry from a Paris bakery, and I thought of all the small things we traded and needed so badly now—cell phones and credit cards and phone cards and iPods. Little plastic things people killed for. Not like when I was a child, and my mother traded bags of oranges and boxes of eggs for long slabs of pork ribs from Mr. Lanier's freshly killed pig.

"Fantine—see, you always trippin like that, breakin off in space," Sisia said, snapping her long fingers over the cards and turning over her hand like she was doing a magic trick. "You want one or not?"

Someone must have stolen them, and paid her with them. I shook my head and pulled into the 7-Eleven parking lot. "You seen Victor?"

When we got out, she was about six inches taller than me in her heels. She glanced at my boots. "You always got the same damn clothes on," she said.

"Yeah," I said. I was tired. "So do you." I was burning up in my long cotton sleeves and jeans, but the night was cooling now. "Victor didn't come by here?"

She walked ahead of me into the cool doorway. "That who you lookin for?" She went straight back to the Slurpee machine, and mixed granular Coke slush that looked like wet brown sugar with a toxically red cherry swirl. I started laughing, I couldn't help it, and she said, "You too good for this shit, huh?"

I made myself one with just Coke. I'd forgotten how the icy sludge rose from the back of your throat to your temples like magic.

"You cannot drink until you pay," the clerk said sternly. He folded his arms over his belly, his handlebar mustache curling black over his brown cheeks.

"Come on now, Mr. Patel," Sisia said. "How I'ma run away in these heels?"

He didn't smile, but he raised his eyebrows and looked at me.

"She okay," Sisia said, and I put a five on the counter. He unfolded his arms. "See by how she dressed she ain't dangerous." She laughed, wet bubbles from the slush.

"You're welcome," I said to Sisia in the parking lot.

She said, "Shut up, Fantine. You ain't about nobody."

I leaned against the car door. The slush pooled in my chest and filled me with cold, like when we were children in my mother's yard and she crushed ice in a bag with a rolling pin and put it in cups for us with smashed mints.

"Tomorrow's five years," I said. "I always wondered if you knew who did it."

"Who caught her back there that night?" she said in a low voice, and then she took another long pull, so that all the red disappeared from the plastic dome of her cup.

"Do you?" I asked. They worked the alleys together, but I always imagined they lost each other when someone got in a car.

A horn sounded from the street, and her whole face changed again. Her braids were gleaming and black, brand-new, and her eyes were dark as licorice. She whispered, "If I knew, I wouldn't tell you. You ain't never gave a shit, and you ain't never around."

She put her cup on the roof of my car and started walking.

"Did you see Victor?" I called after her, and she turned.

"They came by about a hour ago, talkin all that yang. Told them I'd pay up at midnight, and JZ said he couldn't wait that long. Little hard motherfucker. I said you can't bleed a turnip and he said this ain't Alabama. They took off."

They couldn't wait until midnight.

"Took all they stuff with em," she said, sounding sad. The dryer empty. She'd have to find somebody else tonight. "Victor mighta been in the back. I seen another head. Maybe he was sleep. That boy can sleep anytime. You know."

I knew. All the tiny cramped rooms she'd shared with Glorette, getting ready to forge ahead into the night, smoking a reserve rock before they walked and walked to make enough for the next rock, and maybe one more, and if they had to take Chess or someone else back to the apartment, Victor would stay behind his flimsy bedroom door, sitting on the futon with his books and his music and his words.

"Fantine," she said. "You ain't about nobody. You thought you was the shit way back in junior high. That gifted class." She laughed, throwing her head back. Faint white lines of baby powder there as well, in the two creases of her throat. "And we caught you that day and cut your hair."

"That's ancient history, Sisia," I said.

She shrugged. "All you got is somethin tween your legs and somethin in your head. Tell me I'm lyin."

She turned and walked away.

I couldn't tell her I always used the something in my head, but I controlled the something tween my legs, because she didn't care.

EL OJO DE AGUA

I DROVE TWO BLOCKS the other way, to the part of the alley where Glorette had been killed. If Jazen was looking for someone else who owed him money, they must be getting ready to run. But how far?

The back door of El Ojo de Agua was open, and a woman threw a bucket of wash water onto the wild tobacco trees growing near the fence. The water glistened on the shopping carts abandoned there, like rain on silver armor. A little armored burro had carried Glorette from that very spot.

Pounding drumbeats—a lowered black Honda paused at the mouth of the alley and moved on. I got out of the car and walked onto the powdery dust. Video store, nail salon, taqueria—the back doors to each were open, because of the heat. The stinging smell of nail polish remover floated into the hot-oil smell of the taqueria.

This was where Glorette had walked nearly every night. How had it felt, to know eyes were always stalking her? Glorette and I had looked at the picture of our mothers. We knew that what was between their legs had chased them from Louisiana.

No Navigator. Just the fence and the wild tobacco trees where Sidney Chabert found her, their yellow blooms like tiny pencils in the dim light. Flashing blue of televisions in back rooms on the other side of the chain-link fence like lightning.

I touched the tobacco blossoms, the same trees that grew all along the riverbed near our house, and then I saw the cross. Tied to the fence. A crucifix made of Popsicle sticks, fastened together with faded blue plastic twine, the date written in marker on the bottom. August 25, 2000. The numbers like spiders, and a rosary with plastic beads wound around the splintering wood.

A silvery scarf of water flew past me and onto the tree. A woman stood in the back doorway of the taqueria. She put down the wash

bucket and looked at me, then at the cross. Her hand rose to her forehead, down to her ribs, then shoulder to shoulder.

Someone called to her from the kitchen. "Serafina!" She disappeared
inside, and the spilled water rolled along the dry dust of the alley, not
sinking in. The lopsided moon shone through the ferny branches of the
pepper trees.

Glorette used to lie in the groves next to me at dusk, when the sun
turned each orange into a glowing planet. I would never have seen that
if she hadn't shown me. She *felt* everything. Too much. I remembered
her face when she held Victor—it was almost gaunt, as if she felt
Dakar's absence so deeply it had taken away everything underneath
her skin.

Glorette walked in this dust, so long since it had rained that when I
looked down my black boots were golden across the toe. The small
creamy pebble of rock in her hand, in the pipe. I had never seen it. I had
always imagined it glowing like a crimson ember when she inhaled, but
I had no idea what it looked like, or felt like, to be that high, that insen-
sible, that erased. Released.

The moon was three days past full now, moving fast above those
pepper trees at Sundown Liquor. Like someone had taken a nail file
to it.

I stepped on something very hard. Around my feet were pink shells.
Pistachios.

"That boy live on them nut," Unc Gustave used to say. "I go find him,
and he live on pink nuts and Chinese noodle."

Pistachios and ramen. She used to buy him those every night at the
Rite-Aid, Cerise said. Cerise would be in there buying shampoo or getting prescriptions for her kids, and she'd see Glorette carrying a plastic
bag stacked with ramen. Ten for a dollar.

He'd brought his pistachios to my apartment that night, back when
we studied for the SAT. The pink shells like an art exhibit the way he
lined them up on the polished teak—lines of five, lines of ten, while he
said the words. Loquacious. Ludicrous. Lascivious. Then he piled them
on top of each other like cradles—five, seven, and the stack fell over.

I leaned against the car door and cried into my hands. He had missed
the SAT. The last one he could have taken before college applications.
The night before the test, after I'd dropped him off, Glorette and Sisia

had brought two men home, and while Victor was locked into his room studying, they had a fight and one pulled a gun and shot a hole in the window.

The cops took everybody. Victor, too. He wasn't released for a week. His senior year was gone. And Glorette was killed here, a few feet away, the day he was supposed to register for city college.

I got in the car and waited for Victor's voicemail and said, "So it was really your maman who made me into a writer. I mean, I might have genes from Moinette Antoine, or whoever, that made me love words, but it was Glorette. I'm not just telling you this because it'll make you feel better. But you can't feel much worse, so what the hell."

The wash water made a dark shape like a continent in the alley's dust.

"She fell in love with Sere Dakar. This musician. Your father. He took her to the beach one night, I think it was Newport, and you know, we didn't just up and go to the beach when we were little. We were always working in the groves, and half the time Lafayette and Reynaldo didn't have a car that would make it to the beach. But—your dad—he was already twenty, and he borrowed a car from somebody. A Nova. With a good stereo. She told me they had a blanket and they laid on the sand near the car and he played 'Poinciana.' Ahmad Jamal. You must have heard it. 'Poinciana.' She told me that was her favorite song in the world, but she couldn't tell anyone else because we were supposed to like the Floaters and Al B. Sure. Music like that. He played another song. 'Night of a Thousand Eyes.' I think that was Horace Silver. These were names we didn't even know. And—"

I had imagined this many times, after she told me, because it had never happened to me. Never. I had waited and waited, to feel the way she described. For a night like that.

The message stopped, and I called again. "Victor. They listened to this music, and they were lying right beside each other, and when the cassette was over—damn, we had cassettes—she told me the waves were crashing and then they'd hiss. Hiss and sparkle. She said the foam was the whitest thing she'd ever seen, cause it was so dark on the beach. She said the sand was black, real soft, and the foam was like lace that kept disappearing. She never felt like that before and she never felt like that again."

A man walked slowly toward my car. Middle-aged, with olive skin. He kept glancing around, and then cocked his head to see my face in the window.

I turned away. "The cops yelled at them to get off the beach, but sometime that night—that was you. Nine months later. I'm not trying to tell fairy tales—I'm just saying that's what you came out of. When she told me that story, we were seniors in high school. And I already knew I was going to leave. I had seen *Black Orpheus*. I found Brassai and Henri Cartier-Bresson in the library. I listened to Sarah Vaughan and Edith Piaf and Abbey Lincoln. 'April in Paris.'"

Before the man could come any closer, I turned in to the alley, and felt my tires crunching over the gravel, the nut shells. "I am so sorry I didn't let you stay. But come stay with me now. Just call me, so I can know where you are."

This ain't CSI Rio Seco. That's what Sidney had said, when I asked him why he brought Glorette's body to my brothers, why no one ever called the police. "Don't nobody downtown care who killed her," Sidney said to me at the funeral, the small gathering of people on my father's land. "What clues some CSI gon find? Some white chick wearin white pants kneelin in that alley behind the taqueria lookin to see what Glorette ate? Who she done been with?"

But my brothers and my father and Gustave had never found out who'd done it, either.

Maybe Sisia was right, and Victor really was just sleeping in the Navigator, in the dark tinted cavern of the back, with drumbeats shaking the leather seat underneath him.

THE VILLAS

I DROVE SOUTH ON Palm toward downtown, where the county hospital's old brick buildings stood like a factory that fabricated people no one wanted. We had all been born here. I drove up and down the parking lot. No Navigator. I went into the emergency room. About fifty anxious faces looked up at each person who entered—me, then right behind me a woman wearing a housecoat and blue bandanna over her hair, pushing a huge man in a wheelchair. He was missing his right leg. An ancient Mexican woman sat in another wheelchair, tiny and wizened as an apple doll, surrounded by about ten people whispering to her as if she were a queen receiving court secrets.

I waited in line, and asked for Victor Picard or Alfonso Griffin. The woman said no one by those names had checked in.

If they'd gone back to Sarrat, Cerise would have called me.

At the entrance door, a woman said something to me in Spanish, pointing at my butt. I looked back, and a young man with her said, "You're gonna lose your receipt."

A folded piece of paper about to fall out of my back pocket. The poem. When had he written it? Was it about him as a child, watching the helicopter, or now?

The Villas. #24.

I drove past the Riviera and around the corner to Jacaranda Villas. Maybe this was the one. I parked under the old pepper trees. One was filled with bees—the entire trunk hummed in the heat, with no one in the courtyard except two small children getting out a Big Wheel from under the stairs. On the stop sign at the corner, it was written three times: SKEETA.

The same two palm trees in the center of the courtyard, bending toward the south as if bowing. My father had told me, "Glorette live in Jacaranda—sais pas when. We come to get Victor—he settin up there on the balcony. Hungry like a bird."

I went up the stairs. The black slanting numbers on each door, the window coolers like growling white sugar cubes attached to each front window, the trembling white blinds moving aside in two of the windows I passed. Dark fingers held the slats down in an oval like an eye, and then they went blank again.

At #24, the blinds were torn up so badly that they hung like thick cobwebs in the window. I knocked, a flush of sweat breaking out along my shoulder blades. Would Jazen pull a gun on me? Would Victor even be alive? Would he come with me?

A young woman peered through the blinds and said, "What?"

"I'm looking for Victor or Alfonso or Jazen," I said quietly, close to the window, not wanting anyone in the other apartments to hear.

She opened the door, her whole body slanted to the side, her fingers still buried in the hair of the girl sitting on the floor near the television. Videos flashed from the screen—cars leaping, asses leaping, necklaces and curled fingers, but the sound was off. A baby slept on the couch behind the girl, arms flung out as if flying.

"Why you lookin for Jazen?" the girl said, sitting on the couch again. She braided so quickly her fingers danced as if she were playing a saxophone, and the other girl closed her eyes.

"I'm looking for my godson," I said. "He's with Jazen."

"The one just got out?" the braiding girl said.

"No," I said. "That's Alfonso. I'm looking for Victor."

She shrugged, her hands still moving, harvesting hair and pulling it into place and curving the rows perfectly, bending her head to check the line. Then she glanced up at me. "He light? Like you?"

"Yeah," I said.

"They were here a while ago. He says some crazy stuff."

The girl being braided said, "He was talkin bout Akon. Had me bustin up."

"He slept right there for a couple minutes. He was faded or somethin. But the other one, he had a tattoo on his head."

"He was fit," the other girl said.

"Jazen wanted me to do his hair, like right quick, and I said no cause I already had her. She got a wedding tomorrow."

The other girl's eyes were still closed. She was smiling. She was half done—her left side was long perfect braids radiated out in a sunburst from a side part.

"Jazen always tryin to hang here. I told him to come back tomorrow, cause I gotta sleep, and he said he ain't had time then. I thought he'd get pissed, like he do, but he was just like, Shit, and then they took off."

"You don't know where to?" I said, and she shook her head.

I felt huge in the doorway, the metal strip humming in time with the coolers all along the balcony. Where had Victor sat? If I'd invited him to the reading, he'd probably have made them laugh, and he'd be eating breakfast tomorrow with Rick and Tony and me, talking about Gecko Turner in Spain, joking about white kids in Switzerland who wore South Pole and wanted to be Jazen.

Her fingers moved so fast it was hypnotic. The quiet in the room, the heavy stillness of carpet and limbs and the lolling comfort of the other girl's head—it was like an island of Greek sirens.

I gave her my card. FX ANTOINE. My cell number. "Call me if Victor comes back, okay? The funny one. That's who I'm worried about."

She kept one hand in place and took the card. "You live in LA? FX like that crazy stuff they do in the movies."

"Not much craziness to me," I said. "What's your name?"

"Angie." She put the card on the table.

When I had gone down the stairs, she came out to the balcony and called down softly, "Hold up. I forgot—he had borrowed my clippers. The one with the tattoo. Can you tell him to bring them back?"

Clippers? Alfonso?

I drove back down Palm toward the freeway underpass, where we'd walked on that last day of junior high, the day after Sisia had caught me outside school and grabbed my just-finished braid and pulled me toward her.

You ain't about nobody, she said. I cut your hair that one day.

All five of us from Sarrat had long hair—Cerise and Clarette had curls like Spanish moss that hung to their shoulders, Bettina had sun-streaked, thin hair in baby waves along her forehead, and Glorette and I had black Indian-straight hair that our mothers kept braided tightly.

Toward the end of eighth grade, I'd taken the braid out every day before class and let my hair loose down my back. Every day I braided it again before we walked home from school, so that my mother wouldn't get angry. But Sisia said, "Somebody need to snatch you bald, little bitch." The rasp of scissors on my hair, metal vibrating down the strand and into the skull.

I turned west and drove through the older part of Rio Seco's downtown—ancient Mexican restaurant, the dry cleaners, the ancient Singer store where my mother took her sewing machine for repair.

We saw an old man in a hat there one day—a soft brown boat on a bald head the color of a dirty egg.

"Lord, look like Mr. McQuine," my mother whispered, and then she blew air from her nostrils before she put her hand on the glass door below the gold lettering.

"Who?" I said, and she startled.

"Nobody," she said. "Somebody die long time ago."

And once, when it was too hot to sleep in the summer, I had crept out to the porch and lain flat on a damp towel. My parents came out onto the steps and my father said, "Claudine boy in LA. Say he call her."

I listened. Claudine was Bettina's mother. She didn't have a boy.

"The one from Mr. McQuine?" my mother said, sounding shocked. "Here in California? What his name—Albert? Eh, no." Then I stood up and they were quiet.

The Singer store was shuttered. No one sewed now. My phone rang—Victor's name on the screen. I said, "Are you okay?"

There was no reply. I started to repeat it, "Are—" and then heard the voices, the music, as if I were inside the Navigator. I held the phone hard against my ear.

"Why you got your phone open, fool?" Alfonso said. "You can't be callin nobody."

Victor said, "I'm just using the light. Let me check if it stopped bleeding."

Was his voice clotted with pain? Was it only fear? Whose blood—his or Alfonso's? I felt a lurch in my stomach—a roller coaster, a snapping whip.

"Don't be textin neither," Alfonso said. "Don't nobody need to know where we are. Fuck that—I just got out. I ain't goin back."

Back to prison. The nasal voice of Akon: *I'm a soul survivor.* Short brother—the middle-class son of a Senegalese father. Singalee—the first Marie-Therese was from Senegal. I whispered, "I'm right here. Tell me what to do."

Victor said, "Bourbaki," and Jazen said, "Who the hell that?"

Victor was talking to me. I knew it—as if spiderwebs had been lifted from my temples. "Bourbaki," he said again. "That'd be a cool name. For a warrior."

I whispered softly, "But you're not a warrior."

"Sound like a damn sandwich," Jazen said. "Don't be callin nobody. Cops got GPS and shit."

Victor was quiet. I breathed into the phone. Did he know I was here?

"My phone doesn't even text," Victor said finally. "Do you see me pushin buttons? I'm just tryin to see the blood so you ain't gotta turn on the light."

Whose blood?

"Keep it wrapped up, fool," Alfonso said, his voice blurred. Was he the one shot?

"I ain't turning on no light," Jazen said. "Cops don't need to see us. Saint Streets got all them old ladies sittin on the porch seen us go by his house like three times. They callin the cops just cause we DWB."

Driving While Black. In the Saint Streets. Not too far from here.

"At least VP got us some cash," Alfonso said.

"Not enough," Jazen said. "Where your uncle stay? The one you stayed with last time you fucked up."

Uncle? Alfonso didn't have an uncle.

Alfonso said, "We need gas money to go that far."

Jazen said, "Close the fuckin phone, nigga."

Victor said, "You coulda left me at Mr. Thompson's house."

"He a teacher. He call the cops in a heartbeat. Close the phone, I ain't playin."

His voice was secretive. Afraid. Whose blood? Crumbs. He was leaving me crumbs.

But if Jazen had answered the door at the Villas, what the hell would I have done?

"Cerise," I said into the phone. "Where does Marcus Thompson live?"

"What? He's still married, Fantine."

"I just need to drop something off at his house. From Victor."

Children's voices surrounded hers, like a corona of light. "Oh. Yeah, he always hooking up Victor with books and CDs. They live on St. Ignatius." Then she laughed. "Right down the street from that house where you made me swim with them white girls."

SAINT STREETS

MARCUS HAD SAID YEARS AGO, "You know the Saint Streets? I always thought they were cool."

The streets were narrow, shaded with huge carob trees, and the houses were mostly Craftsman bungalows from the early 1900s, with wide front porches edged by stones. The neighborhood was quiet, except for two kids skateboarding and two old women sitting on a porch.

St. Ignatius Street was dark, with old cement-post streetlamps glowing amber between the carob branches. I squinted at the addresses, and stopped across the street from 4454. Kelly Cloder's house—the same blue two-story, flat colonial front, black shutters, the hedges along the foundation like dusty green biscuits in the heat.

It felt like eighth grade.

I had wanted to swim in a pool that day. Not the canal. When we walked up this sidewalk, the yards all crisscrossed with dark hedges, I could hear the pools. The humming of all the filters vibrating in the air just above the sidewalk, near our legs, like the earth was holding in a mindless song.

Was it the first time I lied?

"I love your nation," Kelly Cloder said to me after Christmas, when I'd been moved to the gifted education cluster class after I scored high on two tests. Mr. Dalton, who was young and had a blond braid he tied with leather, had told us to create our own countries.

Kelly Cloder's nation was Royale, a place like Monaco, Paris, and Luxembourg, she said in her presentation. Mountains with ski chalets and lakes with boats. The language was Royale, which had Frenchified words and lots of *e*'s on the ends.

My nation was the island of Cigale, which was what my mother called the hummingbirds that visited her flowers. I drew bays and inlets on my map, because I'd loved those words when we learned geography. Flowers and sugarcane grew for the gross national product. I had seen sugarcane, in Louisiana. Native people spoke Evola, the language of love. Every word was backwards.

Kelly Cloder's eyes were as blue as an old milk of magnesia bottle.

"You must be Hawaiian," she said.

I'd only smiled. Mr. Dalton was saying we needed to know words like *peninsula* and *strait,* because in a few years we'd have the SAT.

"What island are you from?" she said. "I went to Oahu last year."

I'd smiled again and thought quickly. My brothers joked about Maui Wowie—some marijuana Clarette's brother Alphonse said he'd smoked. "Maui," I said.

"That's so cool! You're coming to my pool party, right?" she said.

I talked Cerise into walking with me, but Glorette just shook her head. We had never deviated from our walk to school and home, and when Cerise and I went under the freeway overpass, where pigeon crap and human pee dampened the ground, she said, "I don't even want to swim with white girls."

But she stayed with me as we walked downtown, past the Singer store, and down the sidewalk past big houses, and then into the narrow gap between green leaves. We went around back to where girls were pulling themselves up by the coping. White girls didn't wear swim caps. They just ducked under the water and then lifted their foreheads to the sky, and the water streamed off their skulls and left their hair plastered smooth.

At school, their hair was all Farrah Fawcett wings, blown back in big round curves, but at the swim party, the white girls had small heads like helmets.

A white man stood near the sliding glass door. "Well, you girls must be looking for the powder room." Mr. Cloder held his newspaper. "Oh—you must be the girl from Maui," he said, studying me.

Cerise was frozen in the entryway. He turned to her, and rubbed his first finger on his chin, his chin that looked lavender in the sun, with black dots like pepper. "You, too?" he said. His eyes changed—the pupils and the blue part. What did he see? I saw Cerise—twelve freckles on her cheeks, the baby hairs plastered to her forehead like black lace after our long sweaty walk. Then he moved toward her and put his finger on her shoulder. He rotated the pad of his finger, turned her, said, "Go that way, and you'll find it. You're letting out all the air."

I didn't pay any attention to Cerise when she walked around the pool and navigated slowly near the shallow end, where girls were sitting at the edge, their knees bony like oranges had been sewn under their skin. I knew it was mean. But my hair would be straight as soon as it dried. I dove into the pool. If I stayed underwater, no one would see my old blue bathing suit, the one we'd gotten at Kmart.

Kelly came up behind Cerise and said, "Marco Polo!" and pushed her to deep water. By the time we got out, Cerise's hair matted up like a Brillo pad because the curls had gotten wet, and then dry, over and over. The sun and chlorine and water had pulled everything up tight to the back of her neck, which was pale as tissue. Cerise felt it and said, "My maman gon kill you. For reals."

When we played Marco Polo the second time, Kelly Cloder waved her hands blindly, wildly, and her fingers landed on Cerise's head. "Eeew! Who put a sponge in the pool!"

When we got out again, Kelly Cloder studied Cerise and turned to me. "You're not from Maui."

"Neither are you."

"I was born in Santa Barbara."

"So?"

"You're not Hawaiian. You're black."

"You're so dumb you think they don't have black people in Hawaii? How'd you make it to gifted education?"

I picked up our stuff from the chaise longues that had felt like oilcloth against my legs. I had wanted to lie on something puffy like that. And I had.

When Cerise and I made it home, she told right away. My plan had been to say because it was the last day, we all jumped into the school pool, but Miss Felonise knew her daughter wouldn't have messed up that hair they'd straightened for the graduation photo.

On the porch, Cerise told my mother and Miss Felonise about Kelly Cloder's house, and why we left, and about Mr. Cloder, who'd put his forefinger on that knob of bone when she was heading the wrong way, deeper into the house.

"He touch her?" my mother said, while Cerise's mother plucked at her solid mass of hair. Then my mother beckoned to me with her own forefinger—Quo fa? What happen?—and she slapped me so hard I fell onto the hot wooden steps.

She told us the story of Mr. McQuine. She told us about the three girls, and how the rest of them left except for Anjolie, and she stayed inside, and that my father told her he would take care of Mr. McQuine.

She told us about the car, the ditch, the burning. She told us my father used a piece of wood, and I closed my eyes. Imagined the blood.

During the steady murmur of words, she and Miss Felonise combed out Cerise's giant dreadlock, which took over an hour and required almond oil, warm chamomile tea, and seven pearly drops of Jergens in a bowl.

I hadn't seen Marcus since Glorette's funeral.

He told me that day he'd bought a house. He'd said, "I'm finally having a kid."

Finally. He didn't know and never would that I had carried some of his blood. A baby that wasn't a baby.

I parked across from a shingled bungalow with bright turquoise paint and pale yellow trim, and on either side of the buttery-gold door, big red pots filled with white angel trumpet bushes with their blooms hanging thick like hundreds of celestial instruments.

There were two bikes on the porch. Saronn had a daughter when she met him, and their daughter together would be five now.

I started up the walk, hoping his wife wasn't home. Cerise had said she was beautiful.

I could have married him. I knew he'd go to college. We took honors classes together. But he loved Rio Seco, and I couldn't wait to leave.

Marcus opened the front door and peered at me. "Fantine?" he said, like he missed saying my name, and it killed me. He was holding a shirt twisted like a wet rag in his hands. No hugs, I thought, but when I put out my hand, he said, "Girl, are you crazy?" and pulled me to him.

I knew it. My breasts pressed against his chest. He had a layer of age like an extra soft shirt, a little padding when I put my arms around him, and the feeling inside my hip bones was sharp. I took a step back. The first man who had ever adored me. We came from the same place.

"Hey, expatriate," he said. "What are you doing here? Victor called you?"

"Yeah, he called."

"He left a picture here, a picture of Glorette and some other woman. He said he wanted me to keep it safe. You know what's wrong with him?"

Before I could answer, he said, "Hey, let me get a new shirt, cause it's so damn hot."

He gestured at the wicker furniture on the porch. His back brown, the muscles gleaming when he opened the door and disappeared.

His bare chest moving against mine when we were on the blanket in the eucalyptus windbreak, in the truck bed of my father's broken-down Apache in the far grove, in the abandoned box house when we finally found a real bed. Fantine, he whispered, over and over. I didn't know. I didn't know.

What? I'd said.

I didn't know you were like this.

He meant he didn't know I was so beautiful. He meant he didn't know I was more beautiful than Glorette, there on those nights, when he put his cheek against my neck and said: I didn't know you were the one.

It shouldn't have mattered, that he had thought I was the one. I put my hands on my knees and looked at the street. Marcus had wanted me, and I had wanted out. I left a month later for summer orientation back east.

The screen door slammed. He sat down in the other wicker chair and handed me the frame. The photo from Dimples. Glorette staring at me with those white crescent moons under her night-purple eyes. Hattie's hair shining another moon, silver sickle on her straight bangs. Her wig tonight at the Golden Gopher, glossy and smooth.

"Where'd this come from?" He touched Glorette's forehead. "There's dust along the edges. Like he just wiped it clean."

"Maybe from a museum."

"What?"

"I don't know," I said. I wasn't telling him about Dimples. "What did he say?"

"Kept talking about 'You were right, I hate this shit, it's a minstrel show.' That's what I tell these kids in class, but they don't listen."

"He shouldn't be riding with them. He wanted to stay with me," I said, and then I started to shake.

Marcus pulled the chair close to me and put his arm around my shoulders. "He was sweating bullets, wearing a big jacket. Didn't seem like himself at all. He stayed here a couple times after Glorette got killed. I helped him register for city college. But this time he just asked me for money."

I put my arms around myself. "Did he say what for?"

Marcus shook his head. "He was tryin to joke with me about Superfly. Only game you know is do or die. I couldn't figure out why, and then I remembered he knew what your brothers called me back in the day."

"Sissyfly." I smiled through my tears.

"That's still me." He laughed. "Sissyfly. Gonna make my fortune by and by. Teachin world history and honors econ." He smiled back. Brown lips, brown cheeks, with a reddish tone like molasses underneath. The Thompsons had Creek Indian in them, from Oklahoma. "Sometimes it still feels weird to be at the school where we used to sit in the same classroom. Remember when we had Spanish with Mr. Nickleby, and he hated all the black kids? Alphonse used to tease him all the time. Say, I speak a foreign language, cuddy, I'm *GQ* down, got my Staceys on, get me some mantequilla in my six-fo and we finna book out this country-ass place. See, you don't know what I'm yangin bout."

He touched my embroidered cuff. "Always *GQ* down." He started laughing. "Remember when you were such a jerk after you first got out of college, and I was doing my student teaching? I came by the barn one night to see Lafayette about a car, and you were sorting oranges with your mama and them. You were pissed!"

"I didn't want to be from a farm."

He nodded. "I didn't want to be from a tow yard. But I'm cool with it." He looked out onto the street. "Victor always told me he was gonna live in LA. But you're the only one there. And you're hard to get in touch with."

Glorette stared at me. Wounded.

"He never asked me for money before, but Saronn's had the store for two years now, and he's been there, so maybe he figured I was bankable." He frowned. "He said whatever I had. Saronn's still at the store—we had about thirty people tonight for open mic poetry." Marcus stood up and pulled the front door closed. "I gave him two hundred. He never even got out the car, Fantine. He was in the backseat, with the window open. Like I was a drive-through idiot. Fool drivin—Jazen— I had him sophomore year, and he didn't even look at me. Didn't acknowledge my existence."

I nodded. "We're old."

He pulled two fingers down the point of his chin again and again, mimicking what the older guys used to do when they were trying to talk to a girl. "I remember when all the fellas wanted to rap to Sarrat girls."

"That's what rap used to mean." The carob leaves were green coins above us. "You ain't got no rap—that's what my brothers used to say to you."

He spread out his wide palms, like the homeless man had earlier today, when I was at the party downtown looking from the sky into the alley. "They were right. I only ever talked to you."

That was it. Like all the other boys, he'd wanted Glorette, but then he'd fallen in love with me. The angel trumpets were translucent in the streetlight, like tissue paper. The picture frame was light, and I imagined the paler empty place where it had been. "I'll keep the picture for him. I'm going to see him tomorrow."

Marcus said, "Yeah. You here for the day, huh? I still don't have a rap, but if I did, I guess I could say, All this coulda been yours, baby." He waved his hand over the porch and house, grinning just a little, no teeth, his mouth curved tight. "But you travel all over the world. All this wouldn't seem like much if you were used to Rome and London."

"Looks pretty good to me," I said, but he thought I was joking, and he held out the same hand to help me up. He said, "It's good to see you." His arms went around me, and my face went into the side of his neck— salty and warm and the vein pulsing there. I would have moved into the darker part of the porch with him just like that—my fingers fanned out on his shoulders—but he straightened up and pulled away.

He said quickly, "Hey, can you give me a ride back to the store?"

I said, "No problem."

Marcus ducked inside the door and came out with a canvas messenger bag swung across his chest—ONE LOVE in Gothic letters on the flap.

We drove back toward Palm. "It's by the old theater," he said. I knew exactly where he meant. One night, I took off from Sarrat without telling anyone and walked all the way to the Cinema Paris to see *Black Orpheus.* No one knew I'd already walked home from LA with Grady Jackson. I had seen five or six worlds by then.

Marcus said, "Is that Esther Phillips?"

"'Don't count stars, or you might stumble.'" I didn't sing the rest. *Someone drops a sigh, and down, down, down you tumble.*

Don't sigh.

He didn't. He got out a piece of paper and said, "I'ma put my cell number here. Call me when you find him, or if you need anything. Cause I don't hear from you. Ever."

I felt my eyes hot. "Marcus," I said. "It's not like my life is that amazing."

"Mine's cool," he said, pointing to a store sign that said ONE LOVE. "I'm surrounded by women. I'm just sayin—" He ran his hand down his neck, like men did when they were nervous. "Check it, I love your godson, too."

Love.

"He's the real thing, Fantine. He's one of the smartest kids I've ever had. The first essay he ever wrote for my class was hilarious. He said you'd taken him to the Getty Villa. He wrote about this wrestler's cup. Some kind of stone. The guy's face was all battered, and that was carved into the stone. He linked it up with Snoop Dog's pimp cup, with all the jewels, and his grandpa's coffee mug." He shook his head. "He could be a great writer or record producer or something. But not ridin with Jazen."

Before I could say anything else, he opened the door and turned toward the store. A CLOSED sign hung in the door. But in the light Saronn's face bobbed up and down in the windows near the cash register. Behind her were two girls, and she turned and laughed, throwing her head back.

The big window was framed with purple and green shimmering cloth, and hanging all around were suns—I recognized the Oaxacan suns of blue and gold, and maybe the others were Indian or African. Clothes, jewelry, books in a kaleidoscope behind her. Saronn's face was round and soft and perfect as a child in a Baroque Spanish painting, with gold leaf for her cheeks, gold hair in the short aura of a natural around her forehead. She wore an Afghan tunic, gold as well, trimmed with beads and embroidery.

It was exactly the kind of store I'd write about if it were in LA, or London, or Luzern. She was exactly the kind of woman I'd love to meet there.

She didn't see us. She spun gracefully and moved to the back of the store, and the girl who must have been their daughter saw me staring from the car window. Marcus said, "That's my heart. Sakkara." Then he blew out a long breath. "Damn—I forgot to give Victor something, cause he was acting so strange."

He ran to the door and knocked, and Saronn let him in. He bent to kiss her, and her long fingers cradled the back of his head. The heat rushed again between my legs, and I looked away.

He pushed a CD into my window. *Superbad! The Soul of the City.* The cover featured a brother with sideburns and a natural, bellbottoms and platform shoes, walking past tall buildings. "I got it at the swap meet—one of those cheesy compilations. But Superfly's on there." He grinned at me. "Give it to him when you catch him. You headin home, right?"

"Yeah," I said. "Goin home."

"You not hidin any of your white friends back there, are you?" He grinned. "I remember when Chess and Glorette said you brought home this white guy once, and your pops was trippin."

"He was?" I thought about it. Tony? My father had been perfectly civil to Tony while he was there.

"Hey, your pops and your brothers barely tolerated me the first few times I went out to Sarrat," he said. "And I could feel it. They don't play out your way."

"No, they don't," I said. He put his lips on my cheek for a moment, hot and dry as a biscuit held against my skin. "Be good," he said. "Cause I can tell you're never bad, in your perfect white shirt."

SARRAT

MY FATHER AND GUSTAVE DIDN'T PLAY. The strongest way to put it, when you were from here. Them dudes don't *play*.

It meant they would do whatever they had to do to protect themselves. And their people.

Did it come from the life they'd had, from never actually having time for play, for fun, for leisure? Every moment was work. Every other human might represent danger. Every situation could end in death.

Jazen and Alfonso didn't play, either. They couldn't even sit down and relax in my place. All Victor did was play. He had refused everything else so far.

But I wasn't afraid of my father. It was my mother. The last few times I'd been home, I had seen something shifting and opaque in her golden eyes—my own eyes—something that meant she had moved away long ago from loving me, to trying to understand me, and now the layer of shine in her glances made me afraid she was edging toward a particular kind of hate, because I wouldn't come home.

I grew up in the most beautiful place in the world, and she couldn't imagine why I wouldn't stay there, why I would leave for anywhere else—not New York or Berlin, Brienz or LA.

People who had never been to southern California didn't believe me when I described the layers of hills and mountains rising from haze like golden tulle or tonight's chalky moonlight. They thought the only hill was the one backdropping the Hollywood sign.

Where would Jazen go? He was looking for money—to spend a few nights at a motel somewhere until things got quiet? Where was this uncle they'd mentioned?

The Westside was below me, the trembling neon half planet of Sundown Liquor held high, a police helicopter floating like a big-headed fly in the moonlight.

The river was invisible from here, winding through the dark belt of cottonwood and willow trees. And just ahead to the east—the black quilt of citrus groves.

I looked out the car window at the arroyo that split Rio Seco into two cities, down the cleft of darkness, and then turned on La Reina. Narrow street of my childhood, which led into the woods. A truck came toward me, open windows blaring accordions and trumpets. Ranchero. Men from Agua Dulce. They slowed and squinted at me as we passed each other. No one drove La Reina casually, and there were no tourists.

A CALIFORNIA GUMBO—BY FX ANTOINE

Deep inside a 30-acre grove of Valencia and Washington navel oranges, a gravel road leads to a tiny hamlet, a refuge for a reclusive group of mixed-race people who have rarely mixed with anyone else for decades. Suspicious, clannish, and fiercely loyal, three generations maintain this pristine enclave. They fled rape and degradation in Louisiana years ago. One was repeatedly locked in a homemade wooden armoire for hours at a time while an overweight white serial rapist stalked the road outside her door. One bore a child by that rapist. And one killed him.

So goes the secretive legend of Sarrat, California. I recently returned to my birthplace to rekindle old ties, mourn the early death of my best friend, who was murdered by a person still unknown, sample the wonderful regional cuisine of my childhood, and look for my godson, the orphan child of that murdered woman and a murdered musician. This young man may have taken a bullet to what was left of his—

His heart? His soul? His chest? His leg?

I did it all the time. The words came exactly in the sentences we all used for travel writing. I wrote the story in my mind even while it was happening, because I'd done it so often. And this one was cheesy as hell.

The tunnel of Washington navels rose around the car. I felt the cool shelter and instant silence. The trees were dusty and tired. The canal appeared from the northern side of the grove, the water running high because it was August. My father would be irrigating. I could smell the water, green and slippery. My river. Not the Limmat or the Thames. Not even the Mississippi.

The trees made a nearly impenetrable wall along the road, behind the canal, until a wrought-iron gate appeared in a gap. If a person wasn't looking, he'd miss it. The gate was eight feet tall, with SARRAT in letters across the top, just like a plantation or cattle ranch.

My father had his friend make those letters, in 1965, the year I was born. A man from New Orleans, who used to do wrought-iron balconies and fences.

When we were young, my father actually locked the gate at midnight. The teenage boys who wanted to buy a car from my brothers or fight them over a girl, or the men always trying to sleep with Claudine—Bettina's mama—encountered the huge padlock.

My father assumed anyone who came that late would steal something. A truck, crates of oranges, or a teenager who didn't need to leave Sarrat. Only the adults who lived in Sarrat had keys.

But now all of us were grown, and we came and went, and my brothers were the feared men whose cars or money no one wanted to steal. I turned in to the lane and stopped on the wooden bridge over the canal. The water slid silently beneath me. About thirty feet from the bridge, four paving stones were lined up along the canal bank—where we used to sit to dry off. A small shirt hung like a blue flag in the branches nearby, and a juice pouch sat like a little metal teepee. The kids had been swimming today.

The Corsica rolled slowly down the gravel road inside the hallway of ancient Valencias. The irrigation furrows between the trees were dark and damp. My father had run the water on this section. Someone would be outside, listening to my wheels popping small rocks, wondering if it was Victor, or whoever they had sent out for more ice or beer, or the police.

Even as they were talking and laughing, they were listening. That was how we came up.

The second language. On my face, I felt the air that comes through citrus leaves. The air scented with white blossoms, with orange rind and oil, loud and vibrating with bees, stinging with soot during a freeze.

How I came up. How they do.

At the end of the lane, my father and brothers left an open space covered with gravel for people to park their trucks and cars. It was so they wouldn't get caught in the mud in winter, but also so whoever was out on the porches could see who was coming.

One day when I was ten, I hid under a huge old tree to finish my book and avoid hanging up laundry. It must have been spring, because the side of the barn was covered in wisteria like fat purple icicles, and my mother's house was covered with morning glory and star jasmine. I was reading *Island of the Blue Dolphins.* So when the police car came rolling up the gravel, the radio spitting names out the open windows, I froze in my dark spot under a skirt of branches.

"I thought we were looking for a nigger," the younger cop said. He had sideburns like little brown ladders beside his ears. "Alphonse Griffin."

"Yeah." The older cop looked down at something on his lap, and then ducked his head to look out the windshield. He had mirror sunglasses like a TV cop, and a hairy wrist resting on the window frame. "Look at this place. Like a picture postcard. You got the oranges and the flowers and the big white house. And look right there who's waitin for us. Nothin but boons."

"Boons?"

The older man shrugged. "Boons, coons, jigaboos, burrheads. All the same."

"You know what my grandma used to call them, when we were in Wisconsin? She used to send money to the starving kids in the South. She called em our dusky brethren."

The older cop looked at my parents' house. "I been here once before. They look Mexican, but they're niggers. Alphonse Griffin—just another nigger." Then he put the car in drive. I remembered it so vividly—the engine shifted forward like it was a caged animal taking a big gulp of air. "What a waste of real estate," the old cop said, and then he went down the road to the houses so fast that gravel popped into the leaves around me.

Alphonse was always in trouble, but when she was sixteen, Bettina idolized him. She named their son Alfonso. Now I stood against the Corsica and listened. Clarette's minivan was parked here, and on the other side Cerise's red Miata. Women talking, kids playing. No men's voices. They were down at the barn. But if the Navigator had come through here, everyone had seen them. I picked up the photo of Glorette and Hattie. Brown sugar. Sweet voodoo. I couldn't hand this to Unc Gustave or my father without an explanation of everything that had led up to this moment, to Victor riding with Jazen and Alfonso. Not with me.

I put the photo back on the seat, but Glorette stared at me, stricken, waiting for me to talk to her. To help her.

I felt like a superstitious child—here in this grove where I had once been a superstitious child—but I propped the photo on the backseat so their faces looked out, and then picked up my bag and the messenger bag I'd bought for Victor. Even with the two books inside, it felt light and empty, like an old snail shell.

"The hell—you here already?"

I dropped the phone and my bag onto the gravel. Cerise came around the side of the van, grinning. "Don't even start that shit," I said, brushing off the phone.

"I didn't start it." She was still smiling. Her hair in a huge puffy bun on top of her head, her freckles larger than when we were kids in Kelly Cloder's pool.

I propped my butt onto the hood, and she opened the passenger door and sat in my car with her legs stretched out before her. "Who you hiding from?" I asked.

"I ain't hidin. Just them kids. They never get tired, and it's so damn hot. Been hot for days." She pointed to two plastic bags near her front tire. "I went out for Otter Pops and more Coke."

Children's voices flew like sparrow chatter from my mother's front yard. I remembered the sweet hard stick of ice we'd all chewed on, every summer.

Not only did I not have kids, no one I knew in LA had them. No one in my apartment complex, none of the writers I worked with at the magazines or the *Times*.

Cerise opened my glove compartment and said, "What you call yourself listenin to now?" She pulled out two CDs. "Uh-huh. Vivaldi. Sarah Vaughan." She shook her head.

Victor had tickets to Dave Matthews. I looked down the aisle of night between the trees. Cerise said, "I can't do it. I tried, when you first showed me. But I can't listen to somethin with no words, and I can't listen to them old voices."

I didn't want her to look into the backseat and see Glorette and Hattie. I said, "I brought you a new *Vogue*."

Cerise said, "I just ain't got the time, Fantine. Your stories make me think, and I got all this laundry or work. I look at em quick and tell your maman where you been."

We walked down the gravel. "I didn't see Victor at sundown. He made it back yet?" I said casually, and she shook her head.

"You saw Marcus, huh? I remember when we were seniors, way y'all carried on, I thought that was gon be you."

"Yeah," I said. "Me, too." His arms around me earlier. The baby that wasn't a baby.

I thought how no one I knew now in LA could translate that sentence. Carry on. Is that *you,* girl?

Always paying attention to the words and not the people. My boots crushed last season's dead oranges like hollow black stones. Cerise carried the white plastic bags swaying beside her like water buckets I'd seen a woman carrying in Vietnam. Suddenly I remembered what Victor had said days after the SAT. "All those words I know and it doesn't matter now. Insignificant. Inconsequential. Without consequence. Not to do with sequence."

My parents' house was on a small rise, a white wood-frame bungalow with black shutters painted every other year, and a wraparound porch with the railing painted black, too. The yard lights were on, the way my father kept them on until all his work was done, and the whole of Sarrat was lit bright. On the east side of the house were the fruit trees—apricot, fig, nectarine, plum—and on the west side were the two walnut trees.

But my favorite tree produced nothing but shade. It was at the very edge of the lawn. A huge sycamore with bark like a white and gray puzzle, with those leaves like dinner plates, and two branches that lay a few feet off the ground. My first time in France, I saw our sycamore—the plane trees shading every village square.

Past the tree, a small graveled road led to the eight shotgun houses, four on each side, where grove workers had lived back in the early 1900s. When my father had bought the land in 1958, the worker housing was empty. He and Gustave cleaned and painted the houses, and then my father went to get my mother at the boardinghouse, and they returned for Anjolie in Louisiana.

The porch lights were on at the first house—Cerise's mother, Miss Felonise. The last time I was here, Bettina was still living in the second house, and her mother, Claudine, next to her. Now those windows were dark.

Six kids played in the yard at Miss Felonise's house. They threw a football and ran complicated patterns that took them into the road, twirling and leaping like a strange parade until someone was thrown to the ground.

My mother's house was like a Monet, with each season flowering vivid and wild. In February, the wisteria was everywhere, purple and cool. Then pink jasmine over the porch, and pale blue plumbago at the fence, and morning glory all summer. Tonight crimson bougainvillea starred in a huge blaze over the carport. My mother trimmed plants and flowers every night, shaping the vines into tunnels and shade and curtains.

But in late August, her sunflowers hung dejected. The roses were blackened on the edges of their petals—when I was tiny, trying to water them on a night like this to revive the deep red blossoms, she would say, "Like the devil breathe on them, tite. They fini."

She stood in the doorway of our house. She didn't wave. She never did. She just watched, but I could see her chest rise and fall with a big breath.

She'd been waiting for my father to finish the watering. Maybe for Victor—if someone had told her he'd been gone two days. When she put her left hand up to the side of her neck, and her forefinger rubbed the skin behind her ear, as she always did when she was waiting for the last person to come home late at night, I knew she was surprised to see me.

When I went up the porch steps, she was coming outside. "Near bout eleven," she said. "Sweep out Gustave house before he come back and sleep. They been out to water four nights, oui."

"Hot," I said. "About a hundred, huh?"

"Hundred and four."

She held the broom, the dustpan attached to the top like a flag. My mother, sweeping for so many hours of her life it must accumulate to months. "I'll come over there with you," I said, and she froze. Someone laughed in the kitchen, and someone else dropped silverware in the sink.

I put my bags down on the wooden love seat, but I pulled out my phone, and my mother gave me that look. "I'm waiting to hear from Victor," I said carefully. "He came to see me earlier." She raised her eyebrows. My mother had never turned away a child or an adult from her table or her house. Victor had to come back here. My mother could fix up any injury, or she'd make him go to the hospital.

I went down the steps with her and past the sycamore tree.

It was like a plantation, I had realized sometime during junior high history, and the irony hadn't escaped my parents. Their house had only two bedrooms and one bathroom, but was larger, whiter, and still the big house.

Gustave's yard wasn't enclosed by chain-link, like Miss Felonise's. She had chickens, and small children around, and flowers she didn't like trampled by dogs. She called to me from her porch, "You finally come home for a minute, oui?"

"Hey, Miss Felonise," I said, pausing at her gate. The kids had thrown the football farther down the dark narrow lane.

"They been waitin on you," she said, adjusting her scarf over her forehead. She wore a white towel around her neck—damp, I knew. The heat would break soon.

"I know," I said. "I was working."

She nodded. "Gotta work, bebe. Gotta work."

I followed my mother up the cement walk to Gustave's porch. He had never grown anything in his yard but geraniums and four o'clocks that came up from seed every year around his porch. He used to say, "Out in the cane all day thirty year. Out in the tree all day now. I sit *down* when I come home."

I had come home when I was twenty-two, just before college graduation, when Anjolie died. Complications of diabetes. "Sugar kill her," Unc Gustave murmured. "That sugar." Victor was four. And Glorette— mute and dreamlike, her eyes floating over my face but never landing.

The house was close and hot inside. My mother opened all the windows for the breeze that always came up at night. Each of the houses was shotgun style, with three rooms in a row. Gustave's front room had always been his bedroom, with his double bed covered by a brown comforter patterned with huge pink hibiscus. His television was on a stand near the window. On the TV tray set up beside it was a coffee cup and an ashtray.

My mother opened the door to the middle room, and I saw the kitchen beyond. She returned to the small porch and started to sweep the day's dust and grit from the wooden floor, her back to me. That was how she always began. It was as if she couldn't look at me coming up the steps or into a room, my face full on to see her own. Even as I walked in, she knew I would leave again soon, and so she was already disappointed.

The small fireplace had been swept clean for summer. On the brick mantel were three photos. Glorette graduating from eighth grade, with the pointy-collared Qiana shirt I remembered so well—it had different-sized suns against the black silky material. Gustave and Anjolie on their wedding day, my mother and father beside them. The men in dark narrow suits and jaws held stiff, the women in white knee-length dresses, the little white church behind them, sugarcane on the side.

My mother's broom scraped against the wooden threshold of the front door. Her back was curved, her neck glossy with sweat under the bun shot through with silver hairs. Her arms were still strong, but the skin underneath swayed gently, soft as curtains.

In the photo, her face was slightly blurred. She had never been able to stand still. Her hands were frozen, one atop the other, around the bouquet of spider mums. Her knuckles were already swollen and darker than her pale skin, from all the cleaning and washing and cooking she'd already done, and she was twenty years old.

Anjolie's face was clear and sharp, serene and distant as if she were modeling for *Vogue*. Her neck was long and curved, her eyes dark and tilted upwards, and her mouth—Glorette's lips—full and lush.

All those days in the armoire.

My mother moved into the corner behind the TV, and I said, "I'll do the dishes." I went past her smell—coffee beans and Jergens lotion—into the next room, but then I had to sit down for a minute. Victor's bed.

It used to be Glorette's.

It was where we braided our hair, and played with the Barbies that had sat lined up on the shelves her father put above her bed. The sharp feet in their high heels dangled above us, and Glorette tied scarves from Woolworth's to rings she put in the bottom shelf so they were like curtains. Miss Felonise did all the sewing for everyone, so she made sheer curtains for the two windows on either side of the room.

Tante Anjolie sat in her chair and watched us. That was her job. She didn't sew, cook, or garden. She watched us because we were in danger from wasps, snakes, wind gusts, invisible bacteria, and men who might wander into Sarrat.

I used to see her face suspended there in the glass, her thick black hair like a crown, her huge dark eyes and the way her sand-pale cheeks swelled more each year, and wonder what had happened to her in that armoire. When a car came, she entered the darkness, the wooden door inches from her shoulders, the smell of herself. How long was she closed inside? It was as if her time in the armoire, the blackness and muffled sounds and fear, had made her more afraid than the girls who'd been attacked.

One night, when I was sleeping with Glorette after a party, I heard muffled crying and talking from the front room, and then Tante Anjolie screamed. She said, "Non! Non! Li crazé! Crazé!"

No. He crushed me. Crushed.

Unc Gustave came floating through the bedroom and went to the kitchen, his narrow shoulders in the white tank top, his face shining with sweat. Or tears. I heard her sobbing in the front. Glorette's arm was stiff against mine. Finally she whispered, "If my papa touch her, and she sleep, she start screamin. Nightmares. About somebody lay on her and she can't breathe."

He had never gotten her. Mr. McQuine. But he had. He had gotten inside the armoire and reassembled himself inside her head. Glorette didn't move. Neither did I. We were both imagining what he looked like. Old and fat and his skin. His hat.

Then I remembered Glorette—walking behind me in the junior high hallway, and the hand on her elbow when she disappeared into the janitor's closet. But I didn't know what to say—then or ever.

I ran my hands over my forehead, the sweat and gel in my palms. Glorette escaped into music, after Sere Dakar. She listened for hours to Ahmad Jamal, Yusef Lateef, Miles Davis—all the music he had loved.

Or some days it was Chaka Khan, Maze, Kool and the Gang—all the music she had loved.

The wall was covered with postcards and prints I'd sent from my travels, and posters Victor must have bought from One Love. A print I'd sent him from the Metropolitan Museum of Art in New York— a reproduction of *Joan of Arc,* a painting that looked astonishingly like a photograph, with Joan in a garden, an apparition of herself floating vaguely behind her, leaving the earth. Like Glorette's two selves, I'd thought. Jacob Lawrence, *Dreams No. 2,* the woman seated in a purple chair, her dark arms fallen to the side and hands open at the visions in her head. A poster of Common, and an old one of Digital Underground.

It was a darker, frameless replica of my hallway. Victor wanted to be me.

The bristles whispered on the other side of the wall.

My mother couldn't speak to me yet.

The terrible thing I did to my mother was to go away. In college, I stayed away, always going home for Christmas with someone else because I wanted to see Boston or New York City.

My father had been a traveler all his life, by necessity, and he thought of my movements as survival. He didn't think about whether I enjoyed the places I went. He thought of them as work.

But my mother would never be the same. For the last twenty years, I had come home for a night or two now and then, between trips, or for weddings and funerals. My brothers had married and had children and lived in downtown Rio Seco for a while, but they had still come here nearly every day, and so had Cerise and Clarette.

It had taken me years to learn that my absence was almost as unforgivable as drug addiction or imprisonment. I was not there, for my mother to see and hear and touch, and the reasons were not important. I had met other people like me, working with them on assignment, or at a party or on an airplane, and I knew it wasn't a Louisiana thing, a rural thing, or even a black thing. It was a clan thing.

It was the Moors.

I'd met a Samoan guy who was an actor and never went home to Carson, where his parents had settled when they left the island. An Irish girl who was a singer and never went home to her tiny town in

County Galway. A photographer from Kayenta who never returned to the Navajo reservation in Arizona except for funerals, and once, to take photos to accompany my piece on Monument Valley. When we went to see his mother, she looked at him with the same fierce and palpable resentment as my mother did me.

People like us were not meant to measure success in the same way our families did. We were failures to them. I'd met countless ordinary people in college and during meetings who never went home except for annual holidays, who'd been raised and groomed for boarding school and college and grad school and work in distant cities, and for success measured by conversations about them while their photos smiled from a mantel. A big mantel.

And now Victor wanted to go away. He wanted to be me.

His three pairs of shoes were lined up on the floor like ghost feet ready to run. On the bed were papers, and a black notebook like Harriet the Spy's.

"*Water Music—Funkadelic Aquaboogie. Dance underwater and not get wet*": notes for the essay he'd been trying to tell me about. "*The journey up the Thames—7-17-1717. Persons of Quality were invited. Barges covered the width of the river.*"

He'd written notes on the back page: *Montesquieu 1755 Essay on Taste: "Let us explain our feeling. This will help us exercise our taste, which is nothing else but the ability to discover easily and quickly the measure of pleasure that we ought to find in all things."* His printing was precise as a draftsman's. Below were random lines: "*I take no pleasure in her company, but my slave has provided me with hours of pleasure." "Taste is the drum: Brazil. Woofers. Taste is the flute: England. Sails." Lafayette and Reynaldo and Chess: Your Love Is Like the Holy Ghost.*

My mother reached the broom into Victor's room. She looked up at me quickly, her eyes guarded and shining. "You come home last night?" she said.

"Today." I folded the two pages and slid them into my back pocket.

"You sleep yet?"

"Not yet," I said. "I'm okay." I went through the second doorway into the kitchen.

Unc Gustave lived on the rice and beans my mother brought him, but mostly he warmed tortillas over the burners and rolled them up. There were white webby marks on the black cast-iron fingers of the burner. In the sink were two plates, two more coffee cups, and one spoon. I washed the dishes with a blue sponge he kept in a flowered dish.

My mother opened the back door. She swept the dust and dried rice and small stones from Gustave's shoes out into the darkness, and then she rinsed her hands at the sink.

I handed her the dish towel. She was missing part of her left forefinger. It was a pink nub, blind as a mole's nose. She'd been chopping ribs at a boucherie, when they killed a whole pig with Lanier, who raised hogs on the other side of the river. A lightning strike startled her, and the ax took off part of that finger.

Grady's finger. Buried with Sere Dakar.

Victor bleeding? Or Alfonso?

Her cheeks were soft and smudged as old gold leaf rubbed onto intricately carved wood, like picture frames from the 1700s. Smooth as mine, but with a fine mesh of lines around her eyes from the years of working fields and groves.

"Hundred and four," my mother said again, and from all my summers of childhood, from all the end of Augusts we had survived lying in the front yard and on the porch to sleep, listening to her moving around with the hose, sprinkling her flowers and vegetables and filling the birdbaths, I knew exactly what her next words would be. "Bien try keep everyone alive."

I felt something like lava rising in my chest, into my throat, and I tried to keep it in, so my mother wouldn't hear, but I nearly screamed when the sob came out.

They were driving now. They were listening to Fifty Cent. He was listening to The Who on his headphones. Alone.

The broom fell like a gunshot, thwacking the floor, and my mother came running to me. "What happen? You fall? See—you tired, you ain't sleep!"

No, no, no, I moaned, like a ten-year-old. Like I had when I hid in the tree all day to read and found my mother and father running along the canal, sure I was drowned because no one had seen me for hours.

No. I cried into her shoulder, big crocodile tears she used to call them, and she didn't mean we were faking, she meant we knew we had done something wrong, something terrible, that was her version of crocodile tears, and I had done something I couldn't even tell her, because my mother had taken care of everyone, all her life, my father and Gustave and all the children and teenagers and women who came into her house and put their heads on their arms on her wooden table and drank her coffee and said, Oh, Marie-Claire, no.

I couldn't tell her why I hadn't let him stay. I had to tell my father.

She handed me the dish towel. Smell of coffee in the weave.

Me—the one who never stayed long enough to joke and wash dishes and feed kids, and I'm back for a minute and start sobbing hysterically—what you got to cry about?

"You better sit down. Breeze comin now. Where you been?"

"Switzerland."

"You ain't use to the heat."

I was a tourist.

We sat outside on Gustave's porch. "You ain't eat either," she said.

I used to bring a box after each trip, with a gift from the place and the magazine featuring my piece. I thought my parents would like Tony's photos of Venice or Antibes or Brussels. But once I saw three boxes unopened in my old room. Cerise hissed, "She used to say all casual, You mind to open that one? Where Fantine done gone this time? Cause sometimes from them pictures, no one know where the hell y'all been."

My mother had never learned to read well. She was the only girl. She had to leave school to wash clothes and cook.

"I was in Switzerland," I said, looking out at Cerise's kids. "I went to this little village way up in the mountains. All the houses were dark old wood, and they had names carved into the balconies. Each house had a name."

My mother nodded, looking at her own house, the porch, the bougainvillea lit vivid by the yard lights. "Name like what?"

"Names of flowers, or trees, or a stream nearby. It was like here. All families."

She nodded again. Miss Felonise had gone inside. The breeze lifted the leaves along the gravel road, lifted the baby hairs off my forehead, rushed through cool and startling as it did almost every night. It was like nothing I felt anywhere else, because just over the mountains was the desert. A hundred and four all day, but by three a.m., it would be sixty-two, and everyone would turn over in their sleep and pull up a sheet.

"Grandmère, you got Popsicles?" the kids said, crowding into the kitchen behind us, Cerise's son Tite Lafie at the head. He must be in sixth grade now, looking exactly like my brother. His eyes were brown with flecks of green like torn leaves, his face burnished bronze, his half grin holding something in reserve somewhere behind his left cheek.

"It's almost midnight," Cerise said. "Y'all need to come in and settle down."

"It's still hot!" Clarette's son Rey Jr. said. His head was nearly bald, and Clarette ran her palm over his skull.

"You here early!" Clarette said, getting up to wrap her arms around me, and I smelled the coconut hairdress at her temples.

"Them rugrats wasn't killin each other out there?" Cerise said.

"I didn't see any blood," I said, and then I shivered.

"Get em in the bed," my mother said. She handed me a Coke with crushed ice and added, "You better sleep now."

"Slept some on the plane," I said.

"That ain't sleep," she said, as she always did. Then she made the last pot of coffee, the one my father and Gustave would drink at midnight, and she checked the gumbo.

The huge cast-iron kettle was outside, over the electric burner where she cooked in the yard to keep the heat out of the house. The big black pot on the stove was only the inside gumbo, the one my mother had brought in for people coming this late. For me, and Alfonso, and Victor.

Now he might be wounded, scared to death, and what would happen when he showed up here? Everyone would say, Why you didn't let him stay? Why you couldn't give up one night? Why you so selfish? Why you didn't think of Glorette? That's her son—you couldn't keep him for a minute? That ain't no godmother.

I could write this dialogue as easily as the travel pieces. I closed my eyes and drank the icy dark Coke and felt the burst of warmth and cold collide in my body.

My mother poured the coffee into the silver thermos. It was time to tell my father and Gustave. I said, "I'll take it down to them. Where are they?"

She squinted and said, "Somethin bout gophers where they put that new pipe."

My brothers would be drinking beer. I walked down the road to the barn, where four tall yard lights hung like caught stars above the trees. Those lights shone down onto the ramada my brothers built every summer for shade while they worked on the trucks or the tractor. It was a huge wooden structure covered with a fringed roof of palm fronds.

My brothers, Lafayette and Reynaldo, were not bad men. They just couldn't love Cerise and Clarette as much as they loved themselves and their friends and their trucks.

When we were teenagers, along the river and on the football field and in the shade of the pepper tree at Sundown Liquor and the deeper shade of the ramada looming above us like a cartoon version of island paradise, my brothers held court with Chess and Alphonse and Sidney and Grady and the Thompsons. When I read *Sula* in college, I believed that Toni Morrison had seen the ramada, or the Sundown parking lot. Sula says to her best friend Nel, "Nobody loves a black man more than another black man."

But they wouldn't love Jazen if he'd gotten Victor shot.

My brothers sat at the wooden table, dominoes laid out before them, their shoulders like copper in the strong light, the brown beetles my father called "bêtes de chandelle" swarming around the high lights, and beer bottles glittering with moisture.

It was a scene I had never seen painted. What my brothers would say to me was how could I love a painting, or a song, or a book, more than I loved them? How could I love van Gogh's painting of the woman in a café at Arles enough to leave my own mother, so that I could stand in the Musée d'Orsay, a former train station with wondrously huge clocks overhead, and study the woman's weary power at her own wooden table, so like my mother at her own kitchen table always crowded with sons and daughters-in-law and grandchildren, but not me?

I loved Tony because he knew me better than anyone now. I loved how he still missed Ian and we could sleep in the same room if we had to and talk until three a.m. and then wake up with coffee in Naples and walk for six hours without stopping.

But this was my tribe. I walked past the old cement cistern like our castle tower. There was to be nothing else—no one else and nowhere else—beyond the table, with the light of fluorescent bulb or candle or chandelier, with the faces of those married to us or descended from us.

Our fire. Our compound. Our walls.

Us. If they ever found out who had killed Glorette, they'd wait for the right time and get revenge. And they'd bury the body where no one would ever find it. If Jazen dumped Victor somewhere, they'd get retribution.

"Gustave said Fo-head ain't been home in two days," Lafayette said when he saw us, a domino held midair like a white hyphen in his oil-dark palm.

"Fo-head and Knuckle-head," Reynaldo said. "Why they hangin out together?"

They'd always called Victor Forehead, teased him that his big skull was full of nothing but words and no common sense. And Alfonso? Apply the knuckles to the skull over and over but it made no difference.

Lafayette studied the dominoes. My brothers had been star football players in high school, and now they worked as plasterers. They had that same comfortable quilt of extra years around the waist as Marcus.

My father and Gustave would never have those extra pounds. They would always be wire-thin, coiled with a different energy. Not the joy and abandon of a fistfight after a football game. The wariness of having survived death since they were small children.

I realized Alfonso had the layer, though it was from prison food, but Jazen was thin like my father. He was dangerous. Victor was thin but not dangerous—he'd lived on ramen and nuts most of his life. And words.

The sound of a piano came through the dark trees around us, like spangles of sunlight. Classical. I didn't recognize the song.

"Rey Jr.," Reynaldo said, slamming down his domino. "He got piano camp and orthodontist and basketball and some damn thing to do every minute."

He and Lafayette had been living in the box houses for six months. Plastering work was slow, because all the new houses used drywall and Mexican workers; my brothers ended up working for friends half the time, making a little cash here and there, and Cerise fought with Lafayette about money all the time.

The music stopped, and started again. Tiny golden lassoes. "I didn't know he was that talented," I said. "Where'd he get that?"

"Maybe Clarette's grandpère. They say he played piano in New Orleans. Back in the day."

I looked down the path toward the box houses. Lafayette jumbled the dominoes together. Wash them bones, the older men always said. Who knew how we inherited passion, really? Had Moinette Antoine given me my love for words, because she was a slave who could read? Had Sere Dakar given Victor anything?

I untucked my shirt and fanned air underneath. Lafayette laughed and said, "Look at you." He went into his truck and brought out a bag. "I got em for Lafie. You gon pass out in them long sleeves."

He handed me a three-pack of white strap undershirts. Boys' XL. "That'll fit you, since you still so skinny."

The barn's double doors were half-open. The tractor and crates were against one wall, and the wooden shelves were filled with tools. The canvas sacks for harvest hung upside down, so rats wouldn't nest inside. I went to the other corner, where my father had an old metal sink, and started to unbutton my shirt. On a corkboard was a map of the world.

It was a yellowed antique I'd found during my junior year of college, studying abroad in Dijon. I had kept it in my room for a few years, and then put it in the closet. Pins were stuck in places I'd been.

"Who stuck the pins in here?" I called out the door.

"Me and Reynaldo. Papa asked us to. I thought you started it."

"I never did."

"You didn't care about all the places you went?" Lafayette shouted.

"I remembered them. Marking off places isn't the point."

"What's the point?"

"Being there." I put my finger on the Dalmatian coast, and then near New Orleans. Pula. Why did that name sound familiar?

Olga. That was a town below Azure. In Plaquemines Parish. Those tiny places never showed on most maps. I went back outside.

"Like you tryin to conquer the world," Lafayette said, grinning. "You always been a bagavond." He bent to take a beer from the cooler filled with crushed ice. It was colder than any refrigerator could possibly be.

I remembered the uncle Alfonso had mentioned. I said, "Where's Bettina?"

"She stay in the last box house. Since June."

"Where's her mama? Miss Claudine's okay?"

"She went to Louisiana back in May. She tired a Bettina, too. You should see what them twins did to her old house. Bettina begged Daddy to let her move to the box house. He should kick her out. But ever since Glorette . . ."

Ever since Glorette. No one wanted a Sarrat girl to be lost like that ever again, even if it was Bettina, who had been a lost cause since she was sixteen.

A gunshot sounded from the groves. Then another one.

I listened, but everything was silent now. No coyotes. No night birds.

"You sure that was Papa's gun?"

Lafayette said, "That's the .22. Who else be shootin down here? Ain't nobody huntin rabbit or pig in August."

Reynaldo said, "Gophers. Papa and Gustave ain't gotta eat rabbit or squirrel now. Like all them old stories bout when they was little. They got gumbo now."

The thermos was heavy. I headed down the main road into the groves. I wished my father had a cell phone, so I could call him and say, "Hey, I'm bringing coffee, don't shoot me."

The rows of old smudge pots stood like one-armed soldiers along the path to the shed where my father had kept kerosene for the nights when a hard freeze threatened the crop.

In Los Feliz, my apartment would be stuffy, the night outside full of noise from cars and shouting people. But here, the wind was constant, stirring up the tired leaves and shivering the foxtails. This air come straight from Vegas, my father liked to say. Come down the Cajon Pass with nothin to stop it. Got some cigar smoke and whiskey and sweat in there. From somebody lose again.

He'd hold up his hand and pretend to grab some of the wind. Keep my money here, me, he'd say. Right here.

The furrows between the trees were all damp black stripes in the lighter sandy soil. These trees were run off the ancient canal system, streaming out of the squat cement towers that stood at the head of each row.

The dried foxtails and milkweed were thick in a few places, seeds blowing in the breeze. My father had no help to hoe out the furrows, to clean the weeds as we had done. No way would my brothers' kids do that work, in the summer. It was different for them.

At USC, I had met Jane, who was from a cotton farm in the Central Valley—Buttonwillow. We were the only farmer's daughters, though it took weeks for us to admit it to each other. She asked about the sickle-shaped scars on my wrists. "Orange trees have thorns," I said. When we were in the dorm lounge, listening while the other girls complained about finals, we smiled at each other. Writing Latin terms or doing endless math problems was never going to be as hard as hand-weeding the rows between trees or tomatoes or cotton.

The earth stretched out for miles, it seemed, when we moved between like a child army, hoeing up the foxtails, bending to pull out milkweed.

When I was a senior in high school, and I got sloppy, my father made me come out in the evening and do over my rows. "You miss some," he said, pointing down the aisle of trees to where green weeds were scattered like thin hair. "Go back and pull again."

I had said, "This isn't a plantation."

"Oui," he said, his face never changing. "I grow you."

My boots were loud along the dirt and gravel, and rustlings skittered under the trees. Lizards and snakes were asleep. Night birds. Rats and mice.

A rush of air past my head, and I ducked. The white-faced barn owl that lived somewhere in the eucalyptus windbreak flew overhead, coasting on the wind, and his snowy startled face was above me for a moment, a ghost that used to frighten us all when we were children. Then he disappeared into the darkness.

Rats screamed when they were snatched up from dry leaves that rattled like maracas.

On the other side of the trees to the east, between my father's land and Agua Dulce, was the asistencia, the small church not big enough to be a mission, but a wooden chapel and burying ground. Rebuilt after the 1862 flood, and only used by those of us in the groves. My father and Gustave had buried Glorette there, in a coffin nailed together by the two of them, in the presence only of our family, in a hole dug by my brothers.

It was as if she had never existed. She had never worked, never paid taxes, never put her name on a government list.

"Ain't no need to call the cops," my brothers had said. "We find out who done it."

But nobody ever had.

I remembered standing there with the red rose blossoms, as we all dropped petals into the hole. Victor was stone-faced, gray as a statue, his eyes set into deep smudges. A man who couldn't have enough of her beauty and had to take it away? Or another woman—some woman Sisia said had been competing with Glorette in the alley?

The sky was lighter over the riverbed, and the chain-link fence at the bottom of the incline, that had barbed wire rolled along the top like an endless Slinky.

On the last five acres to the east, my father had put in drip irrigation when an ancient pipe collapsed. The white PVC had been nothing but trouble, he said. Now gophers were eating their way through it, and I could see far in the distance a square of trees that looked half-dead— brown as toast, their leaves probably curled tight as cigarettes.

There was an ancient wooden picnic table out here, next to a small shed that held pipe and old smudge pots. Behind me was the eucalyptus windbreak, where I'd slept with Marcus. I didn't know, he murmured. And then—not a baby, but a collection of blood.

I hadn't sat out here for years. This was where I'd sat in 1983. When I came home in late October, after my first months at college in the Ivy-Covered East.

The brick buildings. My dorm room with radiators like accordion bellows. The journalism workshop where I'd met Skeet Howard. In my mind, to make fun of his arrogance, I called him the Scion of the Midwest. His dark straight hair in feathers along his ears, pale pale skin, Chicago bars and newspapers and how he didn't want to write for a paper, he wanted to own one. Political science and journalism double major. You guys are lame—you can't make money writing for somebody else. The party after the last day, when we all drank from little airplane bottles of vodka. Hey, what are you anyway? The girl touching my shoulder, saying, Fantine Antoine, wow, that sounds European. Does your dad work here at the college?

Yeah.

I heard they hired two brilliant scientists from Portugal and Belgium.

Yeah. I was born in the Algarve region.

Wow—I was born in Sandwich. I hate even saying it!

Later, when I left with Skeet Howard, he said, Algarve, huh? But somebody from your dorm said you were from Maui.

I lived there once.

Why would you leave paradise?

Paradise is subjective, I said.

He wanted to sleep with me, and I'd slept with him because I wanted to try it. Most people were gone for fall break, leaving those of us who stayed for the workshop. I looked at the sycamore leaves underfoot, cradling ice crystals. I had never seen as much glitter as what spread across the lawns all around us. His dorm looked like an abandoned brick castle and I went up to his room with him.

It wasn't like with Marcus. The bed was narrow and the springs were sharp against my back. The whole place smelled like beer. Bottles lined the windowsill.

It was over in a few minutes, and he was panting. Something in my face he didn't like, and I didn't look away. He went toward his dresser—pale buttocks like a marble statue, like a skinny David—and lit a joint. The smoke drifted into the path of the heater and then flew upward like a spirit. Like the spirits of drowned people my father said lived along the rivers in Louisiana.

That's not how I thought it would feel, he said. Being with a black girl.

What are you talking about?

Your nipples are brown. It's brown under your hair. Look down.

My breasts had actually felt big and tender, swaying when I walked. My nipples were sore and darker than I'd ever seen. I folded my arms. Everything on him was red. The flush across his chest. His dick swayed thin and purplish.

I've been in locker rooms. White girls are pink. Everywhere. My sister is pink.

Yeah, nice that you study your sister. But I'm not your sister.

You think you can just make up stories about what you are?

You don't know what I am. I'm going home.

No, you're not. He stood between the beds, blocking the way to my clothes, which I'd folded neatly. Like a good girl. My jeans. The fisherman's sweater I'd always wanted, and never been cold enough to wear at home.

Brown sugar. Shit, that's what you are. Brown sugar.

I hit him in the chest, like a good girl, and that was wrong. I knew how to hit, from my brothers. Should have aimed for the right eye. He caught my wrist and held it tight. Voulez-vous couchez avec moi ce soir, he sang.

What are you supposed to be? Not a rapper.

I'm supposed to be fucking you. Mocha chocolate ya-ya.

I pushed hard against his chest with my other hand. Not raping me.

It's consensual, he said. The Scion. You came up here. You took off your clothes.

The first time, I said, and he fit the fingers of his right hand around my neck. You think the campus cops are gonna ask which time you wanted it?

He put the fingers of his left hand into my loose hair and pulled tight, so that my throat pushed even harder against his palm.

I was pinned down on the floor by his needle dick. Long and thin. It hit something inside me. A sharp pain. The dirty carpet burned my shoulder blades. Oh, yeah, yeah, brown su-gar. Just like a black girl should.

He wouldn't shut up. Voulez-vous of course you do stop faking.

I said the words to myself while he labored, his fingers tight around my throat. I will kill you. I will take you out.

Speak some French, he said. Now. He stuck a finger from his left hand in my mouth.

I bit down hard and he fell off of me. I stood up, but every time I moved toward my clothes, he blocked me. He smiled. Fool. I waited until he turned slightly to pick up my panties. I grabbed one of the beer bottles. Green. St. Pauli Girl.

I swung it at his temple. Where my brothers said the skin was thin. Don't hit no fool on top of his head. Too hard. Yeah. Specially if he got a fro.

He went down like a shot pig. His legs melted.

The wetness on my thighs was already cold. How long would he stay out? No blood on his head. I pulled my shirt on, my sweater. On the dirty dorm carpet his hand was limp and turned upward.

Pink fingers. Curled like june-beetle grubs in my mother's garden under the dead leaves.

His roommate's poster of Bob Marley stared at me. The joint still smoldered. A rush of heat like I'd swallowed vodka, my chest opened up and I wanted to kill him. I felt my father's rage inside me. Enrique Antoine. Holding the piece of wood. Hitting Mr. McQuine in his already-bloody temple. Finishing him.

I crouched down and felt the moisture trickle from inside me. What if he was faking and I reached for the panties and he grabbed my wrist like a horror movie?

I held the bottle with my right hand and pulled the silky cloth from under his knuckles. The panties I'd bought in the city, the first sexy thing I'd ever owned.

His mouth was open. Pink. Red. Kick him where it counts, my brothers always told me. I didn't want to kick that damp shriveled thing. It only did what his brain told it to do. I wanted to kick his brain.

The bottle opener was on his cheap plywood dresser. A dormitory. I'd wanted to be here in the East so badly, in this room, in this sweater like the girls wore in *Seventeen,* with those icy leaves outside.

I touched my finger to the sharp end of the bottle opener. Open. his cheek and see the yellow fat and silvery membrane—like a chicken. He'd never killed a chicken. I squatted beside him and ground my feet into the dark wet spot near his leg.

Good. All your babies are dying here in the nasty carpet beside you.

The tip of the opener on his forehead—a tiny dent that filled with blood—under here was the brain that told him who I was. What he thought he could do to me.

I was an Antoine. Fantine Xavierene Antoine.

I stood and spit on him from high above. My saliva landed on his chest. But I froze—my father had killed a man. If he knew, he would drive his truck two thousand miles and kill this boy. I began to shake, across my back, and I turned away.

I went down the stairs. His car was a Porsche, brand-new and black. He told us in workshop how his father bought it for him when he got into this place. The bottle opener left long jagged pile-ups of paint like crinkly ribbons.

A fleur-de-lis. I made a spiky flower and then threw the bottle opener in the Dumpster.

The bus station was freezing. It took me five days of riding to get home. When I got here, I walked from the downtown Rio Seco station to Sarrat. It was five in the morning, and my father was just opening the gate.

Coyotes laughed in the distance now. My father's truck was coming up the road along the chain-link fence. The coyotes laughed again, their own eerie language I had been hearing all my life.

My father drove a 1985 Chevy truck now. The front grille was a squarer grin of metal than the old Apache's—when I was very small, and the Apache came up the hill toward the house, I'd always make believe a huge fish was swimming toward me in the blurry dusk. Open that mouth wide and swallow us, like Jonah and the Whale.

I pictured the Porsche hood one more time. The flower. Then I waved and stood up, so my father and Gustave could be sure it was me.

My father's left arm rode on the open window, his hand a dark starfish splayed against the white truck door, wary and stiff. Then he lifted it to wave back.

"Look like one them boys," my father said when the truck stopped near the shed. "Thought you was Victor or that other one. One just come back."

"Fonso," Gustave said, getting out of the truck slowly. "That one."

"The tank top," I said.

"Oui," my father said. "Don't look like you, no."

He reached into the cab and brought out two blue coffee mugs.

My father kissed me on the cheek and sat down at the table. My uncle Gustave did the same. I poured the coffee. The wind blew cooler now, and the cottonwood leaves turned themselves over the way they did. My father held out his mug and I took a sip—beyond black, sweet with sugar, a slide of midnight down my throat.

Gustave studied me, waiting.

They looked like brothers now because they were old men. When the Mississippi rose up in 1927 and took away their mothers, Gustave had saved my father's life even though he was seven and my father four, and now that they were so old, their faces had the same severe formality, the same deep grooves like parentheses around their mouths.

There were no childhood pictures of them, though I knew my father had been lighter and a bit shorter, and his forehead more square. But now they had faced the same sun and wind for more than seventy years, and eaten the same food, and made the same movements all day.

I took a deep breath. Their eyes were green and blue, turquoise long buried in rock, and narrowed from all those decades of squinting into the sun and watching.

I told them everything. I started with Victor, that he had come to see me in LA, that he had won concert tickets and found the picture of his mother.

Then I told them about Grady, and Sere Dakar, about the finger and La Paloma. I didn't tell them about "Poinciana," or Gecko Turner. My father got up and brought his bandanna from the truck cab, wiped his forehead. Gustave didn't move.

I told them about Dimples and the Golden Gopher, and how Victor went back for the picture and someone had shot someone else.

"Them boys," Gustave said. His chest rose and fell under the khaki workshirt. Boys. To him, they were not yet men at all.

I told them about Marcus, and the money, and that someone was bleeding.

"They come home, we take care of bleedin," my father said, turning away from me to look at the river. "But what we gon do with that one boy?"

"Jazen?" I said.

"He ain't Sarrat," my father said.

"He grew up in New Orleans and on the Westside," I said.

"Who his grandmère?" Gustave murmured.

I said, "His mother is Juanita, but she went back to New Orleans. He kept asking Alfonso about an uncle. Someone Alfonso stayed with before when he got in trouble."

My father shrugged slowly, and said, "They ain't got nowhere else but here if they want money. Find out who shot who."

Then he looked back at me. "Victor keep callin you, but he don't talk? Like he fear of the other?"

"He calls, which they wouldn't hear, and then he just lets me listen, and he says things that only I would know about. Like he wants me to know where they are."

"What he think you gon do?" My father didn't smile. He wasn't joking.

"I don't know."

He looked back out to the river, and then he got up, and so did Gustave and I. We walked over to the truck. My father picked up his old rifle from the front seat.

"You get the gopher?" I asked.

Gustave nodded. He said, "That one gopher done wreck the pump. A whole acre dry up in three day. He too smart for the trap. A old man. We sit there a long time till he poke his head up."

My father opened the metal toolbox welded inside the truck bed and laid the gun inside. The metal gopher traps were like medieval torture instruments, with their white flags which we always joked about when we were kids. I propped my boot on the old chrome bumper and swung myself up into the back.

The truck bed was still warm. I stretched out my legs as the shovels and hoes and pickax rattled beside me. Fresh dirt on the shovel. The gopher buried in his own hole.

When I'd told my father and Gustave about Victor, about all of it, each image was like a puff of smoke from a pipe, lingering around us. I felt like now that the words were out in the air, the boys would come home, and the men would make things right.

Water was running on one last grove to the west, pouring from the towers and sliding down the furrows, shiny and black as liquid obsidian. My rivers.

When I was small, and cried that my father took Lafayette and Reynaldo to the river to hunt, to catch crawfish in the muddy tributaries, my brothers brought me to the grove closest to the house and said, "Look here, Fantine, you got your own river now."

They had dammed up one of the furrows with rocks and pebbles and a bit of cement, made a stream and poured small stones and even some aquarium gravel to line the bottom, and they must have dumped crayfish and minnows they'd caught at the river into the stream. It lasted only a little while before the water evaporated, but I sat beside it for those few days and nobody could get me to move. I must have been about six. I lay on a blanket, read, and watched the fish dart along the bottom. I heard my brothers laughing in the trees, but I knew that was how much they loved me.

When we pulled up at the barn, my brothers were gone. I got out of the truck bed and said, "I'll see you up at the house."

The big pot outside had been put away, and the porch was quiet. When I got inside, only Cerise and Clarette were in the kitchen.

"Your maman sleep," Cerise said. "All the boys are in the back room, and Danae's sleepin in your room. Lafayette and Reynaldo musta gone for more beer." She was holding a glass of Coke, and I could smell the rum in it.

The gumbo steamed up into my face. Pepper and heat. People who didn't live in places like this couldn't understand how good it felt to eat spicy hot food. We ate in silence, and the heat blossomed inside my chest, radiated along my ribs.

I couldn't stop my brain from writing. If a stranger came here—remarkably unassimilated, folk culture, an enclave—it would be fascinating to New York or LA for the Sunday paper. Recipes could be included—this gumbo which would never taste the same as my mother's, the oddity of how she made her coffee, which would take way too much time to compete with Starbucks.

Who would come here?

The shrimp were pink and tender. The andouille were firm coins of pork and blaze. Clarette and Cerise and Miss Felonise and my mother would have peeled all the shrimp and sliced all the peppers.

Cerise snapped her fingers in front of my face. "So now you gon sleep?"

"Just thinking I haven't had anything this good to eat in a long time," I said, knowing that wasn't enough.

"Your maman make gumbo every weekend," Cerise said.

Clarette said, "Give Fantine a break. She got a hella commute." She grinned at me and raised her eyebrows, those perfectly waxed commas. Her braids were fresh, and she wore earrings that dangled nearly to her collarbone. Clarette worked all day at the youth prison, with no jewelry, loose hair, or loveliness allowed. "She got a breakfast meeting in the morning, right?"

"I'ma skip it," I said.

Clarette said, "I'll put Danae on the couch, then."

"That's okay," I said. "I'll sleep on the couch. That way I can watch for Victor."

Clarette said, "Why he gotta hang out with them? Alfonso so stupid he woulda got killed inside if I didn't watch his sorry ass." There was only inside and outside. Alfonso wasn't going back. He'd done three years. "Got two kinds of fool in him," she added. "My brother and Bettina."

"Them two need to get fixed." Cerise rolled her eyes. "Bettina talkin bout she missin babies. Shit."

"She got two grown and two half-grown," Clarette said. "Alphonse sittin up there on the Westside with nothin but a big-screen. Sleep on the floor half the time. Pitiful."

Then we all stopped. I knew we were thinking of Glorette's empty apartments.

I went to the sink for a glass of water. There were two windows over my mother's sink, and she could see out to Miss Felonise's house, and the road. On the wall beside, I had hung two framed postcards for her. Scenes of snow, frigid in gray and brown and white. A detail of Sisley's *La Neige à Marly-le-Roi,* with the bare trees and snowy field. A detail from Monet's *The Magpie,* just the dark wooden gate, the black-headed bird, and the vivid shadows on the snow.

"Make me feel cool, even the summer," she told me, just one time. She had never touched snow. We could see it, from here, on the San Bernardino Mountains, but she had never wanted to drive there.

I started drying the stack of blue willow dishes—a set of ten, Staffordshire china that I'd bought for my mother years ago in England. The pattern was willow trees and peacocks and a curving bridge over a stream.

"Uh-uh," Clarette said, when I opened the cupboard above the stove. "She keepin em over there now."

"Where?" I said, holding the heavy stack, and Cerise put down her glass with an impatient precise click that said, You ain't never here. You don't wash dishes now. You less of a daughter than we are.

She held open the pantry door. On the wide middle shelf where the flour and sugar and rice used to be were bowls and small plates. I stacked the dinner plates there.

"Danae can reach them to set the table when she's here," Cerise said.

"Your maman shoulder got hurt last month, when she was cuttin that bougainvillea. She want the dishes lower now so she ain't gotta reach up high," Clarette said.

Cerise said, "I heard Bettina let some woman stay with her. And she crept on over to Reynaldo in the middle of the night. Trying to get with him." She looked at me and said, "So you still ain't found nobody good up there in LA, huh?" When I gave her our old look, the one that said, Are you kidding me? she said, "I don't know how you gon go without a man like that."

Clarette said, "Hell, you get so tired you just don't care."

"Not me," Cerise huffed.

"Come work a shift with me at Chino and you won't want to see nothing with that third leg the rest of the week."

"Like I don't work eight hours?"

"I ain't said that, Cerise."

"Well, Reynaldo ain't gon do without. Bettina's messed up." Cerise picked at her fingernails. Red polish chipped off like flakes of chili pepper.

I said, "Remember Tony? He said he had ten years of amazing sex, which was way more than most people get, so he was okay going without now."

"Your gay friend?" Cerise said.

"He's fine," Clarette said.

"Maybe it's different for a man," Cerise said.

"It's different for him," I said. "Because of how he looks at the world."

"Like you?" she said, raising her eyebrows high.

Then a voice called through the front screen door, "Hey, y'all." Bettina came in and let the door slam softly, but she hesitated. "You put that gumbo away?"

"Oh, *hell* no," Cerise said, lifting her hands. "Hell damn no."

"Cerise," Bettina said, in the doorway. "That ain't me, okay? That's they bidness."

"Who the hell is she? She down there right now?"

Bettina shook her head so hard the thin loose hairs around her forehead swayed like antennae. Cerise got up and stood beside the open window, lighting a cigarette, keeping her face to the screened dark.

It was still my mother's house. "Come on," I said, and pulled out the chair beside me. I got Bettina a bowl of rice, ladled the gumbo over it, and poured a Coke for her.

We hadn't all of us sat at this table for years. When we were small, we sat here every day after school, shelling pecans in fall, making pralines to sell, helping snap beans in summer, and doing our homework.

Glorette always sat in the chair at the end. The one empty now.

Bettina's back was bent over her plate. Her fat had collected below her shoulders, pushing out like a shelf under her bra. Her upper arms were round and pink-red as hams. Hams I'd seen hanging in a farmhouse in Italy. But all her weight was above the waist—her legs and hips were still thin, and in her knit shorts and tank top she looked like a prizefighter.

"She ain't been back." Bettina glanced at Cerise's elbow. Her hair was held with a white scrunchie like a tiny Elizabethan collar, the fringe sticking out with static from the wind. "Hey, I got to get my party on now and then, and this brotha from San Bernardino been comin by. He cut a hole in the fence down by the box houses. His sister came one time, and she got drunk."

I thought Cerise would put out the cigarette on her fat shoulder. "Dahani sell CDs, burn you anything for twelve dollars. Custom order. That's how I met him—at the swap meet. You could get oldies, whatever. Remember Glorette's favorite song?"

We all froze. Bettina trying to pull that? I said, "You sure you know it?"

"'Golden Time of Day,'" she said, sucking her teeth at me. "Maze. Yeah, and Chaka. 'Move Me No Mountain.' I ain't never really figured out them jazz songs she liked—the ones with no words—but I been had Dahani make me one with them old jams. Cause I was thinkin about her. For tomorrow. I was gon give it to Victor, you know."

"Victor?" Clarette said.

Then suddenly Bettina said, "Victor need to stop ridin with Fonso and Jazen. He been to college. He need to get married and have some babies."

"What?"

"Fonso already got two. Twins run in our family, no shit. But Victor—" Then she looked at me. "Just like you. College, yeah, all that. But that ain't it. He the only Picard. Gustave people come up hard in Louisiana. My maman use to tell me."

Her maman was Claudine. The first one Mr. McQuine took away. The one who'd had a son.

Bettina said, "Victor the only Picard left—he need to keep that blood in the world."

Before I could say anything else, Clarette said, "You know I can't listen to this. I saved Alfonso's narrow ass three times inside, Bettina. He's so stupid, with that grin like he can do whatever he wants."

Bettina's voice rose higher. "I cain't do nothin with him. You know he hardheaded."

"No," Cerise said now, moving fast, putting out her cigarette under faucet water. "I'm so tired of hearin that. That's it? He hardheaded and we're done?"

"Cerise," Bettina said, folding her own arms so her shoulders rose massive and glistening with sweat. "Lafie and Rey Jr. still little boys. You don't know yet."

Bettina's eyes were green as wine-bottle glass. When we were younger, she was all rosy and emerald and laughing, never working hard in the groves because she saw her mother get money from men and didn't see any need to be different.

Clarette said, "Better hope they're not sellin rock out that damn dryer tonight."

"Victor and Fonso ain't doin none a that," Bettina said.

"They're in the car," Clarette said resolutely, her whole face changed to prison guard. "Whatever he does, if Jazen sells drugs or robs somebody, and they're in the car, that's conspiracy. And Victor? Cops can call him a known associate now." She went into my bedroom, to check on her daughter, and Cerise followed her down the hallway.

I put Bettina's plate in the sink. One grain of rice lay snug against the rim, like the egg case of an ant. I turned my back to the counter and felt the edge dig into my spine.

And when Bettina looked at me—her brows plucked thin as a trail of ants along her forehead—she said, "Well, I ain't even known Victor was in the car till just before I walked up here." She chewed the last of the crushed ice from her glass. "I went outside and he was dead sleep in the backseat."

"What?" I caught my breath, smoke and rum and roux all heavy in my chest.

"Alfonso down there, actin all shady. I don't know what he up to, but he axed me for money, and he taken some clothes," Bettina said, getting up. "I was watchin TV, and I ain't seen Victor."

"They came in the back way?" I said. I bent to put my boots back on. "Alfonso and Jazen have a gun." Dead. Sleep. Which one? Even Jazen couldn't be that heartless.

"Fonso said Victor drank some Bacardi. He said Victor's a lightweight. Fell out soon as he drank it."

I told Bettina we'd take my car. Victor might not be able to walk. And I didn't want to tell my father—Jazen had a gun, and my father's rifle was in the truck.

After we went through the gate and turned on La Reina, I went down the dirt road between our grove and Mr. Sotelo's. His grove wasn't fenced, and my father always mentioned how much fruit was stolen by people who drove down this road and went right in, unless Sotelo and his son patrolled every night.

The chain-link was cut along one pole and peeled back neatly, wired to the next pole.

Bettina started whining. Pitiful. "Uncle Enrique gon be mad. I told Dahani he needed to fix that up and just come on the other way by the barn, but he don't like everybody in his bidness." She was sweating, and now her straightened hair stuck out from her forehead in spikes like a black Statue of Liberty.

The branches hadn't been trimmed, but broken off by his car, so he must have a vehicle he didn't care about. We bounced over the ruts from last year's rain, and turned in to the dirt clearing.

Three small stone houses, built by three Italian men from the Piedmont who had lived here back in 1910, every day nailing pine slats together to make the famous orange crates with labels that people collected now for museums and living rooms. The houses stayed empty all of my childhood. Marcus and I had lain in the middle one, on a blanket scented with eucalyptus oil.

No cars parked here. The road that led up to the barn was smooth and packed from my brothers' two trucks. In the third house, one of the front windows was broken, patched with lines of duct tape that gleamed in the moonlight like a blinding strike of lightning.

They were gone. I shouted at Bettina, "Why didn't you come up and get us right away?"

"I didn't even know you was here, Fantine, okay?" We got out of the car, and she looked daggers at me. "I had company. And they was foolin around with some clippers." Her eyes went to the dark spot on the side of her house. A cement apron, where the box makers had worked, faced south. Food wrappers like dirty snowballs, and piles of black shivering gently in the night breeze.

I went closer. Hair. Clouds of darkness moving toward the edge of the cement. That must have been Jazen's cornrows—unraveled and most of the excess hair cut off.

And on the ground, near the marks of the tires, Victor's dreadlocks— still twisted and curled, like burned twigs scattered in the dust.

"Fonso cut hair in prison, didn't he? They're fucking up Victor's life!"

She shouted back, "How you know he ain't wanted to ride with them? How you know he ain't havin a ball?"

I turned toward the broken window, the Miller High Life cans thrown in a pile along the porch with ants streaming into the keyholes, the trash bags ripped open by raccoons or coyotes and bones strewn in the dirt.

My father hated ants, battled them constantly. Them fromille, he always said. "He's gonna kick you out."

Bettina stood on her porch, her pink shoulders heaving. "You ain't got no bidness here—you don't even live here," she hissed.

"Shut up, Bettina," I whispered. "You're every fucked-up cliché in the world."

"So are you!" she said loudly. "Them little hoops cause you cain't be wearin no doorknockers. Hair all plastered down in a bun like a fake librarian. Wear the same damn clothes every time I see you."

"Fine. I'm a cliché, too," I shouted. "Only one not a cliché was Glorette! She didn't care what anyone thought. And you're disrespecting her by letting Fonso take Victor down." I was shaking, sweating again. "Victor's not a cliché—the only one left."

Her arms were folded on top of her chest, like an old lady. Her face was dripping and impassive under the loose hair that had begun to wilt.

"Where'd they go?"

"Fonso say he ain't goin back to jail again. I heard him say my brother's name. Maybe they gone to my brother's house."

"Your brother?"

"Albert."

That was Mr. McQuine's son. That must be who Alfonso had stayed with five years ago, when he went to Louisiana.

"Where does he live?"

Her shoulders rose a few inches. "Sometime he stay in Vegas. Sometime he stay in Louisiana. I ain't seen him in years." She went inside and closed the battered door.

I turned my car around, slow and careful, but the wheels raised dust that I knew would settle on Victor's lost hair.

"Matin." My father washed his hands at the kitchen sink, staring into the dark. Morning. He wanted to think until morning. One a.m.— nighttime was Jazen's.

"Did you tell Maman?"

He shook his head. He said, "Matin," and went down the hallway.

Cerise and Clarette had gone home. The small hexagonal tiles on the bathroom floor were always the coolest part of the house. I locked the door and lay there on the tile, remembering.

The fever had started on the last day of the bus ride, and when I'd walked home, carrying that suitcase, it felt as if icy October had gone down my throat, as if the crystals floating in the air had coated my skin and then my body tried to melt them.

I sat there and looked at the river, in the warm California sunshine, remembering the paint on the car hood, until my father found me. In the cab of the Apache, my whole body shook and trembled with chills, and my teeth hurt from chattering.

"That cold get inside her," he told my mother when he led me inside, and I remembered thinking, How did he imagine the exact way I felt?

In my old bed, the four windows of the breakfast nook letting in fractured light from the jasmine vines and the sycamore tree, the chills came harder—like sparkles traveling from my bones and belly to dance across my veins.

I lay in the dark now, remembering exactly how much it hurt. Waves of pain between my hip bones.

My mother brought two blankets. She brought hot rum mixed with water and molasses, and made me take two burning sips. Then she sat silently beside me. I was going to be eighteen years old soon. I was not a child.

After a while, my chest felt full of blood, swollen, and I got out of bed to throw up. My mother heard me run to the bathroom. She stood outside this door.

Fantine?

But I had already been FX for two months.

Fantine, bebe, you need help?

Blood seeped down my legs. When I got up, the white tile was pooled with blood. I sat on the toilet and looked down. A dark shining thing fell from me. Not big. Three lobes of an orange. But heavy, like jelly, like nothing I'd ever seen, and before I could look away, it trembled briefly at the surface and then sank.

I smelled the faint remnants of Marcus's cologne on my temples when I dried my face. From his hug.

It had not been a baby. But it would have been Marcus's baby. The Scion had unhinged it from my body. Untethered it. Unmoored it.

I went quietly into my old bedroom.

It had been the breakfast nook, off the kitchen, until I turned ten. Danae slept in the daybed I'd gotten in high school. She was eight. Flung out on the bed in the heat, the black metal fan on the little table beside her lifting the baby hairs at her forehead. I sat on the wooden chair at my old desk. The glass of cool water was on the little table, and crushed peppermints filled the green bowl as they had when I was small.

My mother crushed them so we wouldn't choke on the whole candy when we lay there with the coldness in our mouths, the fan blowing in night air from the screen. And on my desk, the green pottery vase filled with sunflowers.

"Why do you have flowers in every room every day?" I asked when I was little, and she was putting roses in the living room.

"That make me happy," my mother said. Every surface gleaming and shined every day, the floor swept, the white enamel sink polished with Ajax before she slept, or I did. The job my mother had when she wasn't in the fields was holiday cleaning for Mr. McQuine's aunt, in an old plantation house. When she told me about it, while she taught me to clean, I knew she felt superior to that old woman whose shelves were furred with dust and whose kitchen was full of mice.

Danae's outstretched hand opened and closed twice in her sleep.

There had never been a closet in my room, since it wasn't really a bedroom. Four long windows on two walls, then the daybed, and a narrow armoire. I opened it quietly. Heat rushed out, musty and stale. I laid my bag on the bottom shelf.

I had closed myself in here once, after the story of Mr. McQuine. I wanted to see what Tante Anjolie felt, when she was my age. It was black in front of my face, total black at first, and then a hairline of gold at the bottom of the doors. But had she seen that light?

On the top shelf of the armoire, where my old things were piled, was a cigar box. Inside were my report cards and SAT scores, my college acceptance, my first college papers. Some research I'd done on Moinette Antoine, and Marie-Therese.

I took down the box. The beautiful woman wearing a silk gown, her hair in a heavy bun. The Octoroon.

Danae murmured and opened her eyes. "Mama?"

Her eyes moved over my face when I neared the bed. "It's Auntie Fantine," I whispered. "Go back to sleep."

"Who?" she said. "Where's my mama?"

"She went home. She'll be back in the morning."

"Okay," she said softly, and then closed her eyes.

In the far distance, the coyotes still spoke to each other. It wasn't laughing, like people said, or howling at the moon. It was language, with pauses and answers.

I lay carefully beside Danae. Her braids smelled of coconut hair-dress, too. Her mother's favorite. Sweet and light. Her arm was hot against mine. She was the only girl. Like me.

What had I lost? A girl or boy? I hadn't thought about it for so many years. Marcus. I didn't know. I didn't know.

HOME

WHEN THE PHONE MOOED, we both leapt awake, Danae's elbows cracking against the wall, my arm flailing into empty space beside the bed.

"It's okay, it's okay," I said, rubbing her shoulder. "It's not morning."

It was dark. I knelt and got the phone from my jeans. 5:56.

"Marraine." His voice, slurred and soft. Not the same at all.

"I'm right here. In Sarrat. Where are you?"

"I don't know."

I closed the bedroom door softly and went out to the living room. I sat on the couch and looked at the yard, blue and stark in the moonlight. "What do you see?" I said. "Are you on the Westside?"

"I'm in a room. With a baby." He sounded high or delirious.

What was I supposed to say now? Just talk, calmly. "Are you bleeding? Did you get shot?"

"My arm. It's wrapped up in a T-shirt." His voice quavered.

"Does it hurt?"

"Yeah."

Then he was silent. I heard nothing this time. "Where do you think you are? Not at Bettina's? You were there earlier."

"It's a baby in here, on the bed next to me. A little baby. She's sleepin on her stomach. Her butt's up in the air like a white mushroom."

"What do you hear?"

"TV. Lil Wayne." He paused and took a breath so labored it sounded like sand in his throat. "I recognize this light. From the window. Some apartment I been in before." A long pause. "Somebody snorin in the other room. And some girl talkin."

It could be Angie's apartment. "Victor?"

"Yeah."

"Your phone hasn't died."

"I just woke up and plugged my charger in here." He breathed hard.

"I always have my charger and laptop and clothes in a bag," I said. "Cause I'm always on the road."

"Marraine." He paused, as if gathering strength. "I always have *everything* with me."

It went like a splinter to my chest, the weariness in his voice. Of course he always had his things with him—he'd been on the road longer than I had. He'd never had a real place to live all his life. His backpack was his home. I remembered his futon, his CD player clutched to his chest so none of his mother's friends could steal it while he slept. His Converses tied tight, white toes poking from the sheet like ghostly muffins.

"They poured some Bacardi on my arm. It's all torn up. They gave me some to drink. I passed out. It hurts like hell." He breathed out.

"Who shot you?"

"That dude. The one we saw getting tickets."

"Who shot him?"

"Fonso," he whispered. "Fonso said he got him in the arm, too, so I keep thinkin he probably made it to some hospital in LA. But Jazen said we can't go to the ER. Said nobody die from getting shot in the arm."

They didn't know the other boy was dead. "Victor," I said. "Are you at the Villas?"

"I can't get up. I tried. Dizzy. I lost a lot of blood." A silence and a rustling. "My whole arm is on fire. I think he got me in the elbow. I don't wanna look. I had my hand up. Like it would fuckin stop the bullet. Like a stupid movie."

"Why did he shoot you, Victor? What were you doing?"

"Carryin my moms," he whispered. "We went back there, and I walked up there by the door. Then when I had the picture and I got back on the sidewalk, he was right there, in the alley. I was like, Damn, cause he just came up on me."

"With a gun?"

"No. He was on the phone. Then he just looked at me. I heard the car pull up behind me. He musta seen Zee and Fonso. He got all big and said, like, Where you from?"

"Why?"

"Cause that's what they say. Bangers. I knew what he was doin. I was like, Fuck this. I ain't doin this. I'm tired of this shit. So I was like, Darkside. I'm from the Darkside, man. One World."

I heard the baby stir and murmur. Little sounds. I tried to imagine the small form beside him.

"Then Zee had to lean out the window and say Rio Seco. Westside. Loc Mafia."

A single coyote called in the river bottom, far away.

"I started runnin, like, away from the dude and the car. All that where you from—shit. But he pulled out his piece. I threw up my hand, but he got me. And then I heard somebody shoot from the car. Fonso started yellin at me to get in. The dude went down and Zee starts sayin, You know where we from now, fool."

"And you dripped blood on the sidewalk from your arm," I said softly.

"How do you know?" he whispered.

"It was on the news." Wait—I didn't want him to know the boy named Mando had died. Then they'd run for sure, and I'd never find him. "Just that someone got shot, and no further details," I said quickly.

The baby let out the first yelp that meant sleep was over. I said, "Try to look out the window. Just tell me where you are and I'll be there in a few minutes."

The crying started in earnest, and Victor said miserably, "I can't pick her up. I can't even move my arm. It's dead. Somebody's comin in."

The abrupt silence—I hadn't thought about it in a long time, how old black phones like the one my mother still had clicked when someone hung up. A sound. This was just the voice taken away.

I had never opened my parents' bedroom door in my entire life. I knocked and said, "Papa?"

He came out into the hallway. "I think they're on the Westside. He just called me."

The smell of my mother's lotion came from the open door. She said something in French that I couldn't hear, and my father said to me, "Get dress."

The white branches of the huge sycamore outside shone pink from the dawn, and then the sun rose a few minutes later, already hot and gold as syrup spreading through the trees. Over a hundred again today. My head was on fire, too. My eyes felt filled with sap, and I tried to untangle all Victor had told me.

My father came out of the bathroom in work clothes. The dark blue Dickies. My mother did laundry every day—he wore dark green, then dark blue, and sometimes khaki. He said to me, "Quo fa?"

"Victor said his arm is wrapped up in a shirt. That's where he got shot." I kept my voice steady. "They were at Bettina's last night, and then they left. Fonso cut their hair. They must be looking for a place to hide."

The sycamore leaves were turning brown at the edges. They weren't as big this year as the ones Jazen had seen on my table. I said, "It's not like they're holding him against his will. Alfonso's his cousin. He wouldn't kidnap his cousin. He wouldn't hurt Victor. I don't know what it is."

"He ain't never have no trouble, him," my father said. "Them other two always have trouble. They know what they do. They run somewhere."

"They don't even know the boy is dead. At least, Victor doesn't know. But he was passed out last night." My father sighed, his chest rising and falling. The name tag on the shirt—not his name, only La Reina, the company brand, embroidered in thick white script. He always said that everyone in Sarrat knew his name, and if a stranger came, he didn't need to know.

"Get your bag," he said finally in a hoarse whisper. "Don't say rien. Not even your maman. Put it in your car. He might be on the Westside," he said. "Mais, he might be gone. On the freeway."

His eyes moved onto my face. Bright turquoise in the sun, and a series of scars on his left cheekbone like complicated Chinese symbols. Like the tattoos all the boys had on their arms, words they might not even know. My father's skin was marked with slanting cuts that had healed into feathery dark lines. From being beaten with cane stalks when he was small. Unc Gustave had told me once.

"He call you, oui?" he said. "Don't call Gustave, him, don't call nobody else. Call you over and over. Tell you where he is. He got raison."

In the kitchen, my mother turned on the coffee grinder. Under the noise, I said, "I'm the last person to know what to do."

He shook his head. "Gustave can't drive no more. Clarette can't go. She work at the prison. She got a gun. And your brothers—they can't go. People know them. Like they hunt, and them other two feel like a corner. Don't know what they do, them."

"What am I going to do?"

"I goin with you, me. But Victor want you to come. He call, like he leave a rag tie to a tree, in the cipriere."

The cypress swamp. Where my father had taken us when we were small.

My father said, "You talk to him. Tell him a story. How you do. When we find him, we see. See then."

He opened the front door and went onto the porch.

How I did. Tell a story. I put the phone in my pocket and went into the kitchen. My mother had laid bacon out in strips along the wide cast-iron grill. She had a dish towel tied around her wrist, for the popping grease. She glanced at me, but said nothing.

My work had been to tell all those stories about strangers I had never seen again, though I had imagined many times going back to those little towns or ornate apartments or riverside gardens to stay for a month. To really live there. With strangers.

Gustave paused at the screen and said something in French to my father. Then he came inside, and to my mother he said softly, "Dor bien?"

It was what they said every morning. Did you sleep well? Did you live?

My father's work had been to keep his own blood and land intact from strangers. The tribe. The trees. The circle of light at the table. I waited for my mother to pour the coffee.

I showered quickly and repacked my bag. I put on the same jeans, and one of the clean white tank tops under my Oaxacan shirt. I took my own bag from the armoire, and Victor's bag, and for some reason, I grabbed the cigar box with the beautiful woman, too.

Danae was the only one awake, already on the porch in her pajamas, making a bracelet from thread she had nailed to a board. "Who's that?"

she said, looking at the Octoroon. I picked a piece of leaf from her braids, from the pale scalp showing between the rows.

"She's a dancer," I said. "A Spanish dancer."

She grinned. "Cigars are nasty. Daddy smokes them sometimes."

"I heard." I pulled off one more piece of leaf—from their games last night—and said, "Tell your maman I said you look prettier than she does these days. And tell her I'll see her as soon as I come back."

"That's what you always say to tell her," Danae said, pursing her lips just like Clarette. "Then she always says you're a bagavond."

"Cause I always come back." I carried my bags up the road to the Corsica, and my father stepped from the trees alongside to open the door.

PART TWO

They may kill me, baby
Bury me just like they do
My body might lie but my spirit gon rise and
Come home to you

—JIMMY REED

PART TWO

LAPIS

I DROVE PAST THE RIVIERA, shut up tight in the early morning heat, and around the corner to the Villas. We went up the stairs to #24. I knocked softly, and my father stood stiffly beside me, his arms at his sides.

Who did he think would answer the door? Did he have a gun? My heart raced differently this time. Angie peered through the blinds, the TV flashing behind her. She opened the door—no baby. But a different girl sat on the couch.

Angie came out onto the balcony. "They came back last night. But they were trippin." She shook her head. "I told em they had to go. My aunt comin to get her braids done." She looked into my eyes. "They kept callin people. They had a big fight—JZ said, You the only one ain't got nobody, nigga. To him. He said, Talk all that yang and only one you call is your godmother and she don't give a shit."

I laced my hands on top of my head, my whole face hot. "I'm here."

She took a big breath, her chest rising under her tight camisole. "Then the light one said, I got pirates. I got buried treasure waitin for me in Louisiana. My moms told me the first Picard was one a Lafitte's pirates. He slept with his slave and that's us. We got gold. They all laughed and then the fine one—Fonso—he said, Maybe my uncle a pirate, too."

My father was a slight man, but suddenly he felt huge beside me in the doorway, the metal strip humming in time with the coolers all along the balcony. I didn't understand what Victor had said. "Where'd they go?" I said.

She shrugged. "JZ always got somewhere. I'm the only one ever tell him no."

———

I kept seeing the shorn twists of hair like tiny brown Cheetos, lying in the dirt near the box house. I couldn't imagine Victor's skull, naked and glistening.

My father was stubbing out his Swisher Sweet on the sidewalk. The pulsing hole in Victor's skull, the first time I saw him. The place where the bones hadn't fused yet, where the brain was still growing and swelling with the knowledge that someone would pick you up, or not, and love you, or not, and look into your purple eyes, or not.

We sat in the car, pepper tree branches limp as seaweed above us. "You know where Albert lives?" The son of Mr. McQuine, the pale legacy of all those terrible stories, the only tangible evidence that those stories had happened, the child no one mentioned, the boy who would be—he would be nearly fifty now. I'd never seen him, even when we went to Sarrat so long ago.

My father shook his head. "Sais pas. I heard one time he was in Vegas. Vegas three-hour drive."

Sundown Liquor was closed, the posters fading in the August sun, edges of the girls blurring. At the 7-Eleven, a few small-eyed people stalked grumpily outside with their coffee. Sisia would be sleeping until past noon, and so would all the little dealers.

At the Arco nearest the freeway to Vegas, the Sikh owner was in the parking lot, sweeping trash into a dustpan. A smear of dust was a pale gold cloud on his black turban. I drove slowly around the corner to the back area, in case the Navigator was parked there while someone slept. "They need gas, too. But this is crazy. If we find them, what do we do?"

My father said, "See when we see him."

The owner was in the doorway now. I filled up the tank and then I went over to where he stood, his broom propped beside his leg like a rifle. He studied my face—he was darker than me. "Good morning," he said.

"Good morning. Did you happen to see three young guys in a Lincoln Navigator?" I said. "Really early. Filling up, maybe getting some food?"

He glanced past me, trying to see who was in the passenger seat of the Corsica. "Mexican boys?" he said softly, frowning at my face.

"Black," I said. "African American. Three guys—one with short hair, and two bald."

He pulled his chin back sharply as if he were a turtle retreating into a shell. "No," he said. "I did not see them."

"Thanks," I said. There went the eyes. He'd remember if he had.

I drove across the street to the Starbucks. "They don't even know the other boy is dead," I told my father. "I'm going to get a paper."

I picked up an *LA Times*. The photo was on the second page, like hundreds of photos from years of foolish killings. A photographer could publish a book about the irony of their vivid beauty and composition. The shrine, already huddled on the spot where Mando had died. Four candles, glowing dimly—Virgins and angels. Two bouquets, and a framed picture. His face solemn, his black hair glossy and perfect.

Victor had sounded delirious last night. Did he think he was going to die? Expect it, like Alfonso and Jazen already expected it, as if the shrines and sobbing girls were the only possible ending for them? The only end they could imagine, the only one they'd want. Not struggling to pay a mortgage or keep a woman happy or raise kids or even decide what movie to see, like all these people in line at Starbucks.

Cell phones rang like an odd burbling choir. Meetings and appointments.

Shit. I called Rick and spoke low into the phone.

"Rick. It's me. I have a family emergency here, and I can't get back to LA in time for breakfast. I want to hear about the bookstore. And the Dalmatian coast. Some great little villages—I'll do some research as soon as I get a minute."

I called Tony. "Hey, it's me. I have to talk to you, and I can't come to breakfast. Please, Tony, talk to Rick about two more pieces. I need the money. My godson—he's sick, and I'm stuck here in Rio Seco." I looked at the fine weave of the suitcoat in front of me. "Tony. I miss you."

I was every other person crawling forward in line, self-absorbed, as if a beekeeper's net of words covered my face and head. I ordered two plain coffees, added two packets of brown sugar, and brought them outside.

My father was sitting in the car. He sipped the coffee impassively. "They burn the beans and still weak," he said finally. Then we stared into the thick hedge of oleander, and my father said, "Time go by. We gon lose him, oui."

"We can't just take off for Vegas. They might still be here. I'm calling him."

Victor said hoarsely, "Hey. I was sleepin."

"Where are you?"

"Some Arco."

"Where?"

"I don't know. Zee and Fonso in there payin for the gas and gettin food. They left me alone. Cause they ain't worried. I can't fuckin drive. Everybody knows that." And suddenly his voice was anguished. Everything he never had. The phone was hot against my cheek. "Same as it never was," he said. "I never even learned to drive."

"Look for a sign."

"JZ said we all the same now. All three of us."

"If you're headed to Vegas, we're right behind you," I said.

"You wouldn't know me if you saw me anyway." His voice wavered and then he sounded so tired again. "My hair's gone. I got the look. Marraine, I'm gonna die. Either the cops stop us, and Fonso ain't goin back, or some fools see us and JZ's got his gun out, too." Before I could say anything, he went on. "Got so many words for gun. Heater. Burner. Jammie." He sounded like himself for a moment. "Get my gat. That probably comes from Gatling gun. In the movies they talk about the Colt. Six-shooter."

"What do you see?"

"Nothing. The desert. I'm in the back of the car with all these sounds, and all I can do is wait for it. My arm hurts so damn bad. I just want the next bullet to go in my heart. Quick."

We were nearly to Barstow, the Corsica chugging up the Cajon Pass and then along the flatter high desert. There wasn't much traffic heading to Vegas because it was so early.

It had been a little more than an hour. The sun was already intense out here, glaring into the passenger window, and my father rolled up his long sleeves. When the phone rang, we both startled, and he handed it to me.

Victor said, "Hey. You going to Paris today, right?"

"What?" I said. He sounded almost like himself.

"I told you turn off the phone!" Jazen said. "They got GPS and shit. Cops trackin us right now."

Victor made a decision while it was quiet. He put a superior sneer back inside his voice, one I heard him use now and then. "JZ, man, this ain't *Law & Order Cali*. Nobody gives a shit. We're both brown. He ain't from Mexico and I ain't from Africa."

Jazen said, "Shut up before I shoot your sorry ass myself."

Alfonso said, "I give a shit cause I ain't goin back. Stop talkin bout shootin."

Victor didn't waver. "Nothin, Marraine. I was talking bout a TV show. No. Hey, hold on. You at the airport?" Then he said, "She's leavin for Paris in an hour. I'ma talk to her about Led Zeppelin. What—y'all gon snatch up my phone?"

His gamble.

"Fuck that, nigga. But don't be talkin bout yesterday."

It worked. They weren't worried about me—I didn't act like family. My father kept his eyes on the dashboard, almost politely, as if he didn't want to stare at my face.

I imagined the cocoon of the backseat, the swirl of drums and synthesizer and voices all around him. His mouth close to the phone, my ear sweating. Like a lover.

The only thing you can love more than a man is a child. He's not a child. Not my child. Tell him a story. "Led Zeppelin," I said. "'Stairway to Heaven.'"

"Yeah. 'Stairway to Heaven'—that one song where the chick is in the hedgerows."

"Right. And I always think of the stairway as meaning death. The boy died, Victor. His name was Armando Muniz. Will that make it worse? If they know he died."

"The stairway," Victor said. His breath rushed the phone. "All the way to the celestial kingdom, right?"

"We're on the way to Vegas. I think that's where you're going. We'll get you out of here and take you to the hospital."

"You're—" He paused. "For real? You listenin to The Who? 'I don't need to be forgiven.'"

"There he go again," Alfonso said.

"'*Teenage* Wasteland.' He's under twenty-one, he still got a lotta fun."

"But you're not a teenager," I said, seeing what he was saying. "You're twenty-two."

"Big time."

"Prison."

"You got it."

"All because you went back to get that picture of your maman. She's right here in the backseat, you know. I picked up the photo from Marcus Thompson. He's worried, too. Everybody's worried."

"Nuh-uh. Not that song. Same old sound."

"Okay. But figure out where you are, and tell me. We're patient. They'll stop for food or to sleep sometime, and we'll come get you."

"You shoulda told me before," he said softly. "About 'Poinciana.' I never knew. That's fucked up. I woulda gone to the beach and played it. Tried to see it. Sittin in a Nova. Star explosion."

So I wasn't a good storyteller, if I made him angry and sad. My father—his hands on his knees, knuckles huge as walnuts. He had lived a heroic life. Unc Gustave, too. My mother. They had survived floods and cane fields and war and Mr. McQuine. Who the hell was I to tell stories? I had survived Kelly Cloder, the Scion, and college. I had escaped a place where people loved me.

I had nothing but an apartment and other people's stories.

The desert flew past, the engine shuddering. Papa was a rolling stone, Victor had said in my kitchen, only yesterday. He was a child of twenty-two. It was going to be so much work to finish growing him. "Listen. I found your poem. About the helicopter. It's good. I mean, I don't really wish you'd go to college and become a poet, cause they don't make much money and apparently they drink a lot. They do get women. I read your notes about *Water Music*. Look, Victor, you're coming to LA with me. I have room in my apartment, and my friend Tony has a big house right up the street which is empty half the time. You're coming after Dave Matthews." That was Saturday? "So—just be careful and call me."

Be careful? Like I was his mother, sending him out to the yard to play on the swing set?

"Yeah," he said faintly. "Later."

But he left the phone on. It was daytime—no one would see the little screen glowing bluish-bright. It must be lying next to Victor, and since Alfonso said nothing, he must have fallen asleep, while Jazen drove.

I held the phone tightly.

"Damn. Look at them Mescans in the field. Like 120 already out there," Jazen said.

Where would it be so hot? People working in fields?

"They could be Guatemalans or Salvadorans, man." Victor's voice was weary now. The only word for the slow, old-man timbre. "Why you always profiling?"

"Mescans hate us."

"No, they don't."

"Man, that Mescan hated us."

"That guy? He didn't hate us. He was just followin the script."

"Then why he ax the question? Why he step to us like that?"

"Yeah. Why he brandish his weapon, right?" Victor whispered. "Where you from? Why you always goin blackwards, Zee? One Love. One Heart."

"Only white boys listen to Bob Marley, nigga."

"Brothas listen to him all the time, man. One Love. One World."

Jazen didn't respond.

"Nothin but desert out here. Where the hell we goin?"

"Just passed Blythe."

"Blythe?" He raised his voice. For me?

"Man, it's gonna be a long-ass ride if y'all keep on," Alfonso said drowsily. "What happened to the sounds?"

"Wake up, fool. We comin to the river. You need to toss that shit. Got a body on it. We got the new ones."

Victor closed the phone. He was telling me what he could, and that it was up to me now. I was supposed to be in the airport, waiting for my flight to Paris. I was no threat.

They were throwing the gun in a river. Blythe was on the 10, near the Arizona state line. We were headed the wrong way.

It took another two hours to get back down to the 10. My father and the phone were silent. I drifted off into my head—a young woman in the Oaxacan market telling me about the dark glistening heap of mole, how she'd made it that morning even though a malevolent spirit had come inside her bedroom and tried to choke her because her next-door neighbor wanted her handsome husband, who had just bought a cab.

I hadn't driven longer than an hour or two in a while. A trip to Santa Barbara last year with Jimmy Taco. I'd driven to Santa Fe two years ago with Tony. He wanted to photograph the landscape on the way there. But that was for *Condé Nast Traveler*, which had money, and we'd rented a Jeep Cherokee.

My father didn't like people to drive him. He lit another Swisher Sweet. At home, he never sat this way. He crated oranges, fixed machinery, cut up wood, and when he finally sat on the gallery, as he called the porch, he always held a coffee cup. I hadn't driven anywhere with my father in twenty years, since he'd dropped me off at USC after I'd decided I could never go back to the Ivy-Covered East.

But I remembered the trip to Louisiana with Glorette, when we were ten. Last night, riding in the truck bed, I'd felt the air whipping past my neck. Back then, in 1975, we lay in the truck bed in the early morning darkness, wrapped in blankets.

"You want some music, Papa?"

He lifted his chin for yes.

I had some CDs in my bag, in the backseat, but I reached into the glove compartment to see what I'd left there.

"What this one call?"

"Water Music."

He looked at me. "That the one you tell Victor about?"

I nodded. "Written for a king to make a journey up the River Thames. A special song they wrote for him."

The music seemed all wrong, of course, with my undistinguished American car speeding down a highway through hills blackened by a wildfire.

Suddenly my father pointed ahead of us, at the pass near Palm Springs where huge windmills spun. He said, "This way, how we come back when we done killin people. Nineteen forty-eight. They let us go at the base, and we start drivin around California. Nobody goin back to Alabama or Lousana or Missippi."

In the strong light pouring through the windshield, his mustache was two thin lines of black slanting along his upper lip, as it had always been. His forearms were browner than his face, raised veins like cables running down into his hands. He was eighty-two, and still coiled with energy like a man much younger. Gustave had slowed these past five years since Glorette was killed, but my father—the only word I could see was *implacable*. He knew every tree in the groves, every drip line, and he could still see perfectly—well enough to wait for that gopher's small head.

My father said, "Tommy Washington stay in Palm Spring. Missippi boy. Biloxi. He meet a girl work for some lady from Hollywood. They got maids and butlers and gardeners in Palm Spring, but they make em live on the north side. Not side them blankitte."

Blankitte—the white people.

Then my father grinned. "Tommy have ten kids. They can't stop that."

We came through the riven mountainsides close along the freeway now, sand dunes pale as chalk, smoke trees trembling in the constant wind. He said, "I tell Washington when we on the base, you think California different from Missippi? From Texas?"

The music was tinny and small in the rushing wind of the car and the heat like a blow-dryer. My father said, "Four of us get a ride with OC. He from Houston. He say we better go to Los Angeles. So we go, but that too many people. Too many police. On the way back, I tell him let me off in Rio Seco, cause I see them trees. All them orange trees, like Azure. Smell the flowers. It was March. I walk down by the river and make me a camp. Till I know where I can go."

California. Hundreds of towns, each with a place for dark people. The ones you needed to work.

He rested his hat over his eyes. I thought he had fallen asleep. But he said, "You been to the place where that king ride in the boat?"

"Yeah. The Thames."

"You see it again when you hear the music."

"Yeah."

"You live in your forehead. When you tite, toujours." He was quiet, and I didn't know what to say. "Like a TV up there," he went on.

I waited for him to say something about how strange that was, how he and my mother had worried about me. But he said, "Mo tou soule."

I'm all alone.

"I live in my forehead all them year. When I close my eye. I see the water, the river flood up and catch us, and Gustave. My maman. The body float past. All white. Even if they black. The river brown, but the skin turn white."

The sun was unbearable on my face and neck now. I tried to see my father at four years old, standing on a levee after the great Mississippi flood, watching his mother get shot, and Gustave, who was only seven, pushing stolen meat into my father's mouth to save his life.

No music for that. I saw only the water, because I couldn't imagine the rest.

My father was quiet for a long time, and I didn't know whether he slept, or lived in his forehead.

Desert Center was up a long steep incline, and by then it must have been about 110 outside. The smoke trees were ghosts tethered to the earth. My father squinted from under his hat. The mirages of puddle water were big as lakes ahead of the car. I hadn't really slept for two days. I watched the heat gauge, and finally said to him, "I can't tell if we have a problem or not."

He looked over and said, "Radiator. Open them window and turn on the heater. Tou fort."

All strength. The hot air blasted my face and arms, from inside and outside, until my body was covered with sweat and my eyes burned. It was like being in a small metal hell, surrounded by a larger golden hell.

We made it over the summit, and the heat gauge stayed just at the edge of the red.

"We get to Blythe, check that radiator," my father said. Below us, Blythe was flatlands covered with fields, vivid green squares that stretched to the hills. Irrigation sprinklers threw water furiously over the rows, and the canals were wide as freeways.

"Watermelon and cantaloupe right now," my father said, looking out the window. "When I come with OC, it was all cotton. Look like snow. Never pick cotton in Louisiana, mais pick here for a month. Make some money." He shook his head. "People say, California, that the movie and the ocean. All I see was cotton, and then I see oranges. See that same hoe like Louisiana."

I grow you.

We hadn't grown Victor very well, we hadn't helped him enough. But what the hell were we doing? He would call and say he was at Alfonso's uncle's house, and we'd show up and cut him away from the other two, like a calf?

"Papa," I said. "Seriously, how are we gonna find Victor?"

"He find us," my father said. "He have to."

We stopped at a service station, and my father lifted the hood and went inside. I climbed into the backseat and closed my eyes, which felt like dry grits were sealed inside.

Marcus and I lay in the back of the truck. His neck like damp velvet. The wheel well with scratches like hieroglyphics.

Esteban and I lay in the hotel bed in Barcelona. The way his sideburns were not strips of hair but hundreds of tiny filaments and my eyelashes were caught when he rested his face against mine. An entire week. But then I had to leave.

The Scion smelled like beer and something acrid and sharp. His neck flushed red, his ears red. White people were so many different colors. The strangest thing, I'd thought.

My father's voice, and another man's, near the hood. They did a few things, and then the hood slammed shut, and a man with a pushcart said into the window, "Señora, tacos?"

He put homemade salsa on the carne asada. Tomatoes, onions, garlic, and jalapeños. My mother's gumbo. The chopping up of vegetables and meat. Heat to counter heat.

It must have been 115 degrees, with a drum cooker radiating heat nearby, the smoke lingering in my hair. We sat near the cottonwoods edging the parking lot, on white plastic chairs, and a truck radio played Little Anthony and the Imperials. Like Nome in winter, huddled inside an ice house, eating dried seal.

Who would come here? Dark people in the pulsing shade eating blackened meat and listening to music that had no cultural worth to anyone who read what I wrote. *I wanna make it with you . . .*

In the bathroom, I splashed water on my face, smoothed water on my hair, and redid my bun. Purple circles like pansies around my eyes. I called Tony.

"Where are you?" he said. "You bailed on breakfast, and you bailed last night, too. I woke up and you were gone. Usually you turn the movie off for me."

"Did you see the *Times* today? The shooting on page two?"

"I guess. Another bunch of candles and flowers. These kids are crazy. It looks like an Italian chapel on every corner."

"My godson was in the car, Tony."

"Victor?" Tony had gone with us to the Getty Villa, made fun of the cypresses and the gardens. But he'd loved the wrestler's cup, too. "He didn't do anything, right?"

"Whoever was in the car is—" I couldn't think of it. "Culpable."

"No, he's not."

"Tony! I'm the one that put him in the car." The Formica counter was hot under my palms. I told him about yesterday, and last night.

"Now you're in Blythe? What the hell are you gonna do?"

"I don't know." A pink silk orchid on the counter, with curly moss in the clay pot. Like Louisiana—Glorette and I tangling our fingers in what hung from the trees. "Today's five years since Glorette died. And I hadn't even talked to her, not for real, not for years."

"Because you love me." He wasn't laughing.

"Well, that's fucked up."

"Yeah. It is."

"You were easier to love," I said.

He paused. "I mean, most things I see, I imagine how you'd see them. Like a twin, I guess. So stop getting sentimental. And what you're doing is crazy. When my cousin goes on a drunk roll in Philly, I don't go get him. I let someone else do that." He paused. "I'm heading to the studio. Rick probably called you. We talked about the Dalmatian coast. Pula and some other little towns. Very preserved. We could fly into Venice, actually. And we could just go on down to Naples and my grandmother's area on that same trip. Save a lot on airfare."

"Except I'm on a road trip with my father." I looked in the mirror again. Like Ash Wednesday rubbed there around my eyes. "Your grandma and my great-great-great-grandma, getting attacked by rich guys. Wonderful story. But Victor got shot in the arm," I said.

"Why didn't you tell me?" Tony's voice went deeper. "My cousin got shot in the arm in Jersey. If it's the upper arm, you can lose enough blood to die. He had surgery."

"He says his arm's on fire," I said.

"You better hope the bullet didn't sever a tendon." I heard his car stop. "FX. Call me. I can be anywhere pretty fast."

In the car, I opened my mouth to tell my father what Tony had said, but then I realized my father had warned me not to tell anyone about Victor—and the steering wheel burned my fingers. A boy had died for nothing. For three words. I wanted Jazen and Alfonso to be arrested. To stop shooting people. But I didn't want Victor gone, too.

If we did find Victor, and took him, and cops stopped us, we were— what? Co-conspirators? Accessories. What a word.

"Papa, if they left the state, and we help Victor evade arrest—"

My father whispered, "You want him in prison? Boy like him? He ain't no man. He a child."

"What if he doesn't want us to find him?"

"He call again. He ain't give up. So we don't give up." My father finally looked into my face. His eyes were like cold water, like the Swiss lakes. "You inconvenience, oui? After you call your friend in the bathroom? You busy?" He shook his head. "Victor survive all them years with his mama. He ain't finish."

I always pictured the Colorado churning, tinted the red of sandstone like its name, the way it was in parts of Utah. But I'd forgotten that here, under the bridge just east of Blythe, the river was wide and deceptively placid. Bluish green—a color I had always thought of as *lagoon.*

Sleek boats and Jet Skis buzzed around below us, herky-jerky like battery-powered toys. And white people with Ray-Bans and skin tanned to that deep reddish-brown—*cuite.* Not molasses, which you could see in any store. But cuite—the thickened, boiled by-product of sugarcane I'd had in Sarrat, way back then.

Water Music. Violins screnading the barges. Victor's notes: The newspaper reports "persons of quality" as the other celebrants. The date was auspicious: 7-17-1717.

This river was probably littered with guns, bodies, bottles, and even cars.

"Last night, mo pense c'est Victor sit at the table," my father said again. "But I see that you. Toujour by the river, you."

The desert here wasn't beautiful at all. It was bleak, brown, and the small scrub and rocks looked almost like trash strewn accidentally across the landscape. No plateaus or red-tinted stone formations or purple striations. A lot of faded beer cans.

I got out the ancient road atlas from under the seat. I hadn't looked at it in a few years. "How far to Louisiana?" I asked.

"About twenty-fo hour, you drive straight through," he said. Then he took a long time to light another Swisher Sweet. I cracked open the window, which made a layer of hot air mix with the cold. "Depend on what them boys do. And see where we are in Texas."

"Texas?"

He turned his face away and said only, "Oui." His smoke was snatched out of the sliver of open window.

Nothing but dry sandy white riverbeds below each bridge after that.

He took deep pulls on the cigar. I could hear the ember glisten and work. After a long time, he said, "I remember when Sidney Chabert bring Glorette body in the shopping cart, to Lafayette and Reynaldo. We make that coffin, me and Gustave."

"Gustave buried his only child," I whispered.

My father nodded. "Nineteen twenty-seven, his maman stay in the house when the water come. That flood. He never see her body. We up on the levee, where they bring us, wait for the boat. Boat take the blankittes, but we stay on the levee. Dead horse, dead cow, dead pig go by. Then they shoot my maman, and she fall into the water."

She had been holding his baby sister. I knew this. My mother had talked about it a few times, in the kitchen, late at night. The baby was wrapped inside my father's mother's shirt, to keep her safe from insects, and so she could nurse. There was no food.

"She float down. See her back, me, and the shirt rise up. Like—" He lifted his hands from his thighs—fingers curled—like a bubble.

"Rise up so fast. That air. Under her shirt."

The gray course ahead of the car was flat, lines of tar in the cracks like snakes. Snakes in the water, too. My mother had said.

What was her name? The baby? She was only months old. Gustave had killed someone's pig, further down the levee, with a hammer, and then cut up the meat and brought it in his shirt to my grandmother.

She was still my grandmother, though I had never seen even a photo of her. She was the granddaughter of Moinette Antoine.

Gustave squatted by the fire my grandmother made, from splintered chair legs, and waited for the meat. But the National Guardsmen smelled the smoke, and they shot her for the stolen meat.

My father took the last deep draw and the smoke hid his face.

"Never have a body. My maman. Fish eat her body. She have cousine—Marie. They meet two men in Azure—on a boat. Say, come up to Sarrat. And then the one man, he get kill in a bar. Gustave papa. The other one, he just run away. Les cousines, they work the field. Say, When we get pay, we go back home to Azure."

She died for her child. My father closed his eyes and slept like a child, and the tires hummed and the landscape stayed unvarying and brown except for the burned-out hulks of cars abandoned on side roads. Those were charred black as crow wings, and they'd never fade no matter how hot the sun beat down.

He missed the Gila River, which was a dry bed, and the Salt River, a pale channel of sand, but woke up when traffic slowed past Phoenix.

The sun had fallen behind us, to a red suffusion in the smog and haze of the west.

"We in Texas?" my father said, his voice thick with swallowed cigar smoke and sleep.

"No," I said. "Past Phoenix." I had put in Esther Phillips again. I couldn't help it. *Don't count stars, or you might stumble. Someone drops a sigh, and down down down you'll tumble . . .*

Marcus. The smell of him. In my imagination, I moved him to the park below Sacre Coeur, in Montmarte, the shadowy corridors leading up to the church and the winding streets past it. Dark. Not just sex, but his throat, collarbone. The way it had felt, my fingers against his shoulder blades.

But my father said, "That sun go down, you find a place. When we in Texas."

There was a strange hoarseness in his voice. Not sleep, or smoke. Terror. What had he dreamed of?

We were about three hours behind them, maybe more. We'd passed hundreds of miles of scorched earth and bushes like dead coral. How many bodies were buried in the deserts—the Sonoran and Mojave and Gila wilderness? Jazen had sped along this same freeway—did he see a place to dump Victor? Victor was useless to him.

Mando. His picture in the newspaper, on the seat behind me. His hair slicked back. He's darker than me, Victor had said. He was just a boy, too.

The sun edged down behind us, the sky to the east glowing blue and neon almost in the reflection. The other side of sunset. The moon would be more lopsided tonight when it rose.

"Drive all night, we be in Texas in the day," he said, and I could hear the strain in his attempt to remain calm.

"Then we'd better get gas, and eat dinner. Get some coffee."

It had been years since I was on the road with no itinerary and no Tony or Jane or someone to meet. I suddenly wanted the illusion that I could choose something—anything—about this day. "Rick?" I said into the phone.

"You okay?" he said immediately, his voice Mayan coffee charged. "Tony said you were having some family issues."

"Yeah, I'm fine." The fluorescent tubes at the gas station began to pop and hiss. My father was filling up the tank. "I'm in Tucson."

"You went to Tucson? On August twenty-fifth? Who the hell are you writing for? *Satanic Weekly*?"

"No. I just ended up here."

"O-K. For fun?"

"Rick."

"FX. Hey—are you alone?"

"I'm not here to party. I just need a good restaurant. I'm tired of fast food."

He sighed, and I heard fingers tapping on the keyboard. "Tucson—I got something in my inbox about Lapis. Some brand-new restaurant. Check it out, and if it's not too chronically hip or pathetically cute, maybe you can do a short piece."

"I can't write anything right now," I said. "Not right now."

"FX. Are you okay?"

"I am."

He accepted the lightness and dismissal. "Shady. You must have found the Gentleman with a Tie and don't want to tell me yet. So call me. Tony and I made up a good list this morning. And today I got a big press release about some medical spa in Slovakia. Frickin medical tourism. One of the advertisers is hot on it. You want something fixed?"

"Very funny. I'll call you, Rick."

———

My father didn't hate white people. That was simplistic. He didn't hate them, and he wasn't afraid of them.

He thought of them like coyotes. Sometimes he admired them from a distance. He had a healthy respect for their cunning desires, atavistic impulses, and greed. He watched them, studied them, and was at every moment of his life prepared to defend himself and his blood against them.

Aversion. My father's entire being changed when he was around white people. We sat at a small table along the wall, in the bar since it was too late for the restaurant. His body was stiff, his face impassive. I watched him listen. The words all around us as foreign and sharp to him as if I were in—Turkmenistan, surrounded by older men.

I'd have to save the word for Victor. It was the same hardening and wariness in white people, as if shellac replaced sweat and blood, whenever young black men pulled up at a corner. Or when they got into an elevator.

My father sat in a cowhide director's chair. The room was dark except for the ceramic luminarias, replicas of paper bags holding lit candles. So far Lapis meant the electrified blue paint on the adobe buildings, the purple lavender lining the walkways, and the indigo leather on the furniture, with tiny barrel cacti on the table.

"Blankitte love them cactus," he said softly.

My father was like all farmers, all over the world, without his head covering. His face paler than his arms and hands, his neck somehow tender and vulnerable, and he squinted in the dim candlelight.

"Just coffee," he said. "Pas fam, me. Them tacos."

"That was a long time ago," I said. "We have to eat something decent, and then I'll sleep while you drive."

The server came back and smiled, patient and bald and quite cheerful. "The crab cakes are amazing," he said.

I shook my head no. We'd pulled up crabs from traps in the bay near Azure. Never order crab in the desert. "Where you from?" he asked, and I was inexplicably surprised.

"Louisiana," I said, and his whole face lit up like a child's.

"Oh, my God," he said. "I used to work at Tante Zoe's Cajun Restaurant in Dublin. They called it Dublin's French Quarter. We had the best blackened redfish. But it wasn't New Orleans. New Orleans is the most amazing place in the world."

My father's face was secretive and despairing.

"But I'll bet those Irishmen hated hurricanes," I said, smiling back. "Too sweet."

"You know it," the server said. "Hey, there's a hurricane on TV! People are mixing up those drinks right now."

We glanced at the bar screen. Hurricane Katrina was beating up on Florida, the news said. Palm trees sticking up out of water like toilet brushes.

My father waited until he was gone. Then he said, "Give em crazy name. Camille. Nineteen sixty-nine. Camille take out the end of Comtesse."

"Comtesse?"

"House up the river. They have a slave jail. Brick house, four of em. For the ones they steal. Jean Lafitte bring people there. After he steal em from the ship."

Just like that. "Victor mentioned pirates yesterday. To the girl in the apartment."

"When I run liquor, back then, people say Comtesse got spirit. Ghost. The big house fall in the river long time ago—1902. Say them spirit have to stay in the slave jail."

"Could Albert be down there? In Azure?"

My father shook his head. "Albert—maybe Sarrat. Maybe New Orleans." He poked at the polenta when it arrived. "This couche-couche?"

"Kind of," I said. The polenta was formed into a cake and grilled with prominent stripes, with black bean and corn relish on the side.

All grits. All ground corn. The slaves ate couche-couche. "You went in the building?"

He said softly, "I keep liquor bottles in there. Cause people afraid."

"How we doing here? How's that blue corn? Intense, huh?"

I gave him that fake smile, small as the Mona Lisa's, and nodded.

No one cared about our stories, Cerise used to say. When we found out about Mr. McQuine, after Kelly Cloder's party, she told me, "I'm not tellin somebody we got here to California cause a some nasty old white man. Shit."

The bathroom had lapis tile borders. The paintings on the wall were Georgia O'Keeffe–style flowers. Dark irises, nearly black, with sword-like foliage.

In the car, I had put on my white shirt from Zurich, forced my swollen feet into the black boots, and redone my hair again. It was so dirty it stayed flat and docile in the bun, which was fine with me. I wanted so badly to be me again. Just for an hour.

The soap was a vivid blue ingot. Not lavender but musk. I had black musk soap from Provence in my bathroom at home, and linen embroidered towels from Brussels. They made me happy every time I used them.

Suddenly my mother's voice came—That make me happy. The crushed peppermints in a bowl, the sunflowers in a green vase, the bougainvillea like a magenta curtain over the carport.

In the street, shouts rose up, and loud music bumped from cars. Always the same drumbeats, if not the same drivers. Classes must have started at the university nearby.

"Don't you want to call Maman?" I said.

I dialed home and handed him the phone, and walked away. I was still his daughter. Stay out of grown folk talk.

The stunted trees in the courtyard were hung with blue lights. I walked to the sidewalk. CVS. Ben & Jerry's. Bars where noise rushed out like a wet roar. Clothing stores with urban chic and southwestern wear.

The boys in front of me were definitely college freshmen, out having their first week of freedom. One had spiked black hair, glistening like a thousand fishhooks, and his pale scalp showed through in the streetlights. The tender skull. Filling with knowledge.

"Brah!"

Two more spilled out of a bar. "Yo, bro, come in here and let's get fucked up!"

"Bro, I'm already one with the gangaweed, man. I can't handle anymore. The guy in my hall has major stash."

"For real, bro. We're just kickin it."

"Lookin for the hookups, brah. Hey, dog!"

The mass of them on the sidewalk. Kobe Bryant flew in a window across the street.

What kind of jersey had Mando been wearing? I couldn't remember. It was black.

The boys moving past me now. What would they say if Victor and Jazen and Alfonso were walking ahead of them? Or behind. Nervous glances. Hey, bro. S'up, bro. Hats sideways, backwards, forwards. Mando's hat. Mando had gone to pick up free tickets but he had a gun in his waistband. Who had he expected to see but someone who threatened him? Whose territory was this, outside a university, boys like the Scion making their own language out of another language?

My father was beside me, holding the phone as if it were a stone. "That's it?" I said.

He met my eyes. "Rien a dit. We don't find him yet. Gustave say only 100 today. He got the water on."

A girl pushed past me. Her green T-shirt read KISS ME, I'M IRISH.

Slavic. Nordic. Germanic. Gaelic. Italian. Tony and I had joked about these T-shirts. I'd said, "No shirt for me? Kiss Me, I'm Senegalese? Mixed with Burgundian?"

More boys in a crowd, hair glittering and shining, blond waves and black spikes and Armani waistbands showing. All the designer names scrolled above their butts, while they hitched up their jeans. Baggy because they'd had no belts in prison.

One dropped his wallet. "Yo, dog, wait up!" he called.

Jazen. Alfonso. But not. And Victor? In his skinny jeans? They'd still think he was a gangbanger. Loc Mafia.

He was a mutt. Like me. I was his mother now—I felt it behind my ribs, along my shoulder blades, the fear that someone would shoot him again. The physical ache. I wanted him back.

My father held out his hands for the keys, and I lay in the backseat, head on my jacket.

I woke up just before Las Cruces. It was almost four a.m. My father had been driving all night, with the static of AM radio pricking me now and then in the backseat. I sat up and looked at the dark outside, then at the front seat, where my father's ancient green duffel bag was beside him. It was slightly open. His right knee almost touched it. I saw the glint of black metal on top of his clothes.

We were heading for Texas. He had a gun, too, and he made sure he could reach it anytime. The fear I'd felt for Victor raced lower this time, mixed with how scared I was for myself now, like someone scratching at my hip bones.

WEIMAR

A SHADOW STOOD over me in the dark.

"Fantine. Fantine."

It wasn't dawn yet. My father blocked the irritating light that shone from the parking lot into the backseat. I struggled to sit up. The phone thudded to the floor. The backseat was covered with papers and CDs. I had put Victor's notebooks, the ones from his room, in the messenger bag. Had I tried to write notes about Luzern and Zurich? My head was filled with black—like magnetic filings. My tongue felt like a cactus pad stuffed into my mouth.

My phone showed no messages. His voicemail was full. Victor was out there somewhere, lost. Maybe he liked being lost. Maybe he didn't want to be found. Brought back to his mother's old room, with Joan of Arc on the wall.

We were in the parking lot of the gas station in Las Cruces. We had slept for a few hours. It was six a.m.

This was how we had come when I was ten. Glorette and I had slept in the back of the truck during the early morning, covered with sheets and blankets, and then sitting against the cab sipping on the chocolate milk cartons my father bought at the gas station.

We rode up front with my father in the afternoons, when the sun would have cooked us facing west. Lafayette and Reynaldo were fifteen and sixteen, the stars of the Linda Vista High School football team, and the coach said they had to stay for practice that summer or quit. Someone had died, and my father had to help with the cane planting. We were old enough to work.

The cane was razor sharp. It had cut us on the forearms. In college, I'd met girls who sliced themselves shallow with razor blades, in nearly the same place, and I'd touched my own scars—thin and white like threads on my skin, but not deliberate and lined up. The cane cuts were random graffiti on my arms, faded now to invisibility.

The cousin was old—it was her husband who had died. Auguste was his name, and Glorette and I smirked hearing the old people talk in French. We went into the tiny house and he was laid out in a wooden box while people filed past him and filled a saucer on his chest with quarters to pay for his funeral and a band.

We lay cane in the furrows turned by a tractor that my father drove. We ate gumbo and court bouillon with rice. At night we slept in the same bed, smelling of bleach and sun, in the middle room of a shotgun house, while people sat in the kitchen on one side and the front room on the other, talking and drinking coffee for hours.

When I was in college, listening to people talk about their travels, and I began to write about foreign places, I wondered what it would have been like if we had spent that month in Provence, or on an Australian ranch, or in Cambridge. How much of Louisiana entered me, in the dirt I breathed behind the tractor, and the coffee beans ground by the old cousins, and the animals we ate? The chicken twirled like a toy in the hands of the old woman?

My father took his gun from the truck, back then, the first night. A rifle. He and the other men shot rabbits because the fields were cleared for planting. The women skinned the rabbits and the membrane was purple gloss.

Now he had a smaller gun. In the faded green duffel bag near his feet. The same bag he'd brought last time. The bag he'd had since World War II. He was hunting again.

My legs were stiff. My black jeans were damp around the waistband, and too long without boots, so I had to roll them up. Nice look. Went along with the second boy undershirt from the pack.

We ate Danish and drank coffee in the front seat. "We're looking for Albert. Claudine's son. Maman told me a long time ago about Mr. McQuine." My heart beat faster, from my fear to say it. "You killed him. And you have a gun in your bag?"

Suddenly I saw the Scion, lying on the floor of the dorm room. Mouth slack. The blood under his temples pulsing bluish as thin milk.

"So you're gonna shoot Alfonso or Jazen?" I said.

He chewed slowly. "Non. They ain't shoot me."

"Jazen will shoot you, Papa. He doesn't care. That's what he does."
I looked out the window. Red sky at morning. "Did you shoot Mr.
McQuine?"

"I never shoot none of em." He finished his coffee and stared straight
ahead.

"How many?"

"Three."

"You killed somebody in Texas?"

He shook his head. "I ain't had no gun in Texas. Not that time."
Then he slanted his head toward the wheel. "Allon."

I drove across the Rio Grande. The freeway followed the river now.
The water was to the west of us. All those cowboy movies, the Wild
West, the cattle drives and shootouts and John Wayne. My father and
Gustave used to watch them on a little black-and-white TV in the barn.

The duffle bag was in the back now. But the gun could be in the
glove compartment. A handgun, not a rifle for gophers. Had my father
been a knucklehead, a known associate, back in his day? Who else had
he killed?

My father lit a Swisher Sweet. The wind blustered at the open windows. And he was silent.

He would tell me when he wanted to.

Just outside El Paso, we passed a roadside shrine. Three wrought-iron
crosses, painted white, with dusty veladoras and bouquets of plastic
flowers tied to the crosses. Names in plastic-encased circles in the
center.

Had they been driving or walking? They were immortal now. This
was the spot where their spirits had left their bodies. Like Mando's
spirit had left the sidewalk outside Dimples. Glorette's spirit rose from
an alley behind a taqueria. Sere Dakar's rose from a dump along a freeway, and nothing marked his passage.

I could never tell Victor that.

The Rio Grande a few miles from here, where Mexicans swam
across with their belongings in plastic on their heads, taken away now
and then by the swirling current after a storm and who would ever
know where their bodies ended up? Not in the Gulf of Mexico. The sea

where my grandmother's body, with her baby tucked inside her shirt, would have floated to eventually.

No shrine. No flowers. No candles. No bones.

The sun was right in our faces, blinding as a flashlight, when we crossed the border into Texas. I looked at my father. He said, "This West Texas. East Texas, pas meme chose."

We left the Rio Grande behind at Esperanza. A town called Hope.

I played Astrud Gilberto. But I'd never been to Brazil. I had always wanted to, but I'd been afraid. Belize, but not Cuba. Argentina, but not Brazil. A fear of what I would be there, and in South Africa, and lots of other places. The blurred low tone of her voice, the guitar like beaten silver. After a while, my father said, "Where you missing?"

"What?"

"You go somewhere toujour. Where the next place? You miss a plane yet?"

"I'm not sure where I'm going yet," I said. When I came home, he had always hovered near the conversation of my mother and the women on the gallery or in the kitchen, and then hours later he might ask: You eat good there—you never sick? They ain't had no trouble there? Say London got terrorist, oui?

We were in hill and brush country now, with oil rigs grazing like skeletal dinosaurs and cattle huddled in the umbrella shade of oaks.

"Nobody think you terrorist?"

"They think I'm beige. Like oatmeal. Like nothing."

He said, "Nobody ask you?"

"I remember this interview with James Baldwin. One of my favorite writers. He said Greeks and Armenians weren't white until they came to America. They were Greeks and Armenians."

"You go to Greece, what they think you are?"

"Sometimes in Spain, they think I'm Spanish. France, I'm French. Maybe from Marseille. A couple times in England someone thought I was a Gypsy." I looked at the blond grass and stubby bushes, the immense flatness of the land.

His eyes were moving constantly over the landscape, too. Not on me. "Black still black. You in Texas now."

He chewed on the inside of his cheek for a minute, the indentation like a dimple. "You make it up when you in college, no?"

"Yes."

"You lie?"

I nodded. "All the time."

He nodded, too, just slightly, the way he always did. That incline of the chin. "I make myself up. In the Army. Gustave, too. We ain't had no paper. The name in the Bible, and the Bible wash away. No birth paper, rien. Man take us off the levee, blankitte, and keep us at his house for a month. Then he take us down to Azure, and he gone. When we turn eighteen, we get somebody make us a paper." He opened the bag of pistachios we'd bought at the gas station. "Army don't care, back in '42. Take who come."

I held out my hand and he put a few pistachios on my palm. The salt flooded my mouth. "What's the best thing you ever ate?"

"Only one?"

"No."

"Cochon. On the levee."

He had to have imagined the meat. He was four. What did I remember from being four? "What else?"

"They had walnut tree in France. In the war. By the farmhouse. Them walnut cold and they taste good. I sit there, and think of the pecan tree down in Azure. By the graveyard. Me and Gustave find some pecan once at night. We tro faim. We bout ten, t'etre. Put them pecan on the fire little bit." He held the pink pistachio shells like treasure in his hand.

"Glorette and I found pecans like that in the yard. Baked by the sun. Fat and sweet."

He nodded. "Call that nut meat. Pas meat. A seed." He paused. "Sit there all night, watch for German come, and eat them walnut. Think I ever see Gustave again." He looked out the window, and then said, "Eat some cuite, when I come back from the war. And drink some water from a well, real cold once. And one time your maman make a gumbo. A party. I don't know why. Best gumbo I ever eat."

"The best thing I ever drank was black cherry Kool-Aid. It was so hot, that summer. And Glorette and I drank it in glasses with ice."

Then I thought of Victor. Drinking the gangster Kool-Aid.

He said he wanted to be a combination of Zelman and Marcus, a crazy lovely hybrid. A teacher. I reached for my CDs and put in Bob Marley. "No Woman, No Cry."

The first time I heard the song, when I was in college, I saw it all so clearly, as if I had been there—the government yard in Trenchtown, the firelight, the porridge. My feet is my only carriage.

Because I had been there, with Marcus, back when we sat in the beds of two trucks pulled together in the river bottom. Lafayette's boom box playing Earth, Wind and Fire. Bored, broke, playing cards, built a fire, and what we had to eat was tortillas. A whole stack that Glorette and I heated up on an old refrigerator rack. They were so warm and soft—like eating the moon. I sat in the circle of Marcus's arm, and I licked the side of his neck, in the dark. The tortilla, the salt, and the warmth.

I drove for hours. My father drifted in and out of sleep, the seat leaned back.

I remembered how he always slept in the big chair in the living room, sometimes until midnight when the boys finally came home after a football game. I crept out to watch him once, and when I woke him, we sat in the dark together, waiting for my brothers. We looked out the picture window at the garden, the road below. My father said, "Dor bien in the chair. My grandmère do that. Say her maman do that, too. Moinette. Moinette say her maman sleep in the chair. The maman from Africa. Say, sleep in the bed danger. Make you too rest. Say, keep watch."

"For coyotes?"

"Watch for somebody steal Moinette. But she don't steal. She sell in the night."

Was Victor sleeping in the Navigator, curled in the back, Alfonso with his mouth a little open in the passenger seat, and Jazen driving and driving, like me? Had they pulled off on the road, in the shade of a tree, and napped? Like the men in *The Encampment*?

We were all bambopcianti now.

I thought of the next few months. Fall travel—usually cruises and cheaper European trips. The Dalmatian coast. Leaves and festivals. Pumpkins and apples and pecans. Not pecans from a wild tree in a field. Then Christmas season, though usually those pics had to be done the year before—like Paris, the City of Light at the holidays, snow on the bridges. New York decorated. Santa Fe shrouded in white.

My life was absolutely predictable. The Romance of Rome. The Hidden Amalfi Coast. The Art of Country Pub Food. Secret Venice. Belize—the Tamed Jungle.

But I'd never been to New Orleans.

So I left Los Feliz—the Happy Place—to find Victor, who'd watched someone from Boyle Heights get shot by a guy from the Westside of Rio Seco, where all the blacks were forced to live when they came from Louisiana and Oklahoma and Mississippi. And I was headed to New Orleans, where south of the city was Azure, a place named for a white girl's eyes.

The sun was low behind us by seven o'clock. My father woke up changed again, just after I passed over the Llano River.

"We can eat in San Antonio," I told my father. "About an hour."

He shook his head. "Stop at dark."

"We haven't heard from Victor, and who knows whether they'll even find the mysterious Albert. We have to catch up with them."

He shook his head again, just a few inches, like an irritating totem pole god, sitting stiff and staring straight ahead.

"It's cooler at night. People always say it's better on the car."

"Not on the people."

"Papa. I fly and drive all over the world. I've driven all night so many times—I drove through the Alps in Austria once when a hundred cars got stuck by an avalanche, and we had to stay awake so we could move forward."

"Who you with?"

"What?"

"You with your friend. Tony."

"Yeah. So? He's not scared of much, but—"

He cut me off. "Now you with me. You just a nigger."

"Papa."

"We get stop at some gas station, some fool see us and want play—you ain't nobody." His voice sounded like some movie. Echoing and deep. "You not a writer. You with me. You tite souri. For them. They work in the day. At night they got nothin to do. Drink beer and look for souri."

A mouse.

"When you brought me and Glorette, did we drive all night?"

"Non. We stop in Seguin. Somebody farm pecan. But she gone now." Then he cracked a pistachio.

We came into the suburbs around San Antonio. "Up there, by Tyler, a man tell me his grandpère born when they cut open the maman belly. Hang her from a tree. She cuss some blankitte."

Texas.

"Name that baby Boston. I meet him in France. Boston, c'est bien place."

We crossed the Guadalupe River. The sun was nearly gone now, but no moon rose in the windshield. It would come up late. Half-eaten.

My father said, "Fantine. La-bas." He pointed to the big Super 8 sign just outside Seguin.

Inside, the young man at the counter said, "Sorry, we're totally full. Which way you headed?"

"East," I said, over the television blaring in the lounge.

"There's the Check Inn," he said. "In Weimar."

When I opened the car door, the air pulled out a rush of vaguely sweet cigar smoke and salt. The duffel bag was on the floor behind my seat now, zipped again, but he had moved it. "Another hour," I said. "No choice. You want to stop and eat first?"

My father shook his head.

Down the narrow lit path of freeway, surrounded by darkness, by woods and farms and empty night to a town that sounded as if it should feature a castle. Sure as hell couldn't write this one. My father gets psychotically paranoid the minute the sun drops. Let's do a piece on sundown towns. Nigger, don't let the sun set on you in Hawthorne—I'd seen pictures of the old sign just outside LA.

Nothing but that weird blue-black everywhere, the trees like cutouts against velvet, only the high-mounted lights of a few ranches like electrified eagle nests in the distance. I was spooked, too. Spook. Haint. Spirit. The bright people—what Aunt Almoinette used to call them— ghosts of white people who walked along the levee at night.

But I knew better than to say anything about ghosts. It was live people he was afraid of. What if we did get pulled over right now, by a Texas cop? What would my father do? We were actually going to a town called Weimar? Like Nazis instead of Klan?

The sign beckoned like a giant spatula from the side of the freeway—CZECH INN. No way.

It must have been a former Super 8, with exactly the same architecture. Parking lot half-full, and dark except for the brightly lit portico and pillars—a very sad castle. The woman behind the desk said, "We've only got three rooms left. Two queen beds."

That was us.

She was about fifty-five, with brown hair in a very short pageboy, and one of those measured, toneless voices. Her face was perfectly still when she took my driver's license and credit card. "Los Angeles," she said. "You're driving a long way by yourself."

"My father's with me," I said, and then she looked up, over her glasses, like a clichéd librarian.

"Isn't that nice?" she said, and her whole face lit up. I wasn't an LA jerk with a white shirt and platinum Visa and attitude. I was with my dad. I was okay.

I sat on the queen bed closest to the window. Satiny comforters. Metallic smell of air-conditioning and bathroom cleanser. Carpet worn by thousands of feet.

"You think they're already in New Orleans?" I asked.

My father sat in the chair by the TV. He hadn't moved or taken off his boots. "Jazen drive all night?" he murmured. "Sais pas. Maybe he know somebody."

I couldn't picture Jazen and Alfonso having girls all along the route. Were they souris? Mice? Or were they hunting someone, for more money?

I took a long shower. In the steamy bathroom, I put on the last clean tank top from the pack, and my new black jeans, but my feet were not having the boots. Still swollen. I rubbed them for a minute. All that walking I did, miles and miles every day, never bothered my feet, but this driving was killing me. I put on the flip-flops I'd worn at home, the impressions of my soles dark on the straw matting.

Being in a motel made me feel more normal. I wanted to check e-mail. If I couldn't work, I would go crazy. I towel-dried my hair. My father was watching the Weather Channel. "Hurricane," he said. "Come past Florida."

I drank some water. "I hate plastic cups," I said.

He stared at me. "You come home from school, say, That not a cup, that a glass. Lafayette tell you shut up, and you say, That not a carpet, that a rug. Rug don't touch the wall." He unlaced his boots but didn't take them off.

My laptop was out on the bed. "I always figured nobody could steal my words. Not even Lafayette or Reynaldo."

"Oui," my father said. "Somebody can."

"Not once I send them off through that electronic maze," I said, hanging up the towel.

"Tante Monie say you like Jean-Paul."

"When we were down there in Azure?" I said.

"Oui. When you talk all the time. She say you like Moinette boy. The one die. Say he care too much about clothes and talk and he won't—" My father paused. He was still looking at the television. "Go under nobody."

"He wouldn't obey? I thought he lived with her. You said Moinette bought him out of slavery."

"Oui, buy him and then he still have to work. He won't—drop his head." He rubbed the side of his jaw, where tiny silver stubble showed like frost in the blue TV light. "He get kill for smile too much."

I had no response for this. Everybody died, in every story. I looked at the slim hotel amenities folder. "Papa, there's no Internet in here. I'm going to check in the lobby. See if Victor e-mailed me."

But I wanted to write about the Aare River first. Just a few paragraphs.

There was no lobby, only two maroon velour easy chairs and the television near the check-in desk. A little girl with two brown braids tied by yellow ribbons sat nearly hidden in one of the chairs. She waved hesitantly at me.

"My granddaughter," the woman behind the desk said. "I watch her until midnight, when my daughter gets off work."

The little girl had a coloring book and kept glancing up at the television. The woman gazed at me and the laptop. Her forehead was so white that her frown lines looked pink. But then she said, "I could open the breakfast room for you. There's an Internet connection in there. You have to dial up using our number."

"Thank you so much," I said, following her down the hallway to the small room with imitation oak chairs and the microwave and the packets of instant oatmeal. "I won't eat anything," I said, and she smiled.

"You don't look like an oatmeal person," she said. I was startled, but she smiled again. "But there's fruit. In the morning I make coffee and I do put out scrambled eggs."

She left the door open. The refrigerator hummed. Paper doilies under coffee cups. Like a Coen brothers movie. Deceptive? Weirdly comic? But the darkness and fear were upstairs in my room, and outside all around this bright dull room.

I opened the laptop. I saw the Aare River, rushing white through the narrow cleft in the mountains, the path that led all along the Aareschlucht glistening with damp and risen mist and delicate ferns, and the elderly Swiss women in their heels and dresses and thick hose, walking with their grandchildren, whose calf muscles were like apples already in those strong legs. Honoring where the water was born. And then, through the narrow passages of black stone, out a gate, and there was a café with ice cream sundaes and strong coffee.

The small park in Zurich where Jane and I hiked up a steep cobblestone street, overlooking the Limmat moving swift and ruffled. The bronze figures of military-garbed people holding tall pikes, their backs to the water so their faces wouldn't be seen by the invading army coming up the river. The men were gone, to another battle. The women of Zurich put on uniforms and helmets, formed a line of defense, and held their weapons aloft, and the scouts told the invaders to turn around.

That was enough. For now.

I had 226 e-mails. I could write nothing to Jane or Tony or Rick. Their names were in a line down the screen—No Subject. Because we talked about too many things.

Jimmy Taco, My New Thai Piece. He sent everything to everyone: *Oh my God! Tacos de Lengua and Tacos de Cabeza at this new place in Boyle Heights last night! Come for the usual at my place September 1— can you believe August is almost over? Thai Street Food. I'm making skewers but they're not some crappy satay. And if someone can catch the alligator in Lake Machado, we'll have alligator burritos.*

Jesse James Martin: *Get together?* A second one from her: *Neighborhoods of LA? Hermon and Atwater?*

My editor at *Vogue: Oaxaca piece ready?*

What could I write? "I'm in Weimar, Texas, contemplating the ironies of history."

Nothing from V1World—Victor's address. Did he have batteries for his iPod, an outlet for his laptop? He had everything, all the time, he said. Bambocciante for life.

I slid in the first CD he'd given me, keeping it so quiet that I bent my head to the keyboard. "Check It Out: Ironic Mix."

The White Stripes, doing an old Son House song: *I got a letter today said the gal you love is dead . . . When I got there, she was laid out on the cooling board . . .*

Cake, doing Barry White: *Never never gonna give you up, I'm never ever gonna stop . . .* It was torture.

I opened the CD case. Inside was a meticulously folded and stapled booklet. The cover was hand-drawn—four cartoon guys with Mohawks, Afros, spikes, and dreads. The liner notes:

Marraine—This is for you. A copy of something I did just before graduation. Professor Z's assignment: Compare the Crossfertilization. Ray Charles doing country, Run DMC doing Aerosmith. Son House: somebody in class thought Grandpere would know that one. Cause I'm black. I didn't even try. Son House is Mississippi Delta, not French Louisiana. Yeah. Like expecting some Cuban dude from Miami to listen to Tejano just cause their last names are both Hernandez. The White Stripes— ain't no way he's looking at some chick laid out on a cooling board. I saw the cooling board. He doesn't know shit about it.

He'd seen Glorette. Lying dead in my mother's living room, while my father and Gustave built her coffin. My God. Her photo stared at the ceiling of my car now. Breast milk pooling inside her.

I hate Barry White, and I like Cake, most of the time. But this one just doesn't work. He doesn't sound like he wants it. Not really. Not like the older brothers I know, when they want it.

Last one is Led Zeppelin, and Memphis Minnie's original version. Grandpere saw the water. He told me that a couple of times. But art versus technology—Robert Plant and Jimmy Page have the imagination and the hella big sound. It's, like, mesmerizing. Swirls around you like a storm. She had the voice and guitar, basically, and that was it. But she sounds so sad. Her throat holds all this tragedy. So that's Soul—to live the shit? And Art is to use the shit? Like Eazy E and Eminem. One gotta die, one gotta get rich. Blackface. Whiteface. Face up to it. Which one?— Victor Picard 2005

The mournful weird sound of electrified harmonica, reverberating drums like thunder, and guitar riffs whirling around—he was right. The Zeppelin version was amazing. Like being inside the turbulent storm, but then this guy with a bossy high voice is telling a strange story. *If it keeps on rainin, levee's gonna break . . . Mean old levee taught me to weep and moan . . . cryin won't help ya, prayin won't do you no good . . .*

For the last song, he'd written:

Marraine—Under the Bridge is mine. One of the most powerful love songs ever—to his city. Your city? I want to love a place. Not love a person. Again. They die. Peace. VP

Anthony Kiedis sang so softly, *She sees my good deeds and she kisses me windy, I never worry, now that is a lie . . .*

V—I feel like you're ahead of us by three hours, but where? You guys have to stop and sleep sometime, so I figure you're in a motel or someone's house, and you can check e-mail eventually.

You can be a flaneur. You are a flaneur. When I'm in Paris, I think of paintings of the young men who began this. They were called dandies— because they wore all these fancy clothes, and they pulled stunts like walking turtles on leashes down the streets of Paris. They refused to do what was expected. Their deal was to walk leisurely.

Basically, they didn't give a shit what people thought.

We can figure out the money. I've managed all these years to do it. I do what I want. I'll make sure you can do what you want.

I'm kind of a flaneuse. That word never sounds as good. But I'm invisible. Your mother wasn't invisible. She was in some alternate uni-

verse, like she was floating above all of us, kind of amused, always
melancholy, and we could never get her back down.

The Dread Flaneur? That's you.

It will grow back. And you can use your SAT words.

My SAT. Marcus Thompson and I were the only black people in the
study class. The night before the test, there was a freeze. I had to be out
all night in the groves, with the smudge pots. It was January. So when I
got to the test room, I looked like shit. I sat near this girl named Kelly
Cloder. She thought I wasn't black, till she thought I was. She held up
her hand before the test started and said something stinks, I can't con-
centrate, oh, it's the girl behind me, she smells like smoke, isn't smoking
on campus against the rules, shouldn't she have to leave. Slick.

My hair had kept the oily smell, my fingernails edged with soot, my
knuckles filled with black, even the lines on my palm filled in with
darkness. I'd taken a fast shower, but it took days for the smoky residue
to wear off.

They moved me to the back of the room. I didn't care. It just pissed me
off. All those words were in my head. I only missed two questions on the
language part. I scored in the top one percent of the nation. Fuck Kelly
Cloder. I remember thinking that.

I'm not saying the same thing happened with you. But you have all
those words in your head.

Now I sound like a coach in a bad movie.

The Dread Flaneur. I put my head down on the table. Smell of
Windex. Antoine. Picard. If I were going to tell Victor stories about the
past, I'd better get it right. My father and Gustave were not brothers.
Were they even related?

I typed *Moinette Antoine Louisiana* in Google Search. Had I always
lied? Lying was so much more imaginative, so easy, so rewarded.

Twelve entries. There was no Google years ago, the last time I'd
wondered. And I realized, clicking on the first entry, that I'd never
wanted to know too much more than the family stories: how she
learned to read from the owner's blue-eyed daughter while she curled
her hair, how she was sold and ended up in Opelousas, how she bought
a brick building, and her son died but she raised two daughters. I
hadn't avoided her history because she was a slave. No. I hadn't

wanted to think about her particular job, which would have been to make a white guy happy.

The first entry was in Afro-Louisiana History and Genealogy. Slave sale records, hundreds of them.

1814
Moinette
Gender: *Female*
Race: *Mulatresse*
Age (when this record was documented): *17*
Name of the Seller: *Etienne de la Rosiere, pere*
Name of the Buyer: *Julien Antoine*
Grouping: *Sold as individual. Not sold with son*
Selling Currency: *Piastre*
Selling Value: *800*

Seeing her name—solitary like that, no last name—and that she wasn't sold with her son, and that a monetary worth had been allocated—to her cooking? her sexual skills?—sent a sliver of loneliness below my jaw. Under Skills and Trade Information, Personality, and Family Information, there was blank space.

I did the math—she had been born in 1797.

It really did make me shiver. I could touch the words on the screen. Her body sold. Property. Chattel. But had she run away from Julien Antoine, and been branded on the shoulder with the fleur-de-lis? Or from the one who sold her? If this man had held the hot iron flower to her skin, had she been forced to sleep with him—to have his child?

The next entries were court documents, filed in Saint Landry Parish:

At the court held for the Parish of St. Landry at the courthouse on this 20th day of July, 1818, present the Honorable George King, Judge of the said Parish, on the Petition of Julien Antoine praying permission to give liberty to his female slave named Moinette, a Mulatresse, and it being proved to the satisfaction of this court that the said slave Moinette is about 21 years of age and that for the last 5 years she has led an honest conduct and has not ran away nor been guilty of robbery or any criminal misdemeanor whatever and the said slave having been duly advertised as the law directs and no opposition having been made to her liberty, the said Julien Antoine has permission to emancipate his said slave Moinette.

She was free. Why?

The next entry was dated a month later. Moinette Antoine, using that last name now, bought Jean-Paul, quadroon slave, five years old, from Etienne de la Rosiere.

In 1819, she named him as indentured to Julien Antoine. In 1825, she mortgaged him to François Vidrine, for nine years, for $900, to be paid in equal annual installments. But something must have happened.

The Saint Landry Parish Notary Book recorded: *Jean-Paul, quadroon slave for life, originally acquired from Laurent de la Rosiere, sold by Moinette Antoine to Crespin Frozard for $750, on November 4, 1828.*

She sold her son.

I had to stand up, to walk over and touch the microwave. She would have had a fireplace, to cook. She sold her son. Why? She never saw him again? The chill went across my scalp, and I made myself sit back down.

In 1835, she bought Marie-Claire, mulatresse, aged five, from Joseph Ashleigh, trader, Virginia, for $200. In 1840, she bought Marie-Therese, griffone, aged five, from the estate of Philomene Artois, for $100.

She must have had these two daughters with two different men, and then had to buy them. But I'd read it before: the condition of the child follows the status of the mother. A slave woman had slave children. Why would Moinette be required to buy her daughters, if she were free? Why her son?

I closed the screen. How much of her blood was in me? Halfrican. Mulatto was a made-up word. No Latin origins. It was coined from mule. Moinette was a mulatresse, and who was the father of her daughter Marie-Therese, the one named for the grandmother she never met? The grandmother who died after Moinette was sold away?

Who had told me she killed herself?

If a mulatto and a mulatresse produced my mother and father, and they produced us, what were we? Quadroon and sacatra and griffon?

I typed in *Azure Plantation Louisiana.* No results.

I typed in *Comtesse Plantation Louisiana.* Two photos appeared, in a state historical collection. A plantation with citrus trees and a bone-colored fence. Then the house sagging into the Mississippi River, half of it submerged, the shutters still straight, one side in the earth collapsed in a dark slump. Below the photo was a handwritten caption: *Crevasse.* I knew that word—a flood caused by a collapse in the levee.

I closed the photo and pulled up the next entry for Comtesse.

A woman in black leather bondage costume, with a mask, her lips red, her skin golden, her breasts spilling out of the bustier. "Comtesse du Sade. Fulfill your painful fantasy."

Someone stood in the doorway. "Um, is there any water in there?"

I turned around. A man about thirty with a sweat-ringed T-shirt and a baseball cap looked at my face, then at the laptop. I closed it quickly. He said, "Sorry, I was—"

A woman pushed through from behind him. "Just get some ice," she said, dismissing me with a flick of her eyes. Her camisole top was tight, her breasts compressed by the built-in bra and shivering over the top, and when she turned to the refrigerator, the excess flesh of her stomach formed a lifesaving ring above her waistband.

I glanced back—she opened cabinet doors now. Her short bubble of hair was subtly streaked, three shades of caramel and blond. The hotel receptionist came in and said, "The breakfast room isn't open, I'm sorry. You'll have to let me lock up now." Her granddaughter stood behind her, coloring book in hand.

"But she's in here," the woman said, swaying a little. I could smell her breath—she was drunk. What time was it? Her husband said, "We'd better head over to the restaurant," and put his hand on her back like a paddle and rowed her down the hallway.

The receptionist said, "They've been here two days." Her granddaughter put her arm around one of her legs, held on to her like a tree. "A family reunion."

I said, "Thanks for letting me work in here."

"You're welcome. Is your father comfortable?"

"Yes," I said. "He's fine."

But I went out to the car. My hair was a tangle of waves, from the humidity. I opened the glove compartment. Everything looked the same. No gun. Maps, CDs, a little notebook with coffee stains. I kept a packet of elastic bands there, too. I pulled my hair on top of my head but it was like trying to flatten a soft tumbleweed, so I left it in a ponytail to keep it off my neck.

The window was open, but the air sat heavily on top of the car. Had my father put the gun here, and then taken it back out?

Was he sitting with it now?

I didn't want to go back to that room.

I couldn't listen to "Poinciana" yet. I couldn't listen to Marvin Gaye or Al Green, either. I reached inside the glove compartment. Feux Follets. Will o' the Wisp. Transcendental Etude no. 5. Franz Liszt.

The rapid double notes, the mysterious hesitations and then whirling responses. Nicolas Perroy. The pianist I'd had a crush on in France, during my semester abroad.

It was the first piece I'd ever written. Not an essay, not a story. He played in a stone church, in a tiny village above Valreas. Nicolas Perroy's long black bangs had fallen into his face, and I'd realized that was part of the pianist's trademark—the movements of his head and back, his hair dancing, his cheekbones slashing through the light. I wrote about the walls of the church, the candlelight, the cherubim, the music. But I knew feux follets from Louisiana, from the woods where Moinette had lived, where Glorette and I had heard stories from Aunt Almoinette, the dangerous lights in the cypress swamp that wanted to lure you to drowning or madness.

I wrote about the sound of the piano notes as the moving mysterious lights in the trees. Then the reception, with dark red wines and bread and cheese and truffles harvested from the white oak grove a few miles down the road.

Professor Stiegal called me into his office. "You made me fall in love," he said, his lowered glasses like clear spoons resting on his cheeks when he looked across the desk. "I'm going to send this to my friend at the *Los Angeles Times* right now."

My first check. One hundred dollars.

A black Jeep Cherokee pulled into the last space, two over from mine. My car was dark inside, but the parking lot light illuminated me. I rolled up the window, and waited to see who was in the Cherokee. The couple from the breakfast room got out, and stood there arguing quietly. She leaned with her hands on the hood for a moment.

It was eleven here. Nine p.m. at home. I dialed Cerise, and started to get out of the car. She answered before I could close the car door.

"Why the hell you ain't told us what happened?" she said.

"What?"

"Your maman told me come down to the box houses with her. I ain't seen her like that in years. So we go stompin down there, and she has the key. She busts on in and Bettina got that dude up there. Fool from the swap meet."

"Dahani."

"Yeah. Your maman gives him the look. The one could burn wood. She says, 'Get out.' That man like to run outta there. Then your maman told Bettina she better talk. Said your papa told her Victor got shot. Bettina start whinin about ain't nobody called her, and her son said, 'Yeah, Fonso called. He said they goin to On-Ri.'"

On-Ri? I closed the car door and leaned my butt against it, trying to hear her. "What?"

"Your maman said, On-ri too old for that foolish. Said he live in Sarrat. The old Sarrat."

Was there an uncle Henri?

Cerise whispered, "Your maman told Bettina get out tomorrow morning."

The couple walked around the other car, and the woman stopped dead when she saw me.

"Hold up a second," I said, low, to Cerise.

"I thought this motel was decent."

She gave me that look, and immediately I knew what it was. Damn. My hair was an explosion like Spanish moss, curling around my forehead. "Who's she supposed to be—a low-rent Halle Berry?"

"You're a little drunk," he said to her. "This isn't appropriate."

"This ain't Seattle, Gavin. You're not from here. What—she's setting up an appointment?"

I put my palm over the phone, smiled and raised my voice. "Actually, I'm doing a stock trade."

"At eleven?" She held up her wrist. Wow. She had a watch. What a victory. Then she stumbled into her man.

"In Tok-yo," I said, enunciating as if speaking to a small child. "That would be Ja-pan. It's daytime there. Excuse me."

I turned away and walked toward the cement base of the motel sign.

I said to Cerise. "Tell Maman we're probably close to Sarrat. Tell her Papa's fine. He's in the motel watching the Weather Channel."

I put the key in the lock and said, "Papa, it's me," as quietly as I could.

A different gun was on the round plywood table. A short-barreled shotgun. He was cleaning it, with a flannel and a vial of oil and shells nearby.

My father had showered and shaved. I smelled the shaving cream. The room was dank and cold and wet. He wore different clothes, and his boots were laced loose again.

"They're in Sarrat," I said. "At Henri's house. Maman found out from Bettina."

He nodded. "Henri. Claudine uncle." Then he said, "Cinq-heure," as if it were one magical word. Five hours from here? "Sunrise 6:23. We leave 7." He rubbed the oil from his hands with the hotel washcloth. "They don't hunt matin, no." Not in the light of morning. Whatever had happened to my father in Texas, it had happened at night.

"I'm going to call him one more time," I said. "I'll be right out here."

On the floor of the hallway, fluorescent and long as a tiled freeway tunnel in Switzerland, I dialed, and he said, "Yeah." The voice was rough and deep.

"Victor?"

"You still in Paris?"

Not Victor. "Yes. I won't be home for a few more days."

"This ain't him. This is JZ."

I kept my voice steady and cheerful. "You get your braids redone?"

"Hilarious. VP already told me you know what's goin on. Said you heard on the news about that fool. Before you left for Paris."

He actually believed I was in Paris? "Where are you?"

"Where we need to be."

"Where's Victor?"

"Sleep."

"Jazen. What happened in Burbank?"

"We Westside Loc Mafia. He needed to know."

I said, "Jazen. *Loc* is short for *loco*. A Spanish word. Popularized by Tone Loc, remember, the rapper? And *Mafia* is an Italian word. Southern Italy. Are you crazy? You're from the Westside—about forty blocks of the city of Rio Seco. None of that's worth dying."

"I ain't dyin."

I had to stifle the anger. "This isn't time to play games. You need to drop my nephew off at a hospital and someone will come get him." I looked down at the carpet underneath me, the soda or beer spills near my feet like sullen dark clouds.

He laughed. "Oh, you in a fancy-ass hotel in Paris, and you worried about Victor? You don't give a shit. But you send your brothers to come get him, right? I heard about them. Hard motherfuckas back in the *day*. This is the *night*."

"Victor wasn't even involved."

Jazen laughed—one deep bark. "In-*volved*? You a writer and think you know all the fuckin words? He was with the nigga pulled the trigga. That's all they care about. And you ain't his mama."

"I'm his marraine. Godmother. Same thing now."

He laughed again. "Don't seem like it to me. You in Paris. Sisia told me one time, said you act like some white chick. But that's cool—ain't no real niggas in Paris, so nobody bust you."

I leaned against the wall. "You know who I see in Paris? On the subway? Rappers that look like you and Alfonso. Maybe from Algeria or Morocco. Maybe born in France. There's plenty of *brothas* in France."

"They ain't keepin it real cause they don't know what real is," he said, and his voice was suddenly light. I could hear him moving, hear a screen door slam shut, and then a car door open. "Here," he said, his voice distant now. "Your crazy-ass family."

"Hey." Victor's voice was weak. The screen door slammed again. He must be outside.

"Why didn't you call me?"

"You in Paris."

"No, I'm not."

"Yeah, you are."

"Victor, I'm in Texas."

"Whatever."

"We'll catch up with you tomorrow, if you're in Sarrat. You're at Uncle Henri's house. When we get close, I'll call you, and you can take a walk, or go to the store."

"We at some old man's house. But with a guy looks kinda like Tony Soprano."

I tried to picture that. A door opened at the end of the hallway and the same drunk woman came out and looked both ways. Then she walked toward the stairwell, and I heard the ice machine like a frozen waterfall. She gave me a distant dirty look, and then she tripped. The ice bucket dropped. Ice like diamonds along the carpet. She said, "Well, shit," and went back inside.

"Whatever. I gotta take the fall."

"What?"

"Jazen already did time. Fonso been in. They said I gotta do it. First offense. Do about two years. Three hots and a cot."

"Why are you talking like this?"

"I got a bullet in my arm."

"What?"

"It's still in there. But I can't go to the hospital cause then they'll take out the bullet and call the cops to see where it came from. They can ID the bullet and see it's from that dude's gun. Then they'll arrest us."

"We're taking you to the hospital as soon as we get there," I said.

He laughed a little, like his old self. But then he said, "No need. I'm gonna die. Somebody's gonna shoot me again. Every time we go to a 7-Eleven for some food they want to shoot us. Three niggas. That's a gang. Dude behind the counter darker than me and got his hand under the counter. I see his piece. I'm like, Where you from, man?, and he's all suspicious and says Madras and I'm like, Cool, *The Outsiders*. Cause Marcus Thompson gave me that book and the rich white kids wear Madras shirts, which is crazy cause that's like, from India."

I tried to picture the house. "Are you in a driveway?"

"Yard. I guess that's cane all around us. Must be a levee around here," he said. "Led Zeppelin could come by."

"Is there someone named Henri?"

"I don't know."

"Did they give you some rum again, for the pain?"

"Somethin they call lean. Purple drank. Sweet like candy. Snoop Dogg and them all have these fancy cups for their drank. Like kings. Like the wrestler's cup."

A battered face, misshapen ear and lumpy nose, cruel mouth.

"Where's the Constable? The River Dedham?"

"The Huntington," I said. "We'll go."

"I got a 7-Eleven cup right here," he said dreamily. "I'm worth savin now cause you think I'm smart? I'm inculcated with value?"

"Knowledge for the sake of knowledge. A flaneur," I said desperately.

"You thought I wanted to be you? A writer?"

"What?"

"Said you have a present for me."

The messenger bag. It seemed so useless now. "I do. It can hold a new laptop."

"Cool," he said, faintly. "But I wanted to be Zelman. And some Thompson mixed in. Not you."

Wanted? Past tense?

"A brotha could be goofy back in the nineties. Like Humpty, or De La Soul. But now don't matter how I look. So don't even think about me comin to LA. Don't matter if I'm bald or got a fro or dreads. It's all gangsta."

"Kanye's allowed to be funny."

"But he called you a mutt."

"Me?"

"Half girls."

"After all these centuries, how are we still gonna be exactly half?"

No joking. He was breathing harder. Then he said, "You eat good in Paris?"

"She made it?" Alfonso said near him. "Tell her bring me—what they got in Paris? What I want?"

His voice was expansive, generous. No big deal. We shot somebody and now we're on a road trip. Everyone's on a road trip. It's summer. Not April in Paris. August in Louisiana. Too bad I couldn't bring him a young woman from an outlying Parisian banlieu who wanted someone's hand on the small of her back.

Alfonso said, "Bring us some Chanel. Case we meet some ladies."

Victor whispered, "You know what I'm playing on the iPod? The Stones. You never told me why you hate the Stones." He sang, "'Please allow me to introduce myself, I'm a man of wealth and taste.'"

"I saw the Montesquieu quote. In your notebook."

"You hate the Stones."

"I hate one song. 'Brown Sugar.'"

"Wait—that's what it says on her picture."

"Yeah." I listened to him breathe heavily. "She's right here."

He was quiet for a long time. "Jazen, man, his measure of pleasure is he can read a person in one heartbeat. Like—uh. Remember every name in Rio Seco and every dollar they owe."

"And what about Alfonso?"

"He's just—he's just so pretty, he really wouldn't have to do anything if he had the right woman. But he's so pretty, fools are always steppin to him, or testin him."

"And he's got the gun?"

"Both of em," Victor whispered slowly. "But Fonso do the do, yeah. JZ ain't never shot nobody." Alfonso did the shooting and Jazen always got off, I thought.

"A bullet in your arm." I winced. The soft part. I held up my own arm, bent it, tried to see.

His voice broke. "Makes me real. A real nigga."

We breathed in the quiet.

"Don't go," Victor said. He was close to crying. "When I listened to your messages, it was like talking to you. Like we were in LA. In the kitchen."

My heart pounded against my breastbone again. This was how they got you. Children. They made you feel like no one else in the world would compare. Pure need.

"I'm not going anywhere. I'm in a fancy hotel in Paris," I said. "Marble floors and gold leaf on the chandelier."

But then I heard voices down the hall. The guy said, "You can't just leave it here. That's so irresponsible. It's bad for the carpet. It's how mold develops." He bent to his knees and moved along the floor, scooping up the ice and dumping it into the bucket.

Suddenly I saw *Les Raboteurs de Parquet*. The first print I ever bought. A salon or ballroom with white-and-gold-paneled walls, three men on the wood floor, scraping off the old finish with crude tools. The dark varnish shone in the light of the painting. Like irrigation water. I'd stood there before it. Gustave Caillebotte. The men's arms ropy with muscle, the curled shavings collected in a pile. One man speaking, one listening. A grievance, a woman, a meal.

The man raked his forearm to pile the ice and then pushed it into the plastic bucket. He stood up heavily and looked at me for a long time. I looked away. The door closed.

My hair twirling and waving around my face. My nails longer than usual. Fur and claws. That's what Moinette taught Marie-Therese, who taught her daughter, Anjanae, who told me when I was in Azure. Only difference between humans is fur and claws and skin. Same blood inside.

"I'm a nigger right now," I said to Victor. "A high yellow nigger. Neither fish nor fowl. Quadroon. So what are you?"

"Black cracka." He hesitated. His voice was still slow and syrupy. "Last fall, I was in the quad, and football players come up, and one of em was like, Yo, brotha, you got some shoulders. Why you ain't playin ball? I was like, I'm too busy. And then he started laughin. What's your major and shit? He was a big brotha. Frontin for his boys. I said, English literature and history. Double major. He was like, Oh, you a black cracker?"

The hallway hummed. "A *what*?"

"Brotha was talkin all Alabama or Louisiana, and I bet he was born in Rio Seco."

"Maybe he was Cleveland," I whispered, thinking of Grady trying so hard.

"I was like, You know where the word *cracker* comes from? Being so poor you gotta eat crackers instead of bread."

"Did that work?" I said.

"Mayeli walked up then, and this brotha was like, Ay, shawty, you don't want him—he majorin in English and I already speak that language."

I said, "Gotta give him some."

Victor laughed weakly. "You gotta hear Mayeli. She sounds like she's from England sometimes. She was like, I speak English, too, growin up in Teakettle, speak the King's English, speak Creole. But not cracker, nuh, man." He tried to imitate her Belizean accent, and I laughed, too.

"I can't wait to meet her," I said.

"But you won't. I ain't gon make it back to Cali."

"You're a Picard. I'm an Antoine. You got your grandpère's toughness—that man saved my father's life. And my father'd be pissed off if he heard you."

"He lived by the river. He had a boat," Victor murmured.

"Yeah—you want to talk niggas? Every day, my father and these other men would go to the docks where the oystermen kept their boats, and they'd say, I need one nigger."

"What?"

"The oystermen were guys from Yugoslavia. It was after the war, the 1940s. That's what they said. He told me, Every day he was one nigger.

He shoveled the oysters on deck and loaded them into burlap sacks and then unloaded them at the dock. For four years. And then some old man died, and he didn't have sons, and Papa bought his boat. He'd been saving his money, living with his aunt. It was a little boat, he told us. And on the side, the name was *Anna.* For the dead wife of the old man. My father painted it over and then put *One Nigger.* That's what he named the boat. He knew it would piss everybody off. White or black, they were mad. And he just smiled."

"What happened to the boat?" Victor said, softly. A bedtime story. Nice.

"It's still down there, I guess," I said. "I don't know who has it now. I haven't thought about it for years."

"My treasure," he whispered. "From Lafitte's dude. He was Picard. My moms told me. It's for me. Not you."

"What?"

"I'ma crash now."

What did he mean—I wasn't descended from the pirate? What had Glorette told him?

My father sat on the bed, fully clothed, boots laced loosely. The gun was hidden. The storm whirled on TV.

The knock on the door was gentle, secretive. My father moved only his eyes, so I said, experimentally, "Must be the lady from the front. She was nice."

I went to the peephole—what a strange name to still call it. The husband from down the hall stood there, his head bent so I could see the sunburn inside his part. Seattle. Scalp like pink yarn. He said in a low voice, "Are you free now?" He knocked again, gently, two more times. I stood there, frozen. He whispered, "I'm not interested in the mask. All that."

The mask? Comtesse. "Is it only phone sex?" he whispered. I didn't move—I didn't want him to hear me, inches away. He waited a long time. Then his footsteps receded down the hall.

From his bed, my father said, "Who the hell?" The gun in his right hand, flat on the sheet along his leg.

"He was pretty damn lost," I said. In the stiff sheets which smelled vaguely of smoke, I looked at the ceiling.

SARRAT

WE HEADED EAST. The rising sun like a hot dime on a white sidewalk.

"Mo parle avec t'maman," my father said. He must have called her last night.

"You used the room phone?" I said.

"Call collect. Lady at the front do it."

I pictured everyone last night, putting flowers on Glorette's small gravestone at the chapel, and my mother storming down to Bettina's.

Damn—was it Friday? Rick would try not to be pissed, but pretty soon he had to assign the next two issues. Tony—he was always booked, so his agent was going to move on if I didn't make plans. The Oaxaca piece. It was the 26th—rent was due in a few days. All the things I said to Victor in the hallway felt like bullshit. Like I'd spent the night in a bar, talking to a stranger I wanted to impress.

We crossed the Brazos River. Ruffled, greenish brown, and wide under the bridge near the town of San Felipe. Each small town, then dense woods.

The woods of East Texas. Where something had happened to my father.

I knew we wouldn't stop to get gas or eat anything until Houston, where there were black people.

My father couldn't read, but he knew exactly where to go. He remembered every tree, river, bridge, and silhouette. We got off the freeway, filled up at a station, and sat in a Burger King to eat scrambled eggs and hashbrowns like damp shredded paper. The young woman at the counter was sleepy, her cheeks brown and full, and her straightened hair shiny-slick in ribbon curls. "Y'all drive careful," she said.

Outside Houston, after the suburbs faded into the blinding morning, the woods were dark and dense. We crossed the Trinity River in silence.

I turned on a news station. Hurricane Katrina had finished battering

Florida and headed into the Gulf. Someone made a joke about the alligator still eluding the idiots in his lake in Los Angeles.

"Mr. McQuine," I said. Was he the first man?

My father didn't answer. The man who'd invaded my dreams when I was a child. The heaviness of white flesh suffocating me. A pale blue car with dull chrome teeth that chased me down a road. A boy baby white as coconut flesh, with red hair—because for some reason red hair always scared me—biting me on the shoulder.

Victor had bitten Glorette on the shoulder once, when he was just a year old—red dents on her skin. She'd bitten him back and he howled.

The white baby. The place we were headed.

"Where did they hunt you?" I said finally. "Around here?"

We were approaching Beaumont. "Prè Vidor."

Vidor. Famous in the news for not wanting black residents.

"La-bas—Jasper," he said, lifting his chin north, toward my window.

Jasper. Where a black man had been dragged to pieces, chained to a truck driven by drunken white guys.

The woods were lit by sunlight in places. Lacy green. "You killed someone around here?"

"Non. Not here. Mo tou soule." I was all alone. Then he held up his hands. His wrists were crossed.

It took me a moment to realize what he was showing me. They had hunted him. They had caught him. And he'd been tied.

He said no more.

We drove silently over the Neches River, so wide and deep it must be a hundred of my Santa Ana Rivers. The tamed silver thread near my father's tamed forest. Rows and rows of woods that belonged to him. Where he knew every branch, every row, every fence, every gopher, every intruder.

When we crossed the Sabine, we were in Louisiana.

I didn't remember this—I must have been asleep in the back with Glorette—the deep green of rice farms and cane fields around us, and rolling prairie, and more woods. We went north on a two-lane highway. Lush grass, cattle behind barbed-wire fences, and most of all, the solitary live oaks that stood along the road or in a field. They were so large, their branches wandering so far, that I could find no word to fit them. We'd left the manicured perfection of my father's groves and the shimmering impermanence of the desert's smoke trees and the anonymous dark woods of Texas for oaks that looked as if they'd outlived ten generations of people.

We stopped in Basile near noon, and the heat was like an electric blanket. The gas station had a hand-lettered sign that read BOUDIN and CRACKLIN. The older white man who sat on his porch near the stand was dressed in a plaid sport shirt like the ones I saw on hipsters in Silver Lake; he spat tobacco juice into a can, and two lines of brown ran down the corners of his mouth like a faint tattoo.

Near Eunice, I asked, "What exactly are we doing when we get there?"

But of course he didn't answer that.

He said, "Temp passé, they talk on the radio about the bomb."

The 1950s, I thought.

"Say, how you survive when the bomb fall? How you eat? Them Russians." He bit the insides of his cheeks, so that deep dimples appeared in his face. "Pas bomb here. Sometime it's a man."

The bomb is a man.

A bayou covered with green duckweed vivid as neon. My father's voice came as if from a long way. "And some people—they move toujou and everything is them."

They move forever. Like Arthur Graves. The world swirled around them, contracted close to them, ensured their happiness?

"Jazen. He like that. Make a path." My father shook his head. "But I watch, me. Nobody have to see me."

The fields passed. I could watch all day but I wouldn't know what to do. "Papa, they shot a boy," I said. "Alfonso's done it twice now. He needs to be off the street."

"Oui. He do. He shoot somethin. Jamais *kill*, no." The vein like flattened yarn around his temple. "Kill a pig and do boucherie, then you kill. Take that heart and cut that head. Them boy, they only shoot. Like a game on TV. Shoot from far away."

Grady had killed Sere Dakar up close. With his hands. Someone had killed Glorette up close. With his hands.

"Them three," my father said, and I thought he meant the boys. "I never shoot them, me. Kill them with my hand." He held up his right arm this time. Not tied.

"I know," I said, and he turned to me, surprised. "I heard you and Gustave talk about it one night. On the porch." I didn't want to picture it, but I had. Gustave had said, "You throw that match." The car had burned in a ditch.

After a long time, he blew out a skein of smoke and said, "In Texas, I run wine and rum for someone from Plaquemines. Them sheriff get the liquor from my truck. Mais pas tout. He want laugh. Him and them deputy."

They had tied up my father, somehow, and found something comic. His helplessness?

Then my father said, "Maybe Jazen want laugh, too. Laugh at Victor."

I remembered Opelousas. The town where Moinette bought a brick building, and her son, and then two more daughters. Why did she buy them? I thought again, remembering the bills of sale. Why did she have to *own* the children she'd borne?

Somewhere here, she and Jean-Paul were buried. After he was killed for his defiant smile in a cane field. Only game he know is do or die. Superfly. I wished we could stop, look for their gravestones, see the brick home where she became free. It was a great story. And I'd never written about it.

There was no stone for Fantine. She had died on a plantation somewhere near here, but she probably only had a wooden cross.

Past Opelousas, a flock of egrets rose from a cattle pond like moving origami. Green, white, blue. Everything back home was brown and gold and gray by now. Ahead of us loomed the scary bridge over the Atchafalaya. This I remembered, too, suspended above the wide swath of water.

My father raised his chin. Turn here, he meant.

We went north before the bridge. A two-lane road that followed the levee. Somewhere on this levee, my father and Gustave had huddled against each other for warmth while the dead floated past. All these years, in my version of the story I told myself, the Mississippi River had taken away their mothers. But it was the Atchafalaya, swollen by the rains and the Mississippi overflow.

"Say Atchafalaya so deep, Mississippi fit inside," my father murmured, looking up at the levee. A bank of earth, covered with grass. Just a wide wall.

Now I remembered this winding road, small bayous alongside and a lonely house or two. Baton Rouge was half an hour away east.

There it was. Sarrat Road. The old store on the corner, facing that road, where Glorette and I had bought Cokes every evening after we finished helping my father. Like a shoebox, with the faded rectangular façade and the words SEVEN OAKS in a ghostly outline of capital letters.

The name of the plantation house. Mr. McQuine's house, and his father's before him, and his father's before him. A man sat behind the small counter in front, near the screened case that held candy and the old white cooler that held soda and beer. The first day Glorette and I came in, after we got out of the truck bed and reached into the cooler for Cokes, he went to the window, looked at the license plate, and then narrowed his eyes at us and said, "California niggers, hanh? Look same as Lousana niggers to me."

Nothing but cane. Taller than the car, green walls on either side of us, motionless and fierce in the heat.

"Ratoon," my father said.

The language of Louisiana. Ratoon was second-crop cane, grown from the stubble left in the field from the year before. That summer, Glorette and I had followed the tractor my father drove, laying stalks of seed cane in the furrows like purple-green thighbones.

A grass. From India. All the grasses and weeds I'd hoed out of the irrigation furrows in the orange groves. Johnsongrass, crabgrass. The wild oats I tried to boil and eat one day when I was small.

We were surrounded by a huge weed that Moinette and Fantine had cut with cane knives. My father had cut cane when he was only seven, dragging the stalks to a pile taller than he was. He told us this when we complained in the groves.

After about two miles of cane, we came to Bayou Becasse Road, which ran along the water. Brown-black as tea without milk, the oaks alongside leaching their tannic acid into the water. Glorette and I had been afraid to put our hands in, until my father dropped a string with a tiny piece of old chicken meat and a crawfish grabbed it. By the weekend, we had learned to catch crawfish for etouffee.

The bridge was narrow over the bayou, and then we came to the sheltering oaks that defined Sarrat.

The houses were set back from the road, beyond the ditches, which still held some water from rain. There had been twenty shotgun houses back then, and a barn for the tractor, and a few sheds. Behind the houses were the privies.

Now there were maybe ten houses. One rusted roof lying on a tangle of weeds and branches like a sunken raft. My father leaned forward, squinting at the wooden homes. Four had curtains, and metal chairs on the porches. There were two ancient trailers, robin's-egg blue with rust dripping like fangs from the window corners, and one pale yellow trailer that looked brand-new. They were set sideways on the lots so they matched the long narrow shotgun houses.

"La-bas," my father said, nodding toward the last wooden house at the end. "Henri house. That Claudine uncle." We drove over the ditch and into the yard. An ancient car was behind the house, at the edge of the cane fields, so rusty it looked dipped in chocolate. When I got out of the car, the sun felt as if it would split my skull, and sweat ran between my breasts. A white man opened the door. He looked like Tony Soprano without as much belly.

No Navigator.

They shook hands in the front room, which was sweltering. "Enrique Antoine," the man said. "Seen your picture before. Heard a few things about you. But we ain't never met. Albert."

"You stay with Henri?" my father said, impassive as ever.

"I help him out," Albert said. "And this my cousin? Like Christmas round here, people visitin from California. Except none a y'all ever came at Christmas."

We followed him into the second room, where an ancient man roused himself from his bed, a heap of sheet, his gray head wedged into the far corner. "Take your time, Uncle Henri," Albert said.

In the last room, he pointed to three wooden chairs around the kitchen table, which was pushed against the wall. This house was exactly like the one where Glorette and I had slept with the old woman in the middle room. We had eaten on the back steps because the kitchen was so small.

"They kept him up late last night," Albert said, fanning his fingers over three glossy flyers on the table. "My nephew call hisself takin a break from Cali." My father settled into the chair opposite him. Albert wore a cream-colored guayabera, two crescents of sweat below his chest. A cigar in the pocket. We knew nothing about him except the circumstances of his birth. Not whether he was armed, whether he knew why they were running, or what he knew about us.

"I woke em up early and sent em to Baton Rouge," Albert said. "I got a lil hustle goin, for a video shoot. They can make some cash. Pay Henri some rent, if they plan to crash here, like Alfonso did last time. Everybody gotta have a hustle. Even this place ain't free."

He pushed the flyers over to us. "Call hisself Cane Razor," Albert said. A handsome brown-skinned young man with almond-shaped eyes, lines shaved into his eyebrows and two front teeth edged in gold. He wore a Saints jersey. His head was cocked to the side; in his left hand he held a large handgun, in his right a cane knife polished and shiny.

Cane Razor—Soulja Country.
Video shoot August 26.
canerazor.com
Cash prize for fine ladies.
U No Whut U Got 2 Do.

Soulja—Soldier. I said, "What do they have to do?"

"I met the producer in New Orleans. He wanna do a city soulja versus country soulja thing out here. The girls are free. They gotta look good. Dance. Get up onstage and show—" Albert didn't look like much embarrassed him, but he glanced at me and smiled. "What people wanna see. For the Internet version. You got dirty and you got clean."

Great. "And the guys?"

"Get paid three hundred dollars for the shoot. They said they can rap."

I said, "My godson's got college. Back in California. He wants off this ride."

"They'll be back tonight." He looked at my father and then at me again. "I checked out LA few times. California ain't nothin special." He grinned. Albert—what was his last name? Not McQuine. Claudine's son. Did he know what my father had done?

He knew. Albert was all about knowing.

"How you make it?" my father said to Albert.

"Do what come natural." He grinned. Old school. "I'm bringin some props to the shoot. Had big money last year, takin cars to Vegas. Got all these old cars in the fields, in people yards. Chevys, like '56s and '57s. Them Mescan guys in Vegas was crazy, they wanted them cars so bad. Ain't hardly no old cars left in California. I bought the cars off old people, got my friend to hook em up on a trailer, and we took about ten of em out there. Then the Mescans started fightin with some black gang, and I ain't been out there for a while." He shrugged. "They thought I was Italian. But they seen the brothas drivin with me. That was that."

The old man called, "Enrique? Enrique?"

My father got up and went into the bedroom, and they spoke in low French.

Passe blanc. Albert's goatee was brown, the hair straight and fine as a boar-bristle paintbrush. The hair on his head was sparse and combed back. It was the faint rosy pink in his skin. Like Bettina, and her mother, Claudine. He looked straight at me. "I guess you done did Italian, too. Somebody told me you call yourself whatever you want."

"Who?"

He shrugged. He bent forward and said softly, "That boy stay outside in the car and Alfonso said, 'He talkin to his marraine. She in Paris.'"

"Came back early," I said. No way of knowing whether I could tell him about the bullet. Maybe Alfonso had said Victor was the shooter. "Where's the video filming?"

"They checkin locations. It ain't till later, cause the light too harsh in the day, you know? The crew came up from New Orleans. Gotta be that kinda gold light. Say that make their boy look good."

"Who is this kid?"

"Lady used to live down the way. That's her son. But Alfonso look good. They gon use him onstage. And the other one—he ain't said much. Tryin so hard to be gangsta. The light one slept in the car. They said he was drunk. Ain't seen him all night."

His eyes were gray-green as shallow water over cement. Victor was drunk? On the purple stuff? Or passed out from pain?

"Victor—that Anjolie grandson," Uncle Henri said, coming into the kitchen. He had combed his hair and changed his shirt. He had to have been a few years older than my father, but he gave me a strong hug with those thin arms, and he smelled of Vicks.

"Well, Michelle's daughter was sittin in the car with him, so he must got some play," Albert said. "I'ma heat up the catfish she brought."

"Who?" I said.

"Michelle Meraux. Live down there. She cook for Henri every other day."

Henri smiled, his eyes webbed with that ghostly blue of old age, his teeth outlined in gold. Just like Cane Razor. And Henri's cane knife was still in its place on the wall, by the back door. Clotted with sap, unsharpened, the hook like an eyelash.

I wasn't about to eat some of his catfish, since he only had three pieces. The kitchen was a two-burner stove on a counter. I looked in the cupboard, which was the old white-painted metal kind, but the only things inside were a bag of rice, one of grits, and some sugar. The thought of cooking anything, even turning on the burners in this stifling heat, made me dizzy. "I need some coffee," I said.

"Not less you goin to Baton Rouge or back to Krotz Springs," Albert said. "Ten miles. My car down at the barn. Keith putting some oil in. Keith and his brother the only one workin cane. That big company bought all the land about twenty years ago."

Henri said softly, "Cane all the way to the back do. Your house fall down, they plant cane over you."

Albert said, "Michelle cookin jambalaya today. She always got coffee. Tell her I'm goin to the store tonight for coffee and butter and whatever she want."

When I went to the front room, my father was sound asleep in the easy chair. He wore just his white V-neck T-shirt, his skin tanned at the neck. He had taken off his boots. His feet were long and pale. He never wore sandals. His toes were so defenseless next to the duffel bag that I felt a frightened pang in my chest. His head dropped onto his chest. He had been sitting up, dozing, waiting, all his life. All these nights. Now he felt like he was safe—here.

In the bedroom, one suit and three shirts hung in an old wooden armoire whose door was swung open. There was only a picture of Jesus, his face alight, his hands raised, on the wall.

In the kitchen, Albert put his plate in the metal sink. There was one wooden shelf nailed to the wall, with tins of pepper, Creole seasoning, salt, and Red Rooster hot sauce like a little skyline. The old wallpaper was tiny flowers.

A door off the kitchen—a tarpaper-framed addition that must be the bathroom. At the back door, I stood on the three wooden steps and looked out at the cane fields. A row of oaks in the far distance, on a small rise. The privy out the back of the house next door, and two more after that collapsed.

Which house had Glorette and I slept in, that August? The big pecan tree in the back.

It was gone. The yellow trailer had taken its place.

Albert stood behind me. "You off work? On vacation?"

I nodded. "Yeah."

His eyes glinted like bottle glass in the shaded doorway. "Michelle probably know where Alfonso and them went. He took her daughter to help him find pretty faces."

More likely pretty butts, if it was a video. "Meraux? Alfonso's twins—their mama's a Meraux."

"Michelle's niece. She stay over in Bayou Becasse. Where I got my house." He pointed out the window. "We bought ours the same time three years ago. She got the yellow house. We bought em brand-new from this guy I know."

"The trailer?"

"The way you say it." He grinned again. "Where you from?"

"LA."

"Oh, yeah, ain't no manufactured homes there. Out there, y'all call it trailer trash. White trash. But you ain't got black trash. Just niggas. Niggas is niggas. Ain't no need to add nothin else, right?"

"Nobody said the word *trash*." He stood right behind me now, his breath wafting over my shoulder. I went down the steps into the yard. The heat seemed to boil out of the cane in waves, and the patch of

Saint Augustine grass was spongy under my feet. Someone had cut it recently.

"Your maman Marie-Claire?" Henri asked from behind us. He stood in the doorway, bent slightly to the left, his eyes scanning the sky. His voice was clipped and French, like my father's. "Marie-Claire cook every day," he told Albert. "Right there where the house fell. That where we eat, when we come in from the field. She make a gumbo, chicken stew, biscuit, rice. Praline in the fall. Coffee. Get a plate every night twenty cent, fifty cent. No need to cook." He put his hand over his eyes like a brown visor, and then he pointed at the empty yard next door. "That house finis—1995. Marie-Claire, they taken her to California, and jamais see her maman before she die."

Right here. My mother used to sit on wooden steps right here and sort through pounds of rice, pick out the stems and pebbles. There was only a chimney left, a tangle of vines tight around the brick, and a few depressions in the soil. Someone weed-wacked the brush to keep it clean. Because of Mr. McQuine, she never saw her mother again.

I looked back at Henri's house. Was he still working cane when we came that summer? All I remembered was a sea of older faces every night. They all spoke French too fast for Glorette and me. We made up our own language. We'd seen my brothers and Bettina dancing and playing their music at the barn. "Your Love Is Like the Holy Ghost," we laughed. That old Bar-Kays song. "The antidote to fill my soul." We rolled our eyes at the things my brothers said on the phone to Westside girls. "You fine as wine and just my kind. Wait for me after practice. I swear, you killin me."

In the fields, picking up the cane from the flatbed truck, we got through the heat and dust by pretending to be Marvin Gaye. "'How could you be so cruel? Oh, baby—please, darlin, come back—home!'" At the end of a row, we threw water on each other like we'd fainted onstage.

The wooden boards of Henri's house were pearly gray, and with the rusted car, the chinaberry tree, and the old privy, it looked like a Walker Evans photo. What if I'd been born here? I'd been to Charleston—the narrow sideways houses, slave quarters behind. I'd seen tabby houses, slave quarters near Fernandina, Florida. The walls glinting with bits of shell. Once in Virginia, somewhere outside Richmond, I was on a tour bus and someone whispered, "My grandmother used to call that place a breed farm. Raise babies there." It was a rainy, dark day, and the trees were bare and black, the wooden buildings dim and overgrown from the road.

I walked down the road toward the yellow trailer.

The front door was set squarely in the center above wooden steps. A woman opened it. Red-gold hair cut to the scalp and pressed in perfect waves like lace, brown-gold skin and three small moles under her left eye. Two lines on her throat. She was a few years younger than me. She folded her arms and said, "Don't tell me Albert got him a new girl-friend. Who you supposed to be?"

"Fantine," I said. Not FX and not Antoine, because what if she knew about Mr. McQuine?

"You from California, too?"

"Too?"

"Them boys—all that gangsta rap," she said, her face impassive. "Come from LA. I'm tired of it. But my daughter went off with one of em couple hours ago. Took my car."

This heat swarmed like wasps down my shirt, into my throat every time I breathed. "Which one?"

"The one with the cut arm." She studied my blouse from Oaxaca, my too-long jeans and the sandals. "Alfonso just a grinnin fool. Last time he came here, five years ago, he had shot someone and he was runnin. He stayed with my niece and got twins. I don't know what he up to this time. But the light one—he was shady. He didn't want to get out the car. Somethin wrong with him."

"You don't know where they went?" Immediately, I knew it was the wrong thing to say. Her daughter was with them. Now I'd questioned her discipline. Her face closed even further, her chin lifted till I saw the gleam of sweat on her neck.

"So you from LA? Or New Orleans? You with these video people?"

My phone rang, and then died quickly. Tony.

"This ain't the city. Service messed up here. You gotta go up to that headland road, you want to talk to some rap star," she said, and closed the door in my face.

The cane was about eight feet tall. On the narrow service road, the stalks came right up to the dirt. Each row was tightly jammed together, like ratoon cane grew because it had had all year to develop roots. The tops were green and lush, the bottoms already shaggy and brown. Gustave used to have his own sugarcane patch at home—he felled one stalk with a machete and slashed off the leaves in movements so quick Glorette and I couldn't even see, and then sectioned it into cylinders for us to suck out the sweet juice.

I heard birds, and a very faint rumble of someone driving a tractor maybe a mile away. The tall grass from India that had traveled here on a ship and then been turned into white crystals. It rustled. Always. Even in the stillness of this heat.

I walked blindly. The lush green explosions of orange trees, painted on the crates and labels and in the galleries. The women tying sheaves of wheat in France. The gleaners, following the potato harvest in England. The women carrying baskets of peppers on their heads down the mountain trails of Bolivia. Glorette and me, holding the cut cane like batons. And from each joint, a twelve-foot stalk of grass. Cut it down, burn off the leaves, grind out the juice, boil it for hours, to get a white crystal. Sparkling. A cube, in a glass saucer, on a marble table in Paris.

My phone came back on. It was nearly two. I reached the headland road, where the trucks would park to collect the cane when the harvest began. This road was wide and high, winding through the fields and out onto the highway. From here, I could see two roofs in Sarrat, floating just past the green.

My mother—what must she have thought, weeding in the windy aisles between orange trees behind my father, remembering this solid wall of whispering, slashing grass?

All the splinters she had removed. And one night, she'd sewn up Claudine's arm.

Claudine—face impassive if we dared to knock on her door, her arms folded. The right one with two long scars, satin-shiny and keloid-raised, across the soft underside.

"Did she try to kill herself?" I asked my mother before I went to bed one night.

My mother was washing out coffee cups. Her face was incredulous. "Heh?"

"Cut her wrist like that. After she had the baby?"

My mother turned toward me, furious. "She cut that arm break into a car. Some boyfriend in San Bernardino and he take her radio. She break a window." My mother bent her head over the sink again. "You always make up some story. Some romantic story. Nobody kill they own self."

I walked toward the single huge oak tree on the headland road and called Clarette, even though she'd be at work. She was the only one who might understand.

"You know I don't normally have my phone on," she said. "But I'm in the office doin paperwork on a fight. Just like the fights Alfonso got in." She sighed. "Where are you? Y'all find them?"

"We're in Sarrat. Louisiana. Where everybody was born."

"Oh, shit. What are they doin there?"

"Apparently trying to avoid coming back to see you," I said. "At the prison." No shade. It was too far to the oak tree. I turned around, and could see nothing but the sun.

"Don't tell me that," Clarette said, and her voice broke.

"You okay?"

"You know what? I'm tired today. All this stuff I'm doing—piano and book fair and tutoring—what if it doesn't matter at all? What if Rey Jr. decides it's more fun to hang out with Bettina's boys? Cause they havin a ball at your maman's."

I felt light-headed. Shade. I pushed into the row of cane. Shade down the tunnel. I was a rustle, an animal. "I'm the last person to ask," I said. "I don't know shit."

Clarette said, "I should have taken Victor in. But I didn't have kids, when he was little, and then I just concentrated on my own. I feel so guilty—"

"I could've done it, Clarette," I said. The stalks slid over me as I ducked. Glorette and I, hiding from each other. "I was—"

"Nobody expected *you* to do it," she said, dismissively. Me. The selfish travel writer. The bagavond. Shame bloomed hotter inside me. Clarette said, "Just a minute," and then a man said, "You done? They got both of em in holding."

Clarette was facing hundreds of prisoners, and I was whining. "You have to go," I said. "I'll call you back."

But what would I say? I stood still in the cane for a moment. Nobody expected *you* to do it.

I walked back toward the houses. Glorette. I pushed my way down the row of cane behind her and she laughed. Two little animals in the forest. We ran to the gallery and some man was there, delivering something from a truck. He said, "That the one? Anjolie girl?" and the people turned to look at Glorette. He said, "Damn." She froze like a cartoon girl, and I saw what they saw. The heart-shaped face, the huge pansy eyes, the hair in two braids to her waist.

And she turned back toward me—the invisible one, a blurry golden cipher—before she disappeared again into the field.

At the edge of Michelle Meraux's yard, I stopped to wipe the sweat out of my eyes with my sleeve. The embroidered flowers like little knots. She came out of her door and crossed the lawn. "You okay?" she called.

She curved up her lips, just a little. Her lip gloss was pale brown. She was small, like me, but she had a butt when she turned to glance at the trailer. She wore faded pink capris, and then I noticed wet white circles on her knees. "I just did the floor," she said.

"Gotta use the brush," I said. "That's what my maman made me do."

"My daughter won't do it," she said, and suddenly her voice was full of despair. "I tell her to do the floor while I'm at work, and she takes that Swiffer across the linoleum like it means something."

My mother's scrub brush was plastic now, but I still remembered the smell of the wooden one, the straw bristles.

"She just called. She's with those boys in Baton Rouge. Said the one got himself a crazy name was lookin for some paper he dropped in the yard." She held up a small note.

"Victor?"

"No. Scholastic something." She held up the paper. "Wait—that one your son?"

"Yes," I said. "I came to take him home."

And for the first time, it was easy to say. I could see it. A daybed for Victor to replace the low-slung Indonesian chair. A desk instead of the table that held his mother's picture.

She put the note on my palm. I turned to the circle of shade under the chinaberry tree to focus on the small writing. A receipt from Burger King. From last night.

I balanced all, brought all to mind
The years to come seemed waste of breath,

A waste of breath the years behind
In balance with this life, this death.

Who was that? Tennyson?

I had just talked to him last night. He hadn't wanted to kill himself. *If I live, one more thing. Bassi. Indian music and American rappers.*

I felt a sharp sting on my ankle. Then I was standing in flame. A burning like I'd never felt in my life. I screamed and looked down. Tiny ants boiled over my feet as if the earth had erupted, hundreds of them. I screamed and ran.

"No! No!" Michelle yelled at me. "Come here!"

She pointed at my feet and said, "Take off your pants! Now!"

The fire engulfed my legs. I unzipped the jeans and pulled them down, and two ants were on my forearms, biting instantly. I threw the inside-out jeans away from me, and stood in my underwear. Michelle took off her sandal and scraped hard, wiping the ants from my calves and feet. "You gotta unlock their jaws," she said, while I sobbed. My blood was on fire. I fell again, and she pulled me up roughly.

"Get inside," she said. "Stop screamin before somebody call the cops. Albert probably over there laughin right now."

In a bathtub, she poured bleach and water over my legs. The bites were everywhere on my feet, my ankles, my calves, two on my thighs, two on my forearm. Like red sequins. I'd never felt pain like this in my life. The bleach fumes rose into my eyes. Red and white and then black.

I hit my head on the side of the tub.

Michelle's voice was vague and her fingers hard as pliers on my wrists. She said, "You gon faint like some old lady? You ain't gonna die. Here. Put this on your face."

A wet cloth scented with lavender soap.

"Why you wearin jeans anyway?"

"That's all I ever wear."

"Why? Where you work?"

The bleach and water once more. The pain throbbed. Not fire. Like my legs were swelling, like I was rising up to the ceiling on waves of itch already so intense that every nerve opened. Anemones of itch.

"No. Don't touch anything. Put your hands on the side of the tub. I'll be right back. Good thing I was cookin today."

The tub was huge. An old white-enamel clawfoot tub, with silver taps across from my decorated feet. My blouse and jeans outside in the grass. My nephew's tank top soaking wet, my gray underwear spotted with white from the bleach.

Someone knocked on the door, and she said something, and they laughed. Albert? Then a car drove away.

Michelle came in with a blue plastic bowl. "I can't really let you lay on my bed, not like that, so you gon have to stay in the tub for a while." She put slices of white onion on my legs and ankles. They were like discs, sliding off, so she tied dish towels around them to hold the onion tight to the skin. One slice on my arm, which I held like a compress.

She sat in a wicker chair beside the door. "Thanks," I said.

"I'm sorry, but that's the funniest thing I ever seen in my life. If I had Danita's new camera, I woulda taken a video. So you could see it." She started laughing, her earrings swaying. "Albert said look like you did the Funky Chicken mixed with the Freak."

"I've never felt anything like that."

She sighed. "Hope you ain't allergic." She crossed her legs. "I better stay here."

"This is the prettiest tub I've ever seen," I said. "Like a fancy hotel."

She raised her eyebrows. "I got it from the lady I take care of. From her uncle's house. We had to put in one of them sit-down showers."

I leaned my head back on the cool rim. Her air conditioner was working hard, moisture collecting on the bathroom window like dew.

Michelle said, "Look at this. Friday afternoon. When I got this tub, I was picturing some fine man layin up in here. And instead I got you."

I would have laughed, too, if my legs weren't boiling with fire ant venom.

Then her face closed again. "But you probably got all kinda men out there in LA."

"Nope. Nobody worth a tub like this."

She said, "I gotta finish this jambalaya. Get some over to Henri. Then I gotta figure out where my daughter went. With your son." Her voice was guarded. "I worked six-to-six last night. Come home this morning and she's tellin me, 'I ain't never met no one like that.' Starry-eyed shit."

"What?"

"She was sittin up in the car with him for hours. Talkin."

I had to be careful. "He's not a rapper. He's in college."

"Danita's in college, too. Nursing school in Baton Rouge," she said. Her lips folded in on themselves twice, while she thought. "And he rode in with Alfonso. What's wrong with his arm?"

I closed my eyes. The bullet. No. "He's been riding with his cousin, and you apparently know what Alfonso's like. I came to take Victor back to California. He doesn't need to be with them."

"Yeah. Neither does Danita. But she called about two hours ago, and she ain't answered her phone since. She got my car, and I gotta be at work before five." She looked at her phone and put it in her pocket. She imitated her daughter. "'Mama, I ain't never met nobody like him.' I knew I'd have to hear that someday, but I didn't want to hear it today."

"I have my car. As soon as I take these off and get dressed—" The whole bathroom smelled like a New York hot dog stand.

"Them jeans outside covered with ants?" She shook her head and laughed one more time. "Damn, that was funny. I'll get you somethin to wear. And some Benadryl."

The huge skillet of jambalaya was nearly done, low flame popping blue under the cast iron. The apricot linoleum was new—remnants of her wash water trembling in one of the seams near my foot.

In the front room was a living room set, and in the corner was a desk unit with a computer set into a hutch. "That's where Danita spend all her time," she said. "She don't even hardly watch TV now. She was on there this morning, when I went to bed, lookin up this rapper. They got MySpace and YouTube and I don't know what. I try to keep a eye out, but I work all night." She turned to me. "He probably do all that MySpace too."

The lie went like fishing wire around my throat. Victor didn't even have what her daughter had, living out in the middle of the cane fields in rural Louisiana, with a mother who worked all night. Victor had nothing. I'd given him nothing.

"You want some coffee?" She poured me a cup. Community Coffee. The best coffee I'd ever had, except my mother's. She held her cell phone to her ear and said, "You ain't answering. It's been three hours. My car. You got that? My car. You better come to your senses."

She sat on the couch, her eyes narrowed. "Why you haven't called your son?"

His phone didn't even ring. I said to voicemail, "Victor. I'm here in Sarrat. With Danita's mama. And you better call me."

She sighed so deeply it was as if she shrank. "Why she like this one? What's so special about him?" Her arms were folded.

"He's so smart," I said, and then I started to cry.

She said, "He so smart, why he ridin with Alfonso?" Then she pushed herself up from the couch. "Smart, foolish, whatever. I gotta get to work. Dumb old folks like me gotta pay for everything."

I wiped my eyes and looked at the cane outside the window.

She came back from her bedroom wearing a nursing uniform—light blue pants and a blue smock with yellow sunflowers. She held up a pink sundress for me—that crinkly cotton which never got wrinkled because it was always wrinkled.

"Damn, you pale," she said, looking at my legs. "But you got muscles."

"I walk a lot." I slipped the dress over my head, and she handed me fresh underwear. Also pink.

"Walkin in the cane. If you ever worked in there, you wouldn't want to walk in it."

She had no idea who I was. I held out my arms, but the scars were so faded, and I was so pale from Switzerland, that she probably couldn't see what they were. I said, "I worked cane here one summer. That was enough."

Then she nodded. "I don't even chew on it, during grinding," she said. "I just get my sugar at the store."

The jambalaya was spicy, full of andouille sausage, shrimp, and chicken. Peppers, onions, and celery. She handed me a plate, but she said, "I eat mine later. Can't eat right after I cook." She filled three large plastic containers, snapped on the covers.

We took the bowl, a metal coffeepot filled with coffee, and a loaf of white bread down the road. I watched the grass and dirt carefully, expecting to see a huge mound where the fire ants lived. I wished I could have covered my legs—they were slathered in Benadryl, and stunk of onions, and still they pulsated with heat and itch.

Michelle pointed to a grayish bare spot in the grass where my mother's house had been—"See? Ants. I'll tell Albert to put the poison on em. He has to do it every week, and they come right back. Them and the roaches—once we all gone, they'll still be here. And the termites eatin up New Orleans."

Albert wasn't inside Henri's house. Neither was my father.

Henri sat in the recliner, with a fan blowing the air so hard that his hair waved gently. The TV was on, but he faced the window and the road. A violin lay on the couch.

"Albert and Enrique venez a Baton Rouge. Get some truck." He smiled at me. "Mo pas travai vec no engine."

"Why they need a truck?" Michelle asked, bringing him a plate of jambalaya.

He shrugged. In the kitchen, she said, "After he eat, he'll sleep. Naptime at the daycare. Same where I work, bout this time. Then they stay up late, watchin TV."

My father and Albert on the road. She saw the flyers on the table and said, "This where she went? 'U Know Whut U Got 2 Do'? She ain't that foolish." She glanced at her phone again. "She got about a hour before I tear her up."

I was maybe a few minutes away from seeing Victor. From figuring out how to get him in the car. If he was with Danita, maybe it would be easy.

It sounded like she'd fallen hard. For my son.

Michelle drove the Corsica. My legs throbbed so hard I couldn't think. She said, "If they lookin for pretty girls, maybe she went to her cousins."

I couldn't ask her about Danita's father. Then she'd ask about Victor's.

We drove along Bayou Becasse Road for about three more miles. I said, "Albert's got a lot going on."

"Albert come and go. But he's good. He watches Henri for a little while every day, and at night, he checks in on Danita, till I get home."

She turned down a road and in to another collection of old houses and trailers. Michelle said, "Hold up," and ran into a wooden house with a new tin roof and pepper plants around the porch. A heavy woman wearing a black tank top and black shorts came outside behind her, peered at me, and said something to Michelle. Then she reached up and ran her fingers along Michelle's forehead, pushing the baby-hair waves into place.

"My cousin," Michelle said, back in the car. "She just did my hair yesterday. She said she ain't seen em."

We drove along Bayou Becasse Road until we came to a clearing. A huge weathered house, with blank eyes of empty dormer windows above the long porch railing, and dead vines twined around the pillars like something out of Sleeping Beauty. No old rusted car. No one. I turned to look back.

"Seven Oaks," Michelle said, frowning. "I thought you been here before?"

"I never saw it."

"Lady I watch used to live there. After her uncle died. Say somebody killed him. Everybody round here used to work his fields, and after he was gone, somebody else bought the land. They had to get off."

"Get off?"

She pointed down another narrow road. "Used to be houses back there, too. Seven Oaks people. But somebody from Baton Rouge owns all this now. Plowed over the houses and the graveyard. Planted cane. Before I was born—my maman told me."

Did my father know? He knew. It didn't matter. He was saving my mother. And Glorette's mother.

"Where's your maman?" I asked.

"She fell asleep drivin home from New Orleans one night. Partyin down there for Mardi Gras and drove into a tree. Ten years ago."

"I'm sorry."

"Thank you."

At a brick ranch house, a young woman answered the door. She had a flyer, which someone had handed out at the community college in

Baton Rouge. Cane Razor. The website address. I said, "Damn, we could have looked it up on your computer. Maybe it would have said where they were meeting. Is there an Internet café around here?"

"Are you crazy?" She shrugged. "If they in Baton Rouge, we gotta go back down to the highway. No bridge over here."

"Albert doesn't have a phone?"

"He's outta minutes."

We drove in silence until she pulled into a wooden grocery store that said PAT'S PLACE.

"I need some aspirin." Michelle rested her forehead on the steering wheel.

Under an ancient fan, a white woman said, "Quo fa, Michelle?" Just like my mother.

"That girl, Miss Pat," Michelle said.

Miss Pat shook her head and said, "Twenty like kindergarten now, oui? Thirty they still live at home. What y'all want?"

"Oyster po-boy for Miss Titine. She was sick last night, but she's workin today." The woman nodded at me. "This Fantine. She from California."

The woman handed the wrapped po-boy to Michelle. "How Miss Irma?"

"Turn ninety in September," Michelle said. "She got her shows."

We drove back along the river, and she turned on another state road. "Palmetto down there a ways." I was completely lost.

My father had never mentioned a Miss McQuine.

A brick ranch house stood behind a circular dirt driveway. She stopped the engine and looked at me. "So he smart, huh?"

"He graduated from community college with honors. He's going to USC. Next year."

She looked out the windshield. She thought her daughter was in love, just like that.

I looked straight ahead as well, at the oak tree near the house, branches spreading like black rivers in the air. "He wants to be a music writer. That's why he knows so much about rap. But he's not a gangster." I rubbed sweat from my eyes.

"A writer." She gave me a look. "Danita said they went to get tattoos. But your son said he already had tattoos where no one could see em and he didn't need any more."

———

Tattoos? I was still trying to figure that out, and just inside the door was Miss McQuine. She sat folded into her recliner like a flattened paper doll, but her breasts still rose and fell under her knit dress with each breath. She had to be his niece—Mr. McQuine. The living room was dim and cool, the cream-colored drapes drawn over the big picture window, and the old TV in the corner was like a blue fire. Her hair was cotton candy. She smiled at me and Michelle, her eyes black under long soft eyelashes. "You a new girl?" she said. "What a bright dress!"

Michelle said, "She just dropping me off, Miss Irma. This is Fantine."

I said, "Nice to meet you, Miss McQuine." Not, "Do you remember my father?"

She pulled me toward the chair. Her hand was hard and small. "You can stay a while," she said. "The news comes on after *Ellen.*"

"She cain't stay, Miss Irma," said another woman, coming out of the kitchen. "County don't low no guest. You know that." Michelle was bent near the walker, which stood by the recliner. I imagined her here last night for twelve hours, with no one but the tiny woman and the television.

"You put some WD-40 on that wheel so it stop squeakin?" Michelle murmured.

I slid my hand from the cool dry palm of Miss Irma. The other woman took the bowl of jambalaya from Michelle and said, "She taken her medicine."

We followed her into the kitchen. "You must be Titine," I said. She nodded and sat down at the Formica kitchen table to unwrap the po-boy. She was about fifty, with large flat brown arms in the short-sleeved green uniform. A white silky headscarf. She said, "Thanks, baby," to Michelle. "For workin last night."

"I got you," Michelle said, going to the sink.

My phone rang. "We got service here," Michelle said, while I struggled to get the phone from my bag.

"I'm sorry, Tony!" I said, and both women grinned and shook their heads.

I ducked into the doorway, but the old woman smiled at me, and so I wheeled around to the hallway.

"Uh-huh. That must be her husband," I heard Michelle say, and I

wish I could have laughed, but the sound of Tony's voice made everything worse—the bites on my legs, my headache, the endless worrying
about Victor. I was standing in a dark hallway with wood paneling and
old black-and-white photos and murky carpet.

"You just fucking disappeared, FX," he said. "Where the hell are
you?"

"Louisiana. I'm not in a town, or a village, so don't even ask where.
I'm in the middle of a cane field."

He was still pissed. He said, "What the hell's going on? I've been trying to call you and you don't pick up."

Muted noises floated down the hallway, and I saw faces above me. A
photo of Mr. McQuine. It was him. In a suit. A huge man with black
hair combed back from a square forehead. Fleshy lips and perfect
teeth. In front of a white pillar. A porch. With a tiny woman. Miss
Irma. I started to cry.

"I got bit by ants. My nephew has a bullet in his arm," I said through
my tears. "I wish we were in Naples."

I ducked my head and moved away from the photos above me.

He heard me crying. "I'm supposed to be shooting in Palm Springs.
But how close are you to New Orleans? I'm getting a ticket right
now." The soft hollow clicking of laptop keys. "Can you e-mail me your
hotel?"

"I have no hotel. No e-mail. Nothing. I'm about two hours from New
Orleans."

"Wait," he said. "There's a hurricane circling out in the Gulf." More
clicking. "They can't tell the path yet. Okay—got a flight. I'll be there
tomorrow around four. This is enough mysterious crazy shit."

I said, "Tony, there's nothing you can do."

"Always something. Never nothing."

I said, "Tony—" I wanted him to say, "I got you. I *got* you." Like my
brothers. Like Michelle had just said.

"Shut up," he said. "Don't say you love me. Because you've seen the
whole New Orleans scene, so you know how much I hate it."

"I've never been to New Orleans."

"We did that piece about five years ago."

I wouldn't look at anything in the hall but my toes. "No. You have,
but I've never been."

"Look, I'll call you as soon as I get there."

"You in trouble now," Michelle said, but her voice had gone detached. She thought I was married. Whole different story.

"That's a friend," I said. "From work. He's worried because I hadn't called him."

"Your son's daddy?"

I shook my head, and she smiled.

"You want some coffee before Danita get here? Miss Irma always has fresh coffee at six when we change shift so I'm fixin to make some."

Titine said, "Lemme get the paperwork."

They sat down at the table to mark off boxes on a form. The coffee smell filled the kitchen. I stood in the doorway. Titine said, "She didn't want me to do her hair. She want you."

The hair was soft and white. How did Michelle do anything with it? "She got her appointment tomorrow at the beauty parlor."

Parlor? Maybe it was because women in the past had their hair done in someone's house. "Once we braided it," Michelle said to me.

I was startled, imagining cornrows radiating from the pale forehead. Miss Irma called to my shadow, "They got dancing on *Ellen*!"

"Two braids around the top, like the old days."

Two braids of white. Twenty braids of black. Same movements of finger and wrist.

Michelle's phone rang on the table. "Let me put this girl on speakerphone so we can finish up." She pushed a button and said, "You better be here in five minutes."

"Mama!" her daughter said. Voice low and scared. "I didn't know they had guns."

"Get outta there," Michelle said, standing up.

"I can't," she whispered. "I'm right next to the stage. The car's blocked in here. I can't get out. And Scholaptitude's friends got guns, too."

"Danita," her mother hissed. "Where the hell are you?"

"Past Highway 77 is Maringouin Road," Michelle said. "About fifteen miles."

I drove as fast as I could on the winding river road along the levee,

back to the highway, and took the narrow road that followed along
Bayou Maringouin, through another forest of endless cane. Maringouin—a place named for a mosquito, my father told me years ago.

A black Hummer raced up ahead of us and turned down a side road
into the cane. Then a van with VIP Productions painted on the side. A
cloud of dust rose from a place in the fields. Three motorcycles—red
and yellow and black—sped around the corner of a clearing, and
Michelle said, "Right there."

An abandoned set of buildings. An old cane mill with cars and trucks
everywhere in the weedy lot. We had to park at the edge of a field, my
tires slipping in the loose dirt near a cane row. Then another clearing in
the cane, and a rough stage set up in the distance. Soda cans and big
white go-cups everywhere on the ground. Music thumping from the
speakers—a stuttering drumbeat, staccato handclaps, and a deep
hoarse voice shouting, "Cut em down! The choppa or the chete! Cut em
down! The Benz or the Chevy! Cut em down!"

We threaded our way through the maze of cars. On one side, the
three motorcycles were doing doughnuts in the dust, while a cameraman filmed them. There were young girls dancing everywhere, like
they'd taken some drug that made them stand slightly bent, their feet
planted, while their breasts and butts shook and bounced as if electrified. A white cameraman with a brown braid down his back was roam-
ing around filming the girls dancing, close-ups of their behinds. He
zoomed in on a girl in short shorts—the long lens like a wasp getting
ready to land.

"What the hell?" Michelle said, shading her eyes, trying to look for
Danita.

At the edge of the field was an ancient pale blue truck, and Albert
stood beside it while another man leaned into the open hood. Then he
slammed down the hood and brushed off his hands. It was my father.
Five girls jumped into the truck bed and started shaking as well. They
wore bikini tops and cutoffs, and another cameraman moved quickly
to film them.

No Danita. We pushed closer to the stage. The speakers were like
black refrigerators. Maybe she was behind one of them. We were still
twenty bodies away, but I could see three young men in black Saints
jerseys now. Cane Razor held up his hands. "The choppa or the chete—
cut em down!" he was rapping in his deep hollow growl. Four girls

danced beside him, and six huge men wearing jerseys swayed behind him. He held up the shiny cane knife and a black automatic weapon. "The Benz or the Chevy—cut em down! Azz from the country or azz from the city—light skin sista or a black Nefertiti!"

Another cameraman was set up just before the stage, head bent to his equipment. "Wobble for me! You got to wobble for Cane!" the words boomed. "Walk it like a model. Walk it like a dog! Back that country azz up now and make me crazy!" The crowd screamed.

Michelle said, "There. She's over there."

She pushed toward the right side of the stage, where all the production people were gathered. We swerved through the girls, their faces private, concentrating, their elbows hitting me in the sides, and then two huge security guards stood at the side of the platform. "That's my daughter," Michelle screamed at them, pointing to a girl in the crowd at the edge of the stage, holding a small camera.

"Did you sign a release?" one shouted back.

"What?"

"Everybody up there got a signed release. You gotta get back, mamas," he said, folding his arms. We were dismissed.

I pulled an old press pass out of my purse. *LA Times,* I said. "I'm covering this for the paper." He looked momentarily confused, so I grabbed Michelle's arm and pushed around the edge of the stage. Three vans with open doors and equipment, men wearing headphones and baseball caps and T-shirts.

Up onstage, Jazen stood beside a speaker. His Raiders cap and jersey. Then a white man said, "Where's the LA guys? What—it's a West Coast versus Dirty South thing?"

Another guy said, "The bullet's in his arm, I guess. Not even the bicep."

"If it's the chest or back, yeah, that works, but—"

A young black guy said, "How the hell I know what's under the bandanna?" His voice sounded New York.

I heard Victor's voice. I couldn't see him. Then I saw another guy sitting at a table with a monitor. Victor's face. He said, "Elbow ain't sexy. Fonso got the chest, but he been in prison. Time on his hands. I had time on my side."

A girl said, "Don't untie it! It has to stay on to work."

"Danita!" Michelle tried to move toward the stage.

Cane Razor shouted, "Got some Cali souljas up here! LA gon see if the country azz stack up! Oh, yeah, we got it down here!"

Then Alfonso and Victor moved onto the stage from behind the speakers. Alfonso was shirtless, and he yelled, "Oh, yeah!" When he flexed his muscles, the women in the field screamed loudly, and a girl shouted out, "Cali fine!"

They were about twenty feet from us. Victor wore a white tank top and huge jeans. He looked high as hell. Someone onstage said, "Scholaptitude—tell em."

Victor had a microphone. He held the injured arm up like a flag, and winced. "Was a long ride," he said, deadpan. "From the Westside. But I'm Worldwide. I ain't died."

Michelle and I were jostled until we almost fell. I smelled liquor and hairdress and marijuana smoke. Victor said in the same deadpan, "They look inculcated. She look devastated. By the obsolescence of your adolescence. Ask me why I'm peripatetic. All my life I'll say it's genetic."

One of the stage dancers writhed on Alfonso like he was a pole. Her halter top showed dark gleaming skin, and she smiled, eyes closed. "Get that, get her," the man behind the monitor said, and Alfonso flipped out his hands like, More.

Michelle said, close to my ear, "That's Kelli. Danita's best friend."

Victor turned away from the crowd. "I put my back into my livin," hc sang, muffled. On his shoulder, I could see pink circles. "But women want a man bring home the bacon." He untied the bandanna and something fell on the stage.

"What the fuck is that?" someone said. The rappers moved away and one of the girls jumped and said, "Oooh—that's nasty."

One of the white men nearby said, "Get him offa there. He's shit."

Cane Razor stepped forward and bent his knees, swept his arm across the stage and sang, "Out here we got brown cane sugar! I take em coun-tray! I like em chun-kay! But you got to show me what I get!"

Two girls in front of the stage lifted their shirts and breasts fell out of their bras. "Oh yeah—do the titty bop!"

But then someone screamed. Just one note—a lone frightened bird. Two of the big men backing up Cane Razor held up their medallions in the air and said, "We ready, nigga! We always ready! Cali ain't shit!"

They were looking at Jazen. He'd moved from behind the speaker, gun held at his side. "I ain't shit?" he shouted.

Victor didn't move. He looked at them and said into the microphone, "Why can't you just shoot yourself? Why's it better if somebody else shoots you? Lil Wayne shot himself in the chest, right? Save somebody the trouble, man. Just shoot yourself now."

"Fuck you, sorry nigga!" Cane Razor shouted at Jazen. The women onstage screamed, but it was that excited tone—fear canceled by glee, a schoolyard fight.

Jazen shot twice at the stage. Victor leapt off the back, but one of the girls collapsed.

Michelle and I pressed against the tarpaper edge of the stage and held each other's arms tight in the wave of bodies. The music stopped. An elbow hit the back of my skull, and a shoulder knocked me halfway down, but Michelle's strong wrist held me up. "Danita, Danita," she whispered. "Stay where you are. Stay, baby."

People were running, and the bodies fell away. On the stage, two big men were carrying the girl, blood dripping from her leg. It was Kelli. I turned to see the Navigator speeding over the irrigation ditch, four-wheel drive kicking in, and racing through the cane.

Michelle leapt up onto the platform and shouted, "Give me a shirt!" One of the men pushed his tank top toward her and she wrapped the girl's leg tightly with the shirt, then pulled an elastic from her pocket and slid it over the wrap. "We have to call 911," she said, but the men looked offstage, where someone was yelling, "No cops! No cops!"

The two men carried the girl down the steps and put her into a van, and it sped away. Michelle had Danita now, huddled into her arms near the speaker. Danita was tiny, her face swollen, smeared with tears and heavy makeup, her braids covered with a film of dust like cake flour. "They said they were takin Kelli to Baton Rouge. To the hospital."

"Where's my car?" Michelle shouted.

"Over there." She looked past her mother at me, frowning. "Who's she?"

Two young girls were still dancing in the clearing, their small breasts barely moving inside tank tops, their eyes closed. A few more cars were scouring turns in the dirt and heading down the road. Michelle's white Honda was alone now. A hollow loud banging—the hood of the truck coming down again. My father got into the cab with Albert. Albert saw us, and the truck rumbled past to the base of the levee, crushing go-cups and wires. "Cops comin now," he shouted. "Go, Michelle."

Michelle started the Honda. I got into the Corsica. The car bucked and shuddered backwards out of the row. We drove away, past the girls who had stopped dancing, stopped waiting for their moment, and vanished into the cane stalks shaking above them.

I followed Michelle down narrow roads through the fields. No Navigator, no truck ahead of us. If Jazen would shoot at anyone now, what would he do if he saw us?

When we got to Sarrat, she went to her place, and I stopped at Henri's house.

Henri was on the gallery. The silence was immense. I sat in the metal chair beside him, my heart hammering, just as Albert and my father rode up in the truck.

Henri squinted at the grille. "That Philomene truck?" he said to Albert.

"I borrowed it," Albert said.

My father sat on the steps and lit a Swisher Sweet. When Henri and Albert went inside, he said to me, "What I see, Jazen don't care who he hit. Think he in a movie."

Albert came back out on the gallery with a laptop. "They gotta come back here. One them boys left this." Victor's life inside.

"Put your car down at the barn with the truck. They think nobody home when they come back," Albert said.

We walked back up toward Michelle's. My legs were on fire again. Albert's shirt was dark with sweat. "Michelle," Albert called from the yard.

She opened the door.

Danita was sitting on the couch, her lips trembling. Albert said, "I'm sorry, Michelle. Danita, baby, I thought it was a good idea to get the truck, have them girls dancin in the bed. If you call that shit dancin. The promoter from New Orleans was a old white guy. They wanted it like a competition—country girls against city girls."

"Which one were you?" Michelle said to Danita, voice still deadly.

She broke into fresh sobs. "Nothing. They said I was too skinny."

Michelle shot me a look and said, "Them California boys?"

"No, Mama, Cane Razor's people." She held up her digital camera. "Scholaptitude said better have a brain than a booty. It's on here."

"Show me," Michelle said.

Blurry movements and faces. Music reverberated from speakers. Then Victor's face was right there. Paler than ever, his head shorn, his eyes big and dark as plums under the dark brows which looked even more startling because his hair was gone. His left arm was wrapped in a white bandanna near the elbow. He said, "Ain't takin off my shirt," and lifted his good arm to drink from a white go-cup. "What is that?" I said.

"Cough syrup and candy and Sprite all mixed together," Albert said. "Lean. Some nasty stuff. I rather have straight-up Bacardi."

Two men came into the frame. A young black man with headphones, and a white guy with a porkpie hat. "Where are the guys from LA?" the white guy said. "Who's the one with the bullet hole? What the hell smells like bacon?"

Victor shrugged. "You ain't lookin too rugged," the black man said. "I thought you got shot in the chest. It's your arm?"

The white man said, "You wrote some lines fit the script, right?"

Victor said, "Waste of breath, this life, this death." He started to untie the bandanna, and the camera shifted crazily.

"You tied bacon on his wound?" Michelle said. "With my bandanna?"

"He asked me could he come inside and charge his phone, and then I saw the bullet hole," Danita said.

"If we get five minutes of footage out of this whole fucking day I'll be amazed," the white man said off-camera.

I felt like touching the screen, like some country woman who'd never seen a film. Like I could touch his face.

Michelle grabbed Danita's face, like my mother had after I came home from Kelly Cloder's party. Thumb deep in one cheek hollow, fingers deep in the other. "Look at me. No. *Look at me.* You could be dead in that damn field. For what? For this punk-ass fool from California? You had class today!"

And Danita's face hardened, too, under her mother's fingerprints. "So I could take blood outta people arms all day long!"

"You gon be a nurse!"

"And change bedpans."

Michelle thrust her daughter's face away from her. "How you think changing diapers better than changing bedpans!" she shouted.

"Cause you don't do it forever! Like you! Changin that old lady diapers."

"You do it forever if you got two kids like Kelli and now you in the hospital! Fecal waste is fecal waste, Danita. She don't get paid. I do!"

Michelle turned in disgust and saw me.

"Victor's mama said he's in college. And look at his stupid ass today."

Danita shook her head slowly, frowning at me. "He said his mama dead. Been dead five years."

Michelle drew her whole body in, folded her arms, and stared at me.

"He's my godson," I said. "My son now."

But her face had changed. Not the issue of my body. Not a mother. It was different.

"You know what?" I said, to her, to all of them. "Screw this."

I went back down to the barn and got the picture of Glorette from the car.

"This is Victor's mama. She was killed in an alley five years ago. Nobody knows who. She was a damn strawberry. A crack ho, like all the jokes. Her mama was Anjolie. My mama is Marie-Claire. From right here—that empty spot by Henri."

Michelle walked into the bathroom and came out with my jeans, which she'd shaken out and folded, and my white blouse. "Give me back my clothes," she said to me. "I don't care who you really are. I just don't want you in my house."

I sat in my car. The sun was going down—it was around 7:30. I'd left Michelle's pink dress on the small wooden railing. Her trailer was dark. She'd taken Danita to work with her. From the glove compartment, I took out an envelope of museum postcards I kept for when I was stranded on a highway, or in a thunderstorm. A grainy, black-and-white Iturbide photo of a sturdy Oaxacan woman with three live lizards crowning her head, being taken to market, looking out at the world.

I carried the envelope to the house. Cellophane wrappers like dirty glass flowers on the porch. Jolly Rancher candies. "That's what they put in the purple drank," Albert said. "Maybe the crazy one just drop the other two here."

We waited in the living room, in the dark. My father and Henri were in the kitchen. I stared at the road, then the TV. I kept seeing Mr. McQuine's blue car come up the road. The armoire. Anjolie in the utter blackness. Her heart, hidden in the dark, scented wood. Was she afraid that even if her mother hid her there, he would break down the carved doors? Light-bright. Yella girl. Daughter of joy.

Like me.

Like Albert.

"Why didn't you ever come to Sarrat?" I said.

"By y'all?" he said, and stroked his goatee. "Nothin I want out there. Trees. I ain't into trees." He looked at me. "I travel around plenty. Like they say about you. But they had taken me away from my mama, so she wouldn't go crazy. I didn't want to see her for a long time. Till we were both grown." He folded his arms over his belly and grinned, like he was at a poker table. "What about you? Why you always runnin away?"

"I'm a bagavond," I said. "I get bored."

"Some people just don't like their relatives. Rather be in the wind."

"Free therapy. Thanks." For days, everyone had been criticizing everything about me. My clothes, hair, car, life. Everyone—Cerise, Sisia, even Victor. No one expected *you* to do it. You thought I wanted to be *you*?

"In the wind," I said to Albert. "I haven't heard that in a long time."

In the kitchen, Henri played his violin for my father. An old song I'd heard when I was here before. "Bonsoir Moreau, Bonsoir Moreau."

My legs and feet were swollen with ant venom, and I couldn't keep my hands away from the bites. I went to the bathroom, and when I came back I saw that Albert and my father were sitting in the dark kitchen, drinking rum. The cane knife was on the table.

Just after midnight, Albert went outside, the screen door slapping. Then he came back in and leaned over me. "Put this sheet under you," he whispered.

His face was so pale, his flat straight brown hair invisible on his head, and his hand hard on my shoulder. A sheet under me? He was going to—

"Put this on your legs. You scratchin too much. Get infected." He handed me a bowl of something. "Meat tenderizer."

I rubbed the paste onto my skin. I didn't look up at him.

He went back to the kitchen. I sat against the wall for a moment, and then I went to the doorway of Henri's bedroom, hearing him breathe like the rasp of a file.

"You a killer, huh?" Albert said. He tapped something on the wooden table. My father didn't answer. "You kilt more than him?"

"Two more."

"You hunt em down, too?"

"Non. Kill or be kill."

"Yeah?" Albert said. I heard his glass set back down.

My father said, "German. And man down in Plaquemines Parish."

"But not here."

"Kill him here or he might kill one a them."

Albert said, "But you ain't known that. You ain't God."

It was quiet. He was saying maybe Mr. McQuine could have changed. Taken Albert for his son. Or sent him to school and bought him land, at least. Given him—

Not that house.

Albert tapped something again. I moved closer. Cane knife. Where was my father's gun? My father looked up and said, "You thirsty?" His face was impassive. He held out the glass of rum.

I took one hot swallow. Neither of them looked at me. My father walked behind me, back to the front room, and sat in the easy chair.

I woke at dawn. My legs were numb. I heard a car. My father was asleep in the chair, head thrown back, his Adam's apple like stone in his throat.

Albert stirred beside the couch. He'd slept on a blanket, on the floor.

Michelle and Danita were at the door.

I said, "Michelle. I'm sorry."

Michelle bit her lips. Danita said, "They never came back? Victor called me last night. My mama had turned off my phone. But he left me a message."

Michelle cocked her head to the side and said, "He ain't called *you*?"

"I'm not even a decent godmother. He probably doesn't believe I'm here."

Danita held out the phone. The message: "I'm sorry about your friend. Jazen's an asshole. He punched the camera guy and stole the camera. Says he's gonna put the video on YouTube and make some money. But that other dude—DJ Scholaptitude? He's gon be at the Lafitte for one last show. New Orleans. Ain't too many people heard a him. Maybe just you. Thanks for hooking me up with the medical care. I gotta go. Big show. Big show."

She took the phone back and closed it.

"If they gone down to New Orleans, they tryin to stay with my maman in the Lafitte," Albert said.

Danita kept her head down, as if she were praying, and said to her mother, "You gon be mad no matter what. I kissed him. In the car. After I put the bacon on his arm. I leaned over and kissed him. But he just kept sleepin."

THE LAFITTE

"RIGHT HERE?" Albert said conversationally, driving my car off the highway and down a pitted asphalt road. He stopped in front of an old two-story wooden building. A bar—the front windows were boarded up, but a rusted Jax beer sign hung from the eaves. "This where he was parked. The Time Out."

My father said, "This where he come to drink."

"Said you cut the brake lines." Albert put his forefinger inside the goatee on his chin, like a professor studying the board to figure out an equation.

The cane knife was back on the wall. I'd seen it when we left. Did Albert have a gun? Was my father carrying his handgun?

Albert would never say the words—would he? *You killed my father.*

He had said, "I'll take you down to the Lafitte. My maman stay with her niece Inez."

But we were here, in the thrumming heat of overgrown vines and blind windows.

I was in the backseat. Neither of them turned toward each other.

"Oui," my father said. "Wait till he inside. I get under the car with my knife."

"Said that wasn't enough."

"Qui a dit?"

"Henri."

My father let out his breath. "Ça suffit." It was enough.

"No. I didn't even ax who he was till I made eighteen. Then I ax my maman. I found her in Vegas."

My father was silent. Albert spun the wheels on the gravel parking lot and turned down the narrow road again. Away from the highway. We drove into what looked like nothing but ragged forest, and then I saw Bayou Becasse Road. It wound all the way here. Albert said, "Car was wrecked, on the bayou road. Burned up. Where?"

He went another hundred feet before my father pointed to the ditch. "La."

The brakes were gone, the car whirled around the corner and slid into the ditch. But Mr. McQuine wasn't dead. I imagined him bouncing against the windshield of the old car. No air bags. But he was alive.

We sat beside the ditch. Albert waited. Had he been waiting for this moment since he was eighteen? That August in 1975 when my father and Glorette and I were here, he wasn't in Sarrat. But he could have come any time to California and killed my father.

"What—you think I wanted him around? He was gon live to ninety and then die fuckin somebody and deed me the house? Me—a nigger?" Albert laughed. "I just want to know how you did it. I always thought you shot him."

"Jamais shoot a man, me." My father stared at the line of trees beyond the ditch.

He said, "I kill a German in France. Field was plow. Ice in the dirt. Mo tou soule—in the woods look for some food. German come from a bush and he don't shoot—tro peur. I get him with the bayonet."

He looked at the ditch. "There—I get a piece a wood. He barely live, but he open his eyes. I hit him side of the head. That car in the ditch, and gas leak out. A match. And I gone in the woods. Mo tou soule." My father's hands shook slightly when he took the pack of Swisher Sweets from his pocket that said La Reina. Then he said, "Ecoute—how he do them, they can't live. Finis." He lifted his shoulders an inch.

Albert stared at the ditch, filled with weeds now. No one drove here.

He said, "I guess they thought my maman would kill me, or I would kill her. With my face." The weeds hummed with insects. "She was in California, by y'all. I went to Vegas, to LA, and then I come back here. Work with Henri, cause I figure that land mine. But it was the old lady's."

Miss McQuine was sitting in front of the morning talk shows with Titine. Waiting for her beauty parlor session.

He turned the wheel sharply and we went backwards. Just before he pulled back onto the road, Albert said, "I used to go sit in the house. Seven Oaks. All empty. Full a spiders and rats. I went to burn it down once. But then I thought it was funny—see it like that. And he was in the ground. I was up here."

We got back onto Airline Highway, headed toward Baton Rouge. We passed small settlements, cinderblock bars, shacks, plantation roads. Finally Albert said, "In LA, I stole a car once, and they gave me time. I was in the cell with this Aryan dude. They didn't know me. And I tell you, I could talk about niggers good as him. For three months, that's all we talked about."

Victor's cell phone went straight to message—mailbox full. He had his charger. Either he didn't want to talk to me or didn't care whether his phone worked anymore.

At a small road, my father peered north and said, "The river right there. Mulatto Bend Road. They got Slim Harpo bury in that cemetery. He sing about King Bee."

King Bee—I'd heard that before. On a Rolling Stones album?

"Slim never made no money. Drive a truck when I know him. Had a heart attack when he was forty-six. He born the year after me."

I looked out the window at the small settlement. Mick Jagger's lips. Still making money. A story—Slim Harpo's grave in a place named after people like us.

Victor could write that story. Probably better than anyone else, after this trip. We'd come back here. Mulatto Bend. Irony abundant. We drove on the old bridge over the Mississippi. It felt like an hour, suspended over the brown water, the river that made all the others look like sidewalks or country lanes. A mighty force of whirlpools and ripples and barges and bodies. We came down off the bridge into Baton Rouge and Albert got on the interstate to New Orleans.

I settled into my own cocoon of sweat, itch, and funkiness. I hadn't been immersed in water since Michelle's tub. My legs were covered in grimy layers of onion, Benadryl, and meat tenderizer.

A steady stream of cars headed north. Albert said, "Say on TV that storm maybe change its mind out there on the water and come this way. Look like the scary people leavin now. Everybody else mixin drinks. Saturday night and a hurricane party."

By the time we skirted Lake Pontchartrain, drowned cypress in black water on either side of us, the air was damp and heavy again, the sky hard metal hot, with no clouds. Wouldn't a hurricane have storm clouds?

I'd been afraid to call Alfonso. They might take off again if they knew we were close. But I had to hope he was still the boy I knew.

"What up?" He sounded as if he'd been asleep. "Who this?"

"Fantine. Danita gave me your number. Where are you, Alfonso?"

"Where are you?"

"Right behind you."

He yawned. "Why?"

"I'm coming to take Victor back home."

"What if he don't wanna go?"

"He wants to go."

"Maybe you don't even know him." Alfonso's breath was tired and labored. "We in the Sixth Ward now. Lafitte. He gotta be a soulja."

"But you're not. You're from California."

"I been here before. My grandmère up in here."

"Soulja in what war, Alfonso?"

"Just gotta be down. Be a warrior."

"If you ever read history, if you ever got Jazen to read it, you'd see that the Indian warriors, like the Crow and the Apache, they didn't kill their own people. They were out fighting Blackfeet or other guys from down the way."

"You don't get it, Auntie." Loud music sounded vaguely from another room. A thump. "Either they yo niggas or they ain't."

"Where's Victor?"

"I think he in the shower."

He hung up. In the shower? That's what you said when you didn't want to talk.

We had passed through Metairie, and I could see the Superdome like an alien biscuit when Alfonso called me back. As soon as I answered, he said, "He just came out the shower." Then he paused. "But hold up. This ain't good."

He must have put down the phone. "Zee, why you trippin?"

Victor said, "You mean why did he try to punch me? Cause I told him his new tattoo wasn't shit. Why is he loadin his gun theatrically, wavin it around?"

I heard the snick-snicking of a gun. Being loaded.

Jazen said, "You got your first bullet scar and now you think you the shit?"

"My first scar? I got seven scars. You don't know shit about me."

There was a sound like whipping cloth. Alfonso said, "What the hell is that?"

"I got these when I was five. Cause I wouldn't smile. Y'all got tattoos cause you wanted them. You paid to get stuck."

"Who did that to your back?" Alfonso said.

"Some asshole wanted me to smile."

The phone snapped shut.

"They're fighting," I said. "At the Lafitte."

"We just about there," Albert said. The city was spread out before us now. Downtown buildings and hotels mirrored and anonymous as anywhere else, but then the white angel-topped crypts and an oak strung with glittering purple and green beads, and Albert took the car down the ramp for Orleans Avenue.

Vieux Carré to the west. And we went east.

Gingerbread houses, shotgun cottages with fretwork on the porch eaves, wood siding painted butter yellow and lime green and pale blue. The storybook version of New Orleans—an old woman walking with an umbrella and a plastic bag of groceries from a corner store. DANG IDEAL MARKET read the sign.

Albert said, "They built the Lafitte in '41, I think, and my grandpère was one of the first people to get an apartment in there. He worked on the docks at the river."

"Lafitte for colored. Iberville for white," my father said.

Albert laughed. "Yeah, Iberville give my great-great-somebody his land, and Iberville black as midnight now. Scare the shit outta them French Quarter tourists."

On the corner of Orleans and North Johnson, he parked. "My cousin Inez stayed here in the Lafitte all her life. Maman with her." The two-story sandy brick buildings were beautiful, like smaller versions of the famous Pontalba buildings in Jackson Square. My father reached for the glove compartment, but then he glanced up and didn't open it. He looked at me and shook his head. This was not the trees. This was the city.

We walked across the oak-lined median on Orleans, and then the grass in front of the buildings. In the space between two buildings, four young boys peered out warily as we passed. "Little wannabes," Albert said. "It's what—ten o'clock? Early for big wannabes."

I kept hearing Alfonso's voice. Either he yo nigga or he ain't.

The Lafitte had graceful wrought-iron balconies painted burgundy, and porticos over the front doors, and on nearly every balcony or porch were people. Talking, holding a can of soda or cup of coffee, combing hair. Three women peered closely at us from a balcony—they wore housekeepers' uniforms. One saw Albert and her face relaxed. "Hey, baby," she said.

He called back, "Hey, Rachelle."

"Come to get your maman out the storm? They ain't call for no evacuation. Marriott ain't give the day off, neither." She laughed. "Not no Saturday!"

"They got people checkin *into* Marriott—gonna *party*," another woman said.

On the bottom step of the next building, a small girl sat alone, sorting through a bowl of beans. She bent her head, her six twisted braids bobbing like butterfly antennae. She reached into the red beans with two small fingers and pulled out a pebble, tossed it violently to the side.

"Good girl," someone called from inside the door.

"Hey, maman," Albert said, his hands in his pockets, standing at the base of the three steps. The girl looked up at his goatee.

An old woman came out. Not the Claudine I remembered, with thick arms and an angry look. A frail thin woman with hair shorn close to her scalp, and ironed curls like wood shavings along her skull. Her eyes gray as fog—what I remembered as a child. And the scar on her arm a pink satin caterpillar.

"What you been up to?" she said casually.

"Nothin to crow about," he said, and gave her the gentlest hug, his arms barely touching her shoulders.

"That Enrique?" she said, squinting.

My father nodded. He said, "Claudine. Say you sick."

"That why I stay here with Inez. Close to Charity Hospital." She focused on me, and the little girl moved her eyes to mine. Her fingers roamed idly through the beans.

"That Fantine?" She raised her eyebrows. "I heard you was in Paris right now. Alfonso told me." She pulled me toward her in a careful hug. Then before I could ask where Alfonso was, she pointed down, inside her short-sleeved blouse. "They got this medicine go in my chest. Chemo. Call it Red Devil." She smelled of lavender oil and bitter fumes.

It was sweltering inside. On the coffee table were rhinestones of all sizes sorted in bowls, in varying shades of gold, topaz, and huge oblong stones white as diamonds.

Where was Alfonso, if he had told her I was in Paris?

A baby slept in a crib in the corner of the living room, hair in four black clouds held by rubber bands. A radio played low near her. Outside the open door, the little boys were rapping—chants with no music.

The apartment was long and dark and spotless. We walked down the hallway to the kitchen, at the other end, with spatulas hanging from wall hooks and a pan of cornbread cooling on the counter. The back door was open, too. Had the boys run already?

Claudine collapsed into a chair at the kitchen table, and Albert sat across from her, his forearms on the Formica, holding her hands. Then Claudine put her head into her arms and cried, her bare shoulders heaving, the knobs of bone sharp under her skin.

A woman came from the hallway carrying a laundry basket. "Are you Inez?"

She nodded.

"I'm Fantine. We're looking for Victor. My godson. He's with Alfonso."

She said, "They were here for a minute. I went to take a shower." She sat on the couch and began sorting the clean clothes. Three medical uniforms—maybe she worked at Charity. Baby T-shirts and sleepers.

My father looked out the front window. They were somewhere nearby, Victor showing off scars and Jazen loading a gun. This was crazy. This wasn't heroic. Past the porch, little kids were chasing each other under the oak trees in the courtyard.

My father paced near the crib, his face gaunt, etched with lines. We could hear Claudine crying in the kitchen, telling Albert something, her voice halted by sobs. Then he said, "Mo parle vec Claudine."

Inez moved aside the bowls of rhinestones. She didn't look worried. The boys must not have been arguing here. Her hair was amber, too, the rich gold of something found in a tomb. It was straightened and swirled into a stiff chignon.

"I like your hair," I said.

"Uh-huh," she said, distracted.

"What's the color called?"

She looked at me sharply. "Call whatever Teeny decide to put on my head this time."

"It's beautiful," I said softly.

"That's my grandbaby over there, and my other one on the porch. My daughter's at work. She got breakfast shift at the Marriott. Claudine's been helpin out. She can watch the little ones, but she can't handle the bigger kids. She too sick."

Then she said, "That your godson, the one with the bullet?"

My heart stuttered. "Yes."

"We took the bullet out this morning."

"It came out of his arm?" I felt sick.

"Yeah. Infected, too. Somebody tied some bacon on him, I guess, so that was good. The meat musta fallen off, but it pulled that bullet near to the top. That salt pulls out the infection and the foreign body. I got it out with tweezers. I had some salt meat in the kitchen, so I put that piece on there and tied it back up. Pull out the rest of the pus." She glanced toward the kitchen. "Claudine had an old bandanna."

"Where'd they go?"

The little girl came inside with the blue bowl. "Just put it here, Tweety Bird," Inez said. "They serious in the kitchen."

We could hear their voices. My father said, "Pas vrai, pas vrai." Claudine's words were twisted with anger or sorrow—I couldn't tell which. Not true, not true.

Inez said, "Call her Tweety Bird cause of how she ate when she was a baby. But now she watch everything like a bird, too." The girl sat inside the circle of Inez's arms. They sorted out the largest white jewels into one bowl, then slid them into a zip-lock bag. Then the largest amber ones.

"Where did they go?" I whispered again.

She kept sorting. "They made me nervous. He put the bullet in his pocket. Said he needed good luck, and I told him a bullet wasn't no rabbit foot. My grandpère—this his rabbit foot." She pointed to another plastic container, where an old white-furred paw was ensconced with a satin cord. "Said he got it from an old slave man. Caught that rabbit on some plantation right here. Before they build the Lafitte." She held it up in the light. "It was high ground here. A brickyard or something. I always put it on the suit."

"What suit?"

She pointed at the jewels. "Mardi Gras Indian suit. My grandpère used to be an Indian. Now my cousin. I do some of the patches." The baby in the crib sighed again and one hand went up to rub an eye. Her fist was tiny and fierce, pushing near her nose. Inez said, "You got grandkids?"

I shook my head, and she said, "How old are you?"

"Gonna be forty this year."

She laughed. "I'm forty-two. You don't look no forty." She watched the baby. "How he get shot?"

I didn't want to say, until I knew whether or not she would call the police. But before I could answer, she said, "You know what? I'm a nurse over at Charity. I don't even want to know. My daddy and them, they was all Mardi Gras Indians, and they use to settle their fights on one day, when they were out in the street. Now they battle, you know, with the dance. But they didn't just go around shootin people cause they didn't like their shoes or their shirt."

"I know." I waited. I felt poised at the edge of a pool, toppling over with exhaustion, but like the water was so cloudy I didn't want to go in.

Inez leaned over the edge of the crib. "I was in the shower, after I took out the bullet. Claudine said they went to Juanita's. Two buildings down. Juanita's helping Teeny with the meat." The baby sat up abruptly, and smiled. "They say we might get the storm, and they gon cook all the meat today in case the power go out."

I went out to the porch, stood under the wrought-iron portico, and looked two buildings over. A grill had been set up next to that porch.

The Lafitte was its own town. People watched me walking. Like the Villas, or the small villages in France where a castle dominated the hill, the same sandy color as this stone, and the houses on cobblestone streets below. When someone invaded the town, the castle's inhabitants put down the ladder, and only the ones they wanted to save got to climb before the ladder was pulled up and the cliff face was bare again.

But the woman who came out onto her porch with a huge tray of meat smiled beatifically, like an ancient duchess, her face round and dark under the multicolored braids that had been woven into a crown. She must be Teeny. "You lookin for Juanita?" she said. Then she pointed to the balcony above us. "Them boys upstairs like Coyote and Road Runner, can't get along. Getting on each other last nerve."

———

I went up the stairs quietly. I didn't want my father here. With his gun or without. I was nothing. No one. Jazen didn't care about me, and I prayed he'd be glad to get rid of Victor.

A woman answered the door, wearing a white blouse, black pants, and a name tag that said NAPOLEON HOUSE. She had Jazen's slanted eyes and perfect burnished skin, his etched lips. She said, "Who the hell you?"

"Juanita?" I said. "It's Fantine. Glorette's cousin."

She held open the door. "You? I ain't seen you in twenty-some years."

"Me."

She looked at my white shirt, then narrowed her eyes. "I remember you. A braniac. You wore some funny shit to school."

There was a thrift store next to the Paris Cinema. My attempt to look NYC—a beret, a scarf, a jacket in the Rio Seco heat. I'd forgotten that.

She opened the door. A monster loomed in the corner, and I jumped. A Mardi Gras Indian suit, ostrich plumes waving, on a stand. "What you doin here?"

"I came for Victor. Glorette's son."

Juanita took a breath so large her whole chest rose, and then she let it out, her name tag clicking. "Then go on in there and calm him down. He actin a fool."

What about your son? I wanted to say. The fool in chief?

She said, "My son in the shower. He come and go all his life. He been into that bad shit since he little, and I don't have nothing to say to him. I'm goin across the way to check on my other boys and I gotta get to work. I ain't got time for all this drama." She went out the front door. I heard her shoes on the stairs, and heard the women on the porch say her name.

I walked slowly through the exact same layout—front room, kitchen, hallway. A wave of steam came from the hallway—the water was running loudly. The bedroom door was open a slice, and I stepped just to the frame and said softly, "Victor?"

"Yeah?"

No one else answered. I pushed open the door and went inside. He was sitting on one single bed, hunched over, wearing the bright yellow T-shirt from the first day. Black Coral—Belize. His arm was wrapped in a different colored bandanna—almost lavender.

"It's me."

He lifted his eyes to mine and said, "Marraine? For real?" His eyes turned glassy with tears, and then he wiped at his face with the sleeve of his good arm. "My head hurts worse than my arm," he whispered, rubbing his skull. His brain, under the thin so-pale skin. His dreads in the dirt back at Bettina's.

In his swollen left hand, held stiff and awkward like a wooden dipper, were two of the large amber jewels.

Alfonso was lying in the other bed, the sheet up to his bare chest. "Purple drank. Kick your ass next day." His hair was growing back—the stubble thicker, almost obscuring the green tattoo on the side of his head. On his shoulder, a new tattoo—swollen dark letters spelling out CALI, gleaming under Vaseline. A video camera on the nightstand—the one Jazen had stolen.

"Victor," I said. "Let's go home."

He maneuvered his bad hand and opened his pocket with his good hand, dropping the jewels inside. He pulled something from the wall. His phone charger. He put that in his pocket, too, the cord dangling. Then he lifted something from his waistband. A gun.

He didn't point it at me—he propped his elbow on his knee, as if even that arm was tired, and the gun was sideways, aimed over my head. But just the sight of it—I felt the burning sensation in my chest. Where I thought the bullet would strike me. "How was Paris?" he whispered.

"Fine." The gun was a small black revolver. Like two dark chocolate bars glued together. But with a hole facing me.

"I bet it was," Victor said. "That's how I always ask you, and that's what you always say. Before we talk about the real stuff. And then you jet off to the next place."

"I'm not going anywhere now," I said. Every word was a cliché. "Let's just get out of here and go home."

The shower stopped. Victor stood up slowly. He put the gun on the bed and picked up a wallet, pulling it open, extracting a bill with the swollen fingers of his left hand. He winced, and slipped the money into his back pocket. He dropped the wallet on the floor and picked up the gun again.

"Where you headed next?" Victor said, conversationally. "New York? Italy?"

I wasn't smart enough for this. Not with that black hole facing me. Couldn't speak in code. Couldn't speak in French.

"You and I are headed back home," I said.

"The Happy Place?" he said. "In LA?"

Jazen came out of the bathroom slowly, a towel wrapped around his neck. He didn't see us. His head was bent, while he tried to pull his jeans lower, adjusting them below the white boxers, hanging and rehanging them. His braids were gone. On his skull were random thick puffs of hair, wet, uncombed, like a child's. The hat he'd worn in the video had covered it.

Alfonso glanced at Victor, at me, back at Jazen. He was perfectly still in the bed.

Victor kicked the wallet toward Jazen, and his head snapped up.

"The fuck you doin, nigga?" he said. He bent down for the wallet and saw the gun. His eyes flicked at me, then off as if I weren't there. Victor pointed the gun at Jazen's chest.

"Getting my share. Like Jimmy Cliff said. But you ain't seen that movie either." Victor stood with his knees back against the bed, the gun held steady on Jazen, his bad arm bent against his side. "He gave you three hundred for the video. I got shot. Took out my share."

Jazen said, "You ain't about—" and moved forward. Victor raised the gun to the level of Jazen's mouth.

Jazen's chest was covered with tattoos. WEST SIDE LOC in tall capitals like a skyline across his stomach. On his left arm the new tattoo—raised red skin all around the dark green gothic letters: DO OR DIE. The sheen of fresh Vaseline on him, too.

Alfonso hadn't moved at all. He said, "We ain't Indians, y'all. We ain't the damn Crow and Blackfeet, so ain't no need to be fightin each other."

"Funny, nigga—you talkin about my feet?" Jazen swiveled his head.

"What?" Victor said. "You were in Thompson's history class?"

"For a minute," Alfonso said, grinning, cool as ever.

"He gave us a big lecture on the Plains Indians, how they didn't fight within the tribe." Alfonso nodded, going along with it. "But you? You woulda shot me a minute ago, before you got in the shower. Cause you think I ain't about shit."

"You ain't nobody. I'm tired a your mouth. Sarrat nigga think he the shit cause he went to college. Your mama—"

"What?" Victor's voice was low and deadly as a thrown rock. Like Gustave's. Like my father's. I couldn't breathe.

Past Victor was the open door of a closet. A smaller suit of feathers and rhinestones hung there, the same gold and amber as the jewels moving through Inez's fingers. I said, "Victor, this isn't you."

"Really?" he said, and didn't even glance at me. "You sure? Cause you know me, right?" His skin was tight on his skull, his night eyes lost in wells of purple, and the gun looked so small and heavy and foolish in his hand. The bullet in his pocket—small and heavy and foolish, too.

"My mama what?"

Jazen said, "My moms used to say your moms thought she was some fuckin queen. All them fools wanted your moms cause she was light. She had some voodoo."

"Voodoo? Just cause she looked like that? You think she planned that? Way back whoever came from Africa planned to get raped, and then they got raped again, and all that light-skin shit was the lotto?" He shook his head, incredulous.

But Jazen wasn't afraid. He really didn't think Victor had it in him. "My moms said your moms was—"

"A ho," Victor said. "Yup. She was a *ho*. Not like you fools call every girl a ho and trick bitch. My moms lost her *mind* over my pops. Like every day she lost it again. Time I was seven I got it. I didn't look like him. I looked like her. So that made her even sadder."

The burning came back to my breastbone—not fear of the bullet, but shame. Of course he looked exactly like her. Beautiful. But not Sere Dakar's beauty. Nothing of him. And she had told me that once. She'd been sitting at the glass table, and said, "Even his hands." Sere Dakar had big hands, with long strong fingers. He'd been recruited from Chicago to play basketball in Rio Seco, but he'd refused when he got there. He said he wanted to play music.

Victor's sharp cheekbones and long eyelashes and storm-cloud eyes focused on Jazen with pure hate. "My moms had a job," Victor said.

"Every day she got up, drank coffee, and when the sun landed on the roof, she went to work. That's what she told me when I was little. She left me somethin to eat. And somebody sold her the rock. You sold it to Sisia and she gave it to my moms. Or you sold it to Chess or some other dude."

He was nearly whispering now. "Five years since she died, and you guys were down the street. Nobody cared. Pops wouldn't care—he got ghost before I was even born. So grab this gun and shoot me, nigga. See—you happy? I'll call you a nigga and you call me a nigga and we'll keep it real. Fo gotdamnizzle realio! Come on!"

Jazen sounded far away. "I ain't even hearin you. You like Chanel's Chihuahua. Don't nobody listen at you no more." He took two steps toward the bed where Alfonso lay. I flinched, waited for the shot.

"You gon walk away? From a halfrican like me?"

"I'm finna take care my bidness. And you finna sit there and think about shit nobody cares about. All you ever do is think."

Victor shook his head. "All I wanted was a damn ride. And just chill for a day, you know?" He looked right at me. "Maybe a week." He reached behind him to pick up his backpack from the bed, the gun still pointed at Jazen, but his left arm wouldn't work, and the backpack dropped onto the floor.

His face was distorted with pain for a moment. Then he opened his eyes and left the backpack behind. "Excuse me, Marraine," he said, formal, distant, edging into the doorway, his arm touching mine, so close I could smell salt and smoky fat—inside the bandanna? "I got an appointment with a buccaneer."

Jazen moved his foot like a runner, preparing to launch himself at Victor. But Alfonso said, "Naw, man, don't do it."

Alfonso reached under the blanket and pulled out a bigger gun, a wood-handled pistol, and trained it on Jazen's chest. Victor was caught in the doorway with me, his bad arm sealed to my bare shoulder by sweat. Alfonso said, "Let him go."

"You crazy," Jazen said.

Victor didn't move. His skin was hot against mine.

"That's my blood, man," Alfonso said, narrowing his eyes. He held the gun steady at his chest. Egypt and Morocco along his collarbones.

"That's my cousin," Alfonso said again, his voice harder.

"Not your real cousin," Jazen said. "Y'all ain't blood."

Alfonso nodded. "Yeah. We blood family."

Then the room was so quiet I could hear Teeny laughing downstairs, and a car with a stuttered heartbeat in the parking lot. Boom-boom pulsing around us. Victor breathed hard beside me, his arm sliding against mine. Jazen faced the two round holes. The guns that made the silence. And in all our breathing, and waiting, the quiet was the saddest thing—Victor had no words. He said nothing. Then he turned suddenly, his arm left mine and he ran down the hallway. Something fluttered from his pocket onto the floor.

When Jazen tried to move toward the door again, Alfonso pulled off the covers and held the gun steady on him. "Get your stuff, JZ. You got to go."

"How the fuck I gotta go and this my mama place?"

Alfonso said, "My grandma told me your mama don't want you here. She said she done with you. Grandma give me the gun, man. Where the hell you think this old .45 come from?"

Jazen looked at me. His slanted eyes shone in the sunlight through the window.

"I'm done," Alfonso said. "I ain't goin back to jail, man. I'm tired. Longer we ride, more trouble I get in, more time I do." Then Alfonso stood up, in big flannel pajama bottoms with pink hearts. Was Inez washing his clothes?

Alfonso kept Jazen in place. I ran after Victor, as fast as I could with my swollen feet awkward and numb. I heard the front door slam open, and looked out the window to see Victor's shining head move through the smoke of the grill and disappear into the space between buildings.

Alfonso was moving Jazen by moving the gun. I pressed myself against the living room wall, near the Indian suit, so close the ostrich plumes tickled my neck. Jazen was holding the video camera and a sports bag. He jammed the Raiders cap with the pirate logo over his damp hair.

When he got to the open door that led to the stairwell, he turned and said, "You dead now. Not dead to me. Just fuckin dead."

"You the one out there, Zee," Alfonso said, and his voice had a thin line of sadness. "By yourself."

Alfonso closed the front door. He held up the shirred waistband of the pajamas with his left hand. We went to the front window, over the second-floor balcony. We could hear Miss Teeny say, "Where you goin, baby?"

The cap like a black duckbill from up here. The Raiders jersey, black and silver. He had stopped in the stairwell to put it on. He probably didn't want anyone to see his tattoos here. He said, "You see my mama?"

"She went across the yard to get some cayenne pepper."

Jazen went across the courtyard, the opposite way from Victor, and we heard laughter, chanting, rapping. He shouted, "Fuck you, lil nigga. You still a baby."

Then we heard a chorus of laughter, and a car door slam, and the speakers kick in, and what must have been the Navigator drove away.

But Victor was gone, too.

I went back to the hallway to see what he'd dropped. One of the concert tickets. Dave Matthews. For tonight.

Alfonso sat on the couch. The voices and laughter floated up to us. On the coffee table were toys and CDs and video games. "Wait and see if Victor come back," Alfonso said. "After he hear the Navigator take off. He probably hidin in the next building."

Alfonso lay his head all the way back. Thick muscles from lifting weights in prison. Live My Life. "I'm so tired," he said.

He looked exactly as he had on my own couch, a few days ago, as if he wanted to sleep through the rest of his life. What did he dream about? The gun was held loosely on his thigh. The flannel hearts.

"Is Inez washing your clothes?"

He nodded. The sky was still tin gray outside the window, through the branches of the oak tree near the porch. Alfonso had shot Mando. He'd shot someone five years ago, in Rio Seco, and he'd run to Louisiana. Then, when he came home, he was arrested and did his time.

"He's not coming back," I said softly.

Alfonso shrugged, as if his shoulders were sandbags.

I went back to the bedroom and picked up the backpack. Grimy, the canvas blackened with dirt, the straps smelling of salt meat. In the living room, I opened it. Notebooks, deodorant, T-shirt, socks, CDs, his wallet. He had his phone, his charger, the hundred-dollar bill, and the jewels in his pocket.

An appointment with a buccaneer. He kept saying he was the one descended from the pirate—not me. Picards were from Picardy, in France. What was the connection to the first Marie-Therese?

Outside, Teeny shouted, "Hey, now, come on! We gotta get this started." She must be the one who cooked for everyone. Like my mother.

Alfonso put the gun on the couch cushion between us. He flexed his fingers. "Auntie," he said. "I heard it. When she died."

"Who?"

"Victor's moms. Glorette."

"You heard it?"

He nodded. He said, "I was always in the alley then. Cause JZ was at the Launderland. And there was this crazy lady from New York. Called herself Fly. She rode around in a brown van, and she would— you know. That's where she did her thang."

With the men. I said, "She killed Glorette?"

He lifted his shoulders again. "I was in the alley, behind a tree, cause I was—I had to pee. And Glorette was there, like, maybe she was smokin or chillin. The one called herself Fly come up on her and started yellin, and she, like, jerked Glorette around and tied her hair to the cart. Maybe she broke her neck. Or maybe Glorette had a heart attack or some shit. I don't know. I just know when I came out after a while, she was—"

I closed my eyes. Had Glorette been looking up at the sky, then, when she died? Did she see the palm trees? "What did you do?" I whispered.

"I ran. And then Sidney found her. He called your brothers." He ran his hands over his stubble. "I couldn't never tell him. Victor. When he started ridin with us, after she was gone. That's fucked up. That crazy lady, she was around for the summer, and then I never saw her again."

Teeny and the others below us laughed, and someone played the trumpet far away, and the smoke shifted into the window. "Why did you shoot that kid?" I said. "You didn't even know him."

He murmured, "My job. We always ridin. You know. Rollin. What you said about the Indians? I remember the pictures from school. They on horses, ridin all over. The fellas. Huntin buffalo and they had peace pipes and shit. And they was fightin, too."

He rubbed his forehead so hard that red marks appeared. "When I was little, I wanted to play football. Like your brothers. But then when I started hangin with Jazen, it was so easy to make that money. But you know, hangin with Victor—it's like havin some guy from Def Comedy Jam tell me everything. I was thinkin—the other job I wanted when I was about twelve, I wanted to drive a truck. But not by myself. Drive a truck every day, like a beer truck or milk truck, and have a dude like Victor for my partner, and we just cruise all around, make them stops, and chill at the end of the day."

I wanted to be sentimental. Say something movielike—You could still do that now. But he couldn't.

"Can you tell my grandmère I need my clothes?"

"Anybody could come in that door."

"JZ won't come back that fast. He gotta meet some dude in the Ninth Ward."

The smoke rose past the second floor like black ivy. I wouldn't look back at the gun. The Indian suit in the corner watched me, faceless and flat.

Glorette killed by a stranger named Fly. The random act. More not to tell Victor, if I ever saw him again. I felt numb, walking down the steps. What was I supposed to do? Head to Inez's place and say, "Claudine's grandson still has her .45, but now he has to decide how not to die. And Victor's gone."

Miss Teeny was saying to a woman, "Hurricane Cindy was July. Knocked out the power, and then all the meat went bad." She turned over chicken legs sprinkled with seasoning.

"These white girl storms," one of the men tending the coals said.

"Like the Brady Bunch," another woman said, arranging hot links on a tray.

"This one Katrina. Where they get these names? I like to see a Hurricane Shenene. Tell Jamie Foxx go on up there and name the next one."

Everyone laughed. Miss Teeny looked at me. "Hey, now, Juanita said you a reporter."

"You need to do a story on me," the man said, closing the lid on the smoker. "Best barbecue in New Orleans."

I smiled. "My godson—the one in the yellow shirt. Did you see which way he went?"

Miss Teeny gave me a long look. She pointed. "He went toward Orleans. Like he was catchin a ride to the Quarter."

I went across the grass—the buildings curved, I saw now, like the famous town houses in Bath. Claudine sat on Inez's porch in a metal chair, holding the baby a little awkwardly. "Here," I said quickly, thinking of the stent in her breast.

The baby was solid and dense in my arms. She reared back and studied my face solemnly. Her eyes were black as polished hematite, and I waited for her to scream at my foreign status. But then she made up her mind and put her head against my shoulder. Her hair was soft as dandelion fluff against my neck.

I followed Claudine inside. Inez and Tweety Bird were sorting through a new batch of beads. My father sat in the easy chair beside the stand that held the suit. He seemed small and thin, suddenly, next to the huge frame of ostrich plumes. What had he and Claudine told each other? His eyes met mine, and he waited for me to say it.

I couldn't move. The baby was heavy, content, already sealed to my chest, sweat from both of us meeting in the thin cotton. There was no way to ask questions of my father, or explain what had just happened, with the two women watching me.

"Jazen went one way and Victor went another," I said. "Alfonso's over there waiting for clothes."

Claudine looked down at the beads. "Jazen come and go," she said again. "That's how he is. And he need to go, if he still doin what he been doin."

"You know he is," Inez said. "Once they get that easy money, they don't stop." She looked at the TV. A large halo of cotton, twirling in a sea of gray. "They say the storm probably headed this way, so maybe they don't want you to come in." She looked at her watch. "I'ma call Charity. I'm not supposed to work until graveyard. But I better get you to your chemo."

The circular mass moved again and again, on different possible tracks. The blue hole at the center looked as if someone had poked a finger inside.

Two of the intricate sequined patches they'd taken off the suit—one was a buffalo, his massive head lifted, eyeing a warrior who held his arms to the sun.

"Isn't there some place in the French Quarter called Pirate's Alley?" I asked.

"Yeah. For tourists," Claudine said. "Juanita work down there. She probably waitin on the van right now."

I bent near my father and said, "Papa, he kept talking about pirates and treasure. You stay here and see if he comes back. He has Jazen's gun. Alfonso has a gun. Jazen's got nothin right now. But he might come back, too." The baby held on tight to my neck. "I'm going to Pirate's Alley. Maybe Victor's trying to find some map."

The empty crib was imprinted with the baby's shape. And every sound and smell and noise and fear and comfort was imprinted into her, right now, every day here.

And me—I'd had my mother's face to rise up to, when she bent over my crib. Her sunflowers. The vines that twined over my window, making a waterfall of green lace.

We had bought a crib for Glorette. Where had Victor slept, when she lived in that crappy little apartment with Grady?

What had happened to his back?

Inez said people caught rides on the south corner. I caught up with Juanita on the sidewalk. "I need to know where Pirate's Alley is, or whatever it's called."

She sucked her teeth and gave me a look. "You never been here?"

"No."

"That's right. That boy—Glorette son—said somethin bout your daddy and her daddy from the end of the world. Not here." She shrugged. "Nothin but fake pirate Johnny Depp shit all over the damn Quarter. Ain't hard to find." She kept walking on Orleans.

I said, "My car's here. You want a ride?"

She shook her head. "Not with you. You don't know where you goin."

I put my hand on her arm to stop her. "Hey. You used to call Glorette a ho. That's what your son kept telling Victor. A ho and a voodoo queen. That was messed up. Victor didn't need to hear that."

Juanita lifted her chin and moved her arm away from my hand. "What the hell you know? Glorette ain't had no business actin crazy cause some man left her. I got married ten years ago, but I tried my best to raise Jazen before that."

"You had him right after we graduated."

"Yeah. A few months after Glorette had her son. I had gone out to the base and I met this guy. From New York. He kept sayin how pretty I was, my New Orleans accent, all that. How he bet I was Creole. Voulez-vous and all that shit."

"Yeah. I know."

"Only French anybody ever said to me in California. That song."

"I know." Then I said, "So you're gonna blame genetics for how Jazen lives?"

"I'm gonna get to work. And I don't need you givin me a ride, or tellin me anything." We were passing more courtyards with oak trees. "I take the ten-thirty van with Philip every day, and I ride back with my husband when he finish playin. He play trombone."

On the corner was a big white van, side door open, and a thin dark man with sedate, perfect dreadlocks lying on his shoulders. Inside the van were the two women with hotel uniforms. A third woman wearing a sundress got in, sweating heavily under a headscarf.

Pirate's Alley must be the most touristy place in the world, I realized suddenly, and I was embarrassed. I was following someone without any notion of how to find him, and this time it was a huge city. I said, "I'll get dropped off with Juanita."

They each gave Philip three dollars, and I put a five in his hand. He handed me back two of Juanita's dollars, and she kept her face turned to the window.

We left the Lafitte and crossed under the interstate. The 10, the long trail all the way from LA to here, the black belly of a river above us. In fifteen minutes, we were on Basin Street.

He let Juanita and me off on a corner. Chartres Street. The bricked gutters, the stucco walls in all the colors from tourist brochures and ads and photo essays—ocher and rose and soft blue. The balconies, the ferns, the woman driving past with an elegant little black cart and a brown horse—a white brimmed hat on her head. VOODOO TOURS, the placard on the cart read.

No sentences formed themselves in my head. Not easy, not elegant, no descriptions, no narrative. Two men were boarding up an antique store with plywood. Another man was taping windows in an X with electrical tape. Juanita looked up at the sky.

"I was four when Camille came through," she said. "But I don't remember it."

Napoleon House was in front of us. The cupola had shuttered windows, and when we crossed the street, I realized I'd seen this a hundred times in magazines.

The French Quarter, the walls around me, the street a tunnel of pastel shades and lacy black iron. Lady Marmalade, quadroon balls, daughters of joy. I followed Juanita to the back entrance. She checked her hair once more, and started to tie on an apron.

Sweat dripped between my breasts and into my navel—I could feel it there—and even my eyelashes were wet.

She laughed at my face. "You need a beer."

"A Coke."

"People come in all day and drink that Pimms. Specialty of the house. Them white people love it. I cain't stand that stuff."

"You think white people have different taste buds?"

There were only white people at the bar. She said, "They got different hair. Different eyes. Different everything else. Why they have the same taste?" She looked sideways at me. "You hang out with em, right?" She bent down to pick up a napkin someone had dropped, and a man passed by and said, "You better get on it, baby. Bout leven now."

"I'm here," she said. But she was looking at the napkin. Thinking. She said, "Glorette's son—they took the bullet out his arm and then Claudine went to get a bandanna. I remember when I was in California, when them fools first came out from LA to Rio Seco. I saw a guy with a blue bandanna. All that mess about red and blue." She crumpled the napkin in her hand. "Glorette's son said, 'Red or blue kill me in California, but I don't know what kill me here in Louisiana.' She brought over that old bandanna and he start laughin. Said, 'Cool—this a inde-somethin shade.'"

Independent. No. Indeterminate.

Then she said, "Pirate's Alley is two blocks that way." She pointed. "Right next to the church. But ain't no reason for him to go there. Nothin but things to buy."

A crowd of young guys were holding go-cups, and one yelled, "Fuck Katrina! She can't kick a lemon daiquiri!" He threw the cup in the air, and a whipped cloud flew out.

Pirate's Alley was a narrow row of shops adjacent to St. Louis Cathedral. VOODOO WEDDING, a sign said, propped in the entrance. Had someone told me ghosts lived in the alley, the ghosts of a doomed couple, one a pirate, and that's why people were married here, in this place where about ten people were huddled in the shade around the couple, who wore white dress, tux, and top hat?

In front of the church, I sat on a bench. A bedraggled, lost tourist.

You could see the river from here. Moinette Antoine had been sold, not down the river. Up the river.

Sold in a market down in New Orleans, scarred old slaver know he's doin all right. Hear him whip the women just around midnight. Brown sugar—how come you taste so good?

The river was just an absence, in the distance, with a steamboat floating like a wedding cake.

Moinette and her mother, Marie-Therese, had survived by washing and mending and sewing. "Clothes always dirty." Had my aunt Almoinette said that when I was ten? Toujou sale.

The first time I was in Paris, I looked at the paintings of women lavandeuses and thought of the Mississippi and my great-aunt Monie.

The woman van Gogh painted—café proprietress at Arles—she could have been my mother's mother, in Sarrat, cooking gumbo and rice and coffee and cake every day for the people coming in from the cane fields. I remembered that moment, before that painting, and how I saw the weariness in her eyes. Not the demure superiority of the Gainsborough women, in their careful poses and lush gowns.

Art was a moment captured, a piece of a day of the men stripping the varnish from the floor. I was twenty. I was alone in front of the paintings, and I could never talk about them with the people of my childhood. My father and Gustave in the trees, their fingers testing the dimpled rind of the navel crop. My brothers lying on top of the truck to reach into the engine, their legs scissored, their bare shoulders streaked with sweat and oil.

My mother at the table—her work to feed everyone, and listen. Her wrist moving, the muscles in her forearm when she chopped the tomatoes and onions.

My mother saying, "Always talk bout someone sell down the river. But she sell up the river. Marie-Therese. The one from Africa. Cause they down there at the end of the world. Lafitte man find her in the bayou. Moinette mama. She try to drown herself in Bayou Azure. But them pirate come up the bayou with some wine to sell. And they taken her to another place. Sell her, but first she have a baby."

Treasure. He had two amber jewels he must have taken from the suit, and the bullet that had come from his arm, and the gun.

I walked back down Chartres to Napoleon House. It was open now, and a line stretched around the sidewalk. I went back to the service entrance, and waited until someone opened the door to empty trash. "I need to ask Juanita something," I told the same man who'd seen me earlier.

She was carrying a tray with sandwiches. Jimmy Taco had sent us all an essay about layers of meat dripping with green dressing that smelled of olives.

She said, "What?" She winced at the weight of the tray. "I hate sandwiches. I like my meat on the plate, and my rice. Not all mushed together."

"You said Victor mentioned the end of the world."

"Yeah?"

"My papa's from Plaquemines Parish."

"Yeah. Down there. Glorette son was sayin something bout Plaquemines. He want to know how far it was."

Azure was in Plaquemines Parish.

Juanita said, "I told him I never been down there and he said, FX got all those maps in her car. I said, Who FX? He told me that was you. Travel all over the world. And never been to New Orleans." She glanced up at the bar, and put her head down to plow through the crowd.

I hailed a cab that had just let out two people in front of Napoleon House. I got in the back, and the driver pulled away slowly. "The Lafitte, please," I said absently, and he swerved right back to the curb.

"You kiddin me?" he said angrily. His arm was tanned and hairy on the top of the seat when he turned around to see my face. "Hell, no. Where the hell you from?"

I sat there for a minute, in the humming sticky air, his hand flat on the leather. I was not a tourist.

I got out and started walking. Not like a walkin fool, or like myself at all. The hammered-tin sky, the puddles of water, and then under the freeway, my feet like boiled meat, my eyes stinging with sweat.

The white van was parked under the shade of an oak tree. When I asked Philip if anyone else drove, he said, "Yeah, Ricky drive a cab."

"Did you see a kid with a yellow shirt?"

"Ricky call me about a hour ago and say some kid give him a hundred-dollar bill take him to Plaquemines Parish. I was sayin, Man, that's a long trip on a good day. He said, People packin up and business slow—I take him to Mars if he pay me."

PART THREE

Even the smallest of creatures carries a sun in its eyes.

—ANTONIO PORCHIA

AZURE

I HAD FORGOTTEN HOW BIG IT WAS. The end of the earth. The whole of river and sky and marsh and swamp, the wind and grass, and everywhere the woods.

My father's woods. But he stared out the window, impassive, while he drove. No more stories.

What would I say to Victor now? I'd been telling him stories for days—and they hadn't been enough. What words would make him throw away the gun and smile again? Make him say, "Fervid, fervent, feverish, dervish, derivative"?

A hundred miles from New Orleans to the mouth of the Mississippi, they used to say. When we crossed over the bridge to the west bank, the river seemed even wider than it had that morning. The river, the barges and tugboats, the ragged trees along the edge of the water—all seemed still in the midday heat as if under a glass dome.

The bridge was crowded with people leaving the city. We went south, on Highway 23 through Gretna. Traffic was like LA, both sides jammed. The windows were open on the Corsica, and the heat from exhaust, from the asphalt, and from the sky was all around us. Trucks were crammed full of faces, and cars full of boxes and black plastic trash bags like fat pleated slugs pressed against the windows. "You sure we can get back out before the hurricane?" I asked my father.

My father looked at the oncoming traffic. "They headed east to Mississippi or west to Texas. When we find him, we go to Lafayette."

We kept south, past English Turn, then into Belle Chasse. The gas stations were crowded with cars and people carrying gas cans.

"They look scared," I said. "What about Azure? I don't even know who's there, besides Aunt Almoinette."

"Everybody got generator down there," my father said. "On the boats. Not like the city. They used to a storm."

"Where did Albert go?" I asked.

"Went to buy his mama a new fan and get them some can food. Case that storm hit the city. Say he stay there with them case the power go out."

What could they have said to each other at the kitchen table? Albert wanted to know exactly what happened in the ditch all those years ago, but he'd already figured out how he felt about it. Tony's grandmother said, "So who cares how I got the son? I got one."

My mother used to dismiss it, when they talked at night on the gallery and I listened from the bougainvillea hedge. "Temp-passé," she said, scrolling it into one word.

You could only consider the past, and leave it.

The highway turned toward the river again. We followed the water and left everything suburban behind. It came back to me—the liquid smell permeating the air, while Glorette and I were in the truck bed chewing sugarcane stalks we'd gotten in Sarrat. The river to our left, invisible behind the sloping grass-covered levee and the thick woods between orange groves. But you always knew it was right there. You could feel it, hear the tugboat horns or barges banging against chains above you somewhere. To the west, on the other side of the highway, were more woods and groves, and just beyond miles of marsh and bays and canals and swamps where the men fished, trapped, shrimped, and dredged oysters. We had been out there, on my father's old boat.

Plaquemines Parish was the long narrow strip of land that descended south of Louisiana, like the heel of the boot in southern Italy. Every time I looked at a map with Rick or Tony, I always glanced at the birdfoot delta reaching blank and fringed into the Gulf. A place where towns were too small to show up on the maps—they'd been old planta-tions, some of the wealthiest places in the country. Deer Range, Myrtle Grove, Gloria, Naomi. The river had left hundreds of years of earth along its banks, where sugarcane grew.

The finger of land was never more than a few miles wide. A private place, amid the endless expanse of flat earth and water mixed like a mosaic. Not like California, where the hills and canyons and boule-vards and beaches were all so visible and public and famous—the whole world owned LA.

We passed satsuma groves, cattle grazing near the levee bank, and a few houses, some boarded up, some with people in the yards gesturing to cars or windows or just standing and looking at the sky. It was a sunny, clear day, with only a few clouds like dirty old lace to the west.

We drove in silence for twenty more miles. Brick ruins in a tangle of vines, close to the highway. "Sugar mill," my father said, squinting. Past the ruins was a plantation house, white, two-storied, with a red tin roof and railed gallery.

"Woodland," he said. "Somebody buy it."

The house and grounds looked vaguely familiar. I'd seen them somewhere.

"Back by the river, they had the jail. Lafitte put the people he steal in there. Tell them girl, don't wash clothes at the river or bayou. Lafitte men steal you."

The sign showed a horse trotting smartly past. The Southern Comfort label—that's where this house was preserved forever. A bed-and-breakfast. I could tell Rick. A good story, for someone else.

What was the word for a slave jail?

Barracoon. Lots of points for that.

We passed cypress swamp and acres of citrus. After another five miles, a dense stand of woods, with an old dirt road that led inside. My father pointed. "Comtesse," he said. "Back there. House fall in the river, 1902."

The Picard place. The owner called it Comtesse because his wife was a countess in France. He bought Marie-Therese from the pirates—after she left Azure.

I remembered one night when I'd seen Glorette at the Riviera, she'd said, "Hey. You remember when we went to Azure? They had a street named for Picard, and one for Antoine. Bayou named for that little white girl's eyes. A trip, huh?" Then she stood up and pirouetted, and said, "They can name the alley for Sisia. Not me."

The car was stopped. He was staring at the woods. I said, "Papa. Today Alfonso told me he was in the alley when Glorette got killed. He said some prostitute scared her or choked her, or she had a heart attack. And he never saw the woman again."

My father said, "He never tell nobody? Not Victor?"

I shook my head. "I guess he thought there wasn't any point." I felt a shuddering breath roll through me. "Just like the kid in Burbank. No point. Just—" Something I couldn't even name. "You gonna tell Gustave?"

My father looked past me, at the citrus trees on my side. He said, "A stranger."

I said, "Some woman from New York who drove a van. He didn't even know her name."

My father began to drive again. Finally, he said, "Tell Gustave when we get back. But don't tell that boy."

Because randomness only bred anger. The woods and the alley. He didn't look at me. After about five more miles, the road bent slightly. On the west side was Bayou Azure, which was wider than I'd remembered, with two white shrimp boats and several small aluminum skiffs tied to pilings at a wooden dock. My father turned east, toward the river. "A stranger," he said, and shook his head.

Bordelon Road. A narrow asphalt lane, patched with white oyster shells, led into a thick stand of woods. The car bumped down off the highway, onto the rough pale pavement through the trees. The road curved around like a horseshoe, and at the far end was a small wooden cabin. Aunt Almoinette's house, with a red tin roof, and a big yard under three huge pecan trees.

Her house was closest to the levee. We'd walked every day up the path behind her yard, through the woods grown up around the front part of the plantation—the river and the Azure landing, where steamboats used to stop. The abandoned main house was partly hidden in the forest. No one ever went inside—people said there were spirits there. That everyone who lived there had died unhappy.

On the other side, two more asphalt lanes were lined with homes. Antoine Road and Picard Road—about ten ancient wooden houses with hipped roofs of tin and spindly front porches, with wide yards between and a few small boats and some bicycles. Five double-wide trailers with decks and wooden steps. An aboveground pool, and two aluminum sheds near wooden worktables. There were five cars, and people carrying bags and boxes. A battered pale-blue pickup truck had a load of plywood, and three men were sliding off the boards. Then I saw the sheriff's patrol car in the yard.

The officer was about fifty, with a pillow stomach but also big hands and arms, and a black baseball cap. He walked over as we got out of the car. My heart was hammering up in my throat. He didn't even look at me. He went straight to my father and said, "That ain't Enrique Antoine? That you? I thought you lived in California. What the hell you comin south for today, hanh? You head the wrong way."

My father didn't look scared. He leaned against the front fender of the car and said, "That me. How your uncle?"

"Oh, he got the boats all tied down at Empire. He and some old-timers down there say they stayin. I can't make em go." He glanced at me, but then pointed to the old house. "But your aunt needs to go. I'm checkin every house, and she refuses to evacuate. All her animals." He shook his head. "You showed up just in time. These guys say they movin the boats down the Azure Canal to deeper water, but everybody else is just about gone. You need to get Monie out by tomorrow morning." He looked at his watch. "It's past three now. If the storm stays on course, it's comin after midnight tomorrow." He nodded at the men unloading plywood. "Look, this one's the real deal, Enrique."

My father was cool. He said, "Me and my daughter here start packin her up."

"Get out by tomorrow morning," the deputy said. "Most people are headed to Lafayette or Lake Charles. Cause New Orleans looks bad, too."

He waved to the men at the truck and shouted, "Okay, Emile. Y'all get it together now." He said nothing about Victor. He got into his car and headed back to the highway.

A large black dog with a fringy tail held like a flag ran at my father and me when we walked up the slight slope toward the pecan trees. Then three more dogs leapt from the porch of the small wooden house and barked furiously when I stopped. In a yard enclosed by a chain-link fence, red and gold and black chickens paraded around, and one peacock studied us balefully and then turned away. The dogs boiled around me, dancing and leaping, and I froze until a tiny woman came to the door. "Eh, Lord, no, they send you all the way from California? I ain't go, me, so you turn back now. Pas aller, moi."

The same wooden cistern beside the rain-gutter spout, the same sweet olive bushes on either side. And Aunt Almoinette was merely lower to the ground, one of those very small, very old women who were like children again—the entire world revolved around them, and their stories, and their wants. That was why Glorette and I had loved and feared her—she never cared whether we ate or washed or tied our shoes, as long as we listened to her stories.

How old was she? She turned around holding a polished stick. Not a cane. A thick walking stick. "You believe in God now?" she said, to me. "You was tite, temp passé. You say, I don't know God. You say, The Bible just a book."

I said, "I remember."

The house was just one large room, with a small kitchen added to the back, and a tiny bathroom behind that. The front room had a double bed in the corner next to the antique wooden armoire, and an easy chair by the window. The wall was lined with transparent plastic bins of animal food and bowls. The same picture of Jesus from when I was ten: upturned face, soft beard, folded hands. On the fireplace mantel, a few pictures and two small decorative dishes. The wooden stand where you knelt to pray, with a rosary.

She said it again. "You believe in God now?"

"I do."

She sat down and looked out the window, and we had to wait. I knew not to ask her questions, because they would only annoy her.

She used to speak in scripture, that summer, and I'd hated the words and singsong cadence. She said things like "Divided tongues as of fire appeared among them, and a tongue rested on each of them."

She stared at me now. Back then, I'd said, "How do you remember every word?" I had thought, Who talked like that? Who didn't want to make up their own sentences?

And she said, "They beat me when I say it wrong. The nuns in New Orleans. Send me there when I tite, cause I'm so smart."

"They beat you?"

I never forgot what she said. "Beat everybody. But some like to be beat. They cry and suffer when the cane comes down, but I see they do the same thing again so that nun get the cane. They like to stand in front and make a fuss, them girl. Agathe and Marie-Claude. Can't memorize their own name. I memorize the whole book. They beat me cause I ask question. Like you."

Now she reached down to her ankle and moved the string with seven knots. Red string. Like a tracing of blood along her skin. "Had one a these when I went up there, to New Orleans. My maman tie it on. Sister Agnes tell me take it off, and I say no. She cut it off. She make me memorize verses. When I say them, I leave out one word to see she listening. She hit me three times. With that cane." She held out her forearm, and I remembered Glorette and me leaning forward to see the marks. So close I could smell the bleach washed into her sleeve. Her skin was unscarred. But she ran her fingers over the spot and said, "Like three snakes raise up under there. I want to cut them out. They stay three days. I memorize all of Ezekiel and Jeremiah in my room."

My father moved into the room, and she turned to me. "Send you from California. Tu—l'intelligente. Ou est l'autre? Li soeur? La jolie?"

"Back in California," I said. My sister. She meant Glorette. The beauty.

"You ask the question. She the one listen." The dogs settled flat on the linoleum floor, their eyes fixed on her.

My father said in French, "We're looking for her son. Glorette's son. Victor."

She shrugged and shook her head. She didn't offer us coffee. She folded her arms as if we were just the last in a legion of people bothering her, and said, "Ecoutez, they ain't take mesdames at no shelter. Pas aller, moi."

Mesdames? The four dogs. Aunt Monie had always had chickens, rabbits, even a raccoon once, but only had one dog when we were here before.

"Is everyone else going?" I asked, looking at the men unloading plywood from the truck. Five kids were shooting at a portable basketball hoop. Two women had made a pile of food on a picnic table, and were packing coolers.

"Oui," she said, nodding. "Go to Lafayette. Sheriff say I got to go. Mais he don't remember—Betsy knock down some, Camille knock down them place at Woodland. But Azure la-bas—" She pointed toward the river. "Still there. And moi—icitte." Her headscarf was the palest yellow—maybe white gotten old, or marigold gotten faded. Her skin was dark gold, like the oldest gilt frame in a museum, and her nose was strong, with a bump on the bridge. She wore black knit pants and a blouse with turquoise flowers. She pulled on the same short white rubber boots as the men outside. Shrimper boots.

The dog nearest to her, the one who seemed in charge, stood up and stared toward the door. "That Mama," she said. "Les autres, c'est les filles. Coco, Lulu, Zizi." She snapped her fingers and they all stood, electric with waiting. She snapped again and they shot out the door.

"Three thirty," she said. "Mesdames tell time. Three thirty we walk. Toujours."

My father touched her on the arm, and she shot him a look. "Tante," he said. "The boy. Gustave grandson. Gustave fille—Glorette."

"Sais pas, moi," she said, brushing past him.

"La jolie." He touched her arm again.

She stopped and squinted into the yard. "That boy? Mesdames smell his arm."

The salt meat.

"He don't say, Mo fam, he don't say, Mo besoin l'argent. Like all them boy."

He hadn't asked her for food or money. "What did he say?" I asked.

"Say where the cimitaire? I say pourquoi, and he say bijou."

Bijou? Sounded like a name for a little dog. Then I remembered. Bijoux. Jewelry. He thought the buried treasure was jewelry.

The blue truck came toward us. Emile, the one driving, looked vaguely familiar. He said, "We need to take care your house, Aunt Monie."

She nodded, chin high, studying my father. "That Enrique. He the one live out there in California." She shook her head and walked away. My father was not the elder here. He was not a griot. He was just a nephew. The one who left.

There were only two kinds of people. Those who stayed home, and those who left.

My father and I followed her. She walked quickly toward the levee, the dogs racing ahead on the dirt path, swerving into the trees to smell something.

I looked back at her house, the red tin roof and gray weathered wood, set apart now from the mobile homes and shotgun cottages. It had been an old slave cabin. Moinette and her mother, Marie-Therese, had been the plantation laundresses and seamstresses, so they were closer to the front. Aunt Monie had told us that the rest of the old slave quarters were on the other side of the highway, but those houses had all fallen apart over the years.

She called back to us, "I send him up here. See him walk there." She pointed with her stick up the path, and we started up the slight rise.

If Victor was poking around the cemetery, would he still have the gun? Did my father have a gun, too, under his La Reina workshirt?

The main house was like Seven Oaks, and all the other plantation houses that died when their white people died. If a family had heirs, or a good location, they were bed-and-breakfasts or museums. But this was a darkened skeleton of wood, like a ghost ship marooned in the trees. Two stories, set on high brick piers for ventilation, and floods. The front gallery had faced the river, where the boats had landed to bring supplies, and take away sugar. And Moinette.

The back door was a blind keyhole up on the second floor. The stairs that had led to it were gone. The dogs ran under the house. Aunt Monie pointed with her stick toward a tangle of weeds and palmettos a hundred yards away. A small city of white in the weeds.

Cemetery. My father and I walked toward the crypts. My father's eyes moved constantly over the trees, and when we got to the overgrown wrought-iron fence, he picked up a stick and started slashing away at the vines and brush. Victor hadn't been here. No one had been here.

Three crypts. The carved letters blank-eyed as Greek statues. No one came here for La Toussaint and cleaned the gravesite, or painted the names. Bordelon. Bordelon. Bordelon. The blue-eyed girl was inside one.

Aunt Monie hadn't stopped. I ran toward the levee, where she was following the dogs onto the levee road, and caught up with her. "But Marie-Therese isn't buried there."

"C'est Bordelon, la. Up at Comtesse."

"Did you tell Victor that?"

She looked at me like I was crazy.

I bent to catch my breath. The heat and humidity swarmed into my chest. How would Victor walk to Comtesse, even if he figured that out? The levee wasn't a grassy maintained slope here. It was just a mountain of earth, covered with scrub trees and vines and palmettos. But the levee road was clear. You could drive, or walk, for a while.

My father came up the slope. This was definitely high ground. The batture, the wild border of trees and driftwood and trash that stood between the levee and the water, was thick and lush. And the water spread out so wide the other bank was invisible.

I had thought it was the ocean when she brought me here the first time.

The Mississippi. Not blue like the Aare, or black with oil and garbage like the Thames in south London, or green as old jade like the Limmat in Zurich. No bridges or picnics or mallards or ancient walls. The Mississippi was every color. Brown with mud at the edges, green when a chop lifted in the breeze and a tongue of water rose, blue when a flat circle spun for a moment into an eddy.

Stare at the Mississippi too long and them spirit call you drown. That's what Aunt Monie used to say. She ignored us, walking briskly along the levee toward the south, as she probably did every single day at exactly this time, behind the dogs that raced as fast as they could along the road. She was the one who'd made me see the river and the world underneath a world, the first time.

Aunt Monie had whispered, *Attend! You don't know the river, you get too close. But them whirlpool take you down. And them spirit hold you for themselves. Take a boat. Take a girl.*

We walked in silence. If Victor had come up here, and looked at the names on the crypts, and seen that the house held nothing, where would he go next?

I knew the story, from Aunt Monie, but I didn't know what he knew.

Monie had told Glorette and me: *The river bring her. Amina. The one from Senegal. She hold her girl on the boat, all the way from Africa, so no one throw her in the ocean. Then they come up this water. And Amina die from the soldier blue. Marie-Therese live in my house. She have Moinette, and watch that girl all the time. Don't wash clothes in the bayou. Trader steal you. Then Bordelon sell Moinette. Right there at the landing. Marie-Therese drown herself in Bayou Azure. But the spirit push her back up. Dya. The spirit in the water. They don't want her yet. Them pirate come up the bayou and they catch her. Take her to Comtesse.*

She was buried at the place we'd passed.

We reached the old landing. Rotted pilings and what was left of a boardwalk that led off to nowhere in the woods. Past that, along the levee road, cars and trucks were parked in a straight line. The dogs turned around, confused, and ran back toward us.

"She ain't want to raise us," my father said, back in the yard. "Me and Gustave."

Aunt Monie. I said, "I better go to Comtesse and check out the grave-yard."

It was after four now, and the sky was leaden and gray. Three men pulled up in front of Aunt Monie's house and unloaded plywood, prop-ping it against the porch railing. "She won't let us put em up till tomor-row, but leave em there now," Emile called.

He leaned against the truck door and cocked his head. A player.

I put out my hand and said, "Fantine."

He grinned and said, "Ain't it F-X? Look like you, anyway." He made my name a long two syllables, and his grin pushed deep into one cheek. "F-X."

And just like that—like talking to Marcus, or my brothers—I laughed and the words flew out and my whole chest felt warm. "You ain't gotta make it sound like I'm trying so hard," I said. Emile, who had been fifteen when I was ten, who'd already had girlfriends hanging around Azure, sitting on the let-down gate of a pickup wearing shorts and swinging their legs. With his football player's chest that summer, two flat plates of muscle that met along a pale line running vertically along his breastbone. His arms muscled from fishing and dredging oys-ters. I'd had a big crush on him, but Glorette and I were like little wisps of nothing. Feux follets, he called us, when we stalked him in the woods while he built a bonfire with his friends and the girls.

"Have you seen a kid in a yellow T-shirt? Wearing a bandanna around his arm? Walking? That's Glorette's son. He's in trouble."

"And he come down here? Who he hidin from?"

My father spoke in French to the other men. I said to Emile, "Look-ing for something."

He said, "You don't remember when I came to California? You only home for a hot minute that time. Dressed like some fashion model in college."

I frowned. A faded red car pulled up behind him, and a woman shouted, "You gon park up on the levee, Emile? That where you tell Marceline put her car?"

He shouted back, "That blue Thunderbird? Yeah, up there by the old landing road." He pointed toward the river. She drove down the shell road, followed by another woman in a white Suburban.

"My second wife sister."

"Oh, the second one?" I said.

"Yeah," he said.

So easy. "And where's the third one?"

He grinned and lifted his chin up high. "I done gave up." Emile raised his eyebrows. They were thick and winged, arched like Glorette's. He wasn't a Picard. But his skin was the same hammered gold as hers. His eyes were brown, though, and flecked with green. I remembered them. Like agate I'd found on a beach in Oregon once.

"Some funky bandanna tied around his arm? Just about purple? Like he a Prince fan?" Emile said.

"Yes," I said. "And we have to find him. We really do." I didn't want to tell him about the gun—down here everyone had a gun, and a knife, for fishing and hunting. I didn't want to tell him about Jazen, Alfonso, or buried treasure, because it sounded crazy.

Emile had teased me thirty years ago. That was all. But his eyes moved slowly over my face. I put my hand on his forearm, and I whispered, "He's like a runaway child. Runnin wild. Serious."

"Okay, catin. But he could be anywhere. You see how it is." He picked up a piece of plywood. "Ain't nowhere to go round here less you know. He ain't got a boat."

They started nailing plywood over the windows of another house, and I sat in the car, holding my phone, watching clouds move in fast from the south. Black and purple, full of rain. Emile called, "That just rain. But you better not be here tomorrow."

Tony went straight to message. "It's past four. Maybe you're just landing in New Orleans. Tony, I'm not even there anymore. I'm down the river. But I really need you to get two hotel rooms in the city. When I find my godson, I'm coming back."

My father came out of Aunt Monie's house and looked up at the sky. The dangling moss on the cypress began to sway. As the first drops fell, the men kept hammering, and the white Suburban came down from the road. The woman shouted, "Emile! Marceline car ain't on the levee. You got about ten cars up there, but not that one."

Emile walked over to the passenger side. "I tell everyone leave the keys inside cause I might have to move them car after the storm. Who in the hell gon steal that old Thunderbird?"

"Did you see him drive away?" I asked her. "Glorette's son?"

She shook her head. "So many boys round here. And I ain't cook. Think ol lady toujou cook. I ain't no grandmère." Aunt Monie made coffee in a battered metal drip pot, and poured it into two tiny china cups. She pushed one at me and sat at the table. I drank five sips of darkness. "That boy say, My grandmère dead. I say, Well, I ain't take her place, me. He say, You know where she bury? I say, You never read your Bible? Even the wise die, the fool and the stupid alike must perish and leave their wealth to others. Their graves are their home forever. Cimitaire, cipriere."

Cemetery or swamp.

"He say, How many cimitaire? Azure, Petit Clair, Comtesse, Woodland up north. Say, Diamond, Port Sulphur down south. Dead people in the river, in the levee."

He could be anywhere, if he'd stolen the Thunderbird. Aunt Monie listened to the rain, loud on the tin roof. She said, "Some people die in the water and never bury. Enrique know that."

"Aren't you afraid of the hurricane?" I said.

She gave me that imperious look—the one I'd seen on old men in Portugal, sitting outside a tobacco shop, watching young people walk past. An old man, Tio Wilfredo in Belize, who critiqued the way a grandson had brought in fishing nets from a cay.

She said, "So many people come. They all want me go to Lafayette. But I ain't go. Your love to me was extraordinary," she said. "The evening devotion. Samuel 1:26."

"Your love?"

"Mesdames," she said. She looked at the dogs, who lay with their heads up, watching. "Mesdames want love. Jamais money."

The dogs leapt up. "Fantine," my father said through the screen.

"And Enrique," Aunt Monie said quietly, not looking at him but at me. "All day, I make quelque-chose live. All day he make them die."

———

The rain had stopped, and the trees were dripping, the sun hard again. But we had only a few hours until nightfall. Victor didn't even know how to drive.

"I'll check out the cemeteries," I said to my father.

A stolen car and a gun. A bandanna. A pathetic gangster looking for a mythical bracelet.

My father said, "Some them cimitaire you can't drive. They in the woods."

"When I come back, we're going to a hotel in New Orleans. If I can't find Victor, he has to be trying to drive back to California, and he'd have to get gas money."

He shrugged. "I been in two storm. We ride on the boats."

"Papa. We're not riding out a hurricane in a boat. Maman would kill us if we lived. Tony's getting a hotel room. And we should take Aunt Monie."

Emile pulled the last sheets of plywood off the bed. He stretched his arms behind his head, and his muscles moved under the white T-shirt covered with oil, mud, and grime. "A hotel, huh?"

Only the four men, Aunt Monie, and I were left now.

Emile held out his hands wide. "She Aunt Monie! She just made ninety-nine. She ain't gotta be nice. She ain't gotta do nothing she don't want to." Then he bent to pick up the plywood. "But you from California. Your daddy be okay, but you? Regular rain scare the shit outta you. I seen you runnin just now."

I said, "Seriously? You don't even know me. I've been in a blizzard in Maine. I sat on a highway in the Austrian alps for eight hours with a friend after an avalanche. A heat wave in Naples where people were lying in fountains trying to stay alive. And I've been through four earthquakes."

He waited for my father to pick up the other end of the stack. "That ain't a storm."

I pulled onto the two-lane highway. The sun was dangling lower, a blurry explosion in the filthy windshield. Marie-Therese. Slaves didn't get last names. And where the hell would he think the treasure was—buried like some old ghost story beside a tree? Marked with a damn X?

Twice I went down dirt roads and ended up in yards, where brick ranch-style houses were boarded up. The second time, a man came out of the backyard, staring at me, a rifle held loose along his leg. I turned the car around quickly. He thought I was a looter.

My heart was pounding, and I'd had nothing to eat all day. I saw the stand of trees—the road, and went through a gap in cars again. Comtesse. The track was puddled and rough. The levee wasn't far—much closer than Azure. This house had fallen into the river. I got out carefully, looking for a clearing, a grassy area, a cemetery that someone had visited. A black wrought-iron fence, like lace, and six crypts, white stone with angels and crosses and faded plastic flowers and names carved onto the doors. The grass had been mowed.

I looked through the fence. Louise Picard: 1870–1900. Philomene Picard: 1822–1865. Octave Picard: 1798–1821. And three more crypts whose etched names were blurred into nothing. Maybe Marie-Therese? But at those three, nothing was dug up, no marble was chipped or broken open.

Maybe he would look for the second Marie-Therese, Moinette's daughter. I got back in my car and drove south, past Azure, into Diamond, which was a bigger community, with a church. St. Jude's. This cemetery was very large and well kept, and the levee was grassy and bare nearby. It took a long time, but I found the gravestone. Marie-Therese Antoine. "She mechant. Voleur. That why she get what she want," Aunt Monie had said when I was small. She was bad. A thief. She'd slept with whomever she wanted to. I touched the white marble of the crypt, the carved numerals. 1835–1935. The women in our family lived a long time.

I would be forty this year. Sixty more years? I'd be like Aunt Monie. Or I'd get a place in Zurich. Or someday move back to Sarrat, to my mother's house? Not likely. I wouldn't be an old lady anyone liked.

So I'd be Aunt Monie. Great.

I sat in the parking lot, watching the sun get less silver, more gold. I pushed the button. "Leave the digits."

"Victor," I said. "You're in a Thunderbird. Pretty impressive. Except you took it from some woman who's gonna need it after the hurricane. We're running out of time."

The air around the car was heavy as honey. I said, "I'm in the parking lot of the church at Diamond. Here's the deal. Find whatever you think you're looking for and then bring the car here. That way you won't have to see anyone. Except me."

I closed my eyes. "I'm gonna sit here for a while. I'm really tired. But I have one more story about your father. You think your dad played your moms and didn't want you. Nope. You told me Professor Zelman made fun of the Floaters. The Delfonics, the Whispers. What brothers put on when they get serious. Your father hated them. He was a music snob, too. He told me the Floaters were simpleminded. Let me take you to love land. You think he went off to be a famous musician. But Grady, he killed your dad. He was obsessed with your mom."

I thought of all the men, staring at her, thinking they knew. "It was hard to be her," I said. "So hard."

I heard car doors slam near me. Someone went into the church. "One night, Grady stole a car to impress her. She could not be moved, Victor. She loved your dad like that. And then she was a few weeks away from having you, and Grady caught your dad in the parking lot of a club and killed him. He took the body—"

Two little girls with black cornrows and white beads stared at me through the window. Victor didn't need to know about La Paloma. "He took your dad out to the ocean. No one ever found him. I know you're like, Nice story. But Grady told me all this five years ago. Grady's homeless. Your mom left him and he lost his mind. Ended up on the street. I'm the only one he ever told." I took a breath. "I never told anyone because I didn't know which was worse—that your father got killed or that he just disappeared."

The white beads swung like a hundred moons when the girls ran back to their mother's car.

And Glorette? What Alfonso told me wouldn't change how Victor felt. She had been killed for nothing, too.

"Victor. Everyone lost it over love. All three of them. And Danita— she fell hard for you. DJ Scholaptitude." I lay the seat back all the way. "I'm sitting here in Diamond. I love you, okay? I didn't know before. Come on. We need to go home."

I must have slept so deeply that inside my mind went black, as if I were under layers of earth, and my chest felt full of dirt, and I couldn't breathe.

A loud pounding woke me up. They were boarding the windows of the church, and it was dark.

A crown of blue in the dim light of the yard near Aunt Monie's. A huge pot on a portable gas ring. The houses were all blind except for hers. The only light was from her porch, her front window, and two lanterns the men had put in her yard. The heat pressed down on us, but the biggest metal fan I'd ever seen—the size of a small trampoline—blew air over us and kept the mosquitoes away.

Emile said, "He runnin outta time. This boy."

"I know," I said. I looked at the complete darkness toward the levee and the river. There was no moon yet. Night here was night. Like being inside a weird black-velvet painting where only the light around us existed—the burner, the white plastic stack chairs like squat skeletons. Van Gogh but even darker, more blurred than his stars.

Emile said, "This my cousin Freeman and his son Philippe." They shook my hand and sat back down on the chairs. My father came out of Aunt Monie's house carrying a pot.

Emile said, "Guy sold us crab and redfish cheap. He wanted to empty the freezer before he left."

Aunt Monie sliced white onion and green pepper on a cutting board, her fingers still nimble and precise. She gave my father a withering look. "Nobody live without onion. Pepper. And oil. Corn oil right there, in that pot. You call corn a bush or a grass?"

What the hell were they arguing about? He bowed his head and refused to look up.

"They been had this fight before," Emile whispered to me. "She says women raise up things to live, little things, and men kill everything. Men think they're the ones."

She put a wide flat cast-iron pot on the gas ring and fried the fish with the onion and pepper. "Creole tomato. Easter lily. Grow em all here. Bien place, ici. Why go to Texas?" she said darkly. "Why go to California?"

She was still angry at my father for leaving. Just like my mother was angry with me.

Redfish and blue crab. What a title for a food piece. The fish was not blackened but seared in lacy char. The crabmeat was splintery

white and filled with the tingle of salt and red pepper, so spicy my lips
burned.

We had beer from an ice chest. Jimmy Taco would die. All those guys
who wrote about food—this was what they lived for.

Suddenly, just like the day before, I saw other people sitting here, in
this circle.

The old woman from Venice—Signora Passoni, at her long dining
table with the most delicate, perfect handmade fettuccine like a nest of
gold. An elderly woman named Jean in Southstoke, a village outside
Bath, who'd saved every plastic bag and rubber band since the war,
whose dark cottage was cluttered and airless but whose apricot pre-
serves were like golden nectar. A woman about seventy with a red
headscarf, grilling kielbasa at a church festival in Chicago—the best
bursting-open browned thing I'd ever eaten.

What would they say to Aunt Monie, pulling crabs from the pot?
The ancient woman in the mountains outside Brienz? Her granary
built on layers of flat black stones to keep out the rats. Her tiny wooden
kaase-hutli. The cheese had its own house for summer.

"Hey," Emile said. "You left the planet?"

I shook my head. "Just sleepy."

He said, "I gotta move the big truck up to the levee in the morning.
Tante Monie, you got your generator set up, right? We got gas. Where
we takin your animals?"

"You not—"

"Poulets, Aunt Monie. Where you want them?"

She straightened her narrow shoulders in the print shirt. "Take them
on the boat."

He shook his head. "No poulet on my boat."

"Then they go in the truck."

I could see that they'd bargained like this before.

"Peacock on his own."

She nodded. "He fly up to the old house. Where he come from."

My father said quietly to me, "Victor must be sleep in that car."

Aunt Monie took the dogs, who'd been lying at the edge of the yard,
down the street, her pale scarf floating and their dark forms swerving
like fish around her.

———

My father stood up and looked down the narrow road. "I take a ride. See he have a light on. Make him easy to see in the dark."

"He could be anywhere in fifty, sixty miles," Emile said. "You ain't got that much gas left, and ain't no more."

"I find gas," my father said. He started up the Corsica and went toward the highway.

Emile shook his head slowly. "Ain't no more wood left at the store, either, and we got two more house."

"We gotta get that old wood," Freeman said. "Tomorrow."

Freeman and Philippe left in the blue truck, headed down to the dock to their boat. The phone rang inside my pocket, and I jumped. Tony. "Hey," I said. "You made it."

"My flight was delayed. What time is it? I am so out of it."

"Almost nine."

"Shit. Where are you? I'm heading into the Quarter with a guy from CNN. Every reporter in the world is flying in."

"Tony. I'm not in the city. I had to go south. I'm where my dad was born."

"What? That boot of Louisiana thing? You're in the fucking Naples of Louisiana?"

"Yeah. But no mountains and rock."

Emile had turned off the gas ring. He was watching me in the darkness. "So what the hell?" Tony said. "You said everything was out of control."

"Oh, it is." The fan hummed like a giant hive. "Can you get us a hotel in a safe place? Wherever these reporters are going? We'll be there tomorrow."

"This is crazy," Tony said. I heard a lot of noise. "Great shots, though—people are partying like hell. Their faces—this veneer of desperation under the alcohol."

"Tony!" I turned and whispered so Emile couldn't hear me. "Victor's hurt. He's losing his mind. This isn't an adventure. I'm scared."

Tony said, "You don't get scared."

"Yeah, I do."

"Okay. I'll find a safe hotel."

When I turned back around, Emile said, "Your husband made it, huh?"

"He's somebody else's husband," I said. "He's my best friend."

"What they call it? The kids. He your friend with something?"

"Benefits," I said. "Not those benefits." He was pouring something dark as syrup from a blank bottle into a cup, and he handed it to me. Rum? He ran his hands through the loose brown-black curls at his neck.

He leaned back in his chair. "You come all the way down here to find this hardhead? And he don't want to be found?"

Evening Devotion. But my love hadn't been extraordinary. It had been bumbling and random and too late.

The rum was sugar and fire. I drank another cup. The world was hot and black and shivering. There was no moon. Nothing. Only Emile's hand on my elbow, guiding me down the oyster-shell road. The shells crunched like old white pistachios.

"Isn't your house boarded up?"

"Mostly my house is the boat." He grinned. "My first wife left me right before I came to California. She said I love my boat more than I love her. So she lit it on fire."

"On fire?"

"Yeah. Burnt that lil boat up. Your papa's old boat."

"The *One*—" I caught myself.

"The *Almoinette*." He laughed. "The name he paint over the other name. They sent me out by y'all cause they thought she would kill me next. But she took my boys and went to Lafayette."

"Then you got married again."

"Yeah. And I got this boat in '92. But I got divorced in '95."

"You loved the boat more."

"Nothin wrong with that."

"I need to stay here in case Victor shows up."

"Your papa find him."

The water was black, too, but with spokes of silver from the other boat. The bayou headed out to sea. The boat was tall, painted white with black trim, and named *Lady Chance*. "Cross between *Bonne Chance* and *Lady Luck*," he said.

"Why isn't it named for your wife?"

"Real funny," he said, helping me onto the deck.

There were nets, buckets, a huge empty ice chest, and winches that looked like tow-truck equipment. "In the morning, I gotta move the boat down to deeper water. This one spot where the cheniere protects from the wind. We gotta tie em down exactly right, but it's better to be on the boat than in a house. Your daddy told Tante Monie. But she don't like him."

"Why?"

We sat in the cabin, in the two chairs, facing cypress trees swung with tangles of gray moss like hundreds of old women, and the onyx path of water. "I guess she never did," he said. "They had some fight. He was runnin liquor, and then he went to Texas a few times. They say he come back and killed some dude from New Orleans tried to steal his money. He left and she had to hire somebody to help with the grove."

The third man. She'd said dead people were everywhere.

He poured another drink. The rum was like sweet mesh inside my chest. Gold armor. Somewhere on this bayou, the first Marie-Therese had tried to drown herself.

He kept the lights off in the cabin, but he turned the ship's radio on. Static and voices and men talking. "Ain't nobody came to California to get me that one time. I was twenty-four. I thought my wife would come after me."

"She was a Bordelon?"

"Yeah. Bordelon come from one lady. Phrodite. She was here back then. Eighteen and some. She had ten boys. They marry girls from across the river—Nero and Harlem and Bohemia. Them white Bordelon dead—all of em. But the rest of em stay here. You got two, three Picard. Only Antoine left is Aunt Monie. Her sister die, her mother die. Only your daddy. And he gone."

"Aunt Monie's mother—that was Anjanae. She was so old when we came."

He nodded.

"But her mother was Marie-Therese, and her mother was Moinette Antoine."

"Yeah, her mother. But not blood. She came out the woods."

I paused, confused. "The woods? What are you talking about?"

"Yeah. They say some white trader had them on a cart, camped in the woods. Up there by Opelousas. Marie-Therese was five when Moinette bought her. Moinette didn't birth them two girls, she was already old when she got them. She was free." He drank the rest of his rum. "Aunt Monie told me one time. I was a kid. Maybe she tried to scare me. Said somebody could sell me in the woods."

An animal screamed in the water. Then a night bird answered. My father and I were not descended from Moinette Antoine, the woman who got herself free, who learned to read. We were descended from a girl who came from the woods, who probably never knew her own parents.

"And she told you about the pirates?" I said finally.

"Pirates came by here all the time, yeah. Pirates just some dudes with guns and boats. Just gangsters, yeah?"

If the first Marie-Therese, the one born in Senegal, had a child with the Picard pirate, then Victor was her blood. Not me.

"Suppose to be treasure buried all over Louisiana, catin. Yeah, like people used to dynamite places up there around Bayou Teche. You look at tourist books, Lafitte stay everywhere. Everywhere they want to make some money."

Perfect tourist stories. Pirates, swords, jewels, buried chests of coins.

Emile stood up and pulled on my hand. It was like being a teenager again. I stumbled into the steering wheel, and he caught me around the waist. "You look good," he said into my neck. "How you look so good? Not a line on your face."

His lips were on my shoulder. I had no lines because I had no one to worry about. No frowns. I was no one.

"Come on. Down below."

"What?" My own lips brushed his neck when he lifted his head. I could barely stand up.

"You gon sleep in the hotel tonight?" He guided me toward the stairs. "You sure that ain't your man?" His voice was an inch from my earlobe. His breath was warm. "Cause I checked you out way back in California. But you ain't had time for me."

I put my arms around him quickly, spread out both my hands on his shoulder blades. Scapula. Angel wings. That's what my mother called them. You too thin—I see them angel wings. I ran my fingers down the ladder of his ribs, and that made him shiver.

He grinned, his dimple deep into that left cheek again. "Come on," he said.

We lay on the bed below deck. His hands were calloused, the palms lined with tiny hard pillows of skin. He pulled off my tank top, and then lifted off his own shirt. I held his arms in the air and ran my fingernails softly down the outside of his biceps, then along his ribs again, and he bent down like a wire had loosened.

I started laughing, and he said, "Oh, you think you know every-thing?"

He put his hands on either side of my face and traced my ears over and over, then my eyebrows, until I was nearly asleep. Then he circled my waist and lifted me up.

He called at exactly midnight. The phone was in my jeans, on the floor, and I leaned out of the bunk to grab the sound. "I got my ticket right here. You got yours?"

"What?" My eyes felt taped shut, and my hair fell around my face. Wait—Dave Matthews. The ticket that had fallen in the hallway. "Yeah."

He was crying. "It's nine o'clock in LA. They're warming up the crowd. I haven't been this pissed since the SAT. I had a ticket for that, too."

I got up and held my hair off my face. Emile had tangled his fingers in it. He lay on his side, watching me. I put on his T-shirt and grabbed a sheet. Mosquitoes. I went up to the deck, but the utter darkness around the boat was scary, so I sat with my back against the metal door propped open.

"Why'd you have to talk about Zelman?" His voice was mangled with anger and swallowed tears. "You had to bring it up."

"What?"

"Class!" Then he was crying openly. "Zelman would be assigning that essay now. The one where you pick an instrument from your her-itage. Something obscure. They just started fall session and he likes to tell you about it the first week so you can think about it all semester. But he's in fuckin Brazil."

"Where are you?" Tears streamed down my face, too, into my mouth.

"Some trees. A ditch."

"Can't you see anything to tell me where you are?"

"No." He was quiet. "I loved school. When my moms would be passed out, I'd get my pack, my granola bar, and walk to school. First day after we moved, I'd follow some kids my age." He sniffled and said quietly, "Once I followed a bus. I was like—seven. We had just packed up and we came to the Riviera. It was yellow. Like vanilla pudding yellow. And I saw a school bus stop at the corner and all these kids got on. I was scared to get on cause the driver wouldn't know me, so I ran behind it. Ain't like it was going that fast—not around there. But then it got on Palm Avenue and took off. I was runnin and then I didn't know where I was."

"Oh, baby, those kids were getting bused across town?"

"Yeah. So this cop stops. I thought he would just shoot me. Take me out. Cause that's all I ever heard."

"A white guy?"

"Brother. Real light. Said, Your mama Glorette, right, son? Like that. I said, Yeah, and he said, Where y'all stayin now? I told him we just moved to a yellow place. He took me to my old school. It was only six blocks."

"He did know her."

"Yeah."

I heard movement in the water. Something swimming. I pulled the sheet tight around me. The air was warm and wet as a tongue, but I wanted to be covered. "You charged the phone in the car lighter?"

"Yeah."

"What did you find?"

"Nothing. I went to sleep. All those songs about the levee. It's so quiet down here. In the woods. Water everywhere. I can't see shit except the phone."

"Let me come get you."

"Nope. It's my treasure. I'ma find it in the morning. I'm the pirate. Not you."

"I heard."

"I'm her blood. The one from Africa. With the pirate. All those years, you were the smart one, the famous writer, and you told me it was because of Moinette. The smart one. But I remembered my moms told me it was me."

"It is you."

"Aunt Monie told her your mama was like a foster kid."

"Well, my papa is looking for you right now. Maybe he'll see your phone light. You're the tribe."

"Yeah, don't say it. He'd kill for you, boy! I hate when people say that. He'd lay down his life for you, boy!"

"He would," I said. "And all I can do is give you a ride. If you don't believe it's for you, believe it's for your grandpère. They would die for each other."

"Except you live in LA. And I can't go back to the tribe."

"You mean back to Sarrat?"

"Rio Seco."

"Because of Jazen."

"Because of everything."

"You're coming to LA with me."

"Jazen's been to your place, remember?"

"You think he's gonna hunt you down in LA?"

"I don't know." He hesitated.

I said, "With what warriors? Not Alfonso."

But then he said, "He'll get Tiquan or one of the younger dudes."

"They won't come to LA. And you'll be on the road with me."

"If I went to London or Paris with you, I'd still be a nigga. I'd have to keep it real and all that shit."

Before I could answer, he said, "What's a poinciana?"

"A flower? No. That's poinsettia. I don't know." I squinted in the darkness. I couldn't tell him how she died.

"So you thought I wanted to be another version of you."

"I didn't know what you wanted to be."

"Maybe last week. Now I'm done. I heard these little rappers between buildings in the Lafitte. They were singin, My time to leave out this earth. I like that."

"Stop exaggerating."

No music behind him. Nothing but water whispering against the boat.

"So my pops was weak. He got killed by a trashman who wanted to be my daddy. But my moms taught me to be a writer."

"Oh—I thought—"

"You thought I grew up reading your magazines and took some notes, huh? Yeah. But check it—my moms used to lay on the carpet with me when I was little, and we'd look at the pieces of, like, yarn. Imagine being small enough to walk in the forest of the carpet. We saw the crows in the branches and they had purple and gold under their feathers. She told me about the Mississippi when she gave me a bath. Like five freeways of chocolate milk all headed south. That's how big she said it was. And she was right."

"So you're by the river."

"No. I'm in a ditch. Don't ask me where cause I don't know."

We were quiet together for a moment. Then Victor said, "Tonight I was thinking expatriate. You. Like James Baldwin or somebody. You're kinda sad. I wanted to go to college, but then I wanted to come back to Rio Seco. Be Zelman and Thompson at home."

"Why? Why would you want to stay there?"

"Cause I like seein all the places where my moms was. I still sit on the balcony at the Riviera or the Villas. If somebody doesn't look like they want to shoot me."

"But she left you there."

"Yeah. But I remember how it looked, when I sat there. The palm tree and the moon."

The full moon had to be clean, like winter, and trees had to be washed clean by rain, and when the moon rose behind the fronds, and when the breeze moved them, the silver light jumped and leapt from the fronds as if an invisible god held a sparkler.

"I like to walk around and see what she saw. Jimsonweed in the alley. Where she got killed. Those flowers."

"They open up at night. Like a fairy tale."

"Yeah."

His voice was sleepy and faint now. "Your moms, and Auntie Clarette and Cerise, they would feed me, and give me a ride, and wash my clothes. But you were like—an idea. That was cool. But now I'm out."

I was pissed. "An idea? I'm down here the night before a goddamn hurricane chasing you, and you're feeling sorry for yourself and being—fucking histrionic and calling me an idea when I'm right here?"

I sounded like Clarette, and Cerise, and Michelle Meraux when she yelled at Danita.

He was quiet. I imagined him lying in the front seat of the car. "When we were little and there was a freeze, we had to be out all night with the smudge pots. But one night, we couldn't get enough oil so we had to wet down the fruit with hoses. I fell asleep in the truck, and I woke up out there just when the sun was coming up. The light was coming sideways, you know, hitting the ice. Like thousands of ornaments." I saw it as vividly now. "You just carry scenes around in your head, and you try to make them into something. Music or stories or commercials or whatever. That's what you do when you're done with school."

"Yeah," he said, after a long time. "Mine is the palm tree sparkler. But every time I try to see it, there's no moon, or it's cloudy. I see it, like, once a year, and then it just makes me sadder." He wasn't crying again, but his voice was thick with worse than tears. "Makes me want to just kill myself now. I didn't have a gun before."

"Don't say that."

He finally said, "You didn't even try to stop me."

"At the Lafitte? You had the gun!"

"The gun was for Jazen."

"A gun is for anyone it's pointed at, even accidentally. After Dimples, you should know that. Did you get rid of it?"

"No." His breath rustled into the phone. "I was gonna throw it in the river. But I got it right here. If there's no treasure, fuck it. I'm out."

He closed the phone so gently I didn't even know he was gone.

Emile was asleep, his back turned to the stairway. I curled up in the other bunk while the boat rocked slightly in the current. No idea where Victor was, or my father, and nothing to do but wait for the light.

Emile was gone when I woke up. The sun was bright and hot in a line across the floor, and it was stifling inside. On the deck were several cases of water, a box filled with canned food, and candles.

No one was on the dock. I had to walk down the road like a guilty teenager, my hair stuffed into a ball, my clothes wrinkled. Freeman and Philippe were hammering plywood onto Aunt Monie's kitchen window. My father came around from the back of her house, carrying a board. No Victor.

I ducked into the house and stood in the tin shower, feeling the thin skin of metal separating me from the voices outside. Aunt Monie had Lifebuoy soap and Johnson's Baby Shampoo. My hair felt like matted straw. My ant bites were pricks of puckered skin now, like copper rivets on faded jeans. Lovely.

I put my hair in a wet braid and put on the clothes she'd left on the chair. Her clothes. Knit pants in a turquoise shade, and a printed blouse with twirling flowers in the same shade, along with pink and yellow.

She'd left me a pair of rubber boots, too. White. Just to the middle of the shin. Sexy.

I was her.

My clothes were hanging on the wash line next to hers. My white shirts hung upside down, sleeves like broken arms.

Emile stood up from measuring a board and looked at me gravely. He wore faded jeans, boots, and a black T-shirt that said SAINTS FOR LIFE. Fleur-de-lis on each sleeve.

"Saint, huh?" I said.

"Just my team," he said. Not smiling. "Your car on the levee road. We hid it cause the sheriff come by again. You need to go. I don't want him yell at me if you die."

"I'm not his problem." Under his shirt were half-moons from my fingernails. He thought I was his problem now?

He frowned. "You in the parish, you his problem. Aunt Monie!" He called to her, where she was filling water bowls. "Fantine gonna take you. About three hours to New Orleans, and her husband got a hotel room. He told her all about it last night."

"Yeah, cause I'm really dressed for that romantic interlude," I said. "That was Victor last night. I have a kid now." I stopped. Clarette, Cerise, Bettina—all those children. "Yeah. All of a sudden, nothing's up to me."

Aunt Monie looked over her shoulder at me like I was headless. "She don't like dogs, so I ain't go with her, me."

"I don't mind dogs."

"She spend the night with Emile like all them."

All them women? Or she thinks I spend the night with all them men?

"I spent half the night talking to Victor!" I said.

She cocked her head at me. "She talk to him half the night and he don't come, vrai?"

I put my hands on my hips. "If I wanted to go home, I'd be gone. Trust me. I know how to get around, and I know how to find a hotel or an airport. I'm not leaving without him. I'm just as fucking stubborn as she is." I lifted my chin toward Aunt Monie, who blew air from her nose and said, "Ça c'est bon."

She coaxed the chickens into cages with cracked corn. The peacock ignored us. There were twenty-five chickens, in ten cages, and we loaded them onto the blue pickup. My father drove slowly toward the levee road, and we put the chickens into the large refrigerated truck with EB handpainted on the driver door that Emile had parked last in the row of vehicles. "This how he haul the seafood," my father said. "Some men come up from Buras this morning, say them oyster bed already stir up from the current."

The chickens were quiet in the cavernous dark space. They didn't scream, like I thought chickens would. They mumbled, confused, and even I could feel the slight change in the air pressure, somehow, as if the river were breathing harder.

Then we drove the pickup through the weeds and down the narrow path to the old Azure house, knocking down baby palmettos. Emile and Philippe were already there, inside the second floor of the skeletal house, moving like shadows. My father had a crowbar and an ax and a claw hammer. He handed me the hammer and said, "Take wood from here."

In the shell of the old house, we hoisted ourselves up to the second floor, using the studs to climb. The wooden floor was full of animal droppings. Emile was prying boards from the hallway floor, and my father handed them to me. Long pieces of wide dark wood. "Cypress," he said. "Singalee men cut them tree. They build the house back then. 1800. This hard wood. You can't get wood like this. Termite now and different air."

I touched the wall, where the plaster had been eaten away by animals. Inside were smaller boards and between then, what looked like black hair. I shivered violently, all the way through my bones.

My father looked up. "Cheval," he said.

Horsehair and plaster and mud. I didn't want to touch it. I crouched down and stacked up the boards my father halved with the ax.

When we got back to Aunt Monie's, Freeman was sitting in her doorway. "Sheriff come. I tell him you gone."

"Me?" I said.

"Almoinette, too." He kept his eyes on my face.

"I'm staying."

He got up and carried the shotgun he'd had beside him to the truck. Looters.

We nailed the long boards over her front window, and nailed two boards in a cross over those. It was after noon. We ate cold boiled crab and drank the rest of the beer. The heat was suffocating, and the sky looked gray and green at the edges of the south.

My phone made the sparkling sound of a message. It had come in while I was up in the old house with my father. Tony. "I found a room at this hotel on Camp Street. A dump. But it'll work. There's nothing but media and crazy people. You better get your adventurous ass here, though. They're opening the Superdome."

I looked up at my father. "Victor told me he was in a ditch."

He said, "I look in Port Sulphur, I drive down to Buras. He don't know where he goin. Down past Venice, only water. But he come back here. He see the sky."

Aunt Monie said, "Allons. Fini."

Emile and my father left for the boats.

The dogs lay on the porch, their tongues rolling out like pink carpets at a Barbie fashion show, their maple-gold eyes watching every move Aunt Monie made. The house was dark as a cave. Aunt Monie said, "Echelle—ce-la." She pointed to the back of the house, where the bathroom door led onto the tiny back porch. But that had been nailed and boarded shut, too.

"What?"

She mimed climbing. The ladder. It was in the kitchen.

I opened the trapdoor to the attic. She handed up plastic bins of dog food, rawhide bones, and dog biscuits. Then one more medium-sized clear plastic bin, with a blue top. She laid the Bible inside, the rosary, and two small decorative plates. Pheasants and vines. And a carved wooden box, very plain. "C'est tout. Ma vie," she said.

It must have been photos and letters and important papers. I pushed the boxes under the rafters of the shallow attic. There was about three feet of space along the spine of the roof, which was fairly new. Plywood covered with tin.

She filled the kitchen sink with water, and then two five-gallon plastic jugs.

From the trunk of my car, I brought the Octoroon cigar box, my laptop, Victor's laptop in the messenger bag, and his backpack. I put them all in a large plastic bin which she emptied of chicken food in the yard.

"Les poulets très heureuses après la tempête." She actually smiled, looking out into the yard.

Snails and bugs would be everywhere. The tempest. She was still smiling.

We walked across the highway to the orange groves. The boats had been moved further down, vague shapes in the bayou. Aunt Monie picked up a white bucket, and she and the dogs walked the groves. She touched a few green satsumas, working her way to the back, where I couldn't see her anymore.

I sat in the plastic chair near the metal sheds. They gutted and cleaned fish here, and put them on ice. They sorted the oysters, and the shrimp and crabs. The smell was in the wood. The water was like tinted windows. Black. Impenetrable.

Nothing moved.

An engine started, a wasp whine. An aluminum skiff came down the bayou to the dock. My father and Emile got off and went to the metal sink to wash their hands and faces. "Twenty-four lines to tie em down," Emile said. "Right there, the water's deep enough. And the old cheniere is to the west."

The hump of land with hundreds of years of oyster shells and a few bent oaks, where my father had taken us. Where the Indians had lived.

I washed my face with cold water, looked into the speckled mirror. My hair a thick black rope across my shoulder when I wet it and braided it again. The faded ink blossom on my arm. Glorette and I pressing our wrists together. Our hair in one braid, our shoulders tight to each other.

The dogs came first, sniffing the sink and dock to see if anyone had brought fish. Then Aunt Monie. "Regardez—trash," she said, tilting the bucket. "All over the back row. Somebody drive down there."

In the woods at the edge of the grove, near the standing water of the swamp, were two pits, one shallow, one deeper, surrounded by a crumbled brick foundation. Two empty ramen packets, Gummi Bears, and Gatorade. That must have been what was in the Thunderbird. He was eating what he had lived on before. But how long ago had he been here?

Aunt Monie pointed to the pits. "This indigo, here. Where they make the blue for the soldier. That smell, kill the women." Then she pointed down the dirt road. "He ask about cimitaire, I tell him so many dead people, and even a horse bury back here. By the slaves. The quarters back over there, and they bury the people on the other side."

"Why didn't you tell me that yesterday?"

She frowned. "You say you look. You say you look here."

I'd looked in the cemeteries near the big homes. Where white people were buried. I was ashamed to even say out loud how ignorant I still was. I turned toward the trees, heavy with green fruit like ornaments camouflaged in the leaves, my face burning.

My father said, "Too late now." Emile said, "Too dangerous to get stuck on the road with a flat, or in the woods."

It was dusk, and the air turned to the mottled heavy silver of old pewter. The dogs lay down on the dock, confused about why there was no walk. At the far southern horizon, there was an eerie wash of green—not vivid, but like water hyacinth and lichen and moss rising up into the sky.

We stayed in the shed. The small TV showed people lining up at the Superdome. Most of the people carrying plastic bags and crates and children were black, but there were some tourists from other countries, interviewed in halting, jaunty English. I looked for Claudine, Albert, Juanita in the crowd. Had they boarded up their windows in the Lafitte, or would they all go up to the second floor?

Where would Alfonso have gone? And Jazen? Maybe their grandmother and mother had said, No guns, no fighting for tonight. Get your asses in here right now.

My phone still worked. I left a message for Tony. "I'm still here, down in Plaquemines. I'm staying. We're safe. They've done this before."

Then Victor. "Come back here. This hurricane is real. Get the car out of the ditch and bring it back to the levee road. I'm going there right now to leave mine."

———

Aunt Monie headed up the path with the dogs as if nothing were different. I drove my car, tires popping on the crushed shells of the road, to
the levee. It felt strange to gun it up the grassy slope. No one would ever
drive up a freeway embankment back home, crash through bougainvillea and ivy that sheltered homeless encampments and rat nests.

At the top, I parked behind Emile's blue pickup, which was behind
the refrigerated truck. Chickens would sleep forever if it stayed dark
forever, they told us when we were children. If the sun never came up,
they would fall over eventually and die.

I turned my car around, carefully, on the levee road so the Corsica
faced north. I'd be the first to drive back off the levee tomorrow, when
the storm was gone.

Aunt Monie and the dogs were small figures walking north on the
road. The batture of trees and driftwood and trash was washed with
muddy brown water, but only a few feet. That was just the tide coming
in. This used to be the front. I had looked at the gravestones in front.
Where them blankitte bury. The slaves and free blacks were buried in
the back. Nearer to the cypress swamp.

I looked out at the river, and prayed. *Dya*—what Aunt Monie called
the water spirits. I said to the river gods that it had been hundreds of
years since Marie-Therese came up the passageway, and not to let her
blood descendant go back down.

You believe now?

I left the keys in the car, and then I sat on the hood, white boots out
in front of me like someone else's feet, waiting for her.

The old landing, where Moinette had been taken away with a rope
tied around her wrist. A little goat. A little girl. Fourteen. I'd sat here,
watching the tangles of driftwood come down the river, imagining I
was Huck Finn.

A girl in a white dress walked up out of the trees further down,
where the path led to Azure. A teenaged girl. She was white.

Behind her was a fat old white woman in a black dress, huge and
slow. A man followed her, black coat long and skirted around his legs,
and then a pale woman, her head down, as if she looked at her feet.

They moved up the levee and then down the other side, into the batture's trees and debris and they walked across the matted tangle of someone's old fishing nets and I couldn't see them after that.

Blankittes. What did Aunt Monie call them at night, when she told stories?

Bright people. Ghosts.

I couldn't run in the boots. The people were gone. I stumbled fast down the levee road in the darkness that seemed to grow from the trees themselves, to rise from the water, and to have nothing to do with the air. The shaking gathered at my neck like an animal tossed me. Then Aunt Monie's boots were visible, and her scarf, and the dark dogs, who stopped and stared toward the river.

"Eh, Lord," she said, when I told her. "Eh, Lord, nous allons. Rien pour faire—nous allons." She lifted her shoulders to her ears like a frightened child and crossed her arms over her chest.

We'll go.

But it was too late. We'd still be in the car when the storm actually hit. "People see ghost all the time," Emile told her. "You ain't ever paid attention before. Ain't no big deal."

Aunt Monie spoke to him in such rapid French I couldn't follow, and he shook his head. "Fantine and Freeman stay in the house with you, then, and me and Enrique and Philippe run the engines here. I can't lose this boat," Emile said. He wouldn't look at me, or anyone else. He looked toward the west, at the marshes. "All I got."

I had nothing.

I wished I could lie beside him, on the boat. But I lay beside Aunt Monie. She had told Glorette and me stories in the dark. *Marie-Therese, she eighteen. French man come here, to this house. This house. Blond man. Fight or don't. She cadeau. A gift for a week, while he buy the sugar. And she get Moinette.*

Phrodite mama call Moinette a bright hardship. She say, That your only chile? And Marie-Therese say, Take one candle light a room.

I thought I heard rain. But it was Lulu's claws against the linoleum, clicking as she dreamed and whimpered and chased what ran behind her eyes. I wondered if my father paced on the boat. What if it sank, and this house, which had seen so much, stood? He didn't care. Maybe he thought he was on his boat again. *One Nigger.*

"What happened to my father in Texas?" I whispered to Aunt Monie. "Did he ever tell you?"

She was quiet, and then she said, "He tell Emile grandpère. He run that rum, in a truck, and in Texas they take his truck. Take him in the bois. Take his clothes and tie him to a tree. They play with him, chat y souris."

Cat and mouse.

"They play with him," she whispered. "With a stick. Say how big. Like the toy."

I turned my head to the side. My father riding through those woods.

"When he come back, he kill that boy from New Orleans," she said, and then she turned away from me.

The power went out sometime before midnight. The darkness was complete. We were inside our own eyelids. Freeman turned on the battery-powered lantern and went back to sleep in the easy chair, though because he was younger than my father and not used to decades of drowsing upright, his body splayed stiffly and his mouth fell open like a puppet's, his wispy goatee a black cirrus cloud.

Marie-Therese had slept here in a chair waiting for someone to take away her child.

Aunt Monie dozed beside me, but every time the dogs whined or paced, she murmured words to them, and they lay back down. In my small leather purse, diagonal across my chest as if I were walking miles through a strange city, I had my cell phone, my wallet, and my little notebook. She had helped me wrap them in plastic, like sandwiches, in case we had to walk through high water.

The rain started and then stopped, hammering the tin roof. I felt terrified as a child—what if the bright people came here, the only house where there was light?

I couldn't breathe. Not like being strangled, but as if a huge mouth covered me, sucking hard. The whole house vibrated, like a plane rising and falling crazily in the atmosphere. No air. My eardrums felt as if they would burst from the pressure. Emile had bolted boards over the chimney with masonry screws.

"Aunt Monie," I said. "I can't breathe."

"And suddenly from heaven there came a sound like the rush of a violent wind, and it filled the entire house where they were sitting. Divided tongues, as of fire appeared among them," she said, her eyes open to the ceiling.

The house shuddered, sighed, and swelled again. Then the wind hit the side of the house like a bus, and the cistern slammed against the door. Then moaning, moaning—the gods of air and water moaning. A sound no one could imagine. A million throats moaning and filling the world with sound that erased everything else.

Things hit the house. Big things. The house shuddered, bent, absorbed the blows, shuddered again like a person being beaten. Freeman stood at the door, listening. "Trees down. Light pole, gotta be."

Aunt Monie and I got up. She held her walking stick, and went to the kitchen, fumbling for something. She came back with four leashes, clipped them to the dogs' collars, and sat down in the wooden chair like a priestess, facing the cypress-wood-covered window as if she could see something.

The wind tore at the tin roof, screaming metal, and then water came under the front door, sliding inside as if magically, a ghost able to swim through wood and walls. The dogs whined and pulled, and she said, "C'est bon, c'est bon, c'est bien, c'est bien."

Freeman looked at the leashes and said, "We got some rope." He took it off the kitchen table and tied it around his own waist, then mine, and he was reaching for Aunt Monie but the dogs swerved around his legs, staggering him.

Then the back of the house blew off. The bathroom addition. And something so large hit the house that the walls turned and groaned, as if dizzy. The house twisted, and then the water came from the front door and the window, poured into the back from the gaping entry. The dogs were up to their bellies within minutes, swimming.

Aunt Monie was shouting in French—praying or arguing—and while Freeman was tying the rope to her waist, around her bulky blouse, the water rose to our thighs. He tried to grab the ladder, but the lightweight metal floated away, into the kitchen, and then out the back. The chairs, the bed, everything was floating. I grabbed her heavy walking stick and pushed at the trapdoor.

The dogs were swimming frantically, and she called their names, over and over. Freeman still had his feet on the floor. He grabbed Aunt Monie and pushed her toward the attic. The water lifted me in a rush, as if it were alive. I was treading, pushed against the armoire. I grabbed Aunt Monie's elbow and held on, but she was pulled by the dogs, who were trying to get to the floating mattress.

"Hold her!" I screamed to Freeman, and I pulled myself into the attic, my shoulder muscles burning. The water was over his shoulders now. I grabbed Aunt Monie's wrist. It felt like I pulled her arm out of the socket when I dragged her into the attic.

The dogs followed her as soon as she called their names. They leapt up into the space, jostling one another, and then ran frantically over the rough splintery beams, stumbling and barking, knocking over the food containers and not even noticing the food. Fluffy pink insulation flowed in rivers between the rafters, and they waded there and then leapt out as if that were worse than water.

It was dark and stifling in the small space below the roofline. Freeman pulled himself up, his jeans sodden, and lay on a rafter.

The wind moaned and sobbed. Ghosts and obliteration. Sheets of sound that tore into my ears. Then a section of the tin roof tore off, and the dogs barked in looping hoarse circles at the storm itself.

Freeman crawled over to the edge of the hole. I was too afraid to see the air making those sounds. I thought I knew—fierce Santa Anas leaving palm fronds and downed eucalyptus everywhere. My father said we were fleas on the earth and the wind tried to shake us off. Foehn in Switzerland, the rattling hot summer wind of southern France, sandstorms in the desert.

I crawled a few feet to the trapdoor, the rope pulling at my hips. The water was swirling inside the house, choppy as if outside. The furniture was floating. The refrigerator was on its side, stuck at the top of the kitchen doorway like a white coffin.

The water was about a foot from the ceiling.

I crawled to the wooden vent at the front of the attic and broke one of the slats. The dawn was not light—just sheets of rain and howls of air I could see now. The water outside was brown, gray, whitecapped, churning just below the eaves. It was river and ocean and rapids. But actual waves, about three feet, came toward the house, pushing and shoving, and then one pushed the house off the foundation and we spun.

The refrigerated truck. As the house turned, I saw that was what had hit us first—the white truck was impaled on the branches of the huge oak behind the house, cab facing down, like an elephant bowed on its knees.

The house spun again in the current, and Aunt Monie prayed in French. Freeman yelled, "We gotta get out and find a boat. Emile said if it get bad wait for the eye."

The house moved in jerks and shudders and washed up against the pecan trees. It was wedged between two trunks, and we stayed there.

Hours. The wind sucked and pulled at the roof, and the waves pulled at the walls. Then everything calmed as if in a movie. As if a biblical hand had swept over the turbulence. And the sun came out, pale and bobbling, weak apricot, but blinding us in the open hole of the roof.

The eye? The sun?

Freeman and I climbed out onto the slick tin roof and held on to the chimney. The water covered everything except the tops of the oaks and hackberry and cypress. The houses were gone, pushed back toward the levee road, only two roofs visible under the water that still heaved and surged with invisible tides. The dogs surged out of the hole in the roof, and Aunt Monie screamed, "Coco! Non!" Coco tore the leash from her hands and leapt into the water, swept into the current. Then Lulu followed her, and Aunt Monie slipped on the metal roof. Freeman grabbed her by the rope and then tied the excess to the chimney.

Aunt Monie held Zizi in her left arm. And Mama stood stiff-legged, watching the other dogs swim away and then disappear. "Tournee!" Aunt Monie screamed, her voice giving out. "Tournee!"

Come back.

Cows were everywhere, floating on their sides, and other dogs, bellies already filling with air. Snakes swept past, swimming toward trees, moving away like writing in the water. Dead chickens.

A horrific scream. Like a woman dying, being killed again and again. The peacock was alive, somewhere.

A red-brown circle floated close to the roof, glistening in the sun. The mass bubbled and shifted, and I saw white rice inside. Pupae. A raft of fire ants, floating to a new home. I shouted at Aunt Monie to get her legs up and away. I felt faint—the island of ants was eddying near the eaves. If they touched the roof they'd swarm up. I pushed Aunt Monie's stick into the mass and the ants boiled up the wood and I let go. The stick swirled away in the current, pulsing with movement.

The air was completely still. The heat radiant. But then a cow made a strangled sound somewhere, and a boat motor droned like a june bug.

Emile came down the flooded road, level with the tops of the oaks that lined the street. The flat-bottomed aluminum boat—he shouted, "Hurry!" He pulled me off the roof and onto the boat, and then Aunt Monie, who kept holding tight to Zizi's collar. Mama leapt into the boat, and he said, "Hold her!" Then Freeman slid in.

"Coco!" Aunt Monie pointed. Coco had managed to get up onto the cab of the white truck, howling now, and Emile throttled the motor.

"Goddamn," he whispered. "My truck. Two-ton truck. Thirty-five thousand dollars."

Coco howled and whined until we got close, and then she snapped and bit at the air, baring her teeth at Aunt Monie. Freeman reached for her, and she latched on to his forearm with her teeth. Emile said, "She gone crazy," and hit her on the ear. She let go and snapped again, and he pulled the boat away.

Aunt Monie lay flat, facedown, in the boat, tiny and shapeless as a paper doll, her arm around Zizi and Mama, who lay flat as well.

I looked behind us. Azure was gone. Only Aunt Monie's roof was even visible, and two cars that were floating south. A horse swam past, hooves flailing. I closed my eyes. Coco's barking was hoarse and regular now, desperate and chest-deep as the night Victor had croup.

I held on to Emile's back, my face against the wet cloth, and sobbed. Victor was drowned in the car, in the woods, or floating out to sea.

When we reached the boat, the wind had begun again, as abruptly as before. Freeman handed us up to the *Lady Chance* and then went to help Philippe. Emile sent us down to the galley, where we lay on the floor while the boat pitched and tossed and rose up against the ropes again and again. Aunt Monie held the dogs' collars with her gnarled fingers, her face a mask. My father and Emile shouted at each other for what felt like hours. The wind was from the other side now, screaming and tearing at the boat, and the engines chugged beneath us, hot and throbbing, until I threw up again and again in the water sloshing at our feet.

Hours later, the wind finally calmed. Again, the sun came out immediately, hot as a floodlight. I stumbled up the galley stairs.

The world was shredded and drowned. Debris was caught in the cypress trees along the bayou—clothes and plastic and another cow caught in the branches, dead, bloating even now, its neck stretched out like a horrific caricature. To the south, the satsuma grove was gone, leaving only the round tops of trees already brown and dead from saltwater floating like thousands of tumbleweeds. Marsh grass and gas cans and boxes and dead fish moved out in the current, and then the body of a man, floating down the bayou toward the marshes and the Gulf, his T-shirt a transparent bubble of white on his back. My father stared into the water after the body, and leapt into the flood.

Emile and I jumped in after him. The current was strong, but we swam after him. He wasn't swimming. He was floating. He wanted to die. I kicked hard and something submerged cut me on the ankle, a searing pain. I floated in the water, and a gasoline slick lifted fumes into my nose. Then I kicked again. Emile caught him, turned him toward me. We grabbed his shoulders and swam toward the boat.

On the deck, away from the side, Emile wrapped a rope around my father's waist and tied him to a pole. My father opened his eyes, looked at me, and passed out. I sat next to him in the sun, cupped my hand under his nose to make sure he was still breathing. He slumped against the post, and then his chest heaved.

The water. He saw his mother, and the dead cows and pigs and chickens from 1927. The white people swollen and black, the black people washed of pigment white.

Aunt Monie squatted near me and whispered in my ear. "That boy from New Orleans come take Enrique liquor money. Up at Woodland, the jail by the river. Enrique put the knife on his neck. Push him in the water. He go under and Enrique turn his back."

The third man he had killed. A boy. I stayed with my father, while the kaleidoscope that must have been inside his head whirled and slowed.

By late afternoon, sounds rose only from the water, and still nothing from the sky. Drowned egrets hung by their beaks from the chain-link fence around one shed, and I couldn't look off the deck anymore to see what floated past.

My father slumped to the side and slept. Emile and I bailed out the nasty water belowdeck and opened up the door for air. Emile carried my father and aunt to the twin beds, where they both slept, dogs stunned and silent between them.

I sat with him on the deck, in the small shade of nets and winches. He poured Bacardi onto my ankle. I could see the perfect white of my bone. I took one long drink. He wrapped a torn T-shirt around the cut. Victor's bandanna, Kelli's gunshot wound, Michelle and Inez. I stared at the water. No sound except our own breathing. No threads of music from a distant radio, no cars, no bees, no laughter, no bouncing balls, no thumping stereos, no children. No sparrow or hawk or nasal grunt of a coot.

Emile's voice was raspy and guttural, like his throat was lined with stones. He must have shouted all night, trying to keep the boats from capsizing. He took off his shirt and lay on his back and said, "Nothing left."

I nodded. But so little of it had been mine. Except Victor, who had become mine, tied to me now through the stories and whatever love I had tried to give him each time we talked, under the encampment's cloth tent, near a fire, in the tribe. I couldn't believe he survived in the Thunderbird, when trucks had been tossed into trees, and I couldn't bear to imagine him gone. I reached out and put my hand on Emile's chest, and he put his fingers on top of mine.

Oil floated down from the north in veils of black and rainbow slick, then huge slides of tarry thick skin. Rafts of marsh grass collected against the boat, and more fire ant islands. Emile sprayed the fire extinguisher until the foam sank the floating masses that held each other tightly.

His radio snapped static, and came to life. He spoke to someone down in Empire, who said hundreds of boats were wrecked, and two giant menhaden boats had floated onto the highway. Emile said, "Anybody come for you?" and the man laughed.

"Nobody even knows we're down here!" he said. "You think the government cares about us? They worried about the city. New Orleans floodin now. Levees broke."

"How you hear?"

"Goddamn if someone didn't call me. Some cell phone satellite must not a gotten blown out the sky."

Emile stared at me, and then up to the top of a mast. "I'ma climb up here and see," he said. "Go get your phone."

I pulled it from the leather bag, still in the plastic cocoon. I unwrapped it and rubbed it against my filthy print blouse.

When Emile made it to the top, the phone made the sparkly sound of a received message.

"Somebody call you," he shouted. "Call last night at eight seventeen. Say he found it. The treasure."

Comtesse, to the north. The slave cemetery, on the other side of the road, away from the river. The only place left to look.

We took the little skiff. The water was so full of debris that Emile had to maneuver slowly around dressers and stoves and pieces of metal roofing and hundreds of broken tree branches. My chest was hot from the rum. We stayed on the western side of the flooded highway. The cipriere. Where the black people would have been buried.

The boat motor was the only sound. A zipper in the silence.

If he were alive, he'd hear us.

There were no landmarks. No canals, no roads, no barns, no roofs here. But Emile said, "Still got trees."

"You know where you're going?"

"I know. When we go out in the bay, we got trees, and chenieres, to see where the oysters are. Now the whole damn place like a bay."

Then he said, "Oh, damn. No."

At first I thought they were small boats. Metal oblongs, bobbing in the current. With handles. They were coffins. One palest blue, one silver. Then one more, turned on its side against a utility shed. A sleeve, a hand, a leg in black suit pants.

I buried my head in my lap until the motor had whined for a long time.

"That's not Comtesse," he said finally. "Those new coffins. A different cemetery. We got about another two miles. Take forever like this."

It must have been another two hours. We were in a strange foreshortened forest, where Emile had to steer around gas grills and trucks and tires and tangles of clothing in every color snagged up against the oak branches. We had to circle and backtrack around huge tree trunks. Then I saw a dirty yellow rag on a raft of marsh grass. Black coral.

"Is that his shirt?" I whispered. I screamed, "Victor! Victor!" Emile gunned the motor, and I shouted again and again.

A row of black iron spikes, separate, floating in black water. A rise in the earth. A cheniere. Oyster shells and sediment. An island. Oak trees, and three white crypts like tiny garages with their doors left wide open.

Victor was splayed out on a branch of an oak tree, toward the top. His left arm was tied to one part of the branch with a bandanna, his left leg anchored at the knee with a leather belt. His jeans were still on, but his shirt had been torn off. "Victor!" I called, but he didn't move his head. We came closer. His shoulders heaving. He was breathing. Crying. On his back, scars like white rosettes in a pattern. Two circles—the eyes. And five more, in an arc—the smile.

Emile pulled the boat close. I climbed up, the bark scraping my arms. I put my hand on his neck, the burned-red thin neck, holding up the bare shorn head, his cheek etched with scratches black with dried blood.

I couldn't untie the bandanna around his wrist, sodden and knotted so tight. I pulled hard with my fingernails, but Emile handed me a knife and I cut it carefully. Then I undid the belt around his knee.

He didn't look at me. He looked up into the higher branches and said hoarsely, "Where's the other guy?"

I looked up, too. There were snakes coiled in the branches like elaborate jewelry, and above that, a raccoon that stared at us with impassive black eyes.

Victor nearly fell into the boat. He looked terrified of Emile. "Was that you? In the tree last night?"

Emile said, "What?"

Victor stared at me as if he were blind. I felt his forehead. His skull. The place I had been afraid to touch all those years ago. The sun flashed white from his black pupils, and he blinked.

Then he pointed toward the crypts. He said, "She was in there. Then the water knocked out the front, and the box floated out. Like it had a motor. Went all the way down there and disappeared." He pointed east, toward the river.

Marie-Therese. Headed to the ocean, finally. The wind that began in

Africa wanted her back. *Dya,* the water spirit, lifted up by Faro, the god of wind.

When we got back to the boat, my father and Aunt Monie were on the deck, the dogs quiet by her side. Emile and I put Victor in one of the beds belowdeck. He closed his eyes. Emile touched my loose hair. "Jolie," he murmured, and bit his lips. He gathered it in his hands, clumsy and rough, and I pulled back. But he divided my hair into three bunches and braided it loosely. Then he handed me the Bacardi and went upstairs.

I poured rum onto a towel and wiped down the cuts on Victor's face, his chest, and his right arm. Tree bark and pounding wind. On his back, below the horrible grin, were two deeper cuts, about five inches long.

"Things were hitting me," he said softly into the sheet. "Metal things."

He turned over. I took his left arm, where the bandanna had been. The wound was still infected, a long red line like thick-twisted licorice. Inez had taken the bullet out from the swollen part near his elbow, where the skin had crusted over. I poured a few drops of rum there. Victor whispered, "Man, I held my hand up like a Supreme. Like, 'Stop in the Name of Love'!" Then he closed his eyes. "And he shot me anyway."

I dabbed more rum on the bullet wound, and then started looking in the cabinets for bandages. When I turned back to the bed, he was reaching with his good hand deep into his pocket. He pulled out a bullet, and a bracelet, and put them into my hand.

The bullet was small and heavy. Dull gold. On the butt, the word *Super* imposed over an X.

The bracelet was dull and gold, too. A heavy cuff, inlaid along the center with five large rubies. Old rubies, dark red as claret, not the bright created jewels you find in stores now. These rubies had come from somewhere far away, on a ship.

"Tuition," he whispered.

"How are you not my child?" I said.

"I want to be that dude wandering around the library with a beat-up old briefcase, workin on my third Ph.D."

"I had a present for you. Messenger bag. Leather. Soft as butter, from Zurich." I looked up at the sky in the open galley door. "It's in the Gulf now. With my car. And our laptops." That sounded so selfish. "And everything Aunt Monie owned."

"That dude's pissed about his wife's car, huh?" he said, lifting his chin toward Emile.

"Nobody's pissed about a car right now. And it's his second wife's sister." Then I said, "We're only alive because of Emile. And my papa, and the other guys."

"'Out here in the fields,'" he sang softly, eyes closed.

"Those bandannas saved you," I said. Claudine's bandanna, and Michelle's.

"Maybe."

"Your father was watching you."

"From the ocean? Yeah. Right."

Emile came downstairs again. He sat on the other bed.

I said, "Come on, Victor. It's amazing that you lived. Your maman was here all the time, too. She made you come down here to look for the bracelet. If not, you'd be in New Orleans. It might be worse there."

"Worse than here?"

Emile said, "On the radio, they said it's bad."

"Well, I'd rather have her alive and—"

I grabbed his face. Made him look at me. "Cooking elaborate meals for you? Taking you to the library? Who put you up into that tree?"

"Some dude."

"What?" Emile said. "The other guy you talking about when we found you?"

"Some dude was up in the tree. I had dug up this metal box next to the grave. There was a circle carved into the side of her—her little house."

"Crypt."

"Yeah. Aunt Almoinette told my mama about some circle that meant a bracelet. There was only one crypt—wait, tomb, right? There were a lot of old wooden crosses and little graves. But I found the circle, so I dug right there, and I found a box. Inside the box was another box, and the bracelet was inside. With some kinda stuffing. Like moss. And it was already getting dark, so I sat there on top of the—tomb."

"Where was the Thunderbird?"

"I wrecked it in a ditch. That first night. I was trying to find the cemetery and I went off the road. I slept all day in the car." He put his arm over his eyes. "I was layin on her tomb. I figured she wouldn't be mad. It was hot as hell."

He was so thin that his cheekbones were right there, sharp under the scratched skin. "I fell asleep, and then the wind came up, and the water. It wasn't even like a tidal wave, like in the movies. It just, like, came up outta the earth. Like—bad magic. It got up to her name, and I heard a noise, and this dude was in the big old tree. He was, like, waving at me to come up. I jumped into the water, and it was up to my chest, and the wind was trying to kill me. I climbed up on the trunk and there was a hole for my foot, and then a branch. Like the tree in your yard."

The three sycamore leaves on my table at home. Big as hands.

"I didn't look up till I got a branch, and he was up there. He waved for me to come up higher. Then big-time wind. I had the belt. And the bandannas."

"Saint Joseph," Emile said. "He likes oak trees. My grandmère told me about him. He saved her cousin during Camille."

"What did the guy look like?" I said.

Victor said slowly, "It was dark. But he whistled for a while. He sounded really far away. And then he musta fell."

"Or flew." Emile nodded.

He rolled his eyes. "You mean some angel? You believe in that stuff?"

I opened the box of bandages. Emile turned on the battery-powered CD player. Some old song came on. "Maybe it was some guy loved your moms and never could have her. Maybe it was some guy loved Marie-Therese." I put the first bandage on his arm, and then looked again at his back. The burn scars, the cuts, the scapula just under the skin. "Maybe it was your imagination."

I dabbed rum once more on the two deep cuts, and lightly touched the pink rosettes of burn on his shoulder blade—long healed. "You can see the palm tree sparkler in my courtyard, too," I said, to the side of his neck. "It's never as bright, though." His head dropped to his chest, and I ran my hand over the faint soft down of hair growing back.

"Cool," he whispered, and then he lay with his face against the wall.

When I went back up to the deck, I saw pecan trees lying drowned, satsumas' top leaves barely showing, but the biggest oaks were implacable, strung with marsh grass and old Mardi Gras beads and tangles of cloth. The music drifted over us. *We are people of the mighty—mighty people of the sun.* My brothers used to play that song in the barn.

Emile was heating beans on the gas stove. He said, "Them kids hate the old stuff we listen to. They always telling me turn it off."

I called back, "Not Victor. The Dread Prince. He'll give anything a chance."

He was below us. Maybe he was listening.

Emile said, "Look like a knucklehead."

"He's my knucklehead now." In the nearest oak, I could see animals huddled inside the branches, their eyes glittering like black sequins, and in the distance I could hear faint laughter, and I truly didn't know who had saved him.

EAST OF THE SUN, WEST OF THE MOON

FOR THREE DAYS, we were alone in the sweltering heat and complete darkness, Emile's generator humming instead of a thousand crickets and frogs and night birds. Only mosquitoes, so hungry for our blood we had to smear dark mud on our faces to keep them away.

Alone except for the dead. The animals that floated nearby. A baby whose handmade wooden casket had whirled into the stagnant water of the satsuma grove, her skin not black, or white, or brown but lavender. She could have come from anywhere—the water had pushed north and south, the wind east and west.

East of the sun, and west of the moon, we'll build a dream house of love.

My father retreated into himself and said nothing. He lived inside his forehead. I lived right here, on the boat, for once.

Victor sat on the deck, staring at the trees and sky, his arm somehow slowly healing despite the gasoline and oil and bacteria in the storm water. He spent the days writing in my tiny notebook, whose pages had dried into dimpled blank sheets like ancient papyrus.

I had nothing to write.

On Emile's small television, hooked up to the generator, we saw New Orleans. We looked for Albert and Claudine, Juanita and Inez. But in the crush of thousands inside and outside the Superdome, everyone looked like a stranger.

Then Victor said suddenly, pointing to the screen, "Look! Raiders jersey—that looks like Jazen!" He floated facedown near a freeway off-ramp barely visible amid the flooding in the Ninth Ward. The jersey bubbled huge with bloat. Someone had tied his arm to a street sign.

Somewhere in the water and the people was Tony, who would tell me later about taking hundreds of shots of women holding up their babies to the thropping downdraft of helicopters, of men holding up their hands to try and catch food thrown from the sky by soldiers, of everyone holding up their clothes and radios and children to keep them out of the black water up to their chests.

Alfonso called Victor on the third day. Jail was safe—three hots and a cot—so Alfonso had gone to a cop the night before the storm and said he had a warrant in California. The cop laughed, so he broke a window. When the prisoners were evacuated to a freeway bridge, he sat in the hot sun for two days. A bus took them away long before any came for those in the Superdome or Convention Center, because as Alfonso would say later, "People make money off you when you in jail." The bus left them in Baton Rouge, but in the confusion of the holding area, Alfonso slipped through a chain-link gate and walked all the way to Sarrat, to Uncle Henri's house.

On the fourth day, the New Mexico National Guard came up the Mississippi River, their airboats so loud we heard them long before they slowed at Bayou Azure. We knew what we looked like. Aunt Monie and I had washed clothes in buckets of rainwater and scrubbed them with Lifebuoy soap. I wore Michelle's bandanna around my head, and Victor wore Claudine's. In the nervous gaze of the guardsmen, my father and Aunt Monie were impassive, their faces closed as always around strangers, but Victor whispered to me, "Yo, ho, yo, ho."

They took us to a shelter in Lafayette. My brothers and Gustave drove in from California with food and clothing and supplies, and Tony came in the rental car. As soon as we were allowed to return to Azure, we caravanned south.

Aunt Monie's house had lodged against the three pecan trees, off the foundation, and we had to wrestle it back on. But we had plenty of men. Tony, Lafayette and Reynaldo, Emile and Freeman and Philippe, my father and Gustave, and Victor, whose arm was healed. A tattoo of dark satin rope to mark him forever.

We took down the wooden boards of Azure and lay them in a pile. The cypress felled by slaves, notched and pegged, with markings made by Senegalese men. Aunt Monie showed us the ends of the beams, where we saw carved symbols, blackened with age, that her own grandmother had showed her when they went under the house, where people used to store oil and barrels of sugar because it stayed cool.

At dusk we sat on packing crates from the satsumas, near the boards, and Emile made a small fire. Victor lay on his back, looking up at the branches where dresses dangled like moss. My father laid a metal rack over the flames, Aunt Monie made fish and rice in a pot from the boat, and we all ate. The old house was gone, had finally fallen this time, but we were still here.

ACKNOWLEDGMENTS

Deepest thanks to Richard Parks, Katie Freeman, Toni Scott, Denise Hamilton, Holly Robinson, Marisa Silver, Stewart O'Nan, Nicole Vines, Tanya Jones, John Sims and Robert Sims and Loretta Preston, Teri Andrews and Karen Lark, all our Sims family; Revia Chandler and the Aubert family; Jay Neugeboren, Mike Davis, and Monique Verdin; and Rickerby and Paulette Hinds, and the Buckworld One crew.

Mes trois filles: Gaila, Delphine, and Rosette Sims.

Grateful appreciation to the Lannan Foundation and to the people I met in Louisiana.

ABOUT THE AUTHOR

Susan Straight is the author of six previous novels, including *A Million Nightingales* and *Highwire Moon,* which was a finalist for the National Book Award and won the California Book Award. She is a regular commentator on NPR, and her fiction and essays have appeared in *Harper's, The New York Times, Salon, Zoetrope, McSweeney's, The Washington Post,* and the *Los Angeles Times,* among other publications. She has received a Lannan Prize, an Edgar Award, and a Guggenheim Fellowship. She lives in Riverside, California, with her three daughters and teaches creative writing at the University of California.

A NOTE ON THE TYPE

This book was set in Old Style No. 7. This face is based on types designed and cut by the celebrated Edinburgh typefounders Miller & Richard in 1860. Old Style No. 7, composed in a page, gives a subdued color and an even texture that make it easily and comfortably readable.

Composed by Creative Graphics
Allentown, Pennsylvania

Printed and bound by Berryville Graphics,
Berryville, Virginia

Designed by M. Kristen Bearse